I0582989

BLIGHT

E. J. JOHNSON

HEMBURY
—BOOKS—

Copyright © E.J. Johnson 2026

First published by Hembury Books in 2025

hemburybooks.com.au

info@hemburybooks.com

ISBN 9781923517141 (paperback)

ISBN 9781923517158 (ebook)

The moral right of the author has been asserted.

All rights reserved. No portion of this book may be reproduced in any form without permission from the author and publisher, except as permitted by Australian copyright law.

 A catalogue record for this book is available from the National Library of Australia

For April Lee Honeyman

ABOUT THE AUTHOR

Edward Johnson is a first-time novelist who lives in Melbourne. He is married and has two adult children.

He has practised as a barrister specialising in workplace relations law, and spent several years as an industrial officer and tribunal advocate representing members of a large public-sector trade union in Victoria.

Earlier in life, Edward was a teacher in Surrey, England, and in Montpellier, France, where he conducted English conversation classes at the Lycée Joffre. Returning to Australia, he taught French and Japanese at Brisbane Boys' College as their first head of modern languages.

The son of a World War II veteran who spent nearly five years in Changi prison following the Fall of Singapore, Edward is a devotee of military history and is well-read on the decline of colonial rule in South-East Asia.

Drawing upon his career background, research skills and family experiences, his debut novel *Blight* explores the sociopolitical backdrop to Australia's military presence in Singapore before and after its occupation by the Imperial Japanese Army. A faithful reimagining of historic events, *Blight* is a human-centric account of the changing fortunes, concealed truths and psychological damage experienced by a socially diverse range of characters.

Equally passionate about rugby union football and depleting his wine cellar, Edward's knowledge of French wine and viticulture earned him the coveted Vin de Champagne Award in Australia.

I write fiction because it's a way of making statements I can disown.

TOM STOPPARD

CHAPTER
ONE

MELBOURNE, OCTOBER 2015

FOR AS LONG AS I care to remember, in the back of my mind I've always wanted to kill my father – and haven't had much time for the rest of the family, either. However, if I'd once flirted with the idea of actually committing murder, that flight of lunacy had long since been grounded. Apart from the matter of timing, I'd never really thought about how to go about it, and the reason why had become less than compelling over time. Who knows, the impetus to do something decisive might still crop up one day. In the meantime, self-indulgent estrangement has become my fallback position. Quite effective if you're determined to never forget and never forgive – and don't want to talk about it.

What made my father Clarrie so repugnant was the fact that even after all these years, I still couldn't shake off his malign influence, which included his insatiable appetite for bigotry, cynicism and unfailing derision. What was worse, when I looked in the mirror, my physical resemblance to the person I'd grown to despise was some-what unsettling. It was as if by unwittingly assimilating his worst char-acter traits, I'd somehow *become* him. As a father myself, I'd tried hard not to replicate his abhorrent behaviour, but once the venom gets into the blood, well …

They say every child is born without sin, but I have my doubts. I tend to believe my psychological make-up was genetically predetermined, then further deformed by learnt behaviour as an infant. On the other hand, I shouldn't blame heredity entirely, should I? Nature or nurture – who cares? Might as well blame it on the boogie.

I was now starting to question whether it would be that onerous to modify one's personality later in life for a second chance to become a decent human being. After all, I still hoped to be struck down by a rare case of late-onset happiness by using the phone – without having to swipe left and right more than a teenage shoplifter at Highpoint. Perhaps my yearnings were no different from those desperate souls whose healthy relationships had withered, and had resorted to speed dating in search of meaningful connections. For Christ's sake, what the devil was I going to do?

———

I'd been struggling to face up to this chronic malaise for a long time, but there was no way I was ever going to succumb to cyberchondria, frantically searching for negligent advice from Dr Google. I finally decided to seek a clinical diagnosis, all the while thinking that maybe that train had already left the station. It wasn't an easy decision – where I come from, going to a headshrinker still carries a social stigma, spoken about in hushed tones, if at all. It was a confidence-shredder akin to admitting you'd prematurely signed up to become a resident in an aged-care facility.

With all this in mind, I'd naturally not told anyone of my intentions, except my general practitioner, Dr Michael. He had a surname, of course, but it was one of those elongated Polish numbers, full of multiple sets of underperforming consonants, with barely sufficient vowels thrown in to get your tongue around the whole verbal misadventure. Even staff at his surgery made no effort to get it right when organising patient appointments. 'Dr Michael is only available on … Dr Michael isn't in today …' If it wasn't Dr Michael this, it was Dr

Michael that. The staff's adoption of this overfamiliarity had gradually mutated into an accredited form of address.

Michael had told me his name was pronounced *Mick-al* but he'd given in to the insidious tyranny of anglicisation. He'd feared a turnover of his mature-aged, hard-working and experienced staff if he were to constantly chip them about it. He'd discovered long ago that it was the younger, more recently employed who tended to quit working once they'd landed a job. The staff was already copping plenty of abuse from those who'd failed to understand the fundamental purpose of the waiting room. It seemed the words patients and patience bore no relationship, other than being homophones.

Michael was simpatico, though someone with a bit of street cred – who was more of a right-on hipster than me – might have called him cool, even a bit edgy. Out there. You dig, daddy-o? I stopped trying to keep up with the current slang decades ago, when the mediocre was mindlessly glorified as wicked, rad or fully sick – like *beau cul, belle gueule* and the antediluvian, 'That's groovy, man.' They've all gone with the wind.

As usual, Michael didn't muck around with the standard-issue prescriptions – the ones that tell you to use up all the repeats until finished, *as directed*. Whenever I'm given directions, I'm prone to go the opposite way. He knew I didn't want any of that old, production-line stuff, especially when it came to ingesting those reputedly dangerous anti-inflammatories for the pain in my foot. I was grateful that his ultimate response to the illness-dependent was a medical referral – you were sent straight off to a specialist. To employ a type of Zbigniew Brzezinski cold war-speak, it didn't matter if he knew that I knew that he knew I was a hypochondriac, even a bit of a high-maintenance drama queen. Not that he would ever use those offensive, hurtful words.

We both knew I wanted more than some common form of spiritual analgesic and had no qualms paying through the nose to get it from a psychiatrist, rather than having it handed to me on a plate by the parish priest. Not that I'd know much about *that* experience. Even though I went to Church of England Sunday school as a kid, I'd been baptised a Catholic. However, I'd drifted into being what they called a cafeteria Catholic, someone who nibbled at titbits of doctrine from only the limited substantiated buffet. As an adult, married to a mick, I was pushed to stay awake for the Christmas Eve service and had to be lent on to attend the Palm Sunday Eucharist. I was otherwise unschooled in the catechism and the rituals of High Mass with all its bells and smells. It'd take a miracle for me to believe in Jesus, even if I met him personally.

They say the customer's always right, and Michael thought he knew who was right for me. I didn't really have a choice. He had in mind a rather abrupt matter-of-fact physician, one who wasn't into psychological tourism, as he chose to put it. In other words, this practitioner was unlikely to recommend a trip to the Timothy Learys or be interested in administering a hit of psilocybin to speed up a visit to that sunny pleasure-dome with caves of ice. Nor would he be the type of medico who wears a psychedelic bow tie, swanning between patients in adjoining suites, the walls festooned with testamurs and framed photos from the latest fiscally attractive medical conference; the sort of addictive destination that has few adverse side effects.

Nooo. Michael would arrange an appointment for me to see Dr Jacob Mendelson, or *Mr* Mendelson as he liked to be called, a consultant psychiatrist whose standard recipes for the patient, he joked, included a pinch of dry seasoning mixed with a light drizzle of old-school dressing down; one who failed to see the magic in adding mushrooms or ganja to his regimen of ingredients. I wasn't after the taste of red meat, but Michael made this fellow sound way too vegan-friendly for my liking, perhaps the only psychiatrist in town who'd be happy to take your pulse?

He told me Mendelson was a longstanding proponent of cognitive behavioural therapy (CBT), with its strong foundation in neuroscience. Curiously, Michael had heard from other patients that he doesn't particularly like being described as a psychotherapist, and if you're tempted to use the word shrink in his presence … well, don't even think about going there! I've never been accused of having an abundance of optimism, but Jesus Christ, what in the hell was I letting myself in for? Talk about a pinch of dry seasoning! When I heard all this, I thought this shrink could easily be eligible for drought relief.

Apparently, his cognitive approach is a fancy way of saying you do the talking about your feelings and negative thoughts, which are then explored in a collaborative process. 'The diagnostic remedy he serves up may taste slightly bitter, but it's guaranteed to be ethically sourced, non-hallucinogenic and … non-recreational,' Michael smiled.

'What do you mean by that?' I asked, although I already had a pretty good idea.

'First off, don't expect someone demure with a nice pair of legs and lip filler, who dispenses the type of fake cheer favoured by depressed, guilt-stricken criminals and self-indulgent Hollywood celebrities. What you'll be paying for,' he said rather ominously, 'is a doyen of the profession, who's regularly called upon to produce psychiatric reports used as expert evidence in judicial proceedings. To this end, he often collaborates with behavioural neurologists.'

What's his purpose in telling me all this, I thought. This referral was already making me feel decidedly uneasy.

'If he suspects you're someone who's manipulative or finding it difficult to admit you're same-sex attracted, for example, he'll be onto it straightaway. From what I know of his couch-side manner, there'll be no prolonged, psycho-sexual analysis to indulge the patient over multiple sessions. He's also rather sceptical of adults seeking a late diagnosis of ADHD. I suspect he considers most of them have a bad case of ASD – attention-seeking disorder? As the saying goes, you only get one chance to make a first impression, so a further word of advice: don't try to be funny, act defiantly or talk religion. Dr Mendelson is someone who believes the Ten Commandments are authoritative – holy writ – and shouldn't be disparaged in the way some humanists do, by describing them as the ten suggestions.'

Aha. None of this was music to my ears, and I'd reached the obvious conclusion: Mendelson was unlikely to ever be dubbed the Liberace of the lobotomy.

I'm usually blasé when it comes to following recommendations, but some of Michael's endorsement had certainly got my back up. Surely, *I'm* the only one who can attest to my hyperactivity and inability to concentrate? And *who's he* to deny my identification within an autistic spectrum of *my own* choosing? None of this ought to have been surprising, I suppose. According to Dr Michael, Mendelson specialised in disputing the arguments of epithetic psychiatry, especially in cases involving those arraigned for homicide, who decide to plead diminished responsibility on the grounds of mental impairment, which used to be called insanity, or even more shamefully, madness.

'In case you're wondering,' Michael needlessly added, 'Dr Mendelson has also discredited the serotonin imbalance theory and multiple personality disorder, now termed dissociative identity disorder. He decries both as examples of the questionable diagnostic orthodoxies of the psychoanalyst fraternity. He's quite unobservant in that respect.'

Michael shouldn't have bothered telling me all this useless background information. The only thing I was wondering was how long his testimonial was going to take. He wound up saying that Mendelson had recently been consulted to draft opinions on the prospects for rehabilitation of purportedly incurable recidivists on the sex offenders' register.

Yeah, right. Michael likes a joke.

———

I caught the 109 tram along Victoria Parade in Fitzroy and got off towards the Hoddle Street end. The location of Dr Mendelson's consulting rooms barely managed to scrape into the status-rich East Melbourne postcode. His premises were difficult to find, perhaps deliberately so to cater for the anonymity preferred by his sort of patient. It certainly would've been a challenge for those out on day release.

His rooms were situated inside a sprawling, early twentieth-century Federation-style brick residence. It was built upon a deep block of land that looked like it extended all the way to street access at the rear, and the promise of a slightly better aspect. To reach the front door, you entered through a tiny wrought-iron gate, hinged to an opening in the saw-toothed clinker-brick fence. The gate was so low you could easily step over it, if you weren't cursed with bilateral talipes at conception and increasingly crippled by osteoarthritis in late middle age.

Once inside the gate, rather ironically, you followed an unnecessarily winding path laid with crazy pavers. They were once all the rage on suburban patios and internal chimney surrounds, a lasting testament to the tiler's skill in developing a method to deal with the maddening, non-linear shapes by mortaring the multi-coloured paving stones into vaguely harmonious patterns, despite the rough edges.

In the front yard, a balding weed-infested lawn cried out for attention, but obviously not loud enough to attract a gardener. A couple of crumpled Big Mac wrappers chased the breeze inside the fence, blown in – or more likely tossed in – by patrons of the Collingwood fast-food factory just down the road. An ideal landing spot to determine whether society's detritus is recyclable, you might uncharitably remark. And, of course, I did. The metal street number was dangling upside down on the front wall of the house, confirming that the whole exterior was a maintenance-free zone.

The property itself, which had a narrow street frontage, appeared modest and unrevealing on the outside, more Tilda Swinton than Dolly Parton, and pleasingly unhipsterised. There was nowhere for a local braces-wearing barista to chain his fixie for a start. The only indication of the premises' current use was a tarnished brass plaque screwed to the wall adjacent to the side-entrance door. The rectangular nameplate was just large enough to squeeze in the initials of all the psychiatrist's degrees and prestigious fellowships.

It was dimly lit inside, and what I faced directly upon entry was a deserted waiting room, furnished with little more than a half-dozen uncomfortable-looking chairs. They were upholstered in now-faded cabbage-rose patterned cloth and had narrow curved wooden armrests. The varnish had worn off long ago or had possibly been stripped by nervy patients with restless fingernails.

In the room, the setting had been turned to silent, a bit like a padded cell, I imagined. The only thing that disturbed the somnolence came from the traffic outside, which like the phone in my pocket emitted the occasional muted vibration. Someone once told me I'm the sort of bloke who could attract trouble in an empty room, but in this place, I'd be forced to go looking for it. I wasn't expecting to be met at the door by Thelma and Louise in tight denim, boot scootin' to 'Achy Breaky Heart', but hey, c'mon!

I rather annoyingly kept yelling out 'Is anybody home?' before realising the receptionist was tucked away in an obscure alcove up the hallway. When we eventually acknowledged one another's presence, her appearance managed to sing out, 'Don't go lookin' for men's shirts, short skirts in here!' She was no Shania Twain, and man, she must've rarely felt like a woman – perhaps only on odd days? Her hairdo was styled like one of those stiff lacquered wigs worn by Orthodox Jewish women. It appeared to act as her centre of gravity. There was no signage on her desk, but her chiselled features unmistakably proclaimed: *Do Not Disturb*, absent the *Please*.

The dimensions of her intimate workstation suggested that the space might have once served as an oversized broom cupboard, a large closet or a walk-in pantry for condiments and dried fruit, mostly preserved lemons. Her twinset, sans pearls, appeared to have been carefully curated to blend in with the surroundings – redolent of a time colour and fashion had ignored. Today must have been her beige day, like yesterday, and perhaps the day before?

As I handed over the sealed referral, she told me in a cold, standoffish voice to *quietly* take a seat. I sat up straight and filled out the regulation double-sided patient information sheet. The only piece of information it highlighted was a request for the patient's private insurer's details above the place for your signature. The sheet of paper was fastened to a clipboard, to which an uncooperative biro was attached by a length of string. I slipped it back to her on tiptoe, as though returning something I'd stolen. She briefly raised her head, revealing her hollowed-out eyes hemmed in by high cheekbones. In accepting it, she gave me the frozen, burning scowl of a motorist grabbing a parking infringement notice tucked under their car's windscreen-wiper.

Right then.

Not even a spot of lippy, heavy lashings of Tabu by Dana – 'the forbidden fragrance' – or the arrival of the suave Don Draper would have cut through the icy disposition. But I guess he was the wrong type of madman? Maybe she didn't fancy men at all and was a bitter old lesbian who'd undergone humour bypass surgery and preferred to remain in an actual closet? Or was she simply having her usual bad hair day? I think she saw me as just another swinging dick who'd accidentally strayed in off the street looking for the neighbouring suburb's safe-injecting room. But put it this way – I'd have been more surprised if she'd come out than I would have been seeing Arthur Daley's missus – *'er indoors* – sipping a vodka and tonic with Arthur and his minder Terry, at the Winchester Club!

The waiting room was enveloped by that tediously hoovered smell of the late nineteen-fifties. The walls had a picture rail all round, not much above head height, but remained undisturbed by pictures. Would have been an ideal setting for that William Dargie portrait of the young Queen Liz in the wattle-coloured dress. Even one of Namatjira's ghost gums had failed to materialise. Albert's landscapes were ubiquitous in every state primary school and local council chambers in the country, yet most Australians had remained as ignorant of the artist's biographical details as they were of the mushrooms being spawned in outback Maralinga.

These types of paintings encapsulated the artistic, spiritual and political life of the nation in prime minister Menzies' time – a dry, mirthless, and dyspeptic environment, prone to be lorded over by imported vice regals with dinky-di Aussie names like the Viscount De L'Isle. Having nothing else in common with that distant Serenissima, back then if you'd peeped through the slats of your own suburban Venetian blinds, all you'd have seen would have been a dispirited housewife, possibly named Daphne, pulling her squeaky shopping trolley along the footpath, rather than gondolas gently bobbing on the Grand Canal.

Those blinds were very effective in keeping out the light.

It was the time when most children were either bound up tight by strait-laced Protestantism, or alternatively, bogged down by the heavy palm of Rome. Strange as it may seem, it was only the first decade of my life in which I'd struggled to grow up.

———

Michael told me that Mendelson only sees patients on three days a week, and never on Fridays. The rest of the time he was employed as an associate professor and often invited to present academic research papers at medico-legal forums. Judging by the tatty wall-to-wall Axminster in the waiting room, his turnover would certainly need to be supplemented by another source of income.

The small collection of chairs had been arranged in a protective covered-wagon formation around a low coffee table, loaded with heavily thumbed but neatly piled magazines. Some of their pages had been torn out, so they were in no danger of theft. Not a *Vogue Living* or *Country Life* in sight, but plenty of *Better Homes and Gardens* and copies of *The Australian Women's Weekly*, a title once renowned for reproducing the same stories of domesticity fifty-two times a year. Successive editors demonstrated a virtuous commitment to recycling well before the idea became mainstream.

After I endured about ten minutes pressurised in one of the undersized chairs, the receptionist announced: 'Dr Mendelson will see you now.' She said it begrudgingly, as though I were considered unworthy of being granted an audience with the Patriarch in the Temple – a rare concession to a knuckle-dragging, heathen outsider. Jesus wept! I could feel my hackles rising, even if I didn't know what they were, or where in the hell to find them. It was now clear who'd supplied the reading material and may also have advised on the interior decorating.

Without indulging in any eye contact, this latter-day Mrs Danvers pointed unnecessarily to his rooms at the far end of the hallway. Phwoaar! Nothing like this drack sack to deflate the libido. Talk about sexual modesty! She had clearly found her niche in life, but might've benefited from a short stroll along the hallway herself. But this was unlikely. She gave the impression the rest of her body was as immovable as that large wad of hair, which was no doubt bonded to her skull by a thick coating of araldite.

The wooden floorboards in the hallway creaked a little as you'd naturally expect in such an old unrestored period home. The sound was accentuated by my ponderous steps as I stumbled towards the pillory for a session of self-funded flagellation on what felt like my very own Day of Judgement.

I was met at the door by Mendelson, who ushered me towards a bulky, leather chair with extendable footrests. Anxious patients would have found it impossible to assume the brace position. It was the type of recliner that might've been put to better use in his waiting room, or in a dental surgery. This prompted me to wonder what Mendelson might choose to extract – and the pain it might induce without anaesthetic.

His appearance and demeanour nevertheless failed to conform to the stereotype of the man I'd already sketched in my mind. In the flesh, he filled the canvas. He was snazzily dressed in navy blue tailored slacks and a near-matching double-breasted blazer, an aquamarine silk necktie, crisply ironed shirt and chunky gold cuff links – all *de rigueur* if you're impressed by that sort of thing. He was thickset, balding at the crown, and wore a pair of black-framed spectacles with lenses like the translucent glass at the bottom of those old-style quart bottles of milk. It had the effect of enlarging his eyeballs to resemble those of a frightened horse. He did a pretty good job of trying to conceal the built-up shoe on his right foot, as he shuffled sideways onto his chair. *If all else fails, we might swap funny stories about trips to the chiropodist,* I felt like saying.

Mendelson spoke in a deep, resonant voice and had that urbane Mitteleuropa haute-bourgeoisie mien, capable of inducing mild trepidation in a single concentrated stare. I couldn't imagine anyone ever calling him dude, or his responding with glee to a blokey greeting that enquired, 'How're they hangin', doc?'

I'd been foolishly expecting the full monty – a tightly buttoned chaise longue, a casement bookcase crammed with hardback texts and reference materials in the background. I'd also imagined he'd be wearing a tweed jacket with leather patches at each elbow and a pair of shapeless corduroy trousers, both of which formed part of the fastidiously bohemian look favoured by the tenured Freudster. Perhaps a set of framed family photographs, tastefully arranged in tiers on the desk to set the patient at ease?

All these hackneyed preconceptions were conspicuously absent. The images I'd conjured up were as out of date as the sight of a lily-white Geordie on a hot summer's day wearing woolly socks under his

buckled sandals on the sand at Bondi. It wasn't long before my anticipation of a prominently displayed porcelain phrenology bust was also
sadly misconceived. Eventually I realised there was no need for
another large brain in the room that could only ever be used for decorative purposes.

He'd started to examine the referral letter while relaxing in a bendy
Herman Miller chair behind a bulky partner's desk with a tooled green
leather insert on the top. An ageing desktop computer was the only
technological device within reach. I just knew he'd be an analogue type
of guy! His antiquarian taste obviously extended beyond the selection
of receptionist. I could feel my usual bout of cynicism rising – the very
reflex negativity and defiant attitude I'd come here to get rid of –
before he got down to business.

'Well, Mr Roberts, I notice Dr Kuczmierowski didn't mention any
prior history of psychiatric illness,' he said. Michael's surname rolled
off his tongue as easily as if it were a Doctor Smith, Jones or Nguyen. 'I
won't advance a definitive diagnosis at this early stage,' he continued,
'but there's nothing here that points to an acute or chronic form of
depression. There's no history of self-harm, nor any mention of
suicidal ideation.'

'No way, doctor. I'm not into that!' Despite my spirited denial, he
gave me the sort of look that suggested I was only one swallowed
safety pin away from manifesting Munchausen syndrome. *What had
Michael disclosed in that sealed referral letter?* Wished I'd opened it before
handing it over.

'I see you've recently been prescribed medications for peripheral
neuropathy and hypertension, and undergone several orthopaedic
procedures, but those health issues are seldom associated with the type
of prolonged mental ailment that appears to have brought you here.
The obvious question then, is why, Mr Roberts, do you now feel the
need to seek treatment for an apparently self-diagnosed mental condition, which seems to have been well under control? I think we can
dispense with the need for assertiveness training, don't you?'

'I was warned you could be blunt, Dr Mendelson. Well, Dr Michael
reckons it's a type of depressive illness – at least that's what I told him.
But you're right, I've managed to conceal it for a long time. I won't

waste your time, doctor – I'm not going to take any of those old-style medications for depression, anxiety or stress, like Prozac or Ritalin, is it? I've read about their side effects – decreased sex drive, diarrhoea, you can't sleep. No thanks! What I'm looking for is a process to reduce anger and overcome my inability to get rid of persistently negative attitudes and antisocial behaviour. I believe the torment's derived from the bad relationship I've had with that snake Clarrie, my dad.'

'You call him a snake? That's interesting … please, go on.'

'I copped plenty of hidings from him as a child, but mind you, nothing indecent … no sexual abuse or any of the kinda stuff that's thrust upon those altar boys. But, as for emotional abuse? Well, that bastard sure messed with my head.'

'What this is telling me, and I suspect you'll agree, is that you're still experiencing a relatively common albeit sustained form of post-traumatic stress disorder – PTSD – arising from childhood maltreatment. That much appears uncontroversial.'

I responded with a slight nod.

'Perhaps your abusive father came from that generation of men who suffered from their wartime experiences?'

'Yes, I'm pretty sure of that! … and I suffered too. Collateral damage, I think they call it nowadays? He didn't talk much about the time he spent as a prisoner of war in Malaya, which is a bit odd, don't you think?'

'I see. Well, if it's any consolation, the wives and children of many POWs often endured suffering because of untreated wartime trauma. It's sometimes referred to colloquially as barbed-wire disease. The men mostly bottled things up. A good number of ex-servicemen returned to civilian life with some form of undiagnosed mental illness, and the harmful effects on their children are not uncommon. What appears different in your case is the fact that after all the intervening years you still seem to be traumatised by what occurred, as though it happened yesterday? You undoubtedly hold a longstanding grudge and seem to be having trouble coming to terms with the notion of forgiveness?'

'Yes, you're on the right track there, Mr Mendelson, but as I told Dr Michael, it's what I have to put up with that's unforgiving. The nasty thoughts, the anger and defiant attitude keep turning up like a bad penny. I try to cover things up, but deep down I'm mostly on the defensive. Anyhow, I'm pretty sure drugs can't fix it. I suppose I need someone with your experience to get to the bottom of it, as well as providing me with a bit of psychiatric advice on anger management. Are you with me on this?'

'Hmmm … are you sure you're dissatisfied with your self-diagnosis, simply wanting it confirmed by a second opinion, or neither?' he said. My embarrassed silence was met with a look that said, *yes, I thought so.*

'Well, fortunately for you,' he cut in before I could reply, 'I'm in the business of listening and responding to a patient's attempt at self-diagnosis – it's part of what's called psychotherapy,' he said with a straight face, despite his reputed distaste for the word. 'It can be described as a process, and it sounds like what you're looking for.'

I suppose I'm a bit touchy, but it wasn't hard to detect a strong note, if not several bars of sarcasm.

'Any process aimed at reclaiming what might be an acceptable state of normality or emotional equilibrium requires candidness and cooperation. Often, the patient has already formed a close partnership with an undiagnosed mental illness, which may encompass multiple neuroses. Like any relationship with an intimate companion that may no longer be working, it can be surprisingly difficult to break off, unravel or even speak about. And, in common with purely pharmacological treatments, talking therapies on their own are not a silver bullet, a cure, or what the Greeks call a panacea, until that word too became a cliché through misuse.'

'Are you saying it's like being obliged to live with someone you no longer love?'

'Look at it this way, Mr Roberts. Since I mentioned clichés … I've found that one's not always lucky in love, and except in the popular imagination, it's rare at first sight. That's why an arranged marriage, for example, has a lot to offer. Sexual compatibility is something people can work on. Accordingly, the same goes for not persevering with an initially attractive protocol for psychiatric treatment if it's not working. It's natural to feel discouraged when the steps taken fail to live up to expectations. You may need to shop around, and be satisfied with perhaps a less palatable alternative?'

So far, everything he'd said was startlingly unoriginal. 'I can see the logic in all that, but I still don't like the idea of feasting on a smorgasbord of pills, at any stage.'

'I'll remind you from the outset, Mr Roberts, that while it always remains the patient's prerogative whether to follow any recommended course of medication – be it a stimulant, an antidepressant or a combination of both – it is not for the patient to prescribe what is considered the most *effective* treatment. Talking therapies often work better if used in a balanced way, to complement appropriate medication, and vice versa. It's all about gradual healing. Do you have a problem with that?'

'Not now. I suppose that's been part of my problem in the past – not taking advice and being distrustful of authority. But I'm determined to change all that. I like what you said about healing. It sounds funny, but sometimes I feel like I'm limping around with an open wound on the foot, one that doesn't heal and won't respond to a dab of Dettol, and a Band-Aid.'

'Very well. I find it encouraging that you've made the positive decision to finally seek professional help for the management of mental health issues. Keeping silent about these things only makes the condition worse. Unfortunately, even today most men prefer to remain ignorant of the full gamut of therapies currently available to treat depressive disorders. It's derived from their adherence to a type of coercive conformity, which tries to repress the symptoms of psychological injury until its harmful effects are almost irreversible.'

'Perhaps that's the stage I've already reached?'

'We'll see,' he said rather brusquely.

'I rely on the patient opening up with minimal prodding or intervention. As Dr Kuczmierowski may have told you, I'm not the type of clinician who's interested in prolonged handholding; that's more like counselling with a psychologist, who's not given the authority to administer a suitable course of medication. But, as you are no doubt aware, those purely psychotherapeutic sessions come much cheaper.'

'I always say, you've gotta pay if you want quality …' I joked, at the same time appalled by my latest contribution to the steady accretion of clichés and platitudes already littering our conversation. Mendelson remained largely inscrutable, and I kept wishing he'd drop his guard, maybe even lighten up a bit. It didn't help matters that he occasionally came out with the type of psychobabble that was already wearing thin. Perhaps it was no more than a measured dose of performative bullshit, laying on the therapese to justify the exorbitant fees he'd be trousering for services rendered?

'Interpersonal psychotherapy may be an option, but while that approach may prove cathartic, it's generally less effective long-term and runs the risk of overdiagnosis or even misdiagnosis based on certain behavioural symptoms.'

'Uh-huh.' I didn't have a clue what he was on about but replied as if I were au fait with whatever it was. 'I'm not too good with interpersonal stuff, so maybe we can give that a miss?'

'That's fine. Some of my patients have found prior participation in that form of treatment no more restorative than following the contrived wisdom you find on a fridge magnet.'

'Hahaa! Funny you should mention those, doctor. I've got one that has the fully grown Christ holding his shepherd's crook, knocking on an old stable door. The caption beneath reads: Jesus is coming. Look busy. Pretty funny, hey? Almost as good as the one where Jesus is leading his flock over a precipice, except for one black sheep moving in the opposite direction, which says: The Lord is the shepherd I shall not want.'

Mendelson said nothing but looked at me as if to say, *I don't see the point; that's not even contrived wisdom* and *let's have no more irreverence dressed up as childish humour, thank you very much.* And to think I'd already been warned against attempting to be a funny bugger. Undeterred, I kept at it. I can be a cynical, irritating bastard at the best of times … make that *most* of the time.

'But the best one is from Oprah Winfrey: True forgiveness is when you can say thank you for that experience. That piece of magnetic wisdom was an unwanted souvenir from someone who'd made a brief stopover at LA airport and had enough time to pop into one of those cheap and nasty trinket shops in the terminal. That choice of memento certainly tested *my* powers of forgiveness. But Oprah's definitely onto something. She's got almost as many likes for her inspirational sayings as Christ ever registered with all his nifty parables!'

'That's interesting,' he said again. 'I hope you don't expect me to emulate Oprah Winfrey or even the Nazarene Messiah by indiscriminately dispensing forgiveness. I view things somewhat differently, Mr Roberts. It's the individual's task to seek forgiveness before God by offering genuine contrition, not merely saying you're sorry and being thankful for the experience. It's not an unmerited gift from God, but a determination not to repeat the transgression. This is a mandatory requirement of what we call *teshuvah*. It deals with a guilty act that requires restitution, not simply the forgiveness of a sin against a person. It involves true repentance by the transgressor, a recognition of having strayed from God, and then actively seeking atonement. The individual bears responsibility, and the glib expression of regret without more is insufficient.'

That's all well and good, but to my way of thinking, if that's the Hebrew Bible's recommended potion for redemption, it seemed to give off a strong whiff of sulphur. And who *is* this righteous God he's going on about? I'd sooner trust the showbiz confessions of Harry Houdini to release me from the bonds of guilt. Even as someone who had more than a pictorial *Reader's Digest* acquaintance with the scriptures, I'd already been warned not to go anywhere near religion. Mendelson had clearly picked up on my atheistic vibe and was losing me big time, somewhere in the depths of the Torah.

'While I may discount your initial bill today, for any follow-up consultations, prompt payment of my full fee will be all the thanks I need for the experience.'

'Hahaa! That's a good one. I can now see why Dr Michael said we're unlikely to strike up a bromance. He also advised me not to arrive thinking it's ok to behave like Tony Soprano.'

No smile yet. Perhaps he doesn't watch Box Sets on Foxtel?

'Hmmm. Why don't you pronounce his name properly? You surely know he prefers *Mich-al*?'

'Yes, I do. But he's happy to go along with the English version. You make it sound like I'm being disrespectful?'

'Not necessarily. It's that some people might find it offensive if you deliberately get their name wrong. I've recently noticed it's starting to be labelled a *micro-aggression* – you must have detected that an increased susceptibility to take offence has become part of the cultural zeitgeist?'

'Well, I'll be buggered! Where I come from, *macro*-aggressions from the local bodgies were lurking around every bloody corner most days of the week, and twice on Sundays.'

'You oughtn't use that particular expression, either. It harkens back to an era of pernicious discrimination against homosexuals when, as you are no doubt aware, the act of buggery was an indictable offence. There are lots of sensitivities that must be respected, acknowledged and accommodated nowadays, and in any case, certain historically prohibited acts have long been decriminalised.'

Phew! This wasn't at all what I understood as holy writ. It sounded like he'd undergone a progressive, liberal conversion and then purchased a postmodernist, socially inclusive edition of the biblical commandments. Holy Moses! I immediately visualised a resurrected Charlton Heston casting aside his staff and the tablets of stone before reaching for his rifle in disbelief. All of which got me thinking – perhaps I should've added homophobic and misogynistic to the random sample of offensive attributes I harboured. I knew it wasn't an acceptable justification, but surely excusable if you had his only vaguely hetero-normal receptionist firmly in mind?

'I'd rather not explore these issues, doctor. I was brought up in another era. You asked me to be candid, didn't you?'

'That's true. I did, along with being cooperative. But isn't what you experienced during another era the reason you're here today?'

'I see your point.'

'That's good. It was a time when physical punishment was ostensibly used to teach you right from wrong, and the victim was supposed to recognise what the punishment sought to correct. But bigotry and gratuitous acts of physical violence are always morally indefensible, while their effects remain virtually impossible to erase. That said, we can certainly focus on some of the troubling things in your past that may inform your present attitudes. But already it sounds to me like you exhibit what's commonly referred to as an oppositional defiant disorder, or ODD, a propensity to be noncompliant or impertinent at the slightest provocation?'

'That's what I told Michael ... *Mich-al*, in as many words.'

'I'm sure you did. The condition may have stemmed from unsatisfactory interpersonal relationships, unresolved grief, suffering corporal punishment or episodes of bullying and humiliation as part of an unhappy childhood. Any of those causes are more likely to result in what's termed arrested development than the effect of a poor choice of television program, especially those obsessed with gratuitous violence.'

He obviously *had* seen *The Sopranos*, and didn't only replay his old DVDs of Dr Bronowski's *The Ascent of Man*.

'In extreme cases, a personality disorder can render antisocial behaviour and even misanthropy, the default position to explain a patient's attitudes. Neurologists talk of a disturbed patient's prefrontal cortex not being fully developed. As a result, prejudices and bigotry become internalised, become part of the unconscious, embracing any number of negative -isms, touching on sex, race, age, disability, rejection of God, and that immature response to the vicissitudes of life – infantilism. You get the idea.'

Ouch! I didn't have the inclination to unpack all of that – let it go straight through to the keeper. Was he telling me to grow up? It felt like he wanted *me* to apologise for my father's behaviour. As for him bringing up all those -isms? Was he having another shot at me? Michael was right, he seemed totally uninterested in mollycoddling the patient.

And he didn't let up.

'A combination of events may trigger psychological harm, and what we recognise as their predictable sequelae. Some physicians may diagnose what's referred to as borderline personality disorders, which are all derived from differing types and degrees of trauma. With this in mind, we need to explore your troubled psyche to hopefully reveal the root cause of the disorder. In saying that, I'll remind you that I've got little time for prevarication, overacting or the profanity frequently encountered in those crime shows you're obviously glued to on television, for example.'

I sensed that at least one of those failings was directed at me, and not at James Gandolfini's character portrayal. His bluntness wasn't that successful in concealing a caustic sense of humour. He was pressing all my buttons, and might even have a touch of the oppositionals, like me?

'I rarely watch TV, Dr Mendelson. I'm sorry I mentioned that New Jersey crime boss. What you said earlier sounds a bit technical, but I guess that's what has encouraged me to finally come and see someone like you? I've tried Buddhist relaxation mantras, but meditations don't want to work with me. A friend suggested a few sessions on the yoga mat, but I get about as dizzy chanting *ommm* as I do balancing on my head. I can experience a blood rush simply by pressing the remote and landing on the SBS channel – you know, the one that shows sex before soccer?'

My earlier admission of limited exposure to trash TV wasn't looking too credible, so I decided to get off that subject, post-haste. 'And you'll be glad to know, doctor, that I won't go anywhere near those racks of guru-inspired, self-help books – they're about as useful as going to Mass then promising to swallow the homily with a glass of water and several grains of salt at bedtime.'

That might've done the trick. Had I detected the ventriloquist's strangled warble behind his pursed lips? Or was he just clearing his throat?

'A bit of humour never goes astray on the path to recovery, unless it serves to mask an underlying sadness,' he replied, adding: 'And if I laugh at any mortal thing, 'tis that I may not weep,' is a celebrated aphorism.'

'Yes, I know whom you're quoting,' I said. 'It's that notorious romantic hero of Greek independence who was born with a club foot, like Joseph Goebbels.'

'Yes, I was aware of that despicable little man's deformity. Why did you see the need to mention him in the same breath as the great poet?'

'No particular reason. Maybe because they were both damaged goods, and the only physical characteristic they had in common helps explain why they both tried to put their stamp on so many things?'

'What? I hope you don't believe that last comment was amusing. It would've been better to have referenced the late English entertainer Sir Dudley Moore instead, wouldn't it? Less offensive, I'd have thought?'

'Yes, cuddly Dudley, a genuine humorist who never made an issue of his affliction, would have been a better example. I apologise. I wasn't thinking.'

'No, you weren't. Let's move on, shall we? While I might take issue with your choice of words, I wouldn't want to censor your choice of reading, Mr Roberts. You're wise to have avoided books dealing with the current wellness addiction in society. One could justifiably call it the latest *illness*. Its insistent focus on the self seems to be promoting a forlorn desire for permanent happiness and wellbeing. A reflection of the individualistic, godless society at large, no doubt?'

'On the other hand,' he continued, 'I have to say that a growing dissatisfaction with the feel-good industry will inevitably swell my patient list and certainly enrich *my* material wellbeing. In the absence of religion from their lives, many people still mistakenly believe a psychiatrist is the ideal sounding board for all their career setbacks and relationship problems. They hope to extract further meaning from their exhausted tailings of woe – grievance-mining, I call it. Not *you*, of course ... but I digress.'

Oooh, that stung! I decided to play it with a dead bat. For some reason, he was definitely giving me a run for my money in the passive-aggressive stakes.

'You won't be surprised, but I've been dealing for decades with patients who present with similar symptoms to what you've been describing. Quite a number have also made me laugh *and* weep. The causes and complexity of aberrant behaviour may differ from patient to patient, but for those who feel they are being stalked by demons, trying to establish their personal identity, or possess a degree of self-loathing and social dysfunction, symptoms and causation are by and large indivisible.'

I felt as if I ought to have been offended by what he'd said, but he wasn't telling me anything I hadn't already guessed.

'If we decide to go down that path, I can tease out some underlying pathologies you may have sought to avoid by, employing the Socratic method of questioning. We can then jointly examine the probable causes of your affliction and discuss some strategies to address the harmful consequences. To effectively treat your condition, it's important that I encourage you to live *with* the past, not *in* the past – no more running *away* from things but heading *towards* a meaningful and satisfying resolution.'

'A positive outcome will be achieved once you recognise and choose *not* to be the person others see you as. Even those venomous snakes you refer to have no problem shedding their old skin and emerging for the better. You'll also need to suspend your apparent disbelief that a perverse attitude towards life *isn't* a heritable phenomenon. To that end, we'll engage in a type of intellectual inquiry called *psychoanalysis*,' he seemed to emphasise for my benefit. 'Is that the type of consultative process you're after, or did you have some other approach in mind?'

I offered only silence, accompanied by the hangdog look of involuntary approval. What he was proposing was underwhelming, but all the same his strangely hypnotic voice was somehow drawing me in.

'All right. Once we've reviewed discussions and reached a certain point along that pathway, it might then be appropriate to consider a negotiated mental health plan. How does that sound?'

'I'll go along with whatever you recommend,' I dishonestly replied. For a start, I didn't like the sound of the word *plan* one iota.

'That's commendable. One of the methods I apply involves the patient identifying previous traumatic experiences and linking them to their enduring negative thoughts and emotions. It's not a particularly radical approach, except the emphasis is placed on trauma processing. That's all I can promise at this stage. I usually start by asking even the most self-absorbed and emotionally impenetrable patient to tell me five things they like about themselves, in a couple of minutes. Please, go ahead!'

'You won't have to set a time limit there, it might only take ten seconds. On the other hand, I can list around twenty things I *don't* like about myself, and that'll take much longer.'

'Well, that's exactly the point! The nub of psychotherapy and the Socratic tradition may be summed up in the simple expression: know thyself. I won't put you on the spot by asking about your relationship with your mother. Patients who have an ambivalent attitude towards their father seem to get overly defensive when questioned on that matter. Doubtless they fear an unwelcome association with the Oedipus complex, whatever is innocently explored.'

'Thanks for not going there.' Despite saying that, I still felt he was trying to force me into an embarrassing corner.

'I intend going straight to what seems to be the fundamental cause for your being here – the ill feeling you continue to bear towards your father. You seem to feel he's been the bane of your existence or, if you'll forgive me another overworked expression, a scourge on your life. His negative influence is so pervasive that you've effectively *become* him. Is that what you're trying to tell me?'

'You're on the money now, doc.'

'Well, it shouldn't surprise you that repressed animosity, undisclosed rivalry or open competitiveness are not that unusual in father–son relationships. However, in your case, and let's not beat around the bush, I've got a feeling the antipathy goes much deeper than receiving a few smacks on the bottom or not being tucked into bed followed by a good-night kiss? You somehow fear you may have been stigmatised from cradle to grave, unfairly burdened forever by the sins of the father, if I might put it that way.'

'You're spot-on there too, doc. You must've been reading my mail. And, speaking of a good-night kiss – I'd pray to God at bedtime, hoping to keep my father away! The dreaded nightmares came early, whenever I heard the rattle of the razor strop being removed from the bathroom tap. It seemed to me the stronger I prayed, the greater the likelihood of getting a belting. How can you maintain faith in a God who answered your prayers in that fashion?'

'Interesting. Now that I see the scope of your resentment, it may take some time to fully explore, so please, continue talking.'

'If that's the way you want to go, ok then. You'll recall that I mentioned Jesus Christ earlier?'

'Yes, but it seemed a facetious and frivolous remark.'

'Well, my father's teachings never included forgiveness, love or empathy. I wouldn't be so immodest as to suggest even an indirect comparison, but as a similarly neglected, though less forgiving son than Jesus, in contrast to the Christ Almighty and His Heavenly Father, I didn't give a rat's arse whether *my* father art in heaven, was ailing, or complicit in nailing me to a cross. I wanted nothing to do with him.'

'Interesting,' he kept saying. 'Now I can better appreciate that your condition has got *a whole lot* to do with the concept of forgiveness.'

'If you say so. I mean, you sometimes read about people confessing they didn't know who their father was, angling for sympathy. *I was an orphan ... he died an alcoholic when I was a child ... he left my mother for another woman and abandoned the family ... he was a virtual stranger, periodically detained at Her Majesty's pleasure,* and so on. Well, Doctor Mendelson, I would've happily swapped places with any those fatherless souls any day of the week.'

'Keep going ... get everything off your chest. That's the way.'

'My bitterness has not abated. In fact, it has only increased since an old army friend of his, Tasman Walls, got in contact with me a few days ago out of the blue. He didn't offer any specific details in his voicemail, but he hinted at some horrible stuff involving my father that occurred in Singapore during the war and leading up to it as well. The name Sandy Campbell came up more than once. He said Campbell was caught escaping with my dad, and I needed to discover more about this bloke's story. But, you know, I never heard my father ever mention anyone called Campbell, or a Sandy. He couldn't have been much of a pal, you'd have to say.'

I was on a roll. 'Mr Walls said he'd jotted stuff down whenever he could during those war years, in a sort of journal or diary. He said it's very fragile and he'd bring it with him from Brisbane – doesn't trust the post, and its size would make it an expensive delivery. He said he'd decided to visit my father in Bankstown Hospital, after hearing he was really crook. "I'll leave the diary at the closest nurses' station, where you can pick it up if we're not there at the same time," he wound up saying.

'That was the first I'd heard of my father being in hospital. But Walls wasn't to know we weren't on speaking terms, was he? I can't work out why he's taken so long to track me down after all these years and come out with all this now. He gave me the impression the diary contained the usual war stories, but that some of them hadn't been divulged before.'

'Look, Mr Roberts … May I call you Simon?

'Yeah, go ahead.'

'I mentioned a moment ago, Simon, that this might take longer than I first anticipated. It seems we're slowly moving that way. I'll leave you with the onus of coming to terms with your past by focusing on some of the most emotionally charged memories of your father's behaviour, and then asking yourself why they're *beyond* forgiveness? That can be your promise to me. Do you agree?'

'Yes, that's a good idea.'

'All right. We can then examine that process at our follow-up session, if you're agreeable?'

'Okay by me.'

'Please present your recollections any way you like but *do try* to honour your undertaking to me.'

He seemed a little bit cross, and it sounded like he was almost pleading with me. He must've detected I was the type of learner who always marked his own homework. Life would have been a lot easier for these guys in those days when a simple signature could commit an obstreperous patient to the lunatic asylum. It was obvious his favoured line of questioning was getting us nowhere today, and all I'd apparently succeeded in doing was rattling his cage.

'Hmmm, if that's the case, once I get hold of that soldier's diary next week, I might have a good ol' natter with you about what's in it. Maybe it's full of stuff about Clarrie and that Campbell bloke that might help explain my psychological condition – it might even contain the seeds of what I've become?'

'You never know.' Then, frantically moving the mouse cursor around his desktop screen, he said, 'Look, I've had a recent cancellation for this Thursday week – that's in ten days' time. Otherwise, it'll have to be sometime in December.'

'Ok, sounds better than close to Christmas.'

'All right, then. Slotting you in this Thursday week, allows for the early implementation of the antidepressant protocol to which you still seem resistant. Perhaps it's a bit too soon if you have trouble working out whether there's anything of particular significance in those diary entries, so only keep the appointment if you truly believe your attitudes have altered for the better, and you're ready to see me.'

'Sweet as, let's go for it! Perhaps your receptionist can send me a text message with a reminder of the date and time?

'Of course, that's what she's employed to do.'

'Great. It will spare me the job of arranging our follow-up session with her. I don't think she likes me.'

He was visibly unimpressed by my parting dose of chutzpah.

'I'm astonished how she could've come to that assessment of your character so quickly.'

Fortunately, before I had the chance to respond to that unsubtle barb, he continued in his deep, velvety tone of voice. 'You needn't concern yourself with those arrangements – and, by the way, if you hadn't realised already, the receptionist's my wife.'

I had, and it was never a wild guess.

He removed his glasses, rubbed the bridge of his nose, then quickly put them back on. I was taken aback by the thinly veiled hostility but didn't show it. *God Almighty hath sternly spoken,* I thought. It wasn't the time to poke the bear with the pithy rejoinder I had up my sleeve: *Good luck with the arranged marriage, and all that compatible sex you must be still working on.*

I departed slightly red-faced, and without a doubt he'd have liked to have said 'Bugger off!' but couldn't bear the thought of mouthing a macro-aggression. On the other hand, he might've been weighing up the possibility of dusting off his old *Manual of Electroconvulsive Therapy* or presenting me with a copy of *Dr Nitschke's Handbook of Medicinal Cures* should I ever threaten to return. *Hey? Whatever?* ... but all the same, some of that had got me thinking.

Given his expertise, this shrink didn't appear to have made reasonable adjustments in his attitude towards me as a mentally disturbed patient. I could probably self-identify as neurodiverse, or be suffering from ADHD, so where was the display of empathy and the relationship of trust I was paying top dollar for? My job as a creative didn't involve working twenty-nine hours a day down mill, eating cold gravel and living in a shoebox, but it wasn't one of *loorxury*, either! Simply calling my confessions interesting just didn't cut it!

Michael had assured me that Mendelson was not only kosher, but the real deal, adept at illuminating the cause of a patient's neuroses without over-medicalising the diagnosis or treatment. But to me, he seemed nothing more than a walking, talking, rolled-gold placebo. If all I were seeking was moral instruction, forgiveness or to be unburdened of guilt, I could've slinked into one of those curtained-off confessionals that always seemed empty at my ex-wife's church. Or I could've visited the local garden-variety psychologist for some cut-price fridge-magnet wisdom. If all else failed, I might've settled for a cuppa tea, a Bex and a good lie down.

I convinced myself that should there be any more of his polished sarcasm and insensitive finger-wagging at our now improbable second appointment, I'd consider lodging a complaint with the Royal College of Psychiatrists. I might even tick Michael off for his poor choice of shrink – someone who'd turned out to be way too bolshie for my liking.

But I guessed all of that wasn't so cool, was it? Maybe I just needed to chill out ...

CHAPTER
TWO

I RECOGNISED the voice on the end of the line. It belonged to one of Clarrie's grandsons.

'Pop's in hospital and hasn't got long to live, Dad.'

'How'd you find that out?'

'I finally visited your parents, all by myself.'

'What? So you went behind my back ... all that way ... just to find out how they felt about me, did you?'

'No, Dad. I often go to Sydney for my work.'

That was about as far as the conversation went.

It's never too soon to bury bad memories. At least, that's what I hoped, rather than expected. All the same, on hearing this shortly after my promise to Mendelson I felt the burden of completing my home-work assignment being slowly lifted.

After processing my son's news and his betrayal, I was unmoved. Well, not entirely. A bittersweet ambivalence hung around like a bad smell for hours, and it was all the more discomforting for the absence of any sadness at the prospect of the imminent loss of a member of my family. It was something approaching that feeling of schadenfreude whenever you spotted the details of deceased strangers around your own age buried in the daily obituary columns. People generally like to see who they've outlasted, if not outlived?

As I'd mentioned to Mendelson, I hadn't spoken to my father for around twenty-five years. It was undeniably due to my deliberate decision to follow the lonely path of ostracism, and I'd started to experience a lingering guilt about my behaviour. Not too much, mind you. On the other hand, I knew Clarrie's conscience would probably have remained untrammelled by anything as girlish as guilt. The only way our falling-out would've disturbed *his* conscience would have been as a result of the incessant, nasalised hectoring of my mother.

'Why doesn't he ring us, Clarrie? Where's he livin' now? Why's he scrubbed us? I'd like to see his kids … He must blame me for his club foot. But I couldn't help that?'

I later discovered that her harping on in this manner drove him to such a state of barely repressed anger that after a few years any mention of my name was banished from the household. I must admit that I perversely derived a measure of satisfaction from this knowledge of how things had played out. If in the process my innocent mother had suffered damage through his irritation, then so be it. In a partial replication of the long-term imprisonment he'd already experienced during war service, I wanted his torment to be long, slow and ineluctable.

Should I go interstate and see my father on his deathbed in the hospital, or not? I guess I now had no choice if I wanted to get my hands on that diary. For me to go there would be a guilt-laden act of capitulation, knowing he probably didn't give a tinker's cuss whether I turned up or not. Lurking in the back of my mind was that paying my non-existent respects was not only hypocritical but would resolve nothing.

I recalled the protagonist in Camus' *L'Etranger*, an outsider who failed to cry at his mother's funeral. Well, I wouldn't be crying at my father's, that's for sure. But, unlike the enigmatic Meursault, I imagined myself an open book of plausible justifications for my denatured conduct. There'd be no handwringing, existentialist despair in my case. I'd probably show little emotion at my mother's funeral either, but for totally different reasons. Just a sob or two. Quite absurd, really.

Unable to rid myself of all these demoralising thoughts, I decided to fly to Sydney. I'd phoned the hospital and was even put through to the appropriate nurses' station. However, the decision to travel wasn't imbued with any notion of compassion, but impelled by a sort of indolent, almost shameful acceptance of the need to be seen to be doing the right thing. I accepted it under the same duress experienced when told to stand still as a child, despite being overcome by the abrasiveness and smell of my mother's saliva on her tiny, embroidered hankie as she vigorously removed food crumbs from around the corners of my mouth.

Whenever I called Mr Walls's number, he never answered. I left him a voice message saying I'd be there sometime on Monday. I didn't much care whether we crossed paths or not. Opportunity doesn't knock twice, they say, and I decided then and there that I couldn't visit my father in his reported condition without bringing him some sort of parting gift. I accessed a site whose social media handle across multiple platforms was Sicario. Among other things, it had a reputation as a purveyor of the sort of hard-core pornography and firearms only procurable on the dark web. I arranged for my order to be available for pick-up at Sydney airport after midday on Monday.

———

The journey from Mascot to Bankstown Hospital was shorter than I'd imagined. Once off the freeway, the front lawns of familiar suburbs still struggled to be distinguished from a used-car saleyard. I remembered that some of the area's distressed-looking suburbs even affected a royal patronage. Regents Park had never been graced by any regal personage, clip-clopping along in an immaculately varnished landau. Nor were Sloane Rangers or Hooray Harrys particularly conspicuous in the neighbourhood. I guess that's why they dropped the apostrophe. In my day, you'd have struggled to find a park of any description in that suburb – that's if you didn't count the desolate soccer fields full of weeds supporting a couple of splintered wooden goalposts on a lean. As for nearby Villawood, well, it would forever be renowned as the holding bay for ten-pound Poms, a place where young migrants who played guitar either got the jack – or soon got jack of?

One of the main thoroughfares from the city in those days was the pot-holed Canterbury Road. At various spots, the cracked concrete was in pitched battle with the paspalum that emerged in tufts between the curb and guttering and the footpath. And to think they named the local high school after Sir Joseph Banks, captain James Cook's acclaimed botanist and sometime president of the Royal Society in London.

All these bad memories flooded back to haunt me – an environmental reminder of my unreconstructed father.

As I drove the hire car into the hospital's elevated parking area, the forecourt below became inundated with a passing tide of fluttering hijabs. It was as if I'd landed in another country at some unfamiliar point in time, where the only recognisable things left were the names of suburbs I'd hoped to forget. It didn't take long for me to savour the magnificent irony of it all. Here I was at the final digs of Cobra Snake, known as Clarence Stanley Roberts to the New South Wales Department of Births, Deaths and Marriages. I savoured the fact he was now obliged to spend his final hours in God's waiting room, surrounded by descendants and compatriots of those same camel-riders he'd so gratuitously disparaged in my youth.

He'd have been filthy for failing to appreciate until too late that he'd now become a fair dinkum gaijin in his own backyard. The same sort of inexorable dispossession experienced by First Nations peoples, if he'd been capable of grasping the analogy. I knew there'd be no mellowing of his intolerance, such was the visceral nature of his racial prejudice. Not a conventional Balt, reffo or darkie anywhere in sight, upon whom to register his scorn with the pithy judgmental slur. He would've felt deprived of his imagined victimhood, as much as his health. Like the measles, scores of working-class Anglo-Celtic kids were contaminated in infancy by warped parental attitudes. My father injected his viral lessons in prejudice at regular intervals and forced learning by rote had been the favoured form of pedagogy.

Within a generation or so, Bankstown Hospital and its environs had clearly become a microcosm of the changing demographics of western Sydney suburbia. The relocated inner-city poor of the early sixties had been put out to pasture in Green Valley. The former areas had once spawned the bodgies – teenage boys with greasy quiffs and flat-top hair styles, set off by thick-pile sideburns. They'd spend hours blowing smoke rings in fly-infested milk bars, celebrating the boredom of life. Unlike some other post-colonial nations, the only revolutions that mattered in those early rock 'n' roll days were short and sweet, played out at 33 or 45 revs per minute. It was a social environment where parent–child alienation was a common experience. Returned servicemen sat around reliving the past, trying to recover from war service through denial of its long-term effects. Many of those who failed to serve spent the rest of their lives feeling ashamed they hadn't.

After I'd waited for several minutes at the enquiry desk, the hospital clerk finally gestured towards the ward where my father had been transferred. She was completely indifferent when I jovially asked, 'I hope he's ok with a visit. You know, I haven't spoken to him for well over twenty-five years.'

Instead of my words eliciting token sympathy or even mild curiosity, she scarcely bat an eyelid. I thought she must've been recently operated upon and had remained partially anaesthetised? Everything about her said she didn't give a fuck. All I received was a surly downcast look, which suggested nothing could disturb the feeling of bureaucratic tedium that silently raged behind her thick glass screen. *She must get all kinds of nutters in here, confiding things in which she's got zero interest,* I found myself apologising on her behalf.

I started negotiating a path through aesthetically resistant vinyl-floored passageways, along which a few wheezing old men were being pushed in wheelchairs. They were headed for the fresh air in their stained dressing gowns for a smoke, further inflaming their last remaining bronchial tissues. Various doorways were signposted with the names of specialised medical units and consulting rooms. I felt that even for ol' Cobra, this wasn't a very flash place to end one's days, but a whole lot better than starving to death as a prisoner of war, I supposed. Then again, maybe not? At least there you might share a reasonably honourable death among your own kind, not in the palliated company of strangers. You'd still be wearing a military uniform of sorts, rather than kitted out in a crimpled blue smock, waiting to be prodded, poked and inspected during the doctors' rounds like a blood-drained carcass swinging on a hook at Tancred's meatworks.

Pushing through towards the cardiac wing, the bustling corridors could be likened to the alleyways of an Arab souk, but one where the air was not so much suffused with the scent of aromatic spices as by the acrid fumes of heavy-duty disinfectant. I slowly cleaved my way through the stale odours emitted from the pressure-cooked inedible public-hospital food that remained largely untouched on bedside trays. The meals had been briefly inspected – perhaps even nibbled – by the ever-optimistic patients, only for the heat-retaining metal covers to be clumsily repositioned, allowing the half-baked disappointment to seep out.

As I moved further on, the wards started to lose the energising atmosphere of the open-air bazaar and began to resemble the artifi-cially lit quagmire of loss-addicted patrons in one of those twenty-four-hour casinos where clocks are banished. Metal gurneys left their scuff marks on every wall as patients were wheeled towards X-ray or surgery with varying degrees of urgency. Senior physicians and regis-trars were doing their rounds, tethered to a retinue of junior interns, clipboards at the ready, their charts disclosing the latest doses of medications and likely prognoses.

I loitered in my father's vicinity for several minutes, trying to delay the inevitable confrontation.

'Who was that who visited my father a few moments ago?' I asked a nurse nearby. 'Was he waiting for me? He left before I could say anything to him.'

'I'm not sure I noticed,' she replied.

'It was a sad-looking old bloke. He was holding a large parcel – I think I know who it was.'

'Who are you?'

'I'm Simon, Mr Roberts's son. I was told my father's in that cubicle, two down. I'm waiting for the right moment to disturb his peace.'

'Well, your father doesn't usually get any visitors. The person who left was most probably Mr Roberts's old army friend, I think. He doesn't say much. If it was the same gentleman, then he's the one who came in over the weekend, and mostly just sat there. He left during the afternoon handover shift on both days. It's funny, but yesterday he told me he mightn't come back again, and to pass on his message about a diary he intended to leave here. He said it should be given to Mr Roberts's son, when he finally turns up as he promised, sometime Monday. He said he'd leave it at the station down on the left, if the person can prove his name is the one the parcel is addressed to. I assume that's you?'

'Yeah, that's me. He left a voicemail last week and said he'd do exactly that. Did he leave any contact details? There's no-one answering whenever I dial back the voicemail number.'

'No, but you've only missed him by a minute or so. You could probably catch him before he leaves the hospital, if you're quick about it. If you caught a glimpse of him, you would've noticed he's quite frail and not moving that well?'

'No thanks,' I almost had to shout as she glided away on the heavily polished floor.

Now, standing in the corridor a few paces outside my father's curtained-off bed, I crossed paths with a doctor and his impressive detachment of white coats. 'Your father's overall situation hasn't noticeably improved overnight,' he announced without introducing himself. 'It seems,' he said less solemnly, 'there's been a slight improvement in kidney function, and the latest ECG indicates he's in a stable condition.'

Tell someone who cares, I felt like saying. All the while he continued to finger the stethoscope draped around his neck, perhaps to draw attention to the fact he was medically trained, and therefore important? He sounded a bit too cranky for my liking, as if the need to project a congenial bedside manner to an emotionless relative was the last thing on his mind. Which it probably was. His thoroughly bleached diagnosis included a laundry list of other chronic morbidities, which were now starting to kick in. All the while, those in his entourage were nodding in fierce agreement to his interminable list of medical acronyms, their daily exposure to the wash, spin and repeat cycle.

Eventually, I admitted I was the patient's elder son. Obviously, he'd mistaken me for Mr *Norman* Roberts, the younger son, who in my expected absence had no doubt identified himself in the patient notes as the designated family representative during visiting hours. Maybe it was the doctor's first day on the job? At any rate, the overworked quack could probably be excused from thinking that all balding white guys named Roberts looked the same.

My unannounced presence was as much a mystery to me as to the anonymous registrar, whose voice immediately switched into hard-news mode once further relevant data on a clipboard was handed to him, confirming the patient's terminal plight. Perhaps he was as lacking in warmth of the emotional variety as me? As Mendelson had pointed out, I was living proof it would be erroneous for the condition to be characterised as an illness mostly confined to irritable infants and adolescent prats.

As the retinue of medicos moved on to the next cubicle, everything continued as before, each individual blouse blanche taking turns to converse in medi-speak. Perhaps they'd all been taken aback by the air of indifference I brought to the impromptu consultation – they weren't to know I could hardly have expressed concern at my old man's present turn for the worse when I'd so often wished him dead in the past. I hadn't come all this way to seek sympathy or forgiveness – I'd come to see what I'd become.

———

The registrar and his underlings had long departed before I summoned enough courage to pull the curtain back to reveal that embodiment of deeply rooted antipathy, which was my father. At first I felt like a voyeur witnessing a lethal injection on death row. However, I soon realised it was *me* who'd become the victim of my own grotesque behaviour, from which there would be no eleventh-hour reprieve.

There he lay, an emaciated body propped up at fifteen degrees from the horizontal. Despite the absence of the normal trappings of majesty, he seemed enthroned in his own sickness. Tubes were protruding from his arms and chest, the PICC line, a urinary catheter, the saline drip suspended on its own triangular version of the halter and gibbet. A large blue screen with digital read-outs of heart beats, blood pressure and oxygen saturation levels murmured in tremulous blips. Along with the sallow complexion, every aspect of Clarrie's being bore the hallmark of someone slowly expiring.

His attention wasn't aroused until I mumbled, 'It's me, your son ... Simon ... Si ... mon.'

There'd been no rehearsal, since I didn't know what I'd say or how I'd say it. I only knew I didn't want to sound piss-weak or bung on side as he would've put it, by mimicking the mellifluous cadences of Larry in full throttle at the Old Vic. The tone I eventually adopted nevertheless still came across as unnatural and repugnant. It was a register normally reserved for talking to foreigners or tradies over the phone, distinguished by a slightly raised intonation, a bit blokey, louder and slower than normal but distinctly patronising. I was glad the adjacent bed was unoccupied.

I may have repeated that strangely awkward phrase, *your son ... Simon*, a few more times, but it'd probably struck a chord first time round. A pitiless voice inside me wanted to shed any trace of gentility and really sink the boot in.

Well, you rotten mongrel, as much as you'd like to, you can't head for the bathroom now, unhook the razor strop from the tap, fold it over and thrash me around the arse for no reason, apart from your own sadistic gratification, can you? I'd had no problem carrying this memory well beyond the fading welts. *You never apologised, never questioned the emotional damage you inflicted. I don't care if the brutality of the Japanese was off the charts – your PTSD didn't have to become my enduring legacy.* These unspoken words had haunted me for a lifetime.

If only I'd had the courage to come out with something like that earlier, I could've saved myself from a great deal of festering animosity. Yet something inside of me had always seen it as a cardinal sin for a child to physically or verbally assault their parent. Against my strong inclination to do otherwise, I'd convinced myself that I had no alternative but to once again turn the other cheek and harden the heart even further.

Such was my fear of retaliation that despite his morbidity and the intubation, even today I thought the better of swearing in his presence. He wasn't nicknamed Cobra Snake for nothing. From bitter memory, he'd imposed his dictatorial regime within the walls of our claustrophobic Hudson's Ready-Cut fibro home like some de-frocked Tomás de Torquemada. I could still feel the sting of the teaspoon on the side of my skull, one of the regular distractions he enjoyed when he lorded over the kitchen table. His physical assaults hardly ever resulted in bruising unless it was of the invisible psychological variety. From his strategic vantage point at the head of the table, he was easily able to deliver the unexpected flick of the wrist across my ear, as quick as the coiled strike of a viper. To receive a thick ear became as commonplace as brushing one's teeth.

This sadistic ritual occurred with greater regularity whenever he came home a bit full from the RSL. On some occasions, he'd pin me down on the loungeroom floor, ostensibly for a bit of rough and tumble, some innocuous wrestling fun, only to cup his hand over his anus, fart and release the invisible flatus over my face. A variant of this indignity was to be smeared with toe jam from his sweating feet at the end of a hot day. A Neanderthal charm oozed from his every pore, as Professor Henry Higgins might well have paraphrased it in the circumstances. Neither my younger sister nor my brother were ever singled out for similar sadistic entertainment.

These bitter recollections flashed by at lightning speed in my mind. All the while he simply lay there, impotent, the whites of his eyes momentarily incandescent and unblinking at the recognition of something he'd probably never expected to hear or see again in his lifetime. *Fuckin' hell!* I thought. *That's how I'm going to end up looking myself, perhaps sooner than expected?* His familiar, close-set, beady eyes were transfixed on my person for a good half-minute, as though the last remnants of memory were being martialled to process a suitably venomous response to the object of displeasure he was now powerless to assault.

During this time, I noticed the ink had all but washed out of the tattoo that depicted the rising sun-like insignia of the Australian Imperial Force, the AIF, once so prominently emblazoned on his left forearm. I was surprisingly saddened at the sight of his now-withered arm, which often acted as an instrument of fear and undeserved punishment at the table. Half-concealed by the crumpled and slightly soiled bed linen, this former downy limb of arbitrary aggression now lay wasted and seemed to be no more than paper-thin skin over protruding bone. The wrinkled outline of the tattoo was barely recognisable under a mass of finely twisted white hairs. It looked like he was now copping the slow hiding I'd so often longed to personally administer.

Once Clarrie averted the rabbit-caught-in-the-spotlights stare, his eyelids drooped and he fell into a guttural mouthing of vitamised words and hissing sounds. His body language suggested he was struggling with the clear plastic breathing mask, which was attached by tubing to the red oxygen valve on the wall. The side-to-side movements of his jaw resembled the action of someone clearing their ears during a steep descent. This may also have been interpreted as the early signs of asphyxia, the precise nature of his diminishing utterances muffled by the mask that covered his mouth and nose. Stepping forward, I carefully loosened the elastic ties so the mask rested below his chin.

People like to think the terminally ill derive comfort from their hand being held by someone seated at their bedside, irrespective of that person's identity. Maybe it was wishful thinking or the testing of a myth, but I rather coyly attempted to take hold of his liver-spotted hand. It was done with all the diffidence of an acne-faced schoolboy attempting to touch the clammy paw of a wallflower at his first school dance.

Except *this* hand was neither moist nor dainty, but noticeably puffed up by an oedema, and gnarled, mottled and leathery from years of manual labour. As soon as he detected my touch, he moved his hand aside, leaving me with that bitter, unambiguous taste of rejection. No longer an instrument of fear, the hand's sudden reflex movement had become a final act of defiance somewhat at odds with his heavily sedated appearance. I wasn't about to press the matter any further.

One thing you can be sure about with me is that, like ol' Cobra, it was pointless to contemplate the notion of forgiveness if a perceived slight offered the chance for long-term enmity.

When I declined to repeat the awkward hand-holding gesture, his wheezing returned then subsided along with the struggle to convey anything other than medicated grunts. I took this opportunity to retrieve the small phial of powdered Nembutal I'd picked up from Sicario's delivery agent at the airport. I then sprinkled its contents into his disposable bedside cup of water. I put the flexible straw to his lips and, as anticipated, he instinctively sucked the liquid without opening his eyes.

I couldn't be sure he'd swallowed enough to have the intended effect before the nurse arrived. Fortunately, by then I'd already emptied the remaining fluid into the sink and repositioned his mask. After around twenty minutes he lapsed into a deep sleep. There was no need to hear the snap and zing of the curtain rings being dragged by the nurse along the arc of thin metal track to conclude that visiting hours were probably over, once and for all.

I paused to pick up the parcel at the closest nurses' station as instructed. It was more the size of a bookkeeper's ledger than a commonplace diary. It was wrapped in crushed brown paper, loosely tied up with string. At home that evening, I just stared at it for several minutes before placing it on my bookshelf in the section reserved for fiction. Wary of what it might disclose and in keeping with my tendency to procrastinate, I vowed not to touch it again until after notification of Clarrie's death. As a result, my promise of a timely follow-up appointment with Mendelson was starting to look pretty shaky.

CHAPTER
THREE

SYDNEY TO NARRABRI, NEW SOUTH WALES, SEPTEMBER 1939

CLARRIE'S MOTHER had recently passed away when he decided to hit the road. Her death had affected him badly, way beyond his power to articulate the depth of despondency it had caused. He'd heard her suffer from shooting pains in her abdomen, especially of an evening, but was unable to do anything about it. He blamed his negligent father for failing to call a doctor until it was too late. She died of peritonitis from a burst appendix.

Clarrie hated his father's guts for what had occurred, and vowed he'd shoot through from his home on Stoney Creek Road in Bexley, Sydney, at the earliest opportunity. He could make no sense of a childhood that relished the daylight hours of freedom swinging in the trees around Bexley Gully, but which always seemed destined to end most evenings with an undeserved beating. From an early age, he'd thought of home as nothing more than a house of correction.

It hurt him deeply that his father had amounted to nothing and seemed to be doing his best to ensure his son inherited the same legacy. When you're obliged to quit school at fourteen and an absence of self-worth is the prevailing emotion, your attitude towards life tends to take on a negative, deterministic complexion. Clarrie's conscientious embrace of his father's bigotry, and his working-class identification with society's unfair entrenchment of disadvantage, would have made him readily susceptible to the crude polemics of any weekend Marxist on a soapbox in the Sydney Domain. But he'd already been conditioned to hate *commos*, so membership of that loose collective of misery guts was forever foreclosed.

When alone in his shared bedroom, Clarrie would bawl his eyes out for hours on end before all sensitivity was drained from his being, leaving him embittered and virtually inconsolable. It wasn't long before he was planning his escape. With any luck he wouldn't have to set sight on his cruel bastard of a father ever again, happy that little trace of his existence would be left behind.

————

Clarrie was already on the road when he heard Pig Iron Bob's radio broadcast in early September 1939. Prime Minister Robert Menzies had announced Australia's patriotic declaration of war on Germany in support of the mother country, with all the solemnity of a de facto monarch.

With the nation at war, able-bodied working-age men starved of employment enlisted in the armed forces in droves. Now there'd be plenty of cash-in-hand jobs along the road, Clarrie reckoned. He relished the fact he was now on the wallaby, embracing independence as he took to the long paddock to discover his future. A fair bit shy of eighteen years of age, and with a wildly uncertain chance of attaining prosperity, the only contact he had up north was a war widow named Florence Burns. She offered the promise of cheap board and lodgings at Southwick Street, Wynnum, a sleepy Morton Bay suburb east of Brisbane. The address with the home's name Girraween was scrawled in pencil on a crumpled piece of paper. He'd held onto it like grim death ever since clearing out of Sydney.

All Clarrie knew about Aunt Flo was that she was a distant relative in both the geographical and familial sense. Reassuringly, she hailed from a branch of the family tree that was on his mother's side, and reportedly unblighted by zealous religious beliefs and intolerance. As his father had mentioned approvingly, there wasn't even a callithumpian among her lot.

Lugging an improvised swag strapped to a well-worn Gladstone bag and possessing little more than the clothes on his back, he decided to set off from western Sydney, cross the Blue Mountains, then take any old inland route vaguely north towards Queensland. Because of its sheer size, northern Australia still enjoyed a certain frontier – even mythical – status in the thirties. For him, it represented an indeterminate elsewhere, promising a life that offered anonymity and an opportunity to erase bitter memories from the past.

He didn't know exactly which roads led more or less in a northerly direction. His maps were largely word-of-mouth. All he knew was that to the east was the Pacific Ocean, and to the west … well, the countryside stretched forever into the dead heart of the nation, said to be sparsely populated by blackfellas, pioneering graziers, station-hand jackaroos, prospectors and the odd felon on the run. Isolated communities out there were popularly referred to as living beyond the black stump, effectively beyond the law.

By the end of the first week, he'd already worn through a lot of shoe leather and managed to jump on a few slow-moving trains before reaching Lithgow for free. He got used to receiving knock-backs hitching a ride on the way out of small towns and was largely unsuccessful in flagging down anything the further he went beyond the town fringe. He rued the fact he'd overestimated the number of vehicles on the open road during the day and discovered they were as scarce as hen's teeth around dinnertime.

For the most part, he became reliant on cadging a lift from drinkers in the various pubs he dropped into along the way. Sometimes he struck gold and might be taken twenty or thirty miles in a roughly northerly direction. Other times the trip was much shorter, more westerly, the promised distance sometimes curtailed once the driver recognised his passenger was oblivious to the boredom his braggadocio was inducing.

Clarrie's spirits rose every time someone wound the window down, followed by a laconic, 'Where ya offta, sonny?'

'I'm headin' north,' was his stock-standard reply to every phleg-matic hayseed who pulled up out of curiosity in their flatbed truck. It was said with such enthusiasm and conviction, you might have thought it came from someone passionately determined to complete a religious pilgrimage.

Many of the passers-by not driving trucks were travelling sales-men, who mostly kept on travelling. They had no interest in sharing their time with non-paying company, even if the back seat, once loaded up in Sydney weeks before with wholesale merchandise, was now starting to thin out. The truck drivers who did offer a lift were gener-ally grizzled old farmers who weren't going any further than the outskirts of the next small town, grain silo or rail depot, often only a couple of miles down the road.

Occasionally, Clarrie would look over his shoulder, not so much to take in the sparse flora and fauna, or to see if there were any hostile blackfellas lurking around, but to momentarily lapse into self-pity. He was more interested to see whether his childhood was being outdis-tanced than whether adulthood lay ahead.

In the great silence of the outback, he wasn't having much luck fighting against the cruel realisation that no-one in his estranged family gave a fig for his welfare or even knew of his present where-abouts. He was incapable of escaping the feeling of total alienation. Even in the brief company of others encountered in boarding houses, it didn't take much for him to start wallowing in self-pity. You don't need many lessons to grasp you're unloved – and unlovable. However, the obvious reasons for this don't come as easily, and are often denied despite being clear. He had little conception of the opportunity that solitude provided for undemanding companionship, and equally insensitive to the meaning that dwelt within the surrounding landscape.

Unmoved by the spectacle of the fierce cosmology that played out every evening across the immense night sky, he looked upward, but the firmament inspired only desolation rather than intimations of a glorious mystery. Yet it was the daytime that filled him with greater despondency. In order to cope, he'd break into a couple of verses of 'The Wild Colonial Boy' – Jack Dool'n wazis name. The only other song he remembered was 'Wandering the King's Highway', drummed into his head by Mrs Manion, his large-bosomed music teacher in primary school. The refrain, 'As I go, rain or snow, wandering the King's Highway,' could not have been more discordant from what he saw all around.

If you were explaining what you were doing, walking alone on remote country roads, he didn't want to scare the drivers off, so he'd decided never to say Toowoomba was his destination – it always sounded too far away and had too many o's – a bit like the fictitious and faraway Woop Woop. He finally realised maybe they thought he'd never get out of their vehicle.

He'd come a long way since the early weeks around Lithgow when he was still unused to hitching from the outskirts of major towns. It was there that a local bloke had wound down his window and enquired, 'Ben Bullen?', to which he'd replied, 'No, it's Clarrie Roberts.' The car sped off with the driver still shaking his head. It wasn't until the next day that Clarrie passed by the small town named Ben Bullen, twenty miles north. Seeing this, he cursed himself, and after resting his head in his hands for a minute or so, he reluctantly had to admit, *I'm gunna need a betta map and a quicka brain!*

The good thing about carrying a swag was you could suit yourself if you thought any reason was necessary to explain your lot in life. Outback Australia was one of those rare places on earth, outside a monastic cloister, where one's preoccupation with silence was unforced, unquestioned and unavoidable. Country folk you bumped into didn't really care too much about your background, one way or the other. Around that time, there were plenty of itinerant workers who'd gone bush, and for whom a succession of dead-end jobs would be their lifelong calling.

CHAPTER
FOUR

NARRABRI – MOREE ROAD, NEW SOUTH WALES, LATE OCTOBER 1939

IT WAS one of those glorious spring afternoons, with the encroaching nightfall invisibly creeping across a blue cathedral sky smeared with vapourless, feathery clouds. The distant horizon was already tinged by a backlit crimson hue, but all it revealed to Clarrie was that he might be in for a bit of a scorcher tomorrow. Any understanding of the surrounding environment went no further than his unremarkable weather prediction. To say he was insensitive to the fact that the deep silence of the present landscape was crowded with movement, sights, sounds and shapes of real and mythological significance would have been a gross understatement. For him, the meaning held within the animated stillness remained impenetrable. His mental horizon went no further than imagining his next meal.

The dispersed presence of Indigenous Australians, who had no concept of the compulsion to make what was described as a *decent living*, never entered his mind. Nor did he have any inkling of the depredations they still suffered in post-colonial times. Like most non-Indigenous Australians, his understanding of Aboriginal culture remained unreflected and unsullied by feelings of either guilt or curiosity. During long periods of seeing no-one on roads flooded in mirage, he couldn't help but curse his situation. Today wasn't even as promising as those days when he'd tried to cadge a lift from strangers in the bar, only to get the bum's rush. Today was worse. Everyone in the latest pub he'd been booted out of didn't seem to own a vehicle, or else they pretended they didn't.

As he stumbled along, a pair of white cockatoos set off from wherever they'd perched. Their high-pitched squawking slowly faded beyond the hollowed-out eucalypts and withered telegraph poles they usually commanded. There was no gentle, fluted warbling, chirping or trilling from these sorts of birds. They would break into a type of ear-piercing screech as they bobbed their heads from side to side to clean and sharpen the edge of their beaks on the splintered poles. Theirs was the only recognisable noise that disturbed the otherwise blanketing silence, and once their alarm took flight, the heavy sound of emptiness again settled over the land.

He'd already gone some distance beyond the pub and had finished having a long piss not far off the roadside when he heard the clanging sound of an old flat-top truck approaching at snail's pace on his side of the road. It sounded more like a commercial lorry than a truck and looked capable of carting a load of gravel or heavy machinery.

By the time he'd emerged from watering a copse of acacia bushes, the vehicle was lumbering to a stop. It didn't seem like the driver had applied any brakes but had simply allowed the old Bedford to coast to a standstill, tossing up a dishwater-coloured fog of exhaust fumes in its wake. The red paintwork on the bonnet was blistered, and around the dents in the mudguard the colour had been reduced to flecks of paint on bare metal. The hinged wooden tray on the near side was a weathered grey, and here and there it bore traces of what Clarrie took to be the bloodied skin and fur of dead animals.

The driver was gaunt and unshaven, clothed in baggy shorts and a stained blue singlet. The stubble of beard on his face may have been partially trimmed by a sharp object, but it probably wasn't a cut-throat razor. Tufts of unruly black hair grew out of his shoulders and armpits and converged around the nape of his neck.

The driver was slow to open the door, and Clarrie noticed his long, sinewy arms cupped around the sides of the steering wheel like some bloody great orangutan secured to a tree trunk. The top of one of his fingers was missing and the inside of his right forearm was covered with the telltale cuts and scratches caused by brushing up against rusty nails and barbed-wire fencing. Around some of the cuts the flesh was red raw and still weeping. The driver remained hunched over the steering wheel, and had the type of weather-beaten, gravelly face that spelt hardship, if not penury.

'It's a bit late to be hitchin' a ride out here, isn't it, old son?' the voice bellowed through the half-opened passenger-side window. 'Ya seem a bit young for this sort of caper. It's a good fifty mile to the nearest hotel, if Moree's where yaw headed?'

The drawn-out way in which he spoke made the distance seem a lot further. 'Yeah, I know,' said Clarrie, 'but I'd rather sleep rough in a riverbed with a mob of drunken Abos, than stay another night at that rotten pub back there. Most of the shops in the township were boarded up. It looked like they'd gone bung a fair while ago.'

'Ya don't say?' the voice replied.

'Yeah. After pokin' round for ages this morning, I decided to hit the road.'

The driver offered nothing but a silent, contemptuous look.

'The barman seemed to be the only bloke makin' a go of it, even if the place was pretty well empty. I said to meself, it's not only the Abos who've gone walkabout. I should've stayed longer at the Bellata Inn.'

He imagined his chipper delivery would draw a bit of a laugh, but there was an uncomfortable pause, during which the driver tilted his hat and continued to drill him with a deathly stare. The silence was unsettling, even allowing for the fact he could already tell the driver wasn't much of a talker.

He's obviously narked about something I said. Seems reluctant to give me a lift, Clarrie thought. Although he was not normally quick on his feet, he guessed he'd better try a different tack to break the ice – slightly more serious, less chirpy. It was getting late, he needed a lift, and it wasn't like he was stuck in the middle of Pitt Street traffic at peak hour.

'I wondered why the pub was called The Criterion, and why the pub-keeper, a John Henry Palliser, was nowhere to be seen. It was a bit faded, but you couldn't miss his full name in big bold letters on a board above the main door. I got to talkin' with one of the few blokes inside, and he said the barman today wasn't Palliser. It was some new bloke, just fillin' in. No-one had laid eyes on the licensee for quite a while.'

'Is that right?' It's not like John 'enry to go anywhere without sayin' where ee's off to.'

'Well, this old bloke told me Palliser was more like an absentee landlord. Said he was a bit sly … might be off chasin' skirt wherever he can find it, and it's not always round here. Or else he might've headed off to join the army. That'd be right, I said, I don't blame him … might join up meself. He said that's why no-one's too worried about where he's gone – the old cook in the kitchen runs the place anyhow. He also told me the pub's name means the standard. Well, if that's true, then it's a bloody low standard, if you ask me.'

'I *didn't* ask ya, young fella,' the farmer cut in rather menacingly. He'd in fact been in the pub's kitchen at the time Clarrie was punched and then booted out of the public bar. He'd only come into the bar to see what the racket was all about after it was all over. He was told that the young bloke he'd glimpsed hobbling up the road in front of the hotel had been giving lip to Silent Norm Markham, with the predictable consequences.

Norm was the sort of sullen, morose drinker who didn't need much of an excuse to start a blue, even if you only looked at him a bit funny. He got easily offended by cheeky blow-ins and loud-mouthed big-noters, especially if they arrived in tandem. All Clarrie had said to him was, 'It mustn't be much cop livin' in a place like this?' A rather innocuous comment unless the person to whom it was addressed preferred to live nowhere else and thought you were having a shot at them for no reason. Norm was one of those inbred locals who in fact *hadn't* lived anywhere else, if you didn't count the local lock-up. Once he'd taken offence at what anyone had said, or the *way* it was said, Norm went off like a house on fire, the flames not fully fanned until several schooners had been consumed at the end of a session. Because of the hour, Norm had only sunk two seven-ounce glasses of beer. As a result, Clarrie had been lucky to taste only one knuckle sandwich from the burly cow cockie, who could usually be relied upon to deliver a whole cut lunch if it were later in the day. Clarrie had tottered out of the bar, showing no inclination to go on with it, Jack Dempsey-style.

After watching Clarrie's puffy face sink on hearing his unsympathetic responses, rather than bring up the cause of the swollen cheek the farmer gave a twisted smile before he added with a wink, 'But ya can hop in anyway. After ya button-up ya fly, that is.' He took a moment to lap up the sight of his new passenger's embarrassment before asking, knowing full well none had yet been offered, 'What did you say ya name was?'

'I'm Clarrie Roberts, and I'm headin' north to Brisbane. I'll throw my swag over the back, if that's all right?'

The farmer gave a perfunctory nod well short of spontaneous approval, then with a side glance probably thought, *This so-called swag is no more than a couple of rolled-up blankets tied to a leather bag; a hastily put-together bluey if ever I saw one! And it's not going to look much better when the pick and shovel in the back start jumpin' all over it!* It seemed to him the swag's only distinguishing feature was the small collection of seed burrs the blankets had attracted along the way. The whole bundle was strapped to a battered leather overnight bag, which was slung over the shoulder. The bag itself was so misshapen he thought it must have served as a pillow or was used as a crude and probably ineffective weapon.

'You said ya goin' to Brisbane, didn't ya? Well, I won't be takin' ya *that far north.*' He tilted his cattleman's hat from off his forehead with his thumb as he spoke, before yanking it down again to almost cover his eyebrows. The hat's stained brim and creased appearance suggested protection from the elements was only one of the uses it'd been called upon to perform.

'I reckon, young Clarrie, if in fact that's your *real* name, you wouldn't have the bush skills to sleep out in the open in a creek bed for more than an hour or so tops. You'd probably lay awake half the night expecting to be struck on the back of ya skull by one of those Abos with a nulla-nulla as soon as ya dosed off, then left to die?'

That wasn't far wrong, which Clarrie's silence tended to confirm.

'Anyhow, it's not that longa trip to the farm. I can put ya up for the night, if ya like. It'll save ya from sleepin' rough with them Abos, won't it?' Clarrie was not about to refuse the offer, such as it was, and his nodding acceptance was as unadorned as the invitation.

'By the way, me name's Jack Nevins,' the farmer finally revealed. The introduction was plain and simple, spoken out the side of his mouth, and was a long time coming. Indeed, Clarrie suspected that nothing Jack said or did ever occurred without its having undergone a slow process of gestation before arousal. *He's gotta be thinkin' about loads of strange stuff when he goes quiet like that,* Clarrie started to fear.

In fact, Jack was thinking that stumbling upon this unworldly drifter today, could in fact turn out to be quite handy. Nevis gave him another penetrating look as he pushed the sole of his left boot down heavily on the clutch. Both boots were covered in dust and strands of grass and manure. He then started to rev the guts out of the old truck's motor before most of its parts finally set off in one hell of a metallic shudder down the road. It took ages for the smell of the swirling exhaust fumes that wafted back into the cabin to be diffused and disappear.

————

Nevins made no attempt to clear the single bench seat of bits of wire, a clawhammer, pliers, screwed-up paper, rope, a small kero tin or the pair of Stillsons tied to a dry, grease-stained rag. No sooner had Clarrie lifted the assortment of tools and debris from where he was meant to sit, than he was introduced to a pungent commingling of sump-oil lubricant, fuel and body odour. The pong from Nevins's armpits was low octane, but quite possibly flammable.

With nowhere to escape to in the cabin, the intimate encounter with the pervasive, almost visible aromas turned out to be more than a passing acquaintance. To escape its embrace, Clarrie inched as close to the half-opened window as possible. He only realised the glass couldn't be fully wound down after he'd caught sight of the winder on the floor. It was wrapped in the torn remnants of a flannelette shirt. The obvious incentive to reattach the winder in case of wind, dust or rain, was clearly not that pressing an issue for the driver at this time of year, if ever.

In desperation, Clarrie flared his nostrils as he turned his face into the slight breeze, pretending to take a greater than normal interest in the scenery. Unfortunately, the truck's movement created about as much slipstream as the local shire's steamroller, which sat unattended on the shoulder of the road not far beyond where the truck had stopped. There was no sign of the roadworks gang anywhere nearby, a good indication they'd knocked-off work early and had headed towards a liquid lunch at The Criterion. Their custom would probably help lift its turnover, without doing much to lift its standard. It was a Friday afternoon after all – a payday. Those sessions kept isolated country pubs going for the following week and explained why it was the only day when the Aboriginal roadworkers hired by the Boolooroo Shire Council were tolerated in the public bar. 'At least the few beers they can afford will get them off the metho for the afternoon,' was the publican's derogatory excuse for relaxing his usual practice of barring them from entry.

Not having much else to look at, Clarrie noticed that the back of the farmer's hands were smudged with traces of dried blood. On a section of his forearm, set among the hairs, the blood had congealed to form an enormous scab. At the sight of this and letting his lurid imagination stray a little amid the palpable tension, Clarrie hoped it wouldn't be a very long trip down the road to the farm.

'I've been thinkin' about what you said, so listen up while I point somethin' out to ya,' Nevins eventually said in an ominous drawl.

'There're dry creek beds everywhere ya look at this time of year, and drought or no drought, ya won't find any Abos camped there. Might've once. Freshwater streams and creeks mean a lot to 'em, but most've been fished out for years. They know waterholes off the beaten track – same for where they still build fish traps with rocks. Anyhow,' he went on, 'they know where to dig for what they call sweet water in soaks and billabongs and can easily locate rock shelters for the night.'

'Sounds like you know a lot about them,' Clarrie sheepishly suggested.

'I've 'ad *a bloody lot* to do with 'em, sonny. Mostly the ones who live outa town in their gunyas. Others are stayin' in bigga huts on the stations in the district. Bit of all right – proper beds and tank water, and they don't have to hunt for roo meat neither – so good luck to 'em, I say.'

'Well, there were plenty of empty shacks in that town back there, they could probably break into quicka than me,' Clarrie unthinkingly jumped in. His suggestion was treated by Jack in much the same way as his earlier comments – with scarcely disguised contempt.

'Everyone leaves 'em alone, includin' ol' Joe Boyd, the district sergeant – but ee's usually asleep in 'is empty lock-up most days anyway. That useless welfare board officer finally got the message too, when ee came sniffin' round the farm a few months back. An', by the way, I usually hire the same couple of Abos for fencin' work, 'specially this time of year comin' into Christmas. They're good workers. So don't go thinkin' they're all lazin' about in the shade on a riverbank, doin' bugga all!'

Clarrie had no choice but to take it all in and maintained a moody silence. It was the first time he'd heard of Aborigines having a type of close connection with the landscape. In fact, Jack was the first white-fella he'd ever come across who seemed to be standing up for them. But it didn't feel right being taught something he'd no intention of ever wanting to understand.

Then, in a menacing voice that sounded like he was laying down the law, Nevins continued, 'And another thing. I didn't like the way ya said, gone walkabout, neither. You're the only one out here who's walkin' about the place, lookin' pretty well lost and foot-sore, if I'm not mistaken. If not for me pickin' ya up, you'd be flat out gettin' far in those clodhoppers ya got on this late in the day. As I was sayin', the Kamilaroi mob always know where *they're* goin'. You city blokes wouldn't have a clue, but you're wanderin' round in their country right now. Whenever they leave camp, they know where to find what they need to survive without payin' a brass razoo for it neither. An' I'll tell ya – it ain't in the pub.'

Clarrie started to nervously rub his thigh, wondering where all this was leading. He didn't have long to wait.

'When it comes to feedin' themselves, they locate food by huntin' with a spear or foragin' with their diggin' stick – what they call a ganaay. They know the right spots. Probably been doin' it since Adam? Bet you don't know how good goanna tastes after it's been pulled kickin' from its sandy burrow, whacked on the scone, scaled, then smoked and cooked over a fire pit? Or roasted wild pig, eel, bush melon, or yams baked in the hot embers?'

He didn't wait for a response, because he was always going to supply the only acceptable answer – '*Bloody tasty*! Same goes for the spangled perch and bony bream they trap when the streams are runnin'. What they hunt is heaps better and plenny cheapa than the counta meals you've probably been feedin' ya face with every day. What they end up cookin' just takes a bit a know-how, careful diggin' and hard yakka – that's all.'

After this, Clarrie had to relinquish his initial impression that Jack was a man of few words. It obviously didn't apply if you said anything mildly disparaging about blackfellas. *Lucky he hadn't called any of them Jacky-Jacky*, he thought.

'Like I was sayin', Mr Nevins, you seem to know a lot about those tribes, but I've never really struck many Aboriginals on my way here,' he slavishly ventured to say, as his mouth started to water.

'Don't ya be callin' me *mister* Nevins now,' he said, slowly turning his head towards Clarrie, his heavy-lidded saurian eyes barely visible under the sloping brim of his hat. 'I'm not surprised ya didn't run into any on the roads you've been keepin' to. They've got tracks in their head you'll never see – and there's no reason to stake 'em out with pegs like the guvmint surveyor does. As Miriam says, the whitefella only feels ee belongs somewhere when ee's got a piece of paper that says ee owns the land … when ee's just squattin' on it. She says the land *owns her*. Can ya believe that! Where's *your* bit a land, sonny? Where do you belong?'

'I don't have any land, don't wan' it. I don't belong to anyone, an' no-one writes to me 'cause I've got no postal address.'

'If all that's true, no wonder ya look so miserable. I've noticed the corners of ya mouth are always turned down. For Miriam's mob, the land means a whole lot more than somewhere to receive a letter. *Er* feeling of belongin' is somethin' she can up and carry with 'er any time a day. So I hope you've cottoned on by now, we owe 'em a lot of respect. In future, be careful what ya say about things ya know fuck all about.'

What's the bloody point of tellin' me all this? Clarrie thought. *The way he's goin' on about those Abos, it's like he's one of them, or owes 'em a whole lot.* As far as he was concerned, he couldn't see that *he* owed an Aborigine one single thing. They're all lazy layabouts people said – except when they go walkabout or maybe diggin' for those goannas. Clarrie shrugged his shoulders as if to acknowledge his ignorance. Even someone with his flair for insensitivity could tell it wasn't the time or place to argue the toss.

———

A period of deafening silence now broke out within the cabin where, like Clarrie, even the prevailing smell seemed to be holding its breath. Jack bristled at the insulting remarks directed at his white community as well, and it showed. He took exception to the way the only pub in town was derided, where his first cousin was the registered licensee. Ownership of the pub had remained in Palliser hands for as long as anyone in the township and surrounding district could remember. Were cousin John Henry to die unmarried and remain childless, Jack stood to receive a beneficial interest in the leasehold property. At least, it was highly contestable, a visiting notary had told him. Jack believed himself to be possibly the last remaining Palliser descendant entitled to inherit and claim possession.

Nevins therefore had no real objection to perhaps one day signing the white man's piece of paper from the Lands and Titles Office. He'd already seen a certified true copy of his deceased uncle John Cyril Palliser's last will and testament. In that document, Jack's late mother, born Myrtle Palliser, was originally registered as one of the lessors of The Criterion. But she had never shown any inclination to enforce her part-interest, and unlike her publican brother John Cyril, both she and her husband Bert Nevins encouraged the hiring of Aboriginal labour around their property. She'd died not long after her brother. The demise of John Cyril's son, the current licensee, John Henry, could possibly deliver Jack a windfall inheritance with its promise of an end to perennial hardship.

Even if he understood anything about them, old title deeds or the law of succession was not something he was ever likely to speak to Miriam about. Despite his words to Clarrie, Jack Nevins was not immune to the acceptance of a self-serving paternalism towards the Aborigine. He knew Miriam's tribal lore was inimical to the English law of tenure, and it wasn't going to prevail over what the lawyer had told him about the legal primacy of his own claim. Despite Miriam's moral title to custodianship of the leasehold land, like his forebears, Jack chose not to recognise an Aboriginal claim solely consecrated by traditional ownership and what Miriam described as her Dreamin' stories. Rather, he went along with the lawyer's abstruse description of the common law chain of title's status as indefeasible.

Given Jack's surliness, Clarrie thought there'd be Buckley's chance of him staying much beyond the short stint of labouring Jack had in mind to get him started on first thing in the morning. It was also made clear that Miriam was part of the family, and Jack had warned him a few times that there'd better be no disrespect, otherwise he'd find he was *not* heading north, but different parts of him would be heading in all directions, after a swift kick up the arse.

One of Nevins's more favoured Aboriginal workers was Flash Billy Nolan, as he was known throughout the district. He was distinctive for his copper-skinned, lean good looks and superb mustering skills. He was given a permanent bunk in one of the farm's lean-to sheds, despite also cohabiting from time to time with kin who lived in settlements on the fringe of the township.

On the other hand, Billy's relationship with Jack's housekeeper Miriam was not untroubled. She disapproved of his coming and going as he pleased and found him deceitful. She was dirty on Jack for allowing him to take certain liberties around the place, to which he wouldn't normally have turned a blind eye.

Jack accepted that Billy's sense of dignity wouldn't allow him to receive payment for his work around the farm solely in salted meat, grog and the usual dry rations. Billy had heard stories of blackfellas being given poisoned flour by station managers and squatters in the past. So he asked for and received half-decent if irregular pay for his labour. At Nevins's Run, he was such a valued worker that he was also afforded a permanent place at the boss's dinner table.

Two years before, Billy had gone north to work as a stockman on a cattle station around Cunnamulla. By the time he came back, he'd developed into a highly competent horse-breaker and could effortlessly vault onto the back of a moving horse while it circled in the mounting yard. On the right horse he could even make it pirouette. His acrobatic feats as a bareback rider were as good as you'd ever be likely to come across in a travelling circus or at a big country-town gymkhana. Over time, his legs had become slightly bowed, such that even with his two feet on the ground it appeared as if he were still astride a horse, albeit quite a small one.

Billy did nothing to dispel the rumour that he was so skilful with a stockwhip he could remove a smoke from between a man's outstretched fingers with a single crack. Nobody had actually seen him do this, so whoever spread the rumour must've rivalled Billy's familiarity with bulldust. He'd started to walk with a confident swagger, and a reasonably sized, ivory-handled clasp knife – a family heirloom gifted to him from Jack – stuck out precariously at the top of the leather belt around his moleskins. The handle already had the initials BN burnt in. That's why he wore it that way – so everyone could admire the knife and him at the same time.

In Cunnamulla, while he was wary of getting too big a head showing off his riding skills when the bosses were around, he was not as reluctant to do a bit of showboating in front of the womenfolk. If he were smarter, it would have been the other way round – men trust a mug lair even less when their wives express delight at what they see in him. With fewer women to impress at Nevins's Run, when Billy knocked off work and tied up the horses during the fading daylight hours, if he wasn't whittling pieces of wood with his clasp knife, he was occupied oiling its blade. A couple of times a week he fetched his larger, curved boning knife and tidied it up over the sharpening stone outside the woolshed.

Jack had previously taken him on as a farmhand as he claimed to come from the same mob as Miriam, despite her being unaware of any

tribal forebears called Nolan. She was less enthralled by his unexpected return than she'd been by his departure. The coldness of her
welcome only deepened after he'd ridden in on a horse that no black-
fella on an allowance could ever have afforded. She suspected his
move back from Cunnamulla had more to do with his running out of
luck around unbroken fillies promised to other men, than being home-
sick for his Country, or fed up with the paucity of his allowance. She'd
heard the manager up north had supposedly paid him full wages,
though he'd never have seen much of it after inflated food and
clothing costs were extracted – and he certainly wouldn't have had
enough left to purchase such a fine-looking stallion, she correctly
reasoned.

Billy was considered a half-caste under New South Wales legisla-
tion and had decided to shoot through to Queensland when his sister
was forcibly removed from their destitute mother by agents of the so-
called Aborigines Protection Board. She was his only sister and was
eventually taken to the mission station at Brewarrina. There she was
trained in domestic duties and eventually sent by the board manager
to serve a wealthy white family in Newcastle.

While he deeply resented the government protector's systematic
removal of native inhabitants from their traditional lands, it wasn't
something Billy constantly brooded over. The stain of bloodshed that
often accompanied the dispossession had had plenty of time to soak in.
The whitefella's *civilising* process and attempt to eradicate his Aborigi-
nality, had gradually discoloured his whole outlook on life, and the
feeling of injustice needed much less time than settler culture to be
thoroughly assimilated.

———

'Well, you were in the right spot today, old son,' Nevins finally
resumed in a slightly more conversational voice, breaking the threatening silences that'd put Clarrie on edge.

'Before I picked ya up, I'd taken some meat to a bloke in town to
repay a debt. Bloody happy as Larry he was, what with the price of
spring lamb nowadays. You're a bit ova lucky bastard too. This ol'

truck chews up a gallon of juice even before it gets much beyond the cattle grid near the house. Most days it sits idle in the shed. Unless it's a Friday, you'd be flat out ever seeing me on that part of the road back there – an' never in the middle of the week, I can tell ya that!'

Clarrie said nothing but tried to look as if he were grateful by moving his chin up and down ever so slightly. After another long pause, Jack went on. 'Turns out you're *doubly lucky*. When I sighted ya from down the road, ya certainly didn't stick out like one of those useless sundownas we get droppin' in every now an' then.'

'I knew some good would come of not gettin' rid of me old Gladstone bag,' Clarrie responded naively.

'Yeah, if it was one of those blokes carryin' that sort of bag, it'd probably 'ave been stolen and I'd 'ave kept goin'. Most of 'em are only lookin' for somewhere to get a free feed round dinnertime. They usually shoot through first thing in the mornin', without doin' a scrap of work. No-one'll give 'em the time a day in these parts.'

'Well Jack, this is my first time hitchin' in the bush, and except for the locals like you, most of the drivers seem to speed up and keep goin' when they spot me. Perhaps all they see is the swag and think here's another good-for-nothin' bastard like the ones you've been talkin' about. I don't have any money to speak of, and that kit I'm carryin' is all I've got. Me auntie in Brisbane is sure to put me up whenever I get there. But I need to land a job every now and then to earn a quid. I'm not one of those useless sundownas, just turnin' up for a feed.'

'I'll give you that much, cause by the look of ya, I bet you haven't 'ad a decent feed or hot tub in ages.' Nevins struggled to clamp his fist around the rotating knob on top of the floor shift to change out of second gear. Neither driver nor passengers could ever be sure there was a third. 'I'll get the chip heater fired up soon as we get there, so ya can give yaself a good scrub – spruce up a bit before tea. How'd ya feel about that?'

'That sounds good,' Clarrie responded in a voice he hoped would convey the right amount of gratitude and enthusiasm to get back on reasonably amicable terms. 'This old clobba I'm in is about to walk off me,' he laughingly added, still wary about cracking a joke and clumsily trying to convey a sense of friendliness in his voice at the same time.

He appreciated the farmer's grudging generosity, but all the same felt a creeping sense of uneasiness that this rough-as-guts bushie was already dictating things, as though he were his *father*. He really didn't have any choice but to go along with the farmer's terms and conditions whatever they were, and to wherever it was he was being transported.

'Canya lift thirty-pound bags ov wheat onto the back ova truck for a few hours at a go? I've got me doubts.' Then, half-turning his head to give his passenger's unimpressive physique the quick once-over, he added, 'Ya must be flat out weighin' ten stone drippin' wet.'

It was more of a statement than a question and said with a directness that suggested it didn't require an answer. Clarrie thought of giving an ambivalent response, saying he was a fightin' welterweight, or perhaps saying nothing at all to what seemed like a denigration of his manliness. Unaware of what it might entail, he confidently piped up with, 'I can handle any sort of farm work, Jack.'

Nevins knew this young bloke would keel over on the spot if asked to do some mulesing or crutching of the sheep. Fortunately for him, those tasks were finished for the season.

'I used to cart hessian bags full of cokin' coal for the owners of Cosy heaters. You know, the brown-coloured ceramic ones that look like tiny houses. They've got four mica windows on a hinged door at the front, and they're set up on a brick hearth. If you're tempted, don't ever get one – they smoke out the whole room whenever you light 'em up. The driver and me, we delivered bags of coke to hardware shops in the wintertime around Hurstville and Kogarah in Sydney. I was only the offsider, but it was the last regular job I had before I hit the road.'

Jack hadn't come across any city combustion heaters in his life, let alone one that resembled a little house. If Jack's silence told Clarrie anything, it was that he remained unimpressed. He then decided to pad out his rather limited work experience for greater effect, possibly receiving Jack's recognition but no doubt heavily qualified approval.

'I also got the odd job as a rabbitoh, an' had a short stint deliverin' ice with the iron tongs as well. About a month ago, I landed two weeks' work with a gang of fettlers, luggin' ironbark sleepers on the Narromine to Dubbo line. I'll go wherever the work takes me an' do more of less anythin' to earn a crust.'

'Well, that's a change from the useless jobs most fellas on the road claim t'ave done. But I've gotta say, there's not much call for blocks of ice where I'm takin' ya tonight.'

Jack had caught a glimpse of the inside of Clarrie's hands. While they were not exactly the coddled hands of a desk-johnny, even the sunburn and abrasions on the tops couldn't disguise the fact that from Jack's point of view, these were the delicate hands of a city bloke. The more often he complained of the blisters that had now hardened after supposedly working on railway sidings with a gang of fettlers, the more Jack suspected the story was a load of bullshit. He'd never heard of a train line going from Narromine to anywhere else, for a start. *He was probably only a counterjumper in a hardware store that sold bags of coke. The amount of manual work those hands have performed was limited, and its regularity exaggerated*, Jack correctly assumed.

'Look,' Nevins continued, wiping the corners of his mouth with his index finger. 'For now, all I'm goin' to offa ya is a bed off the shearin' shed, some old clothes and regular meals – I've always got a pot of stew on the boil, full of the best scrag-end neck of mutton you'll ever sit down to 'round 'ere. I like the fact you're not just hungry, but also hungry for work. I'll give ya a start tomorrow mornin' – that's if ya truly wanna work hard for yer board, and not plannin' to stand round pickin' ya bum?'

The silent reply had by now become such a commonplace between them that even Jack was quicker in keeping the conversation alive. The persistent thrum of the motor deterred lengthy talking in any case.

'I'm not askin' ya to do it for love. Ya say ya haven't got two bob to ya name. Well, there might even be a few smackers in it for ya, if ya can actually *do* all ya say ya can?'

The way this paid job offer came across, it felt as if he was being thrown a bone with the marrow removed, and for which he ought to be eternally grateful. But although he found the situation unsettling, Clarrie knew he had no choice other than to strike a bargain then and there, if that's what you'd call it. Right now, he had only small change in his pocket and a tenner tucked away in his swag to tide him over if work got any scarcer. Things were already tight, and Jack's offer was the best he'd gotten in over a fortnight.

'Since ya know a lot about rabbits, I'll get ya to snare a few, if ya like? They're payin' good scalp money these days – rabbit's more valuable than wallaby skins, and there's a good deal more of 'em around. Should be easy to properly string 'em up too, what with all ya experience as a rabbita?' he said, his top lip curling up on one side of his mouth as he spoke.

Clarrie thought it better not to reply.

Despite adopting a conversational tone dripping with sarcasm, deep down Jack didn't need much convincing about whether this itinerant could be a useful offsider around his mixed-use farm. He knew from experience that it was often the young and nimble, the lightweight wiry blokes rather than the older, burly types, who'd proven to be the best casual farmhands at the end of the shearing season. All the same, he wasn't sure Miriam would be as convinced as he was about the wisdom of taking in another probably work-shy drifter.

For Jack, it was all about stamina not brawn, and Clarrie looked like he had enough of it to swing an axe for more than ten minutes without throwing in the towel. Whether he would be around long enough to learn how to properly bag a bushel of wheat, and strong enough to lump it onto the truck, was another matter. In the meantime, there'd be a bit of woodchopping to get him started in the morning, he'd already decided. *That's as good a job as any to gauge his usefulness – and I won't be givin' 'im any hessian bags to help 'im carry it to the side of the shed, neither*, he thought.

Jack hadn't picked up the stranger out of a need for company, but Clarrie soon talked about everything that had happened to him on his inland journey to where he was now. It was somewhere in northern central New South Wales, just beyond a region he'd heard was called the Liverpool Plains. Once he'd started, Clarrie opened up like the bellows of a small concertina. For his part, Nevins's conversational skills, like the truck's transmission, struggled to get out of first gear. Both man and vehicle were in no hurry, and both seemed to like it that way.

———

After it had dawdled along the main road for several miles, the truck eventually turned off the bitumen and crunched its way onto a fringe of loose gravel. This soon merged into a narrow, corrugated dirt track, where the truck splintered broken-off tree branches, throwing up stones and raising a cloud of dust in the process. Small stands of manna gums with their shredded, white-powdery bark, clumps of wattle bush, bloodwood trees and patches of brigalow scrub hugged the sides of the single-lane track.

At various intervals, what might have started as small ruts on the surface of the roadway had long since developed into deep fissures. No matter who was at the wheel, they would've been forced to adopt the same zig-zag pattern of movement that Jack employed to avoid them. This manoeuvring task was made easier by the fact the Bedford was pushed to go any faster than thirty miles an hour on any type of winding road, sealed or otherwise.

With his jolting head still facing outwards and into the faint sensation of a breeze, Clarrie could make out through the trees eroded hillsides where the straggly roots of paperbarks and tea trees protruded along the sides of waterless creek beds and gullies. The stratified nature of the exposed soil spoke of a land several millennia deep. The only flowers visible along the way were scattered, purple clumps of bush iris. It was fortunate there weren't too many steep rises, as the truck seemed to labour for breath, falter, then wheeze heavily back into consciousness with every gear change, even on the gentlest of inclines. The greasy hand-crank that jumped around on the floor suggested it might be a struggle to kick the motor over whenever it stalled.

The sole direction post they passed pointed: Waterloo Creek 12m. The black lettering that had once been seared into the white wooden arrow was now so far faded as to be almost illegible. The wood was badly splintered and the sign itself tilted alarmingly towards the ground, neglected.

'What's the story about that old signpost we passed back there, Jack?'

'Not too sure. Must've been a few people killed there. Met their

Waterloo at that creek a fair while ago, you'd have to say. There's still a few broken-up humpies at that place now, but not much else. No-one's ever asked me about it before – none of the locals, anyhow. Doesn't mean anything to 'em.'

His abruptness clearly indicated he wanted to curtail any further discussion around the matter. Clarrie detected the reluctance, and thought Jack might've known a bit more about the place than what he'd let on. They then drove through a couple of shallow rivulets glistening with polished pebbles, the truck's heavy tyres displacing the water in a trickle rather than a splash. The track became rockier and caused the car's body to shudder. What Clarrie thought would be a short trip was taking ages. Nevin's earlier 'Not far down the road,' idle promise was surely based upon his understanding of the country mile – a distance much further than the imperial standard defined. He imagined that a few more of those sharper bangs on the chassis might do it, and in no time he'd be looking at the rocks directly beneath his heavy boots. The thudding continued for that good country mile *and some*. The noise continued to reverberate through the cabin floor until the tyres went over the metal bars of a cattle grid, and the slightly smoother surface that lay beyond.

'This is the Nevins's selection from here on in. It's a bit of an axe-handle block,' Jack finally let out. 'I like to call it Nevins's Run … sounds like I've got more grass feed an' livestock than I could ever handle on my size spread. The name's mainly a reminder of me ol' dad, Bert. He would've loved seein' me makin' a go of it, at the place where he and his father before him was born. Grandad was granted a bit of pasture last century, and Dad got it outright when Grandma died, but you'd never catch any of us Nevins calling ourselves *pastoralists*.'

There was nothing to distinguish any boundaries to the property, and sparse evidence of pasture. Both sides of the road were unfenced and not closely timbered, except for small clusters of stringybarks and white boxwood trees, the bibil, randomly scattered among thorny bush shrubs. His and the neighbouring settler families were a recently introduced species amid the ancient landscape. Like the weed they called

Paterson's Curse, they'd taken root and successfully overrun the native inhabitants.

———

Passing over one final cattle grid, it wasn't long before the truck idled to a halt in a clearing about twenty yards from a pair of lopsided farmhouse gates. Clarrie caught sight of some emaciated horses sheltering under trees in a nearby paddock. Further away, he spotted a marginally grassier area of partially fenced-off land. Perhaps it'd been set aside for agistment, its boundaries well overdue for new fencing.

On the far horizon, above the hazy, uneven outline of distant hills, the distinctive reddish streaks of cloud announced the first signs of the approaching sunset. The only thing moving in the immense azure sky was what looked like a wedge-tailed eagle. It was wheeling effortlessly at a great height, scanning its natural habitat for live prey – rat-kangaroos, bilbies, galahs, rabbits – or else the remnants of carrion already torn apart by dingoes and foxes.

The bird would suddenly soar, then drift downwards in a gyre, swoop and finally sheer away in the air without moving its wings. It circled and danced, seemingly at the mercy of invisible and alternating plumes of colder, then rising warmer air. As it glided closer, it seemed to gather the air in its pinions, splaying the feathers at the tip of each wing. Clarrie envied the bird's freedom and became momentarily lifted in unaccustomed reverie before Jack's lingering smell penetrated his nostrils and brought him back to earth.

Almost as soon as he opened the door of the truck, Clarrie was hit by a swarm of tiny bush flies that came out of nowhere. He struggled to retrieve his swag from beneath the filthy pick and shovel in the tray – he was rendered defenceless by their overwhelming numbers and wasn't far off literally dropping his bundle. Once they landed on him, they resembled a mass of agile blackcurrants, scampering every which way on what he imagined were miniscule, retractable legs. Their reaction time to the threat of a swat was measured in split seconds and contemptuously evaded. They soon carpeted Clarrie's clothing, attracted like a pile of lead pellets to a magnet, leaving no bites or itchiness but proving themselves to be masters of irritation. Perhaps the aroma from Jack's armpits acted as a repellent, because in contrast, his bare arms were hardly visited. It didn't have much to do with any lack of personal hygiene, but Clarrie would soon come to realise there weren't any flies on Jack Nevins, whatever the situation. Like a drowning man desperately threshing around in the sea, Clarrie started to flail his arms in a futile attempt to deter their landing all over his face, especially around his ears and eyes.

Noticing his agitation, Jack slyly remarked, 'You'd bedda get used to 'em, son. You're in cow an' sheep dung country round 'ere. The flies are onto it while it's still steamin', and any dead meat that's layin' round needs to be gotten rid of like a shot before they pick up the scent. Nothin's gunna hunt those little buggers away 'til it pours with rain. By the look of things, ya might be waitin' a while,' he said, glancing despairingly at the sky as he slammed the door shut. 'If we don't get rain in the next two weeks or so, it's goodbye to sowin' a summa crop,' he said, and the sight of the near-motionless vanes on the usually creaking windpump alongside the main house justified his sense of pessimism.

Either side of the gate, a low wire fence marked the perimeter of the larger farmhouse. Clarrie noticed another much smaller dwelling set back from the main household. It was nothing more than a rough-hewn slab hut and not fit for more than one person or a childless couple. It sported an uneven split-wood verandah, and a small brick chimney towards the back looked skew-whiff. Someone had given one of the sides a lick of whitewash a fair while ago but presumably thought it wasn't worthwhile finishing the job.

Between the two was an outhouse, a standalone, isolated fixture, like most country dunnies. It looked like it'd been slapped together out of any discarded wood, nails and corrugated iron sheeting that was lying about at the time. Well-trodden pathways led to its door from all directions. The door had no visible latch or handle, so remained permanently ajar. The inside looked barely big enough to squat on the wooden thunderbox, carefully positioned over a long-drop latrine.

Further back again there were two sheds, the smaller one flanked by a couple of lean-tos. Behind the open doors of the larger shed was the dark outline of a farm tractor. The only part that clearly jutted out was the distinctive grill and the cast-metal lettering of the Fordson brand emblazoned above the radiator. Outside, dotted all over the place like a long-abandoned salvage yard, disused ploughshares, the tines of handleless pitchforks and iron-spoked wheels were left to slowly rust away. Given the lack of moisture, that process would take decades. In the foreground lay the remnants of an old dray turned on its side. It was now reduced to splintered planks in which long grass and husked weeds had taken up permanent residence. Closer to where the truck had pulled up lay a squaring axe, an adze and a length of ironbark that had been half hollowed out to form an as-yet unfinished water trough. It was still waiting for an unpredictable bout of optimism to show up and finish the job.

The noise created by the truck's arrival was drowned out by that of an overexcited pack of yelping dogs. All were restrained by robust, leather collars attached to chains, which in turn were tethered to short lengths of galvanised piping hammered into the ground about ten feet apart. There was no give in the metal or the leather, nor was there any apparent shelter offering protection against the elements.

'Don't worry too much about them dogs. It's only a couple makin' most of the noise, 'specially the ones I'll *relocate* before long,' Nevins grunted. 'But if you don't know already, even those that look a bit crook can still come in 'andy 'round 'ere.'

Jack, as much as the dogs, wasn't used to having guests or uninvited drop-ins. The last visitor was a travelling Afghan hawker, who a few months before didn't make it beyond the spot where the truck had pulled up. He hadn't time to utter more than he was called John Mullah Mohamed before he spotted Jack heading for the truck to fetch his rifle. The sight of this was such a conversation killer that it encouraged Mohamed to hurriedly turn round his cart full of pots, pans and opossum skins and skedaddle back to town with his tail between his legs. His U-turn was so abrupt that various small utensils and parcels of seed pods had fallen out of his overladen cart. Miriam was given the job of clearing things up.

Jack gradually became a lot more talkative than his usual laconic predisposition would have predicted. 'The Queensland Blue Heeler doesn't bark much, but I gotta tell ya, ee's always alert to an unwel-come drifter. That speckled cattle dog over there, ee's gettin' on a bit and slow as a wet week, but still managed to bail up a good half-dozen joe blakes last summer without gettin' bit. Ee's a cunning ol' bastard. Doesn't flinch when ee spots 'em in the long grass – goes for 'em right behind the head. Even knows how to pull a brownie from a crack in the ground.'

Clarrie had earlier caught a glimpse of the butt of a .22 rifle over the back seat of the truck and now guessed that was probably Nevins's preferred way of introducing himself to any stray sundownas, as well as providing the means of relocation for anything too crook, surplus to needs, or both.

As he walked slowly to the front gate, Clarrie cast a sentimental eye over the now prostrate animals. Some gave a slight whimper or the occasional dispirited growl through sullen jaws, which were now mercifully closed and resting upon their extended front paws. The larger ones resumed their slobbering on once-oversized shanks and knuckles, which were presently being whittled down to splintered, dirt-covered fragments of bone. He even spotted what looked like a cow's hoof among the offerings. Any of these bones would have provided not much more nutritional value than a crowbar, and by the sound of the dogs' gnashing teeth, were not half as tender. At the sight of this, Clarrie realised that Nevins must have rationed feed for his dogs in much the same way he dealt in conversation – in meagre amounts requiring lots of patience from the recipients to get to the pith and marrow. He still couldn't help wondering which one of the dogs was the likely candidate for permanent relocation. From their physical appearance and their initial feverish straining at the chains, none seemed in any way disabled. Nor did any appear remotely lacking in the vitality that might otherwise have predicted death from other than natural causes.

'They might all look like healthy workin' dogs to you,' Nevins said as he shortened his stride and glowered towards the now brooding and irritable-looking crossbreeds, 'but they're a bit like human beings – you've gotta live with 'em for a while to work out their true nature. It doesn't take long to find out which ones 'av got the instinct for bein' the most useful round the place, an' them that even their mothers wouldn't feed. I don't mind if they've got a bit of mongrel in 'em, so long as they don't cross the line. You soon learn to read 'em, but not as quick as they learn to read who's top dog round 'ere,' he boasted, looking directly at Clarrie.

'You see one of those skinny sheep dogs over there?' Jack vaguely pointed with the stub of his left forefinger.

'Yeah,' replied Clarrie, feigning deep interest and uncommon discernment.

'Well, the one I'm pointin' to I named Dusty. I always suspected ee had too much dingo in 'im for 'is own good. Used to take 'im pig-shootin' a while back, but ee'd often go missin', so I started to chain 'im up for longer periods every day. Ee recently started nippin' at the lambs in the only paddocks with any sort of pasture to speak of. Just doin' what comes natural, I s'ppose. I've seen wild dogs bite small roos and joeys on the end of their tails to get 'em off balance before goin' for the jugular to finish 'em off. I happened to spot Dusty runnin' a decent-sized ewe in circles 'til she got giddy and dropped in a heap like a sack of spuds. Before I saw that, I'd occasionally come across a few dried-out carcasses in the paddocks. I now think Dusty might've 'ad somethin' to do with that, whenever he went missin'.'

Clarrie hadn't heard this much uninterrupted talk from Jack at any time beforehand. Then, looking towards the heavens, Jack went on. 'Ya might've spotted that eagle-hawk hangin' in the sky as we pulled up?'

'Yeah, it's been circlin' round for ages.'

'Well, it can home in on a dead or lame animal from miles away. It's the same eagle that last week led me to that dazed sheep I was talkin' about. That bird seems to like this place. Miriam calls it maliyan, says it's sacred. Says she can smell it when it turns up – calls it the spirit of 'er past elders, what we call ancestors. I don't know about that, but Miriam says it's 'er Dreamin' stories what makes it true.'

Well, livin' with Jack would sure make her sense of smell work overtime, he couldn't help thinking.

'What I *do* know is when it comes to findin' lost or strugglin' lambs, followin' that bird's path across the heavens is quicka than hirin' a blacktracka. I saw it up close one day – it's big enough to give ya a decent feed, but I don't think Miriam would be too happy if I shot the bloody thing.'

Jack raised his arm and pointed again to one of the dogs. Clarrie wished he hadn't done so with as much flourish.

'No doubt about what did it when I spotted the stain around Dusty's jaws. He'll never change now, once they get the taste of blood. I can't forgive the little mongrel. To keep 'im any longer would be worse than lettin' a fox 'ave the run of the chook house.'

Nevins was pretty sure Clarrie had managed to catch his drift.

'The other bitzer tied up alongside 'im, she walks all over the backs of the sheep, then jumps off, drops 'er back and stares at 'em through the gates and into the pens, ready for tail-dockin'. She's only interested in doin' 'er proper job. Ya can work out for yaself, which one's days are numbered.'

In fact, at a distance, Clarrie still couldn't be quite sure exactly which one of the hapless animals was already singled out for rifle practice and relocation. They all looked pretty dusty.

'I had to put down anotha badly savaged lamb early this mornin',' Jack continued. 'Billy the farmhand got in a bit of practice up north workin' as a slaughterer, so ee came in handy dressin' the lamb and puttin' the best cuts in the safe. As I said before, I'd dropped off a parcel of chops at the local pub before I picked ya up on the side of the road. And I'll tell ya again, you're a lucky bugga! You'll get the benefit of sittin' down to a roast leg of lamb for dinna, not the lumps of boiled mutton I've 'ad stewin' in the pot for a good week or so.'

Nevins had rounded off the conversation in a tone that seemed to betray both regret and generosity for what Clarrie was about to receive. Regret, mostly. After kicking a few rocks out of the way without breaking his stride, he pushed through the waist-high, spring-loaded wire gate with a nudge of the hip. 'Just wait 'ere … you'll get word when ya can go any further.'

Once the gate snapped shut behind him, Jack set foot on a short, earthen pathway. Rock borders on either side defined two narrow beds of recently planted poppies, zinnias and nasturtiums of variegated colours. The flowers were huddled together, as though they felt sorry for one another. They could have done with more than a good drizzle of water to stay upright. Almost everything on Nevins's Run looked wilted. These flowers were non-native species and certainly not drought-resistant. Although they struggled to push much above ground level, their mere presence demonstrated a successful act of defiance by small seedlings, which brought a touch of sad beauty to the otherwise desiccated environment surrounding them. *Whoever planted 'em and tried to keep 'em goin', it's unlikely to have been Jack Nevins,* Clarrie thought.

The only shade in the front yard came from a mature bilaar tree, with deeply scarred bark. Its spindly branches carried more seed cones than leaves. A mound of hard dirt with several holes near the base of the tree signalled a nest teeming with bull ants, a species of insect that derived meaning and its sense of purpose by busily conducting its communal activities largely below the surface; yet no matter how far they strayed, they never got lost.

'Miriam!' Jack called out before a smallish tan-skinned woman emerged from the shadowy hallway of the house. Her hair was lank and lifeless and hung in matted strands. She stood with a slight lean, her shoulder resting on the side of the half-open flyscreen door. The bottom of the door sagged and made a scraping sound on the verandah floor before it could be fully opened. What she was wearing was more like a calico shift than a regular frock with a noticeable hemline. It clung loosely to her figure and dropped mid-way down her calves. Although there was no suggestion of deliberate immodesty, she was obviously unconcerned that the sides of her flat, pendulous breasts were clearly exposed at the armpits.

'this 'ere is Clarrie,' Jack announced in a shouty voice. 'ave a good look at 'im before ya go inside an get 'im a towel. i picked 'im up on the road near the turn-off – reckon ee's a bit lost, an' havin' trouble findin' where ee belongs … probably been kicked outa home, an' not just the pub! ee might be stayin' 'ere for a bit, if ee don't act up and learns to keep 'is trap shut, but I don't know 'bout that yet.'

How come he didn't tell me he knew I got thumped at the pub? Clarrie continued to wonder.

The woman remained expressionless and stared at the stranger with the sort of deep, silent gaze that saw things way beyond his understanding. Clarrie detected a hostile serenity about her. To him it was the look of someone resigned to the fact that life was not going to get any better. Then again, his innate prejudices and lack of real understanding of anything at all about her rendered his first impression and his opinions essentially worthless.

'i'll get 'im to chop some wood out da back, an ee can drive in those new fence posts in the mornin'. ya can show 'im round the place, an 'is bed in the shearer's lean-to while i get the copper goin.'

Then, turning to Clarrie, he issued a mock warning: 'We're a bit short of kindling, so ya might end up with a cold shower under the canvas bucket, if yer outa luck,' he said. 'an' you can get 'im that bar of Solvol near the kitchen sink while yar at it,' he shouted out again as Miriam vanished into the hallway.

'What ya gapin' at, young Clarrie?' Jack said as he turned around and started to walk out the gate. 'Don't be fooled. She may look bashful but Miriam's tough as nails. Don't ever try to put one ova 'er. She picked up pidgin English at the mission and understands the lingo nearly as good as 'er native Gamilaraay. When she came back to town lookin for 'er tribal country, the local mob told 'er about that gnarly ol' tree with the notches, over there by the house. Soon as she saw it, she sat down an' started singin' in 'er native tongue. She wouldn't let me take an axe to it ... said it was full ov songs. She was happy to sit there for days before I agreed to take 'er in as me 'ousemaid. But she's no comm'n gin – won't wear an apron or any outfit that looks like one of those tunics they put 'er in as a kid. I taught 'er 'ow to use a rifle, an' she keeps one 'andy to take care of snakes, especially the black ones she calls nhurraay. But she can sense anythin' else around that's deadly. John 'enry didn't like the sound of that when I first told 'im.'

Then he stopped abruptly and, staring at Clarrie once more he cautioned, 'From the word go, I'll give ya the good oil. She doesn't take too kindly to brash young whitefellas, so don't give 'er any lip. As I said, she's no pushova, an' doesn't touch the grog, not even in the pub. She's got a special cup, puts it on the table, but only keeps it to remind her of what the religious minister called the bad spirit ... said it was part of his devil teachin' that taught 'er to leave it empty.'

'Who named her Miriam, was it that religious minister you were just talkin' about?'

'No. Miri's 'er Kamilaroi name. Means *bright star*, an' was picked out by one of 'er aunties … means she 'as no trouble stayin' awake starry nights like a watchdog. I'm the one that calls her Miriam – bin told it's in the Bible, so that's good enough for me an' she don't seem to mind. Ya now bin warned. She's still bitter at blokes like you for bringin' on the sickness that killed 'er mother. Won't let it happen to the daughter, so look out for what ya say, an' be careful what ya *think* ya might get up to – an' not just at nighttime neither!'

While waiting for Miriam to fetch the towel and what he imagined would be a seldom-used bar of gravelly soap, Clarrie thought it would've been a good idea for Jack to have the first scrub after copping another whiff of his distinctive pong, despite the absence of any breeze. Once Jack had gone and fresh air returned, the woman reappeared carrying the towel and a surprisingly withered cake of Solvol. Clarrie then tentatively moved a few steps inside the gate. Behind Miriam, he caught a glimpse of someone else ghosting around in the hallway. Within a few moments, a young girl emerged from the shadows.

She was slightly taller than Miriam, had much paler skin and was more covered up than the woman he imagined was her mother. She too appeared coy, and tilted her head, giving him a stare that went miles into the distance. Clarrie's stare on the other hand was close range, focussed on her snatch, fully bathing in his geographic obsession with country matters. She then turned more side-on and nuzzled up against the older woman's shoulder, as though unnerved by his gaze.

Jack didn't say whether Miriam was his de facto wife or not and hadn't mentioned the daughter at all until a minute ago. Clarrie soon put two and two together, and his basic arithmetic said old Jack was probably what they called a gin jockey. He soon found out it was an erroneous assumption, an unwelcome reminder that while he'd become reasonably proficient in foul language from an early age, he was never much good at sums in primary school.

'how ya goin', miriam,' he said from several yards away. 'an' who's that with you?' From the prolonged silence he could tell it'd take more than simple, direct questions for her to open up. This was the first time he'd seen a lubra up close, let alone two of them. In the few tribal pictures he'd seen in *Walkabout* magazine, the women always looked as rough as bags – slumped over, floppy-breasted and black as the ace of spades. They were usually sitting on the dirt around a fire, plaiting and weaving things, or daubing bark with ochre, their kids and mangy, lop-eared dogs jinking in the background. These two were different. They were both slender, lighter-skinned and standing upright, shoulders back, for a start. *The younger one wasn't bad lookin' for an Abo,* he thought. *If she wasn't stayin' here she'd get plenny of work as the town bike – that's if any young blokes were actually livin' back there.* Such was the extent of his deeply reasoned assessment of her vocational prospects.

Unlike the older woman, who appeared untroubled by the flies scuttling all over her face, the young girl was intent on constantly swatting them away. Her curlyish hair was bleached by the sun and had a lustre that said it must have been recently washed. The contrasting whiteness of her teeth stood out even as she struggled to suppress the hint of her broad smile, which her first sight of a ginger-haired stranger had naturally aroused. It was a small beam of pure innocence that made Clarrie momentarily forget what he hastily imagined to be the sorrow from which it shone.

Olive face, curly hair and big brown eyes – like them pictures of happy piccaninnies in those boot-polish ads. She's got that smooth skin and the long legs they call modern – right up to date, he smirked. He inspected her as if she were strung up on a hook at a wholesale meat market. *If she were a whitey, she'd be gaol-bait, for sure,* he cautioned himself with a half-concealed laugh.

Surprisingly for someone who revelled in talking the leg off an iron pot, Clarrie didn't know what to say. Miriam saved him the effort. 'We're goin' down to da place where ya gunna sleep – down dere,' she said, waving her hand in no particular direction.

'if ya point it out to me, miriam, i'll settle in by meself … or maybe *she* can show me round?'

'It down da back beside da shearin' shed, but it *me* who take ya dere. When ya go in, help yaself to any ov da ol' shirts an' long'uns dat fit – dere in da lowboy 'side da bed. Den take 'em to behine da wood-heap, over where Jack's gunna fix ya up with a tub a hot warda.'

Clarrie followed Miriam with slow, deliberate steps out the gate. He cast a quick look over his shoulder at the young girl, now standing on the inside of the flywire door. His sly glance didn't go unnoticed.

'you didn't tell me who that girl was with you? she doesn't say much, does she?'

'No, ya darn right. Ya godda lodda cheek – only 'ere five minute an' sound like yer wanna know everythin' an' run da place.' She continued, 'Dat's me daughter Nganuwaay, but I'm not 'er mother. She come from down Singleton way, Wonnarua Country. Before I took 'er in, she 'ad a sister not quite right either, an' da tribe killed 'er when she was young – let 'er die, dey said. But dis daughter stayed alive. She got da name Chérie … sound like da bottla grog, but whitefella who thought it up said it mean, *me darlin.*'

'i just wanted to say hello to her, that's all.'

'Well, she don't say much cause docta in Newcastle, ee says she's a bit deaf an' dumb like 'er sister was. But she hear good enough for housework, ee said.'

'how can you make out what she's wantin' to say, or what she's thinkin'?' he said in a slightly musical voice, more for show than out of legitimate concern or sympathy.

'She hear enough, an un'erstan' if ya look 'er in da face. She uses 'er eyes an 'er arms to tell ya things … dat's good, cause she never learn how to speak da lies like whitefellas do. I bin tellin 'er da Dreamin' stories, learnin' 'er to touch, smell an see da memory livin' all round da land, an in da night sky. When 'er own mother died, all dat was lost.'

Clarrie only caught the things he thought he understood, but even those bits hadn't really hit home. He'd heard the words godmother, orphan, foster child and ward of the state in conversations back home in Sydney and had certainly experienced deficient parenting during his own childhood. He ended up just leering at the motherless daughter, all the time conjuring with her name, which he falsely concluded was probably spelt 'cherry'. It satisfied his preconceptions, so he enquired no further about the spelling. *Miriam seems as grouchy as Jack when I called him mister. I'd better not ask her to do me washin'* was all he ended up thinking.

'Don't ya go anywhere near 'er without me say-so sonny. But if ya 'ave to, make sure itzin da broad daylight an' I'm round. I know what plenny whitefella think of us wimmin not stayin' with dere own mob – call us black belbet. Jack will sort ya out if ee see any muckin' round. And if *ee* don't, *I* will,' she glowered.

'i don't want jack relocating *me*, if that's what you mean.'

'Nah, ee save dat for da buruma … duvva dogs. Ee'll juz give ya a good beltin', won't waste a bullet on ya. Ee knows ya juz anuvva drifta passin' thru, tryin' t'scape da past. All ov dem ave lost dere way … dats 'ow Jack sees it. But if dat no-good, guvmint pratecta shows up again, thinkin' ee can take Chérie away cause she got fair skin an' dat, Jack'll bring out da twenny-two ee keep loaded in da truck. Ee make sure da last fella sellin' stuff don't wanna return in a 'urry. After ee spot Jack's rifle … to see 'im run away, was like ee was tryin' t'scape da present an' not da past.'

'does jack get to use that .22 much?'

'I heard da rifle go off duvva night … but Dusty still alive, izin ee? Might 'ave scared away anuvva hawka, or a sundowna? I dunno.' She curled her lip and said, 'If Jack don' tell, I don' ask. I keep sayin' – none ov ya bilong 'ere.'

CHAPTER
FIVE

NEARLY A FORTNIGHT WENT BY and no-one was more surprised than Clarrie that he'd stayed this long. He'd kept his mouth shut around Jack and made sure he steered clear of the daughter and Miriam's eagle eye throughout the day, and especially on starry nights. Nevertheless, he fancied that sooner or later he'd have a go at getting the girl's cherry. *I'll give 'er somethin' to see and touch for 'er memory ... an' not while she's dreamin', neither.*

Occasionally, their knees brushed under the dinner table, and as the girl didn't do much else than softly giggle, he mistakenly took his clumsy advances as something she liked and even encouraged. It didn't occur to him that he only represented a change in the scenery – his strangeness a matter of innocent, child-like curiosity, and nothing more.

In much the same way, he wrongly interpreted her care when she applied the elders' traditional mixture of clay and ashes to a slight cut on his ankle. He was more interested in her touch than the compound's reputed healing properties. These misleading impressions spurred him on to brazenly seek out the slightest chance for uninvited physical contact. He missed no opportunity to exploit her natural innocence, especially when neither Jack nor Miriam were around, or he thought weren't looking.

He'd started to help her bring in the dry washing, which never seemed to include any item worn by him. The whole time he kidded himself that her ditzy laugh was really a swoon. For all his eagerness for intimate contact, he somehow never got around to helping her with the clothes-mangle. Even after he saw her struggling with the paddle and an oversized wooden peg, she was left to wring out the water from the heavy wet linen dragged from the copper.

Of an evening in bed, he thought of little else but greedily fingering what he imagined to be her soft, moist fanny, or else mindlessly caressing her firm breasts and up-turned nipples. He believed that in no time at all she'd eventually lose her shyness and offer only faint resistance before he really started touching her up. *I bet she goes off like a tuppenny bunger on Empire Day,* he fantasised, every time he saw her.

These thoughts formed part of the recurring and odious delusion that he played out in his bed after nightfall, cock in hand. For him, the act of copulation had little to do with love. Although mostly insensitive to the range of human senses, the tactile was not one of them. It was not surprising therefore, that his most satisfying relationships were those conducted with his own body parts. Besides imagining he heard the muffled sound of Jack's rifle echoing in the distance, little else disturbed the genital fixations that increased his heart rate during the night. Unlike the quality of his fencing work in the paddocks, it was the only type of manual labour to which he could plausibly claim some measure of proficiency.

His nocturnal cravings only increased when, going to the window to investigate an outside noise, when late one evening, he unexpectedly caught sight of Billy leaving the slab hut that Chérie occupied behind the main house. He had a spring in his step and made no attempt to deaden the crunching sound made by his riding boots on the stoney ground beneath. Billy also seemed oblivious to the fact that there was a brilliant full moon, and infinite constellations lit up the heavens. There were stars everywhere, and he must have known the closest constellation never went to sleep. Was it a display of bravado, or perhaps Billy didn't care, knowing he might have had Jack's implied blessing? Stealth was seemingly not a consideration as his distinctive bandy-legged movement was as recognisable by moonlight as it was in full sun.

He's not deliverin' cuts of sheep meat, that's for sure, thought Clarrie. *Probably lookin' to sharpen his blade and get in the saddle at the same time. I bet Jack didn't have that in mind when he told Billy to give me some ridin' lessons this week.*

Far from being deterred or disappointed that Flash Billy may have already beaten him to the punch, Clarrie perversely thought what he spied had all but guaranteed his own prospects for turning his wet dreams into reality – whenever the most auspicious occasion arose. Those prospects weren't looking too rosy so far, but he never slackened off the rehearsals.

———

For the best part of a week, Jack had got him to sink new fence posts and affix the wire enclosing some half-promising pastureland. Miriam had stipulated that his labouring was to take place well away from the girl's living quarters. Fortunately for him, the task was taking so long that there'd been no demand to demonstrate his putative rabbiting skills.

Jack and Billy were too busy rounding up any livestock that had strayed through broken fencing to worry about Clarrie's low level of skill and lack of application to his current job. He was never going to be entrusted with a rifle to shoot a few rabbits in the open, anyway. Instead, Jack got him to set some rusty traps where the cleared land met thick scrub.

In the late afternoons, Billy tried to teach him how to strap, mount and sit in a saddle properly, and to manage the reins before geeing up a horse. Unlike his irritable pupil, Billy didn't shout his instructions – they were effectively communicated by repeated gesture and example, unmistakable facial expressions and his telling use of eye contact and silence.

'I'll give ya this advice, Clarrie. When it comes to trainin' a nag for ridin', it's easier if ya show 'im respect an' teach 'im good manners.' But basic horsemanship, like respect and good manners, didn't come easily to Clarrie. It was on a par with his non-existent ability to skin a bunny.

How'd he get so bloody good? He grimaced every time Billy showed him up by doing basic mounting skills so expertly. *He even says he can work out the age of a horse by its teeth. He's such a smart arse ... must be why they call him Flash Billy?* Clarrie's envious remarks were not far from the truth. Experience had taught Billy the smartest way to get in the saddle was in one very fast, seamless swivel of his arse. All Billy got in recognition of his prowess, however, was a dirty look, especially after he'd chosen an obstinate and bad-tempered nag to be saddled up for practice sessions. It was ironically named after the champion two-miler Peter Pan, because neither endurance nor finishing speed were notable qualities of this lumbering workhorse. According to Billy, he was long in the tooth, and Clarrie naively tried to verify that piece of information for himself while struggling to attach the bridle and bit. The horse almost tore his fingers apart.

All mug punters knew a true thoroughbred came back fresher and fitter after a decent spell, but Jack Nevins's workhorses – when not carting hay or pulling a scarifier – seemed to come back without any corresponding improvement in fitness. With no recent form, poor handling and impoverished connections, like the army regiments of light horsemen, Peter Pan was well on the way to being decommissioned. Billy also failed to tell him that the chestnut gelding was blind in one eye and now spent most of his days propping up a tree.

As soon as it felt a new rider in the stirrup irons, the horse instinctively shied away, moving backwards and sideways in the same motion. In fact, Billy was surprised that Clarrie was able to mount the horse at all, unaccustomed as it was to being saddled up. After ferociously digging his heels into the horse's flanks in frustration when it refused to budge, it would toss its head and rear up like a frisky two-year-old, bucking Clarrie from the saddle. It wouldn't be the only time he was thrown off and landed arse over tit in that first week.

Peter Pan had already been lined up for the knackery, and not for Mr R. R. Dangar's stud farm, an equine paradise down south in the Hunter Valley. This was where stallions serviced broodmares between grazing in honey-dewed paddocks of the finest lucerne. That's where cup winners ended up. The also-rans like *this* Peter Pan could expect at most a nosebag with a fistful of oats before that final rails run to the finish line at the glue factory. But while he might be tired-looking and in desperate need of a farrier, the horse occasionally displayed some ticker. Clarrie's ears had pricked up as his backside hit the ground when Billy laughingly remarked that he might still have one last gallop left in him. On hearing this, he decided that Peter Pan, a nag you wouldn't back as favourite in a one-horse race, was going to be his leisurely ticket out of day labour.

Hopefully, this escape would occur at the crack of dawn towards the end of the week. Although his relationship with the gelding couldn't be described as one of respect, in the sense that Billy had employed it, he felt a growing bond, even a sense of ownership. His only worry was that his leave without notice might turn out to be a little too leisurely, and not unnoticeable – that even if Jack didn't get wind of him clearing out until well after breakfast, he'd still need to get a good head start.

———

In the evenings, everyone ate dinner around the same table. Clarrie had been surprised to see Jack doing most of the cooking and clearing up. It was as though he were following the cook's routine at the pub, where the local blacks weren't entrusted to do either task. *That probably explains why there's no goanna, bush melon or even a slice of wild pig on the menu at Jack's table,* he thought.

However, he did like to serve up what he called Bert Nevins's Irish stew, which he claimed to be part of his family's culinary tradition. It simmered away for days in a heavy, blackened pot on the wood-fired range – the contents repeatedly topped up with more spuds, beans, heaped tablespoons of flour and fresh chunks of mutton and gristle. A billycan full of rust-coloured tank water was thrown in whenever the stew thickened and the stirring spoon got stuck. To Clarrie, the taste wasn't much different to the counter meals Jack had sunk the boot into on that first day in the truck – perhaps a little saltier and more of an overcooked, burnt-meat smell? *No wonder he went on about those tasty goannas; it'd have to be better than his stew*, he couldn't help thinking. He would have suggested an improvement by adding a bit of wild game – maybe some rabbit, if not that plump-looking eagle – but he held back, afraid of being immediately obliged to hunt, kill, skin, gut and cook any or all of them by himself.

He was even more taken aback when, one evening after dinner around the kero lamp, Jack pulled out a wad of pound notes and dropped them on the table. He then proceeded to slowly hand out an equal number of them, one by one, to both workers. Clarrie didn't say a word but thought by the fancy way Jack doled them out in even piles, he must've come into money and imagined himself to be Lord Nuffield. The drawn-out payment of wages ceremony was followed by the sharing of his grog outside on the verandah. He'd even removed his hat for the occasion, revealing his thinning brownish hair and some crusty scabs covering his scalp.

During that evening, after they'd exhausted their third-hand yarns, which came across slightly fresher after a few slugs of rum, Jack let on that he and Miriam were going to town that coming Friday. He said nothing about the purpose of his trip. To Clarrie's ears, it sounded as though he was going there to celebrate something – maybe Billy had told him that one of the elders had forecast the big rain that day? Clarrie was starting to enjoy the growing spirit of camaraderie. Jack seemed to talk more freely, while remaining only marginally less tetchy than usual. He was seemingly satisfied the drifter was following his advice to hold his tongue, even if he was tempted to badmouth anyone or anything on the farm.

But it was when Miriam spoke to him alone the following evening that he finally felt more than a barely tolerated drifter around the place. Jack had told her he was happy Clarrie had learnt to button his lip and had surprisingly developed a soft spot for the dogs. In recognition of this fact, Clarrie'd recently been given the job of feeding them. He liked the power he derived from throwing them portions of carcass – raw lamb shanks on which strands of greasy fleece and dags were still hanging, sinews and offal, or whatever else hadn't already been added to Nevins's permanently gelatinous pot-au-feu.

By now he'd worked out which one of the mongrels was Dusty. He made sure he threw him a special bone, one with some decent meat attached. But he still couldn't fathom why the mutt hadn't already been relocated? He didn't dare ask, as the reminder might well have resulted in a gunshot ringing out later in the day. This pleasing chore had its obvious pay-off – after receiving a couple of feeds, the normally ravenous canines had become less aggressive in his presence. They now did little more than give him a dopey look, even if he approached them day or night, empty-handed.

'Jack says ya asked 'im 'bout dat signpost along da track comin' in?' Miriam started off.

'yeah, it was funny to see that old piece of wood stuck out in the middle of nowhere. it was pointing downwards to a creek – the post was on a lean, the arrow part sort of hanging there, badly splintered. i could hardly read the words. it was good the truck was so slow, or i'd've missed it altogether. jack clammed up a bit when i wanted to know more about the place.'

'Well, I can tell ya now, it's lucky ya was a long way from any Myall Creek sign, cause Jack's kin murder plenny blackfellas ova dere too, in da ol' days. Shot 'em and cut 'em up too, say da papers Jack keeps unda 'is bed. Ee don't like to talk 'bout it much, an' don't like others askin' questions neither ... dose papers call'd it a masska, or some-thin'? Ee might 'ave kicked ya outa da truck dere an' den for askin' too much ... Jack says ee's visited by bad spirits juz tinkin' onit – says it like a snake bite, forever wantin' to suck out da bad blood.'

'I could tell he was cranky about something,' Clarrie thought he had to say to keep her interest up. For someone who never touched a drop, she'd blurted out a lot more than he was expecting, as though she'd thrown that cup away and been hitting the bottle all day.

'One time in da truck, ee even took a shot at dat sign ya saw ... with 'is rifle. I told 'im it no good, told 'im ya can't shoot da place like ya can da fellas who once live dere.... I told 'im dat creek now dead water, no Kamilaroi sit dere anymore. Ee know what I mean, an' say ee done wanna get in a row with me 'bout it – promised ee'll nebba talk 'bout dat sign again.'

'yeah, he got cranky with me about a lot of things on that trip in ... an' now you say all that, it must be he's carrying a curse, or has a guilty conscience?' Clarrie almost choked on the shameless insincerity of what he'd just said. He made things worse by mindlessly adding, 'but it can't be *his* fault for what his relatives did years ago, can it? why should jack say sorry or feel guilty for things *he* never did?'

Clarrie tried to work out why she gave him a filthy look, turning her head instead of answering, but to him her thoughts and feelings remained as unfathomable as ever.

'anyhow,' he continued, having exhausted his understanding of apology and forgiveness, 'jack said he respects you a lot ... i was wondering then, if you an' jack were ... you know, married or somethin'?'

'Nah! We can't 'av no tribal marriage, wouldn't be right. Ee's not part of our mob, an' ee'll never know our ways – da bora ring, da smokin' ceremony, our Dreamin stories – an' I know for sure, da white-fella nebba give back da land ee take, whadebber ee promise.'

'no, not a tribal marriage in the bush, i mean a proper weddin', a fair-dinkum one inside a big church, the organ playin', people singin' hymns, a minister wearin' his collar back the front, everyone puttin' in money ... that sort of thing.' He'd switched off to anything she'd said about native customs, ceremony and affinity with the land, and treated it as a load of mumbo-jumbo.

'Dat's a whitefella weddin' ya talkin 'bout. Nothin' like our show. We don't need no church for dat ... an' we got plenny singin', corro-boree dancin' too. Dey go on for long time outside ... no fences out dere an' unda da biggess roof ya can see. No-one pay to go in an' stay dere neither. Anyhow, ya godda lodda cheek stickin' ya nose in, still wannin' to know more dan what's good for ya ... even wimmin business.'

'he's like a good mate, then?' Clarrie said, still taking little notice of what she'd explained, and clearly eager to expand on his ignorance.

'Jack an' me, we live togebber an' fiddle round some night, dat's all. Ee may be da boss o' dis house, but I always tell 'im, I'm no easy gin like what dey call me behine me back when I go to da pub. I tell 'im John 'enry's not *my* family ... dat man, ee treat us like dirt, like da way dose lepers was treated in da Bible stories we learned at da mission.'

'yeah, that's what i was going to say. jack respects you an' the kamilaroi tribe, what you carry round in your head. "they can even read the sky at night, the rocks on the ground," that's what he said … might have even said the rock walls are sacred, like the eagle? i can't remember. the only thing he didn't mention were those corrob … whateverees you spoke about?'

'*Corroboree*,' Miriam helped him out, and then, adopting a more sullen tone, she went on. 'Jack knows what's good for 'im with me round. It diff'ren' out dere in our Country. We 'ave roots go deepa dan dat bilaar tree ober dere. Ee know nothin' 'bout feedin' 'imself … won't eat da thulii lizard, da bandaarr roo meat, only da settla animal with da hard hoof. Ee can't see da spirit creatures all round. Ee talk like ee does, but only what I showed 'im … like da maliyan-ngu spirit.'

'that's what he was saying. it's that eagle you're talking about, isn't it? he also reckons it helps him spot dead sheep – but i think he made that up.' In what was a turn up for the books, Clarrie was sensitive enough not to tell her that Jack would rather shoot and cook the so-called spirit totem than worship it. But from his recent observations, the wedge-tailed eagle was safe. As Miriam had confirmed, Jack's meat intake likely only ranged from chunks of dried beef to his scrag-end mutton always on the boil.

'I don't know 'bout dat. … da maliyan-ngu warn me to look out for bad tings, like what whitefellas get up to. It were dere when ya turned up at the gate.'

'why's that? was it just for *me* turnin' up? jack's a whitefella, isn't he?'

'Yeah, but sometime ee pretend ee don't wanna be … as I told ya, ee knows ee'd be lost out in da bush without me, if ee 'ad no truck to get 'im back … ee'd be just anuvva settla. Jack no clebba man like da Wirringan in our song. Jack don't un'erstan' da real darkness is what I see in da daytime.'

'i don't follow ya, miriam. you must need jack to protect you during the daytime and the nighttime?' He spent no time trying to unravel what she'd said about Jack's character and dismissed the totemic Dreamtime spirits as a riddle.

'In dis place, Jack may be da boss, but I tell 'im, I'm da chief protecta of me daughter, even if Jack say ee'll put a bullet through 'is cousin John 'enry, if ee ever turn up an' try to lie down with Chérie again. But it's me who'll take care ov *anyone* hangin' round who try.'

Clarrie didn't take her threat seriously, but it'd now become clear that Jack wasn't necessarily the top dog he liked to make out. This helped explain why he never let up about Miriam's tribal knowledge. From what she'd said, it didn't seem like Jack did much digging for that tasty bush tucker, either. What she warned about the possible fate of the randy publican, if he still had designs on her daughter, ought've put the wind up him. The likely consequences of his own lascivious claim on Chérie's affection should've immediately sunk in, but it seemingly only served to strengthen his resolve. As it turned out, the most favourable opportunity to chance his arm soon dropped into his lap, even if the surrounding circumstances were totally unexpected.

———

Well before Jack said he was going to town at the end of the week, Clarrie'd already decided that Friday was going to be his last day at Nevins's Run. He realised that it'd be now or never for a bit of cherry picking. He didn't have to pack his swag; it'd remained untouched in the corner of his sleeping area since the day he arrived. He noticed for the first time the filthy scuff marks it'd picked up from Jack's tools in the back of the truck.

Clarrie had recently taken to giving Peter Pan a good watering and a fresh nosebag first thing of a morning. Remarkably, for an old nag destined for the knacker's yard, today he looked in fine fettle ... maybe even sprightly enough to outpace the wheezing Bedford, if pushed. On the other hand, he recalled another thing Billy had said: that unlike his celebrated namesake, 'this horse is no stayer.' With this tip in mind, Clarrie planned to ride him only as far as the main road – if it managed to get that far. If not, he'd have to leg it from wherever it ran out of puff. So long as he stuck to that rocky track he came in by, he reasoned, he wasn't liable to get bushed. *Once I hit the main road, I'll try to luck my way to Moree as best I can. If Jack follows me, it won't be too hard to put a bit of distance between me and the old Bedford,* was the gist of his meticulously thought-out plan of flight.

Friday came, and he heard Billy leaving early on his own horse, a three-year-old colt called Hallmark. He was taking some of Nevins's sheep meat to the settlement blacks on the town's outskirts. A few generations before, Billy's mob would've roamed the same piece of land, speared the settlers' sheep and, as a result, many blackfellas probably met their Waterloo in bloodthirsty reprisals.

Billy's colt was a real galloper, and like the thoroughbred cup winner of roughly the same name, had class stamped all over him. By taking to open country and lesser-known tracks through some rugged terrain, horse and rider had managed to eat up the 300 miles as the crow flies from Cunnamulla to Nevins's Run in a little under two days. Clarrie had come to admire the lively colt in the yard, who was already over 16 hands in height, and as Jack described him, 'had hoofs like dinner plates.' Clarrie would sometimes look dejectedly at Peter Pan when both horses were together in the same yard, shake his head and think, *if only?*

A little bit later, Jack left in the truck to go to The Criterion for lunch. Miriam needed a lot of encouragement to accompany him. He'd had to remind her it was Friday, but calendar days meant nothing to someone who didn't have a precise word in her own language for yesterday or tomorrow.

'look, miriam, i've told ya before, there's only ever one or two blow-ins there ovva friday. if i hear anyone calling you names, i'll floor 'em. those council workers will probably be there havin' their long smoko as usual, but they're used to seein' you with me.'

'It's John 'enry dat worries me. Ee's always eyeing up Chérie … that's why I telled her to stay at the farm.'

'well, they say ee 'asn't been in the pub for weeks, might 'ave even shot through an' joined the army? so, it's only you and me meetin' the lawyer man … all right?'

It wasn't simply the rough crowd of regular drinkers that was unappealing to Miriam. Although she'd never tasted the grub they served at The Criterion, she wasn't interested in trying it, either. She correctly thought that it'd be no tastier than the ingredients Jack routinely threw into the big pot back home. She was ultimately persuaded to go, as Jack said the meeting with the big man from down south had been arranged to discuss important business. Among other things, Jack said he wanted to formalise his promised inclusion of Miriam as a beneficiary in his long-overdue last will and testament. He told her it was called a conditional bequest, and to her surprise, Billy might even get a look in too. 'She may not be legally married and can't read legal documents, but if nothing else, your gin can serve as a credible witness to all sorts of things,' the lawyer had tried to reassure him.

If Jack thought his proposal might somehow square the ledger with his family's occupation of her native Kamilaroi land, he was mistaken. Miriam had more than an inkling of his true motivation.

———

That Friday morning was like any other, maybe more overcast, but events would soon make it unlike any other. Now alone on the farm, and after taking the best part of an hour to feed and saddle up Peter Pan – and even longer to harness his own courage – Clarrie stole into Chérie's pokey bedroom in the slab hut.

Once inside, he backed her onto her rickety iron bed, which was not much bigger than a child's cot without the rails. He immediately started to put into effect the grotesque sexual imaginings he'd rehearsed for nights on end. The young girl initially responded quite meekly, as if she were utterly defenceless, perhaps accustomed to cousin John Henry's or even Billy Nolan's similarly rough-hewn, amorous techniques? She offered token resistance to his wandering hands, but otherwise remained motionless, emitting the occasional muffled groan in reaction to his unpractised fondling.

But when he engaged in none-too-subtle pelvic thrusts against her groin, there was nothing implicitly consensual about it, and she instinctively recoiled. The narrowness of the bed meant she was brutally backed against the wall. As he discovered, simulation of sexual intimacy on a squeaky bed doesn't always live up to expectations when push comes to shove. Despite his feverish attempts to rein her in, she was as unresponsive to his urgings as Peter Pan had been, and similarly resistant when he attempted to get in the saddle. But he refused to relent, unable to restrain his feverish breathing and the primitive sense of his own entitlement that the growing lump in his trousers seemed to authorise.

Whether or not he would've used more physical coercion to induce her compliance became a moot point. He gave up and went limp once he felt a warm sensation trickling down his inner thigh. He thrust her aside as he sprang off the bed and began furiously rubbing the moist stain left in outline on the inside leg of his light-coloured strides. The piece of cloth he'd hastily picked up from the floor was normally used to wipe the grate on the stove – any drying effect was surpassed by its capacity to leave smears of greasy soot on whatever it was rubbed against.

Chérie had turned her face to the wall, discarded like a child's bedraggled toy doll. She was left sobbing deeply in delayed shock. Unable to really howl, it sounded as if her mouth were filled with sodden balls of cotton wool, sluiced with phlegm.

Clarrie sheepishly stood there, not so much feeling apologetic for his repugnant behaviour as deeply humiliated by his premature ejaculation and the black streaks that marked the spot. A picture of desolation, he felt ashamed that he hadn't properly gone on with the job – *something Flash Billy had likely performed without once falling off*, he silently cursed. He had to swallow the unpleasant fact that he'd remain a virgin, the dud stud he'd already been cruelly labelled by the one and only previous female he'd brazenly molested. This cowardly behaviour ran counter to the impression of virility and tales of carnal knowledge he liked to embellish in the recounting every time he found a gullible ear in a public bar.

Outside, the dogs had begun barking. Like Clarrie, they were easily aroused, but unlike him you could guarantee they'd keep it up, uninterrupted. Standing side-on to the window, his heart still racing and his face pinkish all over, he spotted the local sergeant, Joseph Boyd, poking around outside.

Boyd had arrived in an old Morris Cowley that had been crudely modified in a Moree workshop – a simple, steel-framed canopy had been installed atop the tray to serve as an enclosed police van. It had a metal rail inside to which a set of handcuffs could be attached, but there was no rigid back door, let alone a lock – only canvas flaps that were loosely fastened from the outside. A wire grille covered the rear window behind the driver's cabin, and a small gap between the two allowed air to flow in.

Although the covering was tightly laced to secure it to the frame, for a hard-bitten crim the van would have been as escape-proof as a cardboard box, whether he were cuffed or unrestrained. But around here, the absence of a solid door, bolt and padlock didn't matter so much. The van's only regular occupants were not dangerous villains, but those who offended public order by causing affray or using abusive language due to intoxication.

The converted pick-up was as squat and sleepy as its driver. It was so small it had trouble accommodating a bruiser like Norm Markham, whenever Norm played up a little too heatedly and the launch into schooners had rendered him anything but silent. But it was much more amenable to someone of Clarrie's modest size and present sober disposition. So far as he was concerned, the van seemed a far safer bet on which to abscond than the alternative proposition, already saddled up and nosing the water trough, a likely candidate for that last-minute scratching.

While Sergeant Boyd was engaged in his haphazard snooping behind the tractor shed, Clarrie made his move. Without so much as a backward glance at the young girl who was now curled up, foetus-like on the bed, he grabbed his swag, sped through the doorway and scurried towards the back of the van. On the way, he noticed broken columns of bull-ants heading in a frenzied, zigzag pattern towards the bilaar tree ... something was happening.

After carefully opening the bottom flap, he squeezed in by lifting up one side of the tarpaulin canopy. Once inside, he tried to spread himself out as flat as a pancake, sharing the floor with various clumps of loosely bagged produce and the fur from animal skins. These had been gifted by locals in lieu of unlevied fines and the promise of unrecorded misdemeanours. Shreds of whatever lay there soon stuck to the inside leg of his trousers, now soiled in the same place three times on the same morning.

It was almost pitch-black inside and practically airless. At the approach of someone familiar, the dogs had done no more than get up and gently rattle their chains, accompanied by a mellow and non-threatening, *grrr*. Clarrie had paused just long enough to release Dusty from his collar. At first, the mutt didn't know what to do with its newly found freedom. He sniffed the air for a few moments before loping towards the scrub in a circuitous, disoriented fashion, going everywhere and nowhere at the same time. He'd spotted Clarrie slipping into the back of the van and went over to investigate. Clarrie recognised his plaintive whine. The dog circled the vehicle for a few minutes before Clarrie felt assured he wasn't about to jump in the back with him.

After what seemed like several minutes, the dogs started up again when the unfamiliar figure of Joe Boyd ambled back in their direction. Amid their sustained yelping, Clarrie overheard most of the details in the loud, one-sided conversation Boyd was having with the distraught young girl. She'd finally emerged from the hut, still quivering and unaware of Clarrie's present location.

'the last time john 'enry was sighted, sherry, he was on the main road round a fortnight ago … i spoke to jack on the way here this morning, but he said he knew nothin' about it, hadn't seen hide nor hare of him. jack told me to keep goin' to the farm and question the drifter, he called him, the one who's been stayin' here workin for cash in hand. not an ounce of goodness in him, jack says … *and* he noticed what looked like blood stains on the drifter's swag as the young bloke grabbed it from back of the truck when he first arrived.'

He paused for several seconds but was undeterred by the lack of any coherent response – he was used to holding one-way conversations with his usual drunken guests. 'jack reckons the drifter might know somethin' more about it, after being kicked out of the pub round the time john 'enry was reported missin' … goes by the name of clarrie roberts … an' said to ask 'im if he'd seen john 'enry come by, and that maybe billy can help too when ee gets back?'

There was still no answer to his hearsay speculations, or his fishing for some form of admissible evidence to support them. Clarrie feared he would go on like this until the cows came home, or even worse, their owner did.

'sherry, i know ya sorta promised to flash billy, to be 'is woman an' not John 'enry's gin, as everyone says. that's right, isn't it? so maybe billy'll mention to you where the drifter's gone, when ee turns up?'

Chérie's sobbing had ended, which gave him renewed optimism for a response. 'where do ya think he's snuck off to?' he found himself repeating, 'that good-for-nothin' clarrie bloke, i mean? is that 'is horse saddled up ova there? he can't be far off then, an' on foot. do you know where he could be hidin'?'

As he headed back towards his van, Sergeant Boyd noticed Dusty nearby. 'one of yer dogs is on the loose out 'ere, so you'd bedda tie 'im up before jack gets home and gives him that relocation he's always on about.'

The young girl was not asked at all about the cause of her reddish, watery eyes and obvious distress, and was unable to convince the sergeant she didn't know where either of the men were.

Looks like she's got them glassy eyes most gins round 'ere 'av got, but it's usually the older ones, was Joe's spurious diagnosis, mulled over for all of three seconds. Sergeant Boyd's empathy and interrogation skills were as rudimentary as his scouring the farm for clues. Even if he suspected the girl had been the victim of a sexual assault, that'd likely be the end of the matter. *She was a decent-lookin' lubra after all, and 'ad probably been puttin' it about for some time,* would have been the gist of his forensic assessment. That is, if he ever thought about filing a report of his suspicions in the first place. This type of attitude was bereft of morality but enjoyed wide currency across an otherwise devout Christian nation.

Even though he understood she was mute, it took him a fair while to get tired of fruitlessly waiting for her to offer any indication of Clarrie's whereabouts. He gave up his futile endeavours once the relentless snarling of the dogs started to get on his goat. Much to the nervous occupant's relief, Boyd finally got inside the cabin and turned the motor over. Before moving off, he shouted through the window that he'd return tomorrow around teatime, when hopefully they'd both turn up hungry and he could nail them on the spot. He'd failed right to the very end to comprehend that everything he'd said had literally fallen on deaf ears.

What a lying ol' bastard Jack turned out to be, Clarrie seethed through gritted teeth. *And he goes and tells the copper that I'm no better than any one of them lazy, worthless drifters he talks about, after all. Looks like he's using me turning up out of the blue as a person to blame for that publican's disappearance.*

He wasn't slow to sense the serious nature of the deep shit into which he'd now been plunged. He quietly muttered a torrent of expletives. He had little else to do but attempt to piece together what he thought had probably occurred. Those thoughts came thick and fast and crowded his brain. He'd formed the wrong answers even before the relevant questions had been posed, while he anxiously waited, stifling his breath and stretched out stiff as a corpse in the back of the van.

But there was nothing like the thought of one's own disappearance to concentrate the mind. He understood that if he couldn't shoot through before she returned, once Miriam saw Chérie bawling her eyes out and moving her arms around like a windmill to the sound of his name, his immediate future would be looking pretty bleak. Things would only get worse should the girl start pointing to the stains around his groin. He'd be sure to cop more than one haymaker from Jack's long, hairy arms, and after receiving a good kicking, he feared his nuts would probably wind up being as useful as Peter Pan's. Although well short of being hobbled by guilt, he had to admit that Miriam was dead right – he didn't belong here! For the moment, all he could really think about was hugging the floor ever more closely, spread-eagled and determined to stay as still as a blue-tongue lizard basking on a rock in the winter sun.

As the van's tyres shuddered over the first cattle grid, he sensed the weather was changing. It'd started to spit. Pressed hard to the floor, his cheekbones absorbed every concussive bump from the dislodged rocks along the road. The noise rendered him incapable of hearing the dog panting alongside as it kept pace with the van. Large raindrops had now started to plop with increasing regularity on the tarpaulin roof, and as the side of his head was repeatedly slammed against the metal floor, he never thought he'd be so looking forward to his own relocation.

CHAPTER
SIX

AS HE HEADED TOWARDS BRISBANE, whatever little money Clarrie earned cleaning out farm sheds, repairing barbed-wire fencing or humping bales of hay, was soon pissed up against a succession of beer-garden walls. But on the upside, he made sure he got good mileage out of embellishing those brief labouring experiences whenever the occasion arose. Getting a lift became easier once he realised that truck drivers pulled up more often if you had a mangy-looking dog in tow.

The pubs north of Moree were usually fitted out with custard-cream tiles or had wafer-thin, grubby Feltex glued to the floor. The stench of stale beer announced its presence to passers-by well before they reached the frosted-glass doors at the entrance. He had to leave Dusty outside every one of those pubs for hours on end, until one day the dog decided to no longer stick around. Inside, the premises were usually inhabited by small clusters of barflies nursing a flat middy at any hour of the day. These blokes were always open to a yarn with the latest blow-in who was dirty on the way things were going in any place in the world you'd care to name. They became Clarrie Roberts's natural audience.

'Didn't ya say you'd spent time round Moree,' one old geezer called Sidney said to him in The Royal Hotel in Tenterfield.

'Yeah, but not that long. Things were pretty crook, so I shot through when farm work dried up.'

'Well, what dya thinka this?' he said, waving the *Gwydir Examiner* in front of Clarrie's face. 'It says here … the mutilated body of a local publican was discovered in a ditch last Friday at Waterloo Creek, 20 miles south-west of Moree. Police have arrested and charged a local farmer and his part-Aboriginal son with murder.'

Clarrie pretended to show little interest, but his ears were burning.

'It goes on … "District Sergeant Joe Boyd was alerted to the grave's location by the farmer's housekeeper, who later identified the farmer as the owner of the firearm involved in the killing. The corpse was partially exposed, and the flesh bore the marks of scavenging animals. The victim had not only been shot, but there was evidence of a crude attempt to decapitate him. A small knife engraved with initials was found nearby, but if used as a weapon, could not have produced the type of long, curved wound found around the victim's neck, our reporter was told."'

'You can read the rest for yaself, if ya want?'

'Not that interested, Sid. You wouldn't credit it, mate. Looks like nowhere's safe these days … can't trust anyone, especially those half-castes,' he said, all the while thinking, *Jack must've tried to put one too many over his gin? And fancy being taught to ride a horse by that murderin' smart-arse Billy Nolan … or was it Billy Nevins? Losing his knife an' gettin' caught wasn't too flash, you'd have to say?*

From then on, the only thing he could think about was that there'd probably been no need to turf out his blood-stained Gladstone bag from the copper's van, after all.

His circumspection in relation to this horrific murder story was unusual. Such were his rabid views on most topics, controversial or mundane, that he soon attracted a small gathering whenever he got into a late-afternoon shout. Once he'd had a few middies, any semblance of decorum took a hammering, He told everyone he was an expert on everything bar love, marriage and backing the gee-gees. To these he'd now have to add one more – brutal murders in the scrub. Although he still relished telling made-up stories of riding the Melbourne Cup stayer Peter Pan, he was now less forthcoming on where it occurred, who owned it, or revealing its last-known destination.

In the public bar at The Royal, long-term customers like Sid were honoured with a modest brass plaque bearing their nickname. Tin-plate troughs beneath the footrails acted as receptacles for cigarette stubs while also providing the chronically uncouth with a convenient spittoon. Clarrie spent several weeks on the road dropping into dozens of these country confessionals and had no trouble ingratiating himself with any old soak crying out for company. It didn't matter that most of them believed he hadn't yet grown into his underpants. Most evenings, he'd stagger upstairs to the first-floor accommodation, full as a tick. The hotels were often called The Imperial, The Empire, The Prince Albert, or even the more improbably named, The Palace. Given the repeated appearance of these names, even the least nationalistic traveller was under no illusion as to where their allegiance should lie during wartime.

Clarrie learned to get in early if he wanted to order the cheap cuts of meat, gravy and three vegies you could reliably expect as an evening counter-meal. But he steered clear of stewed mutton. These meals were often put together by semi-retired shearers' cooks, still stout of frame but by now gone in the legs after years behind the hobs. Varicose veins decorated their soft, fleshy calves like the wispy, tinted-blue lines on a roadmap.

Located in a prominent position on the mirrored shelf behind the bar, directly facing the till, patrons were sometimes welcomed by the same eye-catcher on a thin cardboard sign – WE TAKE CHEQUES accompanied by an illustration of the enlarged hindquarters of a pig, followed by the words – WE DO.

Witty bastards.

Clarrie'd run out of money, shoe leather and half-plausible stories by the time he reached Brisbane in mid-December 1939.

CHAPTER
SEVEN

THE FIRST THING Clarrie noticed on reaching Brisbane was the river's impressive shoreline. It was burgeoning with colonial mansions constructed by its home-grown, successful men of commerce. From Hamilton to Highgate Hill and around the sweeping bend to Bulimba, at this time of year gardens were canopied in early flowering poincianas and jacarandas. Backyard paw-paw trees bent over with the weight of their mottled yellow fruit, which dangled in clusters like swollen testes beneath their modesty-protecting leaves. Towards dusk, squadrons of bats left a sooty trail across the sky over Woolloongabba as they homed in on the backyard fruit, their silent sorties shredding the flesh to its seeds before anyone inside was even aware of their presence.

Brisbane seemed no more than a big country town. It was a place where the suburban land was measured in perches, a quaint imperial dimension like rods, poles, links and chains. Other than in Queensland, you only ever came across these arcane units of measurement on the back of school exercise books in primary school. That's how come kids down south, who hadn't yet mastered their times table or avoirdupois weights, already knew a cricket pitch was twenty-two yards or one chain in length.

Clarrie's destination was Wynnum, a sleepy bayside suburb, about which a non-resident might be offering praise by describing it as comatose. Most days the foraging squawk of seagulls by the shore, or the insistent, unbroken drone of cicadas at twilight, were the only things that penetrated the silence. Bathed by gentle sea breezes during most of the year, every home sported a lush green, sub-tropical garden. Even the scatty looking staghorn ferns sucking the sides of trees appeared to be in rude health. The same couldn't be said for the weatherboard houses – a local council by-law must have decreed that you could paint them any colour, so long as it was a peeling, sun-bleached white.

Florence Burns's home was a traditional wooden Queenslander. It hadn't been painted in quite a while and stood well above the ground, supported by towering stumps with metal capping at the top. A lick of black creosote at ground level was applied to stop white ants in the soil from reaching the floorboards above. All sides of the surrounding verandahs were screened by white lattice panels. Her home was named Girraween, and it dominated the neighbouring dwellings from the top of Southwick Street. It resembled an ageing dowager in a large, ribboned bonnet attending a country fair. Its elevation made it too windy to attract much of the insect life that invaded the evening serenity of those who lived further down the hill.

Growing up in these places, the kids learnt to build things with broken sticks and fashion imaginary roads for toy cars in the powdery dirt around the stumps. They would defy prohibitions by playing with matches from disused wax vesta tins, igniting the dregs from disused containers of kerosene, while on their knees they bashfully explored the appearance of each other's bud-like genitalia. The shadowy presence of concrete wash tubs among the forest of bare stumps was the only jarring element in this childhood world of dark imaginings.

If only I'd grown up around here – these little blokes don't seem to have a care in the world, Clarrie would reflect while watching them at play in the streets. On weekends they went bare-chested, or their torso partially covered in loose, cotton singlets. Their short pants were hitched up around their narrow hips by unreliable elastic waistbands secured by a large safety pin, or reliant on a couple of extra buttons over the fly. If there were a big enough group of mates and ring-ins, they'd play cockylora or have a game of cricket in the backyard using dented garbage bins as an improvised wicket.

This was the grandest of times – tearing around with runny noses and grazed knees in the fading daylight, the fun only curtailed by the shrill call from mothers over paling fences to come home for tea. Where Clarrie had played as a child, should he have failed to acknowledge a similar call, he could probably expect a belting, 'When ya father gets 'ome.'

———

Down each side of Flo's house was an array of sash windows with highlights in patterned pink and green coloured glass. Most of the panes were cracked. The ropes in the sash windows, whether through accident, laziness or design, had been painted over, making them as stiff as iron rods. A few of the push-out casement windows hadn't lived up to their description for decades. However, Clarrie's skills as a glazier extended no further than replacing a chipped louvre in the bathroom.

There were very few curtains around the house, except for the flimsy and dust-riddled lace ones above the green enamel sink in the kitchenette. Clarrie thought the curtains might well dissolve into a fine powder, if they were ever thrown into the copper for a good soak. The bakelite canisters scattered around the kitchen shelves looked as if they hadn't been used or rearranged in years. All of this indicated that Flo had lived alone for some time, and in somewhat straitened circumstances. Her war widow's pension, supplemented by her undeclared part-time sewing and alterations pin money, barely kept the wolf from the door.

Nevertheless, within a short period of time, the modest surroundings had started to feel like a real home to Clarrie, and he'd little else to do than explore every nook and cranny. After kindly taking him in as family, Florence tried everything she could to discourage him from joining the army. She started to treat him like the son she'd never had and began to wait on him hand and foot. He was still in two minds about the lure of overseas service because it would mean turning his back on someone whose kindness towards him was genuine, and who'd sought no recompense. Unlike his childhood experience, he was now not only seen but also invited to be heard in adult company. *For Christ's sake, Flo's even offered me one of her Ardath cork-tipped cigarettes,* he said to himself, feeling special. He was aware she kept her smokes tucked away in one of the yellowing newspaper-lined drawers in the mahogany sideboard. They were only brought out on special occasions, just like it advertised on the packet.

It was on this same sideboard that Clarrie noticed a traditional sepia-framed wedding pose, the man rigidly standing with his spouse seated by his side. As he drew closer to the photo, both bride and groom appeared to be no longer looking towards some distant point in the room but seemed to be directly focused on him. Slightly unnerved, he moved on to another photo, showing a huge contingent of soldiers from the first Australian Imperial Force in Egypt, the Pyramid of Giza in the background. Somewhere among that sea of innocent faces was that of Flo's deceased husband, Keith Burns.

———

The summer turned out to be the best of seasons in Wynnum. Clarrie liked the way Florence routinely dressed in light cotton frocks with bright floral patterns. They were pulled in at the waist by a thin belt in matching fabric, and the way she dressed put him in mind of his mother. Like his mum, she smelt as though she'd sprinkled a flask of cheap 4711 Eau de Cologne all over herself first thing of a morning. *Then again, perhaps that's what all elderly women smelt like*, he thought, recognising the wafts of familiar scent caught by the salty, light sou'easters coming in over the bay. Every now and then a rogue gust caused the pleats in her dress to billow, as both settled in like a mismatched Darby and Joan on enormous wicker chairs on the side verandah. They shared pride of place with a canvas-covered squatters' chair, its elongated, swivelling rests designed to hold up your outstretched legs as you reclined. Clarrie would often claim the chair on bright, sunny mornings, decked out in fresh clean clothes, his cheeks still flushed from his leisurely hot bath. Lying back on the chair like Little Lord Fauntleroy, legs dangling over the sides, he would imagine himself a well-to-do landowner, sipping a mug of tea under his bull-nosed roofed verandah. The stuff of urban daydreams.

From the potted frangipanis and the huge Bowen mango trees to the even more corpulent Moreton Bay figs, everything about Flo's backyard at this time of year evoked a feeling of warmth and fertility. Of an evening, he learnt to relax around the Astor Mickey wireless, listening to ABC news broadcasts delivered in fruity tones by imported Oxbridge announcers. Settling back on a lounge chair adorned by an embroidered antimacassar, he allowed himself to crack a rare smile at the reassuringly demotic yarns of *Dad 'n' Dave* and the assorted drongos who serialised Snake Gully. Most nights he would have an ear out for the six o'clock pips, announcing the latest British warnings on the deteriorating military situation across Europe to even the most remote Australian household.

But, for all that, he was steadfastly resistant to acknowledging Girraween's lasting appeal. It was as though he were afraid of embracing this new sense of belonging, and something was eating away from within. This would lead him to inevitably forsake what would turn out to be the closest he'd ever get to experiencing an idyllic way of life.

CHAPTER
EIGHT

BY EARLY JUNE 1940, Clarrie's restlessness for moving on had become more persistent. He didn't want to turn his back on Aunt Flo and tried hard to suppress his usual combative nature in her presence, but he was sick and tired of living without a purpose, feeling like a *déraciné*, an up-rooted soul, telling strangers he was from nowhere in particular. Ashamed of his past and unburdened by family ties, personal allegiances or any sense of nostalgia, he'd convinced himself the army would look after all his undiscovered needs.

'You're too young to get involved in all this army talk, Clarence,' Flo was forced to say more regularly, and when the issue came up again one night, she became increasingly cranky. 'Goodness me, you haven't turned eighteen yet,' she went on. 'Why don't you start to enjoy life, find yourself a nice girl, try to get an apprenticeship and save some money?'

Clarrie was stung by all these suggestions. He was certainly reluctant to talk of female attachments and affairs of the heart, and was glad Flo seldom chose to venture any further around *that* topic of conversation.

'Without a trade, you'll end up with nothing to fall back on in life, unless you plan to stay in uniform forever?'

He squirmed at being spoken to like the adolescent he still was but was loath to admit it. Although he recognised the common sense in what she was saying, he'd have been hard-pressed to openly acknowledge it.

'What if you get wounded? You could be writhing on the ground in serious pain for hours before the stretcher-bearers got to you.'

He was somewhat surprised by her uncharacteristically morbid comments, and after he padded that away as improbable, she tried another tack – a more self-effacing approach, designed to appeal to the male-provider instinct. 'Look, if you stay, you can continue to have the run of the house. I really need a man to paint the whole place, inside and out. The sills are so splintered you can see traces of the original undercoat and primer. You said anyone could paint a house, remember? There's dry rot everywhere, and some of the windows are stuck. You must have noticed these things?'

'Yeah, I have. But that's a job for a proper tradesman, not someone like me.'

'Well, there's lots of other odd jobs that need doing. I can't get any of the few local tradesmen to come round, without going into debt, that is.'

Clarrie genuinely craved her affection and wanted to help, but after what he'd been dealt in childhood, he didn't find it easy to express much empathy as an adolescent. As a result, Flo's heartfelt concern for his welfare ultimately proved to be ineffectual – like water off a duck's back. However much she tried to discourage his bleak outlook on life, it seemed he would invariably draw upon an inexhaustible well of undefiled resentment. She came to realise that while he was like everyone else in being young only once, unlike others he was probably gifted to remain immature forever. She marvelled at his endless capacity for bitterness and gradually came to recognise that her sharp tongue rarely hit home.

'Look, Flo, I really like it here,' he admitted. Then, with a conciliatory turn of phrase that was completely out of character, he said, 'And you've been like a real mum to me.'

That's the only thing we seem to agree upon, she thought.

'You've given me more than a roof to sleep under and three good feeds a day. But you know I still haven't got two bob to rub together, and there's no-one I know well enough around here to bite for a few quid. It's like when I was between jobs on the road. Sometimes I didn't have enough to honour a shout or buy a raffle ticket in the pub. I don't want to loll around the house and bludge off you any longer, Flo,' he said, trying to hold back any sign of the small tears welling in the corner of his eyes. 'I'll get looked after in the army, get regular meals and paid for a fair day's work. I'll be able to dump these civvies for a set of fresh khakis and decent leather boots. I'm not sure I could knuckle down and really make a go of anything else ...'

Flo remained silent throughout, finding herself surprised that she should care so much about someone who was, after all, only distantly related.

'And, talkin' about shelter,' he resumed, 'I could tell you a few things about the flea pits I had to put up with for months last year, but they'd turn you off your next meal,' he said in a jokey sort of way, trying to lighten the mood. 'Sleepin' rough in a deserted humpy or in a makeshift lean-to like I had on one of the farms I worked at would've been a safer bet. One of the pubs I stayed at was called The Criterion. All that was in the room was a wobbly iron bed with a stained mattress, a filthy mat and a set of drawers that wouldn't slide open. The wooden floor sloped down from the door, and you could see the dirt outside through a gap in the corner, where the wall had come away from the skirting boards.'

'There you go again, Clarence,' she interrupted, more than a touch of irritability creeping into her conversation. 'You're talking a load of tripe. A little hardship on the road doesn't give you the right to be so disagreeable. To hear you talk anyone'd think you had the world on your shoulders. Don't imagine for a second your sleeping conditions will be any better in the army. Do you know much about camp stretchers, erecting a canvas tent in pelting rain, or bivouacking in a slit trench?' Pressing the point as though she spoke with authority, she dryly added, 'They'll almost certainly be less comfortable than those dreary hostels and hotel rooms you say you were stuck in. Maybe not as many fleas, bedbugs and spiders – if you're lucky, that is.'

She raised her voice a little more, and then really went to town on him, using a bit of the coarse language and unrelenting negativity he was used to dishing out. 'There'll be beds full of snorers, the heavy breathing of blokes playing with their whatsies, or blowing off in the middle of the night right under your nose.' She couldn't bring herself to utter anything cruder.

'Hey, that all sounds pretty normal to me, Flo.'

She pretended to ignore his childish response. 'That's not all. You'll get issued with those khaki hair shirts to wear day in and day out, a prickly overcoat to match, and never get to sleep-in again. I'm telling you, you'll soon appreciate the clean sheets and your smooth mattress compared to the lumpy straw-filled ones you're sure to cop in the barracks. There'll be no broken biscuits to dunk in your hot tea, and you'll have no time to comb your hair the way you do here morning, noon and night, trying to look like some sort of Hollywood Loverboy in the talkies?'

Clarrie was not expecting to be verbally assailed in such a robust fashion. What he'd always disliked most in life was censure, and Flo was ladling it out in big dollops.

'And, more importantly, there'll be no-one around like me to wait on you, like I've been doing since you showed up on my doorstep around Christmas, out of the blue. I've gotta say, you were a bit on the nose, carrying only a couple of tied-up blankets, and with the backside out of your pants.' She also wanted to say, *you're an ungrateful little bugger, aren't you? You've hardly had to lift a finger the whole time you've been staying here!* But she'd never had to scold an unruly child in her life and was resigned to the fact that it was rather late to start now.

Sensing he'd hit a raw nerve and surprised by her vehemence, Clarrie backed off a bit, turning his head slightly to conceal a nervous, swallowing action. 'You might be right, Flo, but as I said, the reason I want to join up is not because I'm sick of stayin' here. Watching those nippers playing on the road makes me wish I'd grown up in this place. But, you see, it's mainly because I've run into lots of old-timers, who say only Abos, shiny bums and commos don't want to see a bit of action in the war. A fella like me doesn't want to be mentioned in the same breath as any of those rotten bludgers, does he?'

Hearing this, she desperately wanted to point out that the Aboriginals he called either boongs, coons or Abos, had been around for a very long time. She knew they'd had fewer opportunities to get an education and earn a decent living than even the most illiterate and unskilled Irish and Chinese immigrants, who'd been arriving penniless by the boatload for almost a century.

She'd slowly come to realise that Clarrie's belligerent stance against even the most reasonable of propositions she advanced had somehow become ineradicable. *Whoever said those people who find thinking difficult are the same ones who rush to be judgmental, must've had someone like Clarrie firmly in mind,* she'd now concluded. The way he averted his eyes and the slight shrug of the shoulders whenever she tried to engage his attention said everything about him. It was for this reason that despite her inclination to challenge his irritating assertions, she often held back the scathing denunciation they deserved.

'Anyhow, it'll be a bit of an adventure won't it, Flo? I didn't escape me ol' man an' head north, just for somethin' to do, an' I don't wanna join up just when the action's all over bar the shoutin'.'

She bristled at the sound of these words, reflecting on how her husband Keith had said the same sort of thing before leaving for active service in the 1st AIF, just a month after their marriage. He ended up being shelled at Pozières and didn't survive shipboard repatriation. It seemed to her that Clarrie, like her husband, had blindly subscribed to the fledgling Australian society's dominant view of masculinity meant being obliged to serve the mother country in bloody warfare? Flo wanted to make the point that engagement in war had repeatedly shown itself to be the most efficient widow-maker known to mankind, and although implacably opposed to warfare, she decided to let it go. *Clarence was fortunately still single, and one ought to be grateful for small mercies,* she reasoned.

'I know the citizen militia won't be conscripted to fight overseas until it's a last resort, so bugger that for a joke. I reckon the hardest part will be gettin' accepted into the regular army in the first place.'

This gave Flo a momentary cause for optimism, which immediately proved misguided.

'There's no way I'll fail the medical, but I'm not game to front up again to the same recruiter in the city without any papers. Wouldn't it slay ya? He said if I couldn't lay me hands on a birth certificate, then a bona fide related adult must vouch for my meeting minimum age requirements. He said if you've got no immediate family, like I made out, then it could be a guardian ... maybe someone like you, Flo?'

She'd never thought of herself in this way before and was more than a little disappointed that he hadn't told her of his recent visit to the Brisbane City Hall recruitment centre. Whatever ruse he was attempting, she realised all too well that he was living in a fool's paradise, impervious to advice and sound reasoning. There must be no child more miserable than a homeless orphan, she thought, unless it's someone like Clarrie, who'd chosen to be one. She couldn't help feeling he was swapping an unhappy past for an even worse future, but to espouse a pacifist cause in June 1940 was about as popular as spreading diphtheria.

'You've made up your mind, I can see that, and there's nothing I can do about it.' By now she'd relinquished any attachment she might've once had to the idea of treating Clarrie as a wayward adolescent who'd eventually come good. 'I suppose joining up is better than you moping around the house all day if you don't get your way,' she said with an air of resignation. 'I don't know how you'll cope taking orders – being told what to do? Even if you've got more front than McWhirter's store in the Valley, being disrespectful won't do you any good in the army. They soon sort out the ratbags.'

If Clarrie was in any way moved by her well-intentioned advice, he didn't show it. He gave her a sort of weak, parting embrace, moving his chin away to avoid eye contact and the possibility of a goodnight kiss. It was the action of someone who shunned any expression of tenderness. All he did was give her an unemotional and graceless, 'I'm turnin' in now ... see ya in the mornin', Flo.'

She'd reached the end of her tether trying to reason with a young man who exhibited all the maturity of a ten-year-old. *He'd come to no good, no matter what, and remain someone who could attract trouble in an empty room*, she sighed. In many ways, she'd be glad to see the back of him.

Yet, despite his coldness and apparent ingratitude, over the next few days she even toyed with the idea of borrowing a plausible birth certificate from an in-law, so he could assume a false identity. Ultimately, she agreed to sign a statutory declaration form as his guardian, attesting to his reaching the threshold age for eligibility to join the infantry. Her readily verifiable Wynnum address and respected status as a war widow was good enough written proof for the recruitment officer.

She needn't have worried too much about perjury – truth is said to be the first casualty of war. Army recruitment officers weren't particularly interested in the administrative niceties of cross-checking the personal information of a volunteer soldier. Willing and Able became the most commonly acceptable names for being issued with an AIF number, a Lee Enfield .303 and a serge uniform. Clarrie's identification number was QX9682, and he was assigned to a battery unit in the field artillery. He couldn't wait to emblazon his left forearm with a tattoo depicting the rising sun badge worn on the upturned brim of his slouch hat.

And so, on 21 June 1940, Clarence Stanley Roberts placed his child-like signature on Attestation Form A.200, falsifying his date of birth and adding Florence Burns as next of kin. The final section contained the oath to: 'Well and truly serve our Sovereign Lord, the King, in the Military Forces of the Commonwealth of Australia in the present time of war … and to resist His Majesty's enemies and cause His Majesty's peace to be kept and maintained.'

Learning this, Flo was finally reconciled to the fact that her visiting man-child was now on his own, unlikely to return. It's said that hope springs eternal in the human breast, but she'd given up the ghost trying to work out who the person was that Clarrie didn't want to become. Nevertheless, impelled by a type of maternal instinct, Flo quickly decided to contact a few friends and relatives she knew were already in uniform, or were intending to join up. She'd get them to look out for him, were they to wind up in the same outfit. She was resigned to the fact that wherever Clarrie went, self-inflicted trouble was sure to tag along.

CHAPTER
NINE

REDBANK AND CALOUNDRA, QUEENSLAND, JULY– DECEMBER 1940; HMT *QUEEN MARY*, FEBRUARY 1941

WITHIN A MATTER OF DAYS, Clarrie had become part of the newly formed 2/10th Field Regiment, engaged in battery training at the Redbank Army Staging Camp, 20 miles west of Brisbane. His regiment then spent three months on manoeuvres, firing live ammunition into the Brisbane Valley behind the coast at Caloundra.

The regiment was made up almost entirely of volunteers from country towns throughout Queensland – timber-workers, cow cockies and shearers, with a fair sprinkling from the citizens' militia domiciled in Brisbane. Clarrie was thrown in with a lot of guileless young men like himself, around the same age, as well as experienced, mature men with grown-up children of their own. The latter were drawn from a wide variety of occupations, trades and professions he'd never come across before.

Some of the city-based volunteers had fought in the Great War and were old enough to be his father. Apart from the usual assortment of no-hopers who'd soon be discharged for 'conduct to the prejudice of good order and discipline', most claimed they were dead keen on seeing active service overseas, and the sooner the better. Their money was on eventually facing the Hun and the Ities in North Africa as reinforcements for the 6th Division, which was already stationed there.

'I wonder where we're off to, Clarrie?' Gunner Tasman Walls asked in his usual laconic fashion, running his fingers through his full head of hair.

'Your bet's as good as mine,' said Clarrie, 'but the other day I spotted what looked like gas masks being loaded onto trucks. You know, the ones used in the trenches in the last war?'

Although he fancied himself a bit of a Lothario, good-looking sheilas didn't find him at all attractive. For a start, compared to Tassie's healthy crop, his reddish-brown hair was dull and thinning. He'd self-consciously described it as auburn to the captain guiding him through the enlistment form. It was as though that colour were a desirable attribute, something that would distinguish him from the ordinary infantrymen, while not being quite ginger enough to earn the endearing nickname, Bluey. Sometimes, he imagined himself a youngish Fred Astaire without the brilliantine, and the only personal object he treasured was a tortoise-shell comb he referred to as his bug rake. Clarrie already sensed he was congenitally destined for his father's premature baldness. Unsurprisingly, he envied the handsome matinee idol Robert Taylor, dressed in a tuxedo and ready to melt the glacial aloofness of Greta Garbo.

Clarrie often wondered how he'd managed to click with Tassie Walls so early in the piece. He was grateful for the show of mateship when most other blokes, in common with the young ladies, seemed to give him the cold shoulder. He liked Tassie's unassuming, taciturn nature and thought him to be the last fella he could ever imagine big-noting himself about anything. If Clarrie had ever been introduced to the quality, he would have recognised it as humility.

'Yeah, but where do you think we're goin' to be sent?' The tone of Tassie's simple question about their probable destination suggested it was intended to be taken half in jest and meant to invite a response that was similar in kind. But Tassie already knew that an easy-going, jocular response from Clarrie would be hard to come by.

'Haven't got a clue where we're goin', but I can't see the need for gasmasks in the African desert, can you? You can bet your life, sooner or later we'll be proppin' up the Poms in some other place where they're already in strife,' he asserted, exercising his deep attachment to cynicism. 'I reckon it'll be a bit like bloody Churchill at Gallipoli again. We're being sent in to do the dirty work after the Pommie generals have stuffed it up.'

Tassie was slightly taken aback by the crude attempt at editorialising, especially from someone so young and with so little formal schooling. To him, Clarrie seemed to have subscribed to the naive belief that to be Australian, you had to dislike, if not mistrust, almost everybody from anywhere else in the world. Since his defining characteristic was an uncanny ability to fall out with anyone in the world who tried to befriend him, Tassie found himself the sole exception to the rule.

'I hope we don't come a gutser like the diggers did in those days,' he proclaimed, bringing one of his now familiar tirades to a welcome conclusion.

Tasman Walls was a few years older than Clarrie, rather heavy-set and much more thoughtful before airing his opinions. He'd been apprenticed to a printer before he joined the army and already knew his way around several skilled trades. In civilian life he'd taught himself to draw and paint, and had a reputation as a talented jobbing artist, with a studio of sorts at the back of his family's home in Herston, close to the centre of Brisbane. Relatives boasted he was a pretty cluey bugger, good with his hands, read a lot, and as fair dinkum as they come. His brother Maurie called him an autodidact. 'He could've done exceptionally well at school and gone on to uni if he'd had the inclination,' he'd crow.

Tassie was as measured in expressing his inner emotions as in airing his political beliefs, but above all else, he was slow to anger, totally lacking in bile. When the conversation invited a grievance, he was happy enough to let his silence do the talking. He discreetly maintained a black leather diary that he'd personally bound at the printing works where he'd been apprenticed. The few who accidentally spotted it might've mistakenly thought it a family Bible. Any discussion of religion with Tassie was implicitly discouraged, which worked out well for their continuing friendship, since Clarrie reserved a special contempt for anyone who merely whistled, 'Onward, Christian Soldiers, marching as to war.'

Yet for all his circumspection around his religious beliefs, Tassie's disposition and generosity of spirit suggested someone who possessed an inner peace, the type of meditative frame of mind that didn't need to look to heaven for guidance, solace or salvation. Gunner Walls was more than comfortable in his own skin. Perhaps it was something shared by all those who embraced the idea of a charitable, God-like spirit at large, unmediated by the dead hand of clericalism. *Not everyone needed to grizzle like a child, or wear their atheism on their sleeve*, he often said to himself, with no particular individual in mind, of course.

In further contrast to his new cobber, Tassie had a respectful relationship with his own father, and while he sometimes appeared lugubrious and a bit of a loner, he certainly wasn't on the lookout for an antidote to whatever under-parented complex was gnawing away at Clarrie's psyche.

None of Tassie's mates from Brisbane could quite fathom out why Tassie had decided to befriend this homeless, surly young bloke from down south. Most simply suspected he'd taken him under his wing as he might've done with a limping, stray dog that had accidentally wandered in through his open front gate. And there'd be plenty of looking after to do, as Clarrie always led with his chin when it came to expressing his views. He'd already gotten into a few scrapes, and like all young tearaways, after a few beers had brought on the proverbial Dutch courage, he continued to foolishly believe he could go toe-to-toe with the heavyweight boxing champion Jack Dempsey, in his prime.

On several occasions, he came within a bee's dick of being thumped for rubbing up a local tough the wrong way, but with a bit of fast-talking he'd often managed to emerge unscathed. However, there were other times when talking got him nowhere, especially when he disputed the fact that he'd failed to honour his round of beer. On these occasions, he unwisely elected to settle the matter with a few rounds behind the pub – and seldom returned to the front bar to brag about a successful outcome.

In almost every hotel bar he visited, it was if he were auditioning for a fat lip, and there was never a shortage of touchy drinkers willing to provide further alterations to his facial features. Traces of scar tissue around his chin were a fair indication of his past acquaintance with those who held a contrary view of his claims to bare-knuckle prowess. Finding himself in the army, it wasn't long before Clarrie's attitude of surly defiance brought him to the attention of Battery Sergeant Major Stratford 'Nobby' Cruickshank, the enforcer in his regiment.

Although he would never openly admit it, deep down this military hard nut believed the presence of the odd larrikin in the ranks was not always a bad thing for troop morale; someone with fire in the belly who was never likely to kiss the rod, as he liked to put it. Such a character might help to ginger up any slackers, and act as a kind of pressure-release valve when things got dicey. Cruickshank could sense that like the previous cohorts of Australian infantrymen sent abroad, the predominantly young men of the 8th Division would likewise be in for a rough trot before they knew it.

On the other hand, Nobby had been around long enough to know that smart-alec civilian volunteers like Gunner Roberts could also imperil the safety of others during the heat of battle. A lackadaisical attitude to discipline could spread like wildfire and be disastrous once engagement with the enemy was on for young and old.

Although he might have had a soft spot at times for Clarrie, Cruikshank was also concerned that his inability to respect hierarchical authority did not augur well for the young man's physical or emotional survival. *Rather than wanting to knock everyone's block off, he should learn to pull his head in,* was Cruickshank's homespun analysis of the conduct required. With that in mind, he was going to keep a close eye on this wiry little bugger for his own good, and if he gave any further lip to the non-commissioned officers, the NCOs, he'd be on to him like a ton of bricks. Experience had taught him that there were only so many times you could polish a turd.

———

It wasn't that long after basic training in the Brisbane Valley had ended that gunners Clarrie Roberts and Tasman Walls wound up together at the South Brisbane Railway Station on a journey to Circular Quay in Sydney, heading for overseas service. They were both officially part of one of the three artillery units of the 2/10th Field Regiment.

Embarkation was a slow affair. Thousands of regular troops, the medical corps, engineers, mechanics, food supplies and tons of armaments had to be ferried to the former ocean liner *Queen Mary*, moored at Athol Bight in Sydney Harbour.

'These Sydney fellas are lucky,' Tassie said, 'they've probably spent the last few nights rolling around in the cot with their girlfriends, not crammed into those upright, sagging leather railway seats we had to sleep in. What about you, Clarrie, have you got a special sheila in town? You're from Sydney, aren't you?'

'Nah, there's no-one here to wave *me* off, that's for sure.'

The actual destination was not something the top brass ever shared with the non-commissioned personnel. But it was clear with the last-minute issuing of Bombay bloomers and mosquito nets for covering the hat and face, that the 8th Division was probably *not* headed for the desert. The doubters still believed they were more likely to be setting off to the Mediterranean. After all, a boatload of diggers had gone that way only a few months before, and quite a few of their mostly unmarried brothers and pals had already been preparing for hostilities in the Levant since the declaration of war.

Gunner C. S. Roberts didn't care one way or the other as any destination was preferable to odd-jobbing through impoverished country towns. Towards the end, he'd come to realise that those communities had become denuded of any men under thirty. A quick look around the troops assembled on the quay provided ample evidence of where they'd all gone.

On Sydney Harbour, the late summer light danced upon the oil-slicked water, only occasionally disturbed by the gentle wake of the Manly ferries and the small barges that chugged in and around the port's many coves, jetties and inlets. Some were heading up to warehouses and factories sited along the navigable stretches of the Parramatta River. Clarrie's brief nostalgia for his life in Queensland extended only to noting the absence of those magisterial Queenslanders around Hamilton and Highgate Hill that jostled for importance as they hugged the steep escarpments on one side of the Brisbane River. He'd jettisoned his life in Wynnum like he'd done with his old clothes.

Within a matter of minutes, any cynical jibes about the cramped sleeping conditions on the converted ocean liner kept their own company, as several battalions of footsloggers started to file on board. They did so with such alacrity that their rifles and bulging kit bags appeared weightless as they were slung over their shoulders, their slouch hats brought to attention and jauntily secured by leather chinstraps. All the soldiers could do was wait for the massive ship to weigh anchor, followed by the anticipated bellowing from its steam horns signalling their departure.

It was late afternoon before the military personnel and inventory checklists were signed off and the last of the ship's hauling ropes and nets of supplies were finally lifted on board. The refitted juggernaut set off at high tide and made its way out through the Heads laden with what the parochial and jingoistic newspapers described as the flower of Australia's youth.

That first evening on board, the ever-present rancid smell of oil and diesel conspired with the spray from the waves to accentuate the trepidation that filled the air. In their quiet moments, each one of the infantrymen in the suffocating holds below deck hoped he'd be brave and not be maimed by bayonet or suffer the misfortune of having his dick shot off! If you were an Officer, that's how you got the Distinguished Service Order medal (the DSO), they'd only half-heartedly laugh. Otherwise, they were determined to live up to the nation's bloated expectations as worthy inheritors of the 1st AIF's heroic legacy.

To boost morale, an entertainment committee was set up with a battalion commander as its president. They organised film and newsreel screenings, followed by slapstick comedy routines hastily arranged and performed by the unselfconscious. These impromptu comedy acts and amateurish music recitals occurred every day during the two-week voyage. They say laughing is the most effective cure for the pain of loneliness you feel in the company of strangers, and Clarrie would've agreed.

When these amateur shows failed to raise the spirits, the only other distraction apart from games of two-up and playing euchre and pontoon, were the ritual competitions among those who sought to outdo one another with their bawdy limericks and off-colour jokes. Gunner Roberts indulged his practised flair for the latter, helped along by the prejudice-infected anecdotes he'd picked up from a host of disreputable characters he'd cosied up to in pubs on his overland journey to Brisbane. His imperfectly recalled renditions of 'Eskimo Nell' and 'Foreskin Fred, the Bastard from the Bush' kept sections of the mob baying for more until lights out every night.

For Gunner Roberts, entire evenings were spent absorbing other soldiers' seemingly inexhaustible store of yarns laced with obscenities. This pastime helped disguise the fact he had no-one to write to, except perhaps his Aunt Flo, when and if he got around to it. Everyone said letter writing helped allay anxieties, so one evening he thought he might try to write a letter to her. However, that's as long as the thought lasted – one evening.

The fact that so many foolhardy men on board had escaped being discharged on the basis that they were unlikely to become an efficient soldier, was a clear indication of the under-manned state of the regular army at the declaration of war. There was little confidence that a significant number of the recently enlisted could fight their way out of a wet paper bag, let alone resist a well-trained, determined enemy. It was widely accepted that many of the volunteers wouldn't be able to count to twenty-one without removing their trousers.

The youngest recruits had pinkie-white cherub faces, and of a morning they felt obliged to lather up like a Santa Claus, cautiously trying to remove the few threads of bumfluff from around their chin with a cut-throat razor. Be they man or boy, wiseacre or simpleton, all were shit-scared of what lay ahead. Few expressed any genuine enthusiasm for the inevitable engagement in warfare, and even with those that did, it was mainly bravado. Only fools were unafraid of death, and despite outward appearances suggesting otherwise, the out and out foolish were seriously outnumbered in the ranks.

A lack of training and the minimal resources allocated to the regular army in Australia over the previous decade was certainly not conducive to imparting high levels of morale and battle readiness within either infantry command or among the footsloggers. One freckle-faced weedy kid named Danny O'Dea appeared so out of place that the hairy-chested cruelly speculated he'd probably pee himself at the first sound of a shot fired in anger; that if he'd remained home, he'd still be wetting the bed. 'Give us a rendition of "Danny boy",' they'd yell out in the dark. This was the least offensive of the infantile forms of teasing and ridicule he had to endure.

The only person Danny hit it off with who didn't treat him like a sickly pipsqueak was Tommy Quinn, a tan-skinned nuggety bloke who was disrespectfully referred to as Chocko. Although this particular use of the vernacular for a half-caste was generally accepted as a harmless piece of barracks' humour, it never carried the same tinge of affection that Bluey or Carrot Top bestowed upon the ginger-haired, or Snowy upon the blond and blue-eyed. Everyone knew private David 'Di' Morgan as Taff, and even the vile bog Irishman Donal McBride took no offence at the inevitable Paddy. He swore it was preferable to being called Donald, which really got his Irish up.

Tommy Quinn was smart enough to cop it sweet, because as sure as water flows downhill, had he bristled about his nickname, you could guarantee there'd be no shortage of shit-stirrers ready to rib him even more from then on. That's why he was advised to stay well clear of Wally Leffler's crew. The only time Clarrie had spoken to him was when he was boasting that he was glad he'd finally pissed off from his father, someone he wished he'd never known. All Tommy could say was they told him at the mission station that his father had pissed off, but the only person *he* ever wanted to know *was* his father!

Not that Chocko was often directly confronted with his overtly racist nickname as he had a dubious reputation for being as silly as a two-bob watch and probably punch drunk. No-one tested the other rumour that he would fight like billy-o if you taunted him too much. Like all hearsay evidence these rumours were another example of the unreliable, word-of-mouth notoriety that accompanied Tommy's arrival on the *Queen Mary*. Danny hadn't helped things by letting on that after leaving the Aboriginal mission at Cherbourg in Queensland, Tommy had gone a few rounds with Jack Hassen, a handy middleweight who'd toured with Jimmy Sharman's boxing troupe around the New South Wales show circuit. Jimmy recognised a sucker at first sight and quickly signed up the itinerant, penniless Tommy on the strength of that one plucky performance.

However, Danny was less than forthcoming with respect to Tommy's overall fight record. Tommy 'Black Magic' Quinn was his sideshow moniker, but as his drum-beating, step-right-up spruikers soon discovered, it was way beyond the powers of a black magician to build a career as a pugilist, if he had a glass jaw. Towards the end he became just another prematurely washed-up pug with a crooked nose – a travelling punching bag for any half-sozzled young buck who fancied his chances dropping an Abo to the bloodied sawdust floor of Sharman's Big Tent. The odds of Tommy Quinn surviving two three-minute rounds unbruised considerably lengthened whenever the young hopeful was egged on by his mates or had just picked up a rootable sheila he was keen to impress. These types of bouts hardly ever went the distance.

Tommy's noticeably erratic behaviour could probably be put down to an undiagnosed case of Tourette's syndrome rather than the repeated thumping he'd taken in the ring. The occasional irrational outburst and involuntary tic had managed to escape the mandatory disqualification that the possession of flat feet attracted at the recruit-ment centre. In any case, he was unlikely to be knocked back as a volunteer for military service as no Aboriginal was on the electoral roll, and there were no records kept of their births, deaths or marriages.

Either way, whatever his medical condition, one look into Tommy's drowned eyes was enough for most everyone to steer clear. He was adrift in a world where he was not just alienated from his traditional culture but could never be part of the white man's ways, either. His mob had been sporadically picked off by white settlers in reprisals following livestock theft and now he'd signed up for another thump-ing, this time in support of the agents of his people's subjugation. This cruel irony was permanently lost in the cranial fog.

Tommy was therefore both feared and derided for the otherness his race represented in the whitefellas' eyes. On the newsreels at the flicks, the audience was far more used to seeing a royal with four-in-hand in Windsor Great Park, hooves clip-clopping to the orchestral soundtrack

118 E. J. JOHNSON

of Empire, than witnessing the grainy shots of a corroboree in the red dirt, febrile legs pounding to the syncopated resonances of clapsticks and the didge. If those same whitefellas had overcome their inherent prejudices then, like private O'Dea, they would have discovered that Tommy was basically harmless, not just homeless in his own country.

Besides the obvious malingerers, there was also a fair smattering of honest toilers and rough diamonds in the volunteer ranks. They were the ones without either past accomplishments or future prospects, devoid of dreams beyond surviving the imagined injuries they hoped to avoid down the line. Like the war of attrition in the trenches on the Western Front, their brief lives were likely destined to be a quick succession of heroic failures, with possibly an unmarked grave in another no-man's-land their only recognition.

Nevertheless, whatever their background, the soldiers of the 8th Division would gradually forge an esprit de corps that they could never have signed up for in civilian life. The common thread was an undivided loyalty to one's mates, adherence to a set of unarticulated democratic values, and a robust attachment to the prevailing mythology of a brief but heroic military heritage. This was a Holy Trinity of their own, which would take precedence over their more tenuous allegiance to God, King and Country.

CHAPTER
TEN

THE VOYAGE to Singapore would take more than a fortnight, but by the end of the third day, once the ship had entered the Great Southern Ocean, the constant swells hastened the first inklings of seasickness for everyone on board.

Meals were taken in shifts with hundreds of others, packed in like sardines in improvised mess areas called dining saloons. Those soldiers who hadn't got their sea legs often saw their undigested meals at least twice a day. Many spent sleepless, sweat-filled nights staggering around like the town dipso between triple-tiered bunks, swinging hammocks and the indescribable shipboard latrines. It was impossible to escape the sweltering heat on the claustrophobic lower decks below the ship's waterline or the throbbing of the massive turbines that rose from the bowels of the engine room directly beneath.

When it came to handling the choppy seas in the Roaring Forties, the sooks self-identified straightaway. Confounding early predictions, the stripling Danny O'Dea was right as rain. Every morning he'd jump out of his hammock looking as fresh as a daisy. That's the funny thing about seasickness; you can never be sure who'll be first to go green around the gills, or who presents with no ill-effects at all. For those who can't take it, once the swirl of giddiness sets in and the mouth starts to water in a dribbling reflux, the initial vomiting progresses to merciless dry retching. There was no respite for some, especially when the sou'westerlies picked up, and even ships as bulky as the *Queen Mary* would shudder and gently list from side to side. This was a big problem for those herded down onto F deck, where the swell lapped the bolted portholes.

To look at Private Alexander Campbell, you'd reckon he'd be strong enough to hold a bull out to pee. He'd decided to drop the name Alexander overboard, saying he was always known at school as Sandy. It wasn't long before Wally Leffler, a former bookie's penciller who'd been warned off several metropolitan racetracks, had ridiculously characterised him in as a typical non-betting, tight-arsed Scot.

Campbell's muscular physique suggested he'd be handy packing down in the second row or at full forward, and if you were a betting man who hadn't yet caught on, you'd probably back him to be the last man standing in a bar-room brawl. Indeed, quite a few of the men had seen the Nazi torchlight rallies at Nuremberg on the Saturday matinee newsreels and thought that if ever there was a raw-boned country boy – complete with cowlick and the Nordic features that were straight out of Leni Riefenstahl's casting book – it was Sandy Campbell. Were it not for his archetypal Aryan traits, the only plausible alternative mythology at one's disposal might have thrown up the Greek god Adonis.

The sight of this rangy cow cocky on all fours, praying over the latrines on his first night at sea was definitely something to write home about. It was only earlier in the day that he'd confided to anyone who'd listened that in the past, he'd relieved himself in some fairly ordinary redback-infested thunderboxes around Dalby. 'The most I ever copped were a few splinters in the arse,' he boasted, which got just enough laughs to draw them in. It had become part of his false persona to project himself as a real he-man, happy to be known as Big Sandy from the Bush. However, nothing had prepared him for his complete loss of composure at sea, or his close acquaintance with the appalling condition of the maritime bogs. If you'd asked Campbell about it, he would've said that until now he'd always taken cloudless blue skies, droughts and flooding rains in his stride, but you could keep your bloody jewel seas all to yourself!

Those seasoned troops who'd also become a little nauseous below deck were not unsympathetic towards his plight. They correctly reasoned that there wouldn't have been too many 15-foot swells on the Condamine River for Campbell to contend with. But a few others delighted in his suffering. One of the least sympathetic was Corporal Mervyn Nethercote. 'Get a load of that big mummy's boy over there,' Merv said to his mate Wally Leffler. 'He's as crook as a dog.'

'Yeah, I've noticed, and it'll only get worse,' Wal replied.

'I've said to ya before, Wal, I find Big Sandy from the Bush a bit too flamin' neat and educated for my likin'. Did ya notice him all dressed up at last night's concert? Looks like he's spent most of his life fingerin' his piano, not workin' the land like he makes out. What's he gunna do when he has to fire 'is rifle at the enemy? He'll 'ave to quickly face the music when that happens,' he laughed.

'Yeah … an' it's always hard to get a Jock to lay a bet, is what I keep thinkin'.'

Normally, if Merv offered his jaundiced view about things, the response was generally inaudible. But whenever he referred to Campbell as 'that lovely boy', accompanied by vulgar hand gestures, it invariably drew sustained laughter from Wally and his reptilian hangers-on.

Before the outbreak of war, Merv had been a fully paid-up member of the Boilermaker's Society. He was an elected official of the union and an old-fashioned standover merchant, the sort of uncouth, lumbering thug who wouldn't have thought twice about farting in church. Merv skited that he'd only ever managed to darken the pews in a church on a single occasion, and that was for a comrade's funeral – a long-serving union shop steward.

Campbell had done himself no favours when engaged in his usual blokey banter. At some point he'd let slip that he came from a family of pastoralists who grew a bit of wheat and ran a large sheep and cattle station west of Dalby, on the fringe of the Darling Downs in southern Queensland. He soon discovered there was nothing more guaranteed to provoke the aggrieved urban working class, than hearing someone was part of what was unthinkingly denigrated as the landed gentry.

'You would've thought with his boarding school education and grazier family ties he would've walked into officer training college,' Merv sneered, unable to relinquish his unexamined ideological prejudices against perceived privilege. This type of attitude often cropped up among the communist sympathisers on board whenever Campbell foolishly let on about his family background. The truth was, no matter how much cow cockies struggled to earn a quid, anyone who owned a decent-sized plot of land in the bush was likely to be considered by urbanised, impoverished Australians as an undeserving wealthy member of the bunyip aristocracy.

The few who were genuinely puzzled often wondered what Sandy's *real* story was. But they soon realised that Big Sandy from the Bush wasn't the only one on board who was untalkative about their private life. A quick look around was enough to suggest that more than one was probably hiding or running away from something or other – most probably themselves.

Tough luck for anyone who remained curious about his private life – now sick and nursing his pride, Campbell clammed up about any personal matters to anyone from here on in, no matter their level of genuine concern. He sported a sullen, hangdog expression throughout the day and sulked like a big kid during the night. Not even cocksure Gunner Roberts was game enough to dig any further. Potty-mouthed Clarrie was also fighting off his own bouts of upset tummy as one of the medical officers uncharitably chose to diagnose it, knowing full well he'd get a rise. Before long, his feeling of queasiness would also see him joining the chorus of bilious men heaving over the windswept gunwales up on deck. Gunner Roberts was really fed up now, and constantly made this known to his now increasingly unsympathetic, single-member audience.

'I can't wait to get off this fuckin' pleasure cruise, Tassie. I've had a gutful of all this pitchin' and rollin' around. I'm strugglin' to imagine anyone forkin' out hundreds of quid for a ticket, when this huge rust bucket was a luxury ocean liner. It's almost as bad up here on deck doing physical jerks and lifeboat drills as it is cooped up down there.'

'Look, Clarrie, none of us are seafarers, we're not cut out for this. With seasickness, it's mostly mind over matter. You need to concentrate and keep lookin' at the horizon *above* the swell. You might be feelin' crook, but I think you're more worried about being called a big sheila if you admit it, aren't you?'

'That's all right for you to say. You must have a cast-iron gut. I haven't. But you're right, I don't wanna end up sulkin' in the corner like what's his name, Lord Jockstrap over there, sweatin' like a navvy.'

'Come off it, Clarrie! Where'd you pick up that expression – in one of those country pubs you're always on about? What would you know about navvies? His name's Sandy, and he's had a big come down. It'd be a bit of a mongrel act to lay into a bloke when he's on the ground, wouldn't it? A *real* kick in the guts! He's goin' through a bit of a rough trot, but he'll come good well before we hit dry land. You can bet on it.'

'By the look of 'im I don't think he can,' said Clarrie, 'and now you've said that I *will* bet on it. Let's make it double whatever you've got on ya right now says he'll be crook 'til we finally get off this tub, wherever that is.'

All Clarrie would've been able to muster were a few coppers and threepenny bits, had he owned up to it.

'All right, I'll see what I've got,' said Tassie. He fossicked around in his pockets and among the dirt and loose fluff managed to come up with fifteen bob in silver, mostly deeners and florins. 'When *I win* this bet, it'll be a pleasure to rub your nose in your poor judgment of Sandy's character. You keep sayin' you've got no dough, so when *you lose*, I guess you'll have to put the bite on Wally Leffler for a loan.'

'You're on,' Clarrie replied, shaking hands. 'That'll work. Wally's never short of a quid, but borrowin' from him will cost heaps in interest, if you want a surer bet.'

Clarrie wasn't expecting his challenge to be accepted. Although Tassie was difficult to read, other soldiers could sometimes see he struggled to conceal his unease at his cobber's volatile streak of working-class uppishness. This time it rankled. He was getting fed up with the young bloke's permanently disagreeable attitude. He'd already witnessed it firsthand on numerous occasions, and if pushed, he'd probably have put it down to the boy's deep sense of inferiority. *I think he's wrestlin' with some unresolved grief, and bad experiences with his father at home. He certainly doesn't like to talk about it*, was as far as Tassie pondered the matter. Whatever the cause, in Clarrie's case coiled aggression lay in wait beneath the surface, and it didn't take much provocation for it to rear its ugly head. It seemed not only to Tassie, but anyone else who happened to be within cooee at the time, that no matter what the point of contention was, Clarrie always argued his prejudices from a finely balanced position; that's to say, from the point of view of someone with a chip on *both* shoulders.

After ten days at sea, it was clear the Indian Ocean was scarcely more calm than Australian waters, and Clarrie's cynicism likewise showed no signs of abating. 'I bet the toffs up above are stretched out on proper bunks, havin' a good ol' time downin' their noggins of Red Mill rum,' he bitterly remarked, but after failing to get a reply, his mind soon drifted elsewhere.

'Bloody hell, Taz, what I wouldn't give for one of me auntie's roast dinners and a cold schooner of Resch's right now.' His mate just chuckled half-heartedly, not wishing to engage in Clarrie's fondness for self-pity. He preferred to get on with his own thoughts, rather than remind him that Resch's wasn't on tap in Queensland, let alone on board the *Queen Mary*.

While Clarrie didn't appear to be lacking in personal loyalty or bravado, he was a total stranger to notions of discretion, forbearance and self-reflection. He was slow to accept that officers were, as a matter of objective fact and military law, his legitimate superiors. Nevertheless, his cynical observations on shipboard life summed up the unexpressed feelings among many of the recently enlisted soldiers of the 8th Division. Most had never lived at close quarters with heaps of other blokes before and quietly resented being put through the wringer on a stiflingly hot, jam-packed boat on the high seas.

Once the ship had veered nor'-nor'-west from Fremantle and anchored briefly off Trincomalee in Ceylon, it was officially confirmed where the long-rumoured destination would be. The distribution of quinine tablets to control malaria had served to erase any lingering doubt. Word had spread that the Imperial Japanese Army was likely heading towards the Malay Peninsula, and the 8th Division was on course to meet that threat.

Like Gunner Clarrie Roberts, many of the soldiers on board had left school at around fourteen years of age, generally before sitting their intermediate certificate exams. As a result, you could wager that most of them wouldn't have been able locate Malaya or Burma on any map of the globe that didn't have a smattering of British Empire crimson all over it. So far as familiarity with Singapore Island itself was concerned, most would say you could only get there via the road depicted in the recently released movie starring Bob Hope and Bing Crosby. Soldiers didn't care if the fantasised exotic locations were produced on film sets and the botanical gardens of Los Angeles, and some even believed it'd be a sure thing to bump into plenty of Dorothy Lamour lookalikes in flowery sarongs once they disembarked.

In a similar vein, prevailing cultural ignorance and stereotypes meant that little was known about the composition and character of the Japanese army among the Australian armed forces at that time. Most wouldn't have been able to distinguish a Japanese national from anyone else of oriental appearance working in the kitchens, market gardens or laundries back home. Racial prejudice was a product of its time and place, and soldiers born after WW1 were largely unaware of the lengths to which colonial politicians had gone to discriminate against non-European immigrants long before Federation. The corollary to this was that it shouldn't take too long to defeat an inferior Asian enemy, and in next to no time they'd be riding home on the pig's back.

Around midday on 19 February 1941, the troop carrier coasted into the port of Malacca. Once it anchored, those on board were captured by an indefinable, contrasting sensation that alternated between fear and a restlessness for the impending war. As they trudged down the wooden gangways in the oppressive heat, their haversacks and .303 rifles felt somehow heavier than they'd been at Circular Quay barely two weeks before. Campbell had remained crook right up until the final disembarkation – Clarrie's pocket was now 30 shillings heavier, but he felt none the happier for its presence.

CHAPTER
ELEVEN

JAHORE STATE, MALAYA, LATE SEPTEMBER 1941

BACK IN 1940, Clarrie wasn't long into his basic training at Redbank on the western outskirts of Brisbane before a few stirrers in his artillery unit detected his thin skin. The baiting only increased once the regiment reached Malaya and eventually established its base at Mersing, on the north-east coast of Jahore. The same bunch of stirrers knew that it remained easy to upset him with a play on his initials, ridiculing C. S. as an acronym for Cobra Snake.

Private Richard Stiff was labelled Stiffy but was indifferent to the crude innuendo. While this derogatory nickname was entirely predictable, like the shortest bloke on board answering to Lofty, both were basically unimprovable. However, at the slightest mention of Cobra Snake in his presence, Clarrie would be sucked in and invariably offended. Whether it was slithering on its belly in the long grass or being mesmerised by a swaying flute on the overcrowded pavements of Delhi, to be likened to a deadly fork-tongued serpent went way beyond insult or derision – it was a direct assault on his notion of courage and manliness. It might've been an echo of his father's fulminations over the dinner table, but the viper had become closely associated in Clarrie's mind with satanic evil. In short, he wasn't going to cop it sweet, and the ensuing altercation only served to underline in the sergeant major's eyes Roberts's natural propensity for attracting trouble.

'Orrright, who started this?' Cruickshank snarled through his tobacco-stained teeth, having got wind of a disturbance in the mess hall. Nobby had a habit of getting up close when giving troublemakers a mouthful and those in the firing line couldn't help but wonder if his missus, if he had one, was immune to halitosis. No matter the distance, those discoloured, malodorous fangs were his most arresting feature, if you didn't count the uncommon girth of his neck. His bottom row of teeth was not simply discoloured by nicotine but was also missing several, and the remainder seemed worn down to not much more than a bed of inflamed gums. By any measure they were an insult to oral hygiene. There were several gaps in the top row as well, but those that remained looked as splayed as cricket stumps after a wicketkeeper's overenthusiastic glove-work to produce a dramatic run-out. His snaggle-toothed grin would have been slightly comical but for the slither of gold filling glued to the side of one of his remaining cuspids. This produced the curious effect of rendering his smile both fearsome and fleetingly attractive at the same time.

'It was me and Lenny here, sir,' uttered private Wally Leffler, who made sure he got on the front foot by owning up before Cruickshank started applying the screws. Lenny said nothing and wore a fixed grin across his square-jawed face so you couldn't pick it as being self-satisfied or simply advertising stupidity.

'We was just geein' 'im up about nothin' in the yard, and after we finished eatin' ee went right off 'is rocka.' As he spoke, Leffler nervously shifted his weight from side to side as if busting for a leak. 'Came straight at us like a bull at a gate. It was a case of self-defence, Sergeant Major, sir. We woz quakin' in our boots ... had to protect ourselves, didn't we? Gotta say for a bloke 'is size, ee's not backward in comin' forward.'

'Leffler had it comin', sarge,' Clarrie cut in. 'He was havin' a go at me name.'

Cruickshank was inclined to sympathise with Clarrie's explanation. He thought Wally was a little bit too pleased with his slavish turn of phrase and had already recoiled at the way in which he'd dobbed in private Len Kelly as co-offender. Experience had taught him that while Leffler might know how to start a blue, he was the sort of bloke who relied on the misplaced loyalty of someone like Kelly to finish it off.

Within five minutes of first meeting Leffler at Redbank Camp, he'd realised that this bloke had tickets on himself. Large ones. He was often overheard boasting of his success in chasing the sheilas, hardly ever receiving a knock-back. He'd started work as a pastry cook and baker by trade and sometimes got a laugh when he said that he'd left a few buns in the oven over the years. Lenny only cottoned on to the meaning after he'd heard the tasteless jest several times. Leffler had claimed to have rooted at least a dozen sheilas before he enlisted. He couldn't be certain – 'Might've been a baker's dozen,' he'd laugh. It didn't matter what they looked like – 'I'm up for anything,' he'd brag, claiming his new uniform had only served to increase the number of ladies who willingly succumbed to his charms.

With his chest puffed out, Wally thought he was king dick despite the scaly wart on the side of his nose that sported a smallish tuft of red hairs. Unless this disfiguring facial feature was mysteriously alluring to the female gender, its obvious repulsiveness would suggest Wally was being rather economical with the truth. The sergeant major prided himself on being an astute judge of character, and from the outset he considered Wally a bullshit artist, a sideshow-alley spruiker and a small-time wheeler-dealer all wrapped up in one. *He must've joined up to avoid being arrested by the coppers; that would be the only explanation why someone like him is standing here before me today,* he correctly speculated. Being a practical type of person, the reason Cruikshank had taken an instant dislike to Leffler was quite straightforward – he knew it'd save time. *Intuition's a funny thing,* he'd say to himself in these situations. *It's a reliable gut feeling, and it comes naturally. No-one ever needs to teach a dog to have a sniff before cocking its leg against a tree, do they?*

Private Leffler was already known for working the system. After quitting the bakery he'd eventually found employment as a form spotter for an SP bookie before enlisting and now ran an unauthorised two-up school behind the barracks. Would-be participants were charged five bob to get in. It was supposed to operate on the sly, despite loud calls of 'Come in, spinner!' lasting for hours. Leffler devised any number of lurks to entice his superior officers to turn a blind eye to his dealings, especially his procurement of things they were unable to get hold of through legitimate means. With his reputation as a betting tout, Wally had little trouble attracting a following of dyed-in-the-wool gamblers, along with the most disreputable members of his regiment who'd suddenly materialise like a cloud of blowflies trailing a dunny cart down the road.

Len Kelly was his prime recruit. He'd been so well trained that he just nodded like a donkey when Wally recounted his version of the punch-up. Suffice to say, Len could always be relied upon to back Wally to the hilt and, in this instance, to appropriately downplay any element of provocation. Cruickshank knew these two blokes were as thick as thieves, and he had no time for the nodding Lenny. He made it clear he wasn't going to muck around with any of their concocted explanations. As he spoke, his face didn't break into one of his fearsome, short-toothed grins, but the skin noticeably tightened and his eyebrows narrowed, as if he were straining hard to lay a cable or squinting at something annoyingly reflective in the distance. After copping a withering tirade, all three were summarily disciplined, including Len, who hadn't thrown a punch but was someone Cruickshank thought would probably have gone in for the king hit, if he'd been called upon.

Most people steered clear of Kelly, believing him not the full quid. He was already up against it because he was presumedly a mick, a rock-chopper of Irish immigrant descent, and therefore of doubtful loyalty to the British Sovereign. Beneath his basin-cut hairstyle, Lenny's ears appeared as if they'd been lowered and fastened to his head like a pair of wing nuts. While not exactly what you'd call a complete imbecile, he was the sort of bloke who couldn't read a Ginger Meggs comic strip without moving his lips or resist shading in the empty boxes when presented with a crossword puzzle and a blunt pencil. He generally had nothing to say, but when he did, whatever came out was no more incisive.

'All ovya are confined to barracks for the rest of the day. And you can say goodbye to any leave approval for at least a month.' Cruickshank's punishments always failed to consider the finer points of causation, let alone the relative apportionment of blame. 'Over that time, you'll drag the 25-pounders through the undergrowth and practise changing their wheels in the mud. Then I'll personally supervise yur spit 'n' polish detail in the latrines for the next week or so. You'll soon wish ya were peelin' spuds all day and come to understand the true meaning of … *fatigue,*' he said, sucking in the air through the remnants of his teeth before dramatically emphasising the word. He assured them his leniency in this instance wouldn't be repeated, and if there was any further buggerising around, he'd do everything by the book and recommend his superiors lay serious disciplinary charges. 'Then again, I might feel charitable and give ya a choice,' he warned them, almost as an afterthought. 'Instead of official disciplinary action, you could both volunteer to be ironed out by me, one after the other … an' it won't be a book I'll be throwin' at ya!'

Neither prospect was appealing, but both soldiers knew they'd opt for being hauled over the coals by the military tribunal rather than the certainty of Nobby giving them both a hiding, even with one hand tied behind his back.

'Save ya fightin' for the bloody enemy,' he scowled, 'an' remember, ya part of an army outfit that'll rely on self-discipline for its survival.'

Both thought these last words a little contrived, and in view of his threats, almost certainly disingenuous. They were pretty sure Cruikshank really didn't give a fig who started the fisticuffs and probably wished both had suffered far more serious injuries than were presently visible. They knew, however, that he would rectify this deficiency if they played up again.

'Nobby's throwin' 'is weight around as usual,' proclaimed Wally in a muffled voice, rounded off with his customary belch. 'Like I've said before, when it comes down to threats, I reckon he's all piss and wind,' he asserted with the authority of someone who had a long acquaintance with the condition. Wally was mindful enough not to offer his deeply reasoned opinion of Cruickshank until well after the sergeant major had finished the dressing-down and had stormed out of the mess hall. In truth, both he and Clarrie had not unreasonably suspected from the shape of Nobby's conk and his less-than-fetching smile that he'd probably gone the knuckle more than a few times before, out the back.

Once Lenny had slowly processed his master's closing words, he obediently brayed his approval in the absence of a stubby tail to wag. A casual observer might've confidently agreed with Cruikshank that Lenny was the type of person who possessed little more depth of character than what was apparent to the naked eye.

————

On only the second day after his arrival in Mersing, Private Alexander Campbell was unexpectedly relieved from regular morning training exercises with his unit. In contrast to Clarrie's ongoing inability to fit in, he'd kept his nose clean since arriving in Malaya and had never come close to committing any act of insubordination. He was having a yarn with Tassie when he was summoned to the nearby quarters of Major Bernard Wake, Regimental Medical Officer (RMO).

Wake was an army doctor in his mid-to-late forties who'd already given distinguished service as a medical stretcher-bearer on the Western Front in France. He'd come over to Mersing from his base with the 2/9th Field Ambulance at the Australian General Hospital (the AGH) in Malacca, to meet up with his old friend and comrade-in-arms, Lieutenant Colonel Thomas Manning. Both had served together at Villers Bretonneux in early 1918 and had remained on the battlefield until the armistice was declared.

Campbell didn't know what to expect. The feeling that descended upon him was akin to the one he'd experienced while waiting outside the headmaster's office at St. Andrew's College in Brisbane over five years before. On that occasion, he'd been required to explain his participation in an embarrassing boarding house incident, that'd almost resulted in his expulsion.

'Come in Campbell,' said the major, resolutely clicking his heels together as he extended his hand rather than saluting. 'I'm told your mates call you Sandy. Is that what you prefer to go by, rather than Alexander, or even Alex?'

'Yes, sir. People seem to find Alexander a bit too formal, with too many syllables. Most of my cobbers think it's a bit too la-di-da.'

The major's temporary office was sparsely furnished and the air hung heavily with the sweetly dry aroma of pipe tobacco. One of the walls was dominated by a detailed map of Malaya that was emblazoned with legends and those thin, squiggly contour lines Campbell recognised from his geography lessons illustrating the steep gradients on Mount Bartle Frere in North Queensland. On the only wall that was unadorned with Australian military insignia hung a portrait of an uncomfortable-looking King George VI, all trussed up in his marshal of the Royal Air Force uniform.

Wake was lanky and slightly stooped, and his sinewy frame and ungainly appearance belied the fact that he'd excelled at athletic games in his younger years. His face was pockmarked and as deeply lined as the military map nailed to the wall but was dominated by an impressive, aquiline nose. This facial characteristic lent him a certain authoritative bearing that sat easily with the respected status he enjoyed among his fellow medical officers and associated staff.

'At ease, then, Sandy. Take a seat,' Wake motioned with a curt wave of the hand. 'You know who I am, don't you?' the major enquired with a slight pout of the lips. At this point Campbell hadn't much of a clue.

'I've seen you on parade, sir, but no, I don't recognise you, not really. I know you're in the medical corps, but I haven't taken much notice of anything other than troops going out on manoeuvres, the mozzies everywhere and the constant humidity.' He was rather disappointed with the indifferent reception his admittedly rather clumsy attempt at light-hearted humour had been accorded.

Campbell didn't know whether taking a seat was a test of his personal initiative or not because the only seat in the room, other than the major's, was occupied. He had to remove a thick ledger tied with a woven braid to effectively comply with the direction. The desk itself was piled high with manila folders filled with what he imagined were medical records, scattered among bundles of scuffed army manuals and bits of military paraphernalia looking for a home. He continued to gingerly assemble the remaining materials from around the designated chair before transferring them to the least precarious space on the major's desk. Despite ransacking his memory, he remained completely baffled as to why he was supposed to recognise one of the medical corps' senior officers, particularly one not directly attached to a field artillery regiment.

Now fixing his gaze on private Campbell as if he were lining him up in the sights of a rifle, the major continued, 'You might be surprised to learn this, but I'm distantly related to all the Campbells, through your mother Mollie's side of the family – the Buttenshaws from Goondiwindi. I'm rather disappointed your father didn't mention the Buttenshaw-Wake connection, because he must've enquired about my presence over here, prior to your embarkation. It just so happens I was also a boarder at St Andrew's a few terms ahead of Alasdair before the last war. We haven't had much to do with one another since then, I'm sorry to say. During the twenties I trained as a doctor in Victoria before undertaking a fellowship in Edinburgh. I eventually returned to Melbourne to set up a medical practice. Colonel Manning and I are old friends, and he persuaded me to sign up to the army's medical corps. Unfortunately, I lost contact with many of my relatives who remained in the bush in Queensland. You know how things go.'

Campbell hadn't been around long enough to know how many things in life went at all, and his memory was working overtime trying to piece together what would soon be revealed once the major resumed the one-sided conversation. He now vaguely recalled childhood mention of a distant relative down south, who practised a surgical specialty that was virtually unpronounceable and totally meaningless to a child. But that was the sum of his dim recollections.

After taking a stride or two away from his desk to key the door, Wake adopted a less military tone of voice. As he collected his thoughts, the spikey ends of his otherwise impressively bushy moustache stuck out like a caterpillar wriggling above his upper lip. The impression of a living organism was accentuated whenever he appeared to use the tip of his tongue as an improvised toothpick.

'Once your training was completed and you were entrained from South Brisbane to Sydney, Alasdair contacted the Divisional HQ by telephone in Sydney. He no doubt remembered you can't take Queensland out of the boy, because your father lost no time reminding me that

I owed him a few favours from our old schooldays together in Brisbane. After sharing some brief reminiscences, he told me the purpose of his call was to touch upon an unsavoury incident during your final term at the college. It involved one of the unmarried housemasters, Stuart Buchanan. He was also my history teacher, and Alasdair and I, along with all the other boarders, used to call him Pudding Face.'

'He's still called that, sir,' Campbell sheepishly interrupted.

'Yes, I know. I was astonished to learn that until recently, he was still on the staff. You'll excuse me, Sandy, if I digress a little? In my time there, the class clowns used to bait him quite a bit, even if he didn't always know it was going on.'

'Maybe he did, but didn't really care?' Campbell hazarded to say.

'You could be right about that, now I come to think of it. Anyhow, it so happened that Buchanan was quite fond of a young fellow called Carstairs, a snotty-nosed boy who always shot his hand up first, no matter whether he knew the answer or not. I can't recall his Christian name – boarding school was a place where a boy's family name was what he went by. A bit like the army, and possibly some of those Italian Renaissance painters. Anyway, it was obvious to everyone in the class that he was the teacher's pet. Carstairs was also renowned for being a masturbator of prodigious energy, unrivalled throughout the dormitory. Even being told by everyone he'd go blind failed to deter his habits. While he was around, there was little doubt where your missing socks had ended up. We eventually threatened to publicise his nocturnal pastime to the wider college community.'

All this still goes on, Campbell thought.

'Not that his exploits were completely unknown, mind you. In fact, by the number of jibes that followed him around the college grounds, it would be more accurate to describe knowledge of Carstairs' handiwork, if I might put it that way, as an open secret. He was the only boy who the head of the boarding house, ol' Pudding Face himself, as it turned out, had ever made lie on top of the bed covers for twenty minutes after evening prayers in winter as a form of punishment.'

'He never tried that on me, sir, even though I used to muck around a bit after lights out as well.'

'Is that so? I'll come to that in a minute. I'll continue with what I was saying, if I may?'

'Go ahead, sir.'

'Eventually we coerced Carstairs into asking Buchanan some obscure historical questions in class so he could get back in our good books, as it were. If my memory serves me correctly, the question had something to do with the dissolution of the Cistercian monasteries under King Henry VIII. We knew Buchanan would jump at the chance as he often boasted about his extensive knowledge of Tudor history. So long as the questioning didn't touch on the fate of Henry's many wives, we reasoned – he'd already covered that to death. No, 'The more arcane, the better I like it,' was the memorable way he used to put a challenge to us. So, no doubt that's why someone came up with the topic of the way in which the Protestant King treated the French order of farming monks.'

Where's all this leading, Campbell continued to ask himself but understandably failed to broach at any stage.

'We eagerly feigned interest in the reply to Carstairs' well-rehearsed questions, but it was all carried out facetiously. Fortunately, Buchanan, innocently or otherwise, provided us with an uninterrupted historical discourse on the matter, which must have taken him a good ten minutes to deliver.'

'You're kidding, major? It's hard to believe he was so easily taken in?'

'Once again, and I'm again relying heavily on memory here, Buchanan must have rattled on right up to the bell. This had the desired result that he forgot to collect the draft essays that everyone in the class except Carstairs had failed to complete in prep the previous evening. Our ploy had worked perfectly.'

'You were certainly game, major. All we got up to in class was a bit of paper-darts throwing and farting behind his back. I remember one morning Mr Buchanan correctly picked out the only boy in the class with two surnames as the likely culprit who'd let go a real rip-snorter. Without missing a beat, Pudding Face said, "Saville-Sneath, that's the smartest thing I've heard from you in months." We all had a laugh, and I think everyone had a lot more time for him after that.'

'Hmmm, it's now clear to me there was more to him than met the eye,' said the major, adopting a more measured tone of voice. 'In those days, we enjoyed coming up with cruel nicknames like Pudding Face on a regular basis. I recall that for one unfortunate lad, whose family name was Strangways, there was no real need to create a nickname if you added a common vowel in the middle. The senior monitors would always pick on the most vulnerable to bully. They'd give out punishments like sitting naked on the lavatory seats for thirty minutes in winter to warm them up for the rugger boys before morning training. For some strange reason, Strangways was often singled out for this type of maltreatment.'

'It's not hard to figure out why, major?'

'Yes, I shouldn't have made it so obvious. This type of tradition, followed by the communal cold shower often resulted in severe chilblains. It was a shameful, cruel practice of which I now greatly disapprove, and regret having enjoyed at the time. We tended not to think of the masters as ordinary human beings, either. I suppose like all unfeeling schoolboys, at that stage I had no idea what lasting devastation to one's personal appearance, like severe childhood eczema, would have caused in Buchanan's case, let alone the mental damage. He must've been getting on in years during your time there, wouldn't you say?' said the major, offering Campbell a rare opportunity to get a few words in edgeways.

'I couldn't tell you, major. Mr Buchanan was balding, and his jowls were always blotchy and lumpy. But then again, I suppose most of the masters looked old and wrinkly to us.'

'That's all by the by,' replied Wake, now eager to get the purpose of the meeting back on track. 'What's important is that your father has ongoing concerns for you, especially in light of the type of boarding house mischief in which you were reportedly engaged in your final year. The name Buchanan and his dubious reputation around certain matters also came up in our little chat. But unlike his unhealthy interest in Carstairs' notorious habits, whatever occurred in your case, didn't simply involve playing with oneself under the bed sheets, or a bit of bastardisation of the weaklings. Need I go on?'

Campbell all the while sat there slightly unnerved by the unexpected dredging up of the past. It was clear that the major gave credence to the longstanding rumours that Buchanan was a pederast and possibly homosexual, as both were obviously indistinguishable to his way of thinking, but couldn't come out and say it.

'This led to your father's request for me to keep a close eye on you. When it comes to a matter involving the family's honour, any compromising incidents need to be forcefully handled with the utmost speed and discretion. Alasdair also briefly referred to your sharing accommodation in Brisbane after you left college, with a much older man he'd never met before. I gather he disapproved of the arrangement. He said you didn't go back to the farm in Dalby until your elder brother got married. Your father sounded a bit disillusioned with both his sons.

'There's little time to sow your wild oats, sir. You must have gone through similar experiences yourself, major, when you were my age?'

'Yes, and they're impossible to forget, Sandy. Anyhow, in relation to the school incident, Alasdair told me that Buchanan has since retired on health grounds, as they say. That alleged misbehaviour at college, as I've said, appears to have been more serious than acting the goat, a bit of harmless tickling or a pillow fight in the dormitory that went too far. I'm not here to rake over past actions and improprieties, beyond what I've mentioned today, and I daresay you won't be too keen for me to do that either.'

Campbell offered no response to the rhetorical invitation. It was the first time the major had witnessed such a large-framed soldier shifting restlessly in his seat like a puny, frightened schoolboy anticipating physical punishment. He looked across the desk to make sure Campbell hadn't crossed his legs in an effeminate way and wa relieved when he saw both hands resting on his knees.

'As I've indicated, Sandy, as far as I'm concerned, this matter will *not* be raised again. Whatever's been said today stays in this office.'

Campbell inhaled a large breath of air that deterred him from protesting his innocence, which at this advanced stage might have been unappreciated, discredited, or even worse, entirely disbelieved. He was aghast that his father had divulged to a relative stranger a boarding-house lark that had gone too far, but which he'd simply witnessed from the sidelines. And it had occurred years before! Nevertheless, he considered it preferable not to pursue the negative implications further, fearing the major might break his promise and launch into an ill-informed, moral denunciation of the schoolboy misconduct.

Wake swivelled in his chair once more, then brutally dislodged the remnants of burnt tobacco from the bowl of his short-stemmed briar pipe. The ashtray was fashioned from the mangled casing of an artillery shell, crudely beaten into a shape that was reasonably fit for its current purpose. Reaching for his tobacco pouch, laden with the contents of the now empty tin of Murray's Erinmore Mixture on the desk, he then plugged the bowl of his pipe by firmly tamping down the loose strands with the stub of his yellowed thumb. Throughout this procedure, Campbell couldn't help but notice Wake's large hands. They looked more likely to grip the handle of a crosscut saw than the sides of a scalpel, more suited to the orthopod than the oculist.

He then lit up and puffed away, before finally revealing the ultimate purpose of the meeting. 'Do you know what sort of work a medical orderly does, Sandy?' he resumed, without waiting for or indeed expecting an answer. 'Well, I'll tell you. Starting today, I've reassigned you to the position of my personal assistant, attached to the 2/10th Australian General Hospital. I've been thinking about this course of action for quite a few months now. Over that time, I've made several enquiries about your character since your arrival in Malaya. Your immediate superiors told me your application to assigned duties and interactions with the personnel in your regiment are irreproachable. That was very reassuring, and I've since sent a letter to Alasdair to that effect. My commanding officer, Lieutenant Colonel Manning, supported my proposal without pressing me for the underlying reason. In keeping with your new role, HQ has done everything necessary to have you promoted to the rank of lance bombardier.'

'Wow, that's a bit of a mouthful, sir. I think it's like a lance corporal, isn't it?'

'Yes, it's not a hugely significant promotion. The colonel insisted on getting rid of the word private before your name; that prefix has only ever referred to a soldier deprived of rank or office,' he said.

'That's never worried me, major.'

'That's good to hear, but your opinion is beside the point. Even though he's a learned man, I happen to disagree with the colonel about this matter of rank. In civilian life a consultant surgeon is officially addressed as mister, not doctor. The former sounds fine. It reflects the humble beginnings of the discipline of surgical medicine, its essence captured by the saying that titles do not reflect honour on men, but rather men on their titles. Over here I'm a major in the 2nd AIF and intend to discharge my duties with honour and integrity. Though some do so grudgingly, like all soldiers I must follow the orders of my superiors. Part of your new job will be to handle some of the administrative paperwork we officers tend to find rather menial and tiresome. I bet you can also drive any sort of vehicle, and you've probably been doing it on the farm in Dalby for donkey's years, haven't you?'

Campbell managed to sneak in a barely audible yes while the major briefly paused to take in a breath. He realised his father had already told Wake that he'd learnt how to handle trucks and old tractors, well before he could read and write.

'Some of the Brits have brought over their own personal batman, as they're called, to provide a comparable level of assistance. But seeing I'm one of the Senior Medical Officers attached to the 22nd Brigade, I'll also be wanting you to undertake some basic medical duties as well. Our mobile medical corps is a bit top heavy with men in their thirties and even forties. I've discovered recently they're not all that fit, and I suspect may be lacking the necessary vigour to carry out their critical duties with speed and efficiency when under fire. Most of your new, younger colleagues hail from Melbourne like me, or from regional Victoria, but I'm sure it won't take you long to settle in and learn the ropes. I don't know what your drop punt was like in rugby but just show 'em you can handle centre half-forward or the role of ruckman if you want to have a run in your new unit's football team. You may need to throw your weight around to gain their confidence.'

He paused to relight his pipe. It was a reminder to him that he'd spoken for way too long, and it was time to draw matters to a close. 'Although you'll be routinely called upon to drive an ambulance, helping set up an advanced dressing station will also be part of your new responsibilities. How do you feel about that?'

Things were happening so fast that Campbell's mouth remained agape throughout. He was still processing an intelligible response when the major cut in again, avoiding a satisfactory explanation as to how a barely trained infantryman could be expected to carry out such an unfamiliar role from the word go.

'I know what you're thinking,' said Wake, still fidgeting with his pipe as he leant back, gently rocking in his squeaky captain's chair. 'You don't have to concern yourself with how official protocols have been set aside. The whole process has been expedited. I've already ordered delivery of your replacement kit. You'll find it in your temporary quarters across the way. Tomorrow, I've arranged for you to get measured and fitted out with new uniforms at Charlie Wu's, our regimental tailor in Endau. It'll be something befitting your rank and status as my assistant. One of our officers, Captain Peters, who's familiar with the area, will drive you there.' Finally finishing his monologue, Wake now addressed him in an abrupt fashion about the conduct he expected of him from here on in.

'Let me be frank with you, lance bombardier. You're only to say you've been pressed into service in the Hygiene Unit as my non-commissioned assistant, temporarily transferred, if you like. You're not to discuss how I've managed to pull a few strings to get you this position, nor disclose the reason for its occurring. Is that understood?'

'Yes, sir.'

'Good. If anyone gets their nose out of joint at your swift elevation through the ranks, I'm sure you'll be able to handle it. If not, direct them to my office where they can discuss the matter further with Sergeant Major Cruikshank. I'd be surprised if they're not already aware that Nobby has a way of quickly resolving complaints. He's been a godsend – though I don't think our Lord God had anything to do with his current duties. He can be abrasive at times but doesn't discipline by swearing or uttering profanities. His approach is to employ the only four-letter words with which laggards and the insubordinate alike are often unfamiliar – *hard work*.'

'Yes, some of the usual shit-stirrers have said he's good at ordering that!'

'I'm not surprised. If Cruikshank wasn't so efficient and in such high demand, I'd order him to attend the Special Dental Unit. That's an assignment he's so far managed to avoid. By the same token, I'm going to demand *your* discreetly shutting down any talk of this matter with your mates, preferably before it starts. If you do that, Nobby's services may not be needed at all. As I've said, you're to confide in no-one. Is that clear?'

'Yes, that's fine, sir,' he replied, still squirming self-consciously in his chair like a nervous, quietly behaved child. 'But I reckon some of the blokes will want to know how I landed this promotion, sir? Most of the country boys who volunteered with me – they'll detect it in a flash if I'm bullshitting them.'

Wake reacted to this plea to modify his instructions as if he'd not been spoken to at all. It simply underscored the fact that this dispensation from his usual infantry duties was more in the nature of an irrevocable order than a humble request. Feeling like he had no say in the matter, Campbell just sat there like a stunned mullet. Any further questions were settled with silence and a raised eyebrow and what Campbell perceived to be a rather limp-wristed handshake, given the circumstances. A rugged, half-smile eked out of the corner of the major's mouth as he escorted his new flunky to the door. Campbell thought there might've been a touch of smugness on the major's face, the type of self-satisfied look that says, *remember, I've got something on you!*

'Be here on the dot after reveille tomorrow, ready for the trip up to Endau,' he finished in a sombre tone. He withdrew his enormous paw from Campbell's shoulder to unlock the door, finally offering a salute. The major's bent-arm action seemed instinctive and rather slow in its execution. *Thank God I at least got a casual salute this time*, he thought, still feeling uneasy about everything that had occurred.

———

Ambling back into the yard he rejoined Tassie who was still leaning against the back wall of the officers' quarters. A cigarette paper was dangling from his bottom lip as he carefully rolled his Log Cabin flaked-leaf tobacco in the palm of his hand. He hadn't moved an inch from the spot where they'd only recently parted company.

'Well, *that* was a turn up for the books,' Campbell said in a buoyant tone, suggesting something of consequence had occurred. 'Guess what? The major and I had a good ol' chat, and he even started calling me Sandy. He's decided to assign me to non-combatant duties from now on. But get a load of this – I've also been promoted to the rank of lance bombardier! I can't wait to record all this in my little notebook!'

'Well, blow me down. What do ya mean?' enquired Tassie, an unfamiliar strain of anxiety creeping into his usual drawl. 'You've lost me already. From what I can tell, you weren't in there long enough to have a decent yarn about anything? Like the rest of us, you haven't seen much active service, never sighted the enemy, and you've only been in uniform five minutes. How can you get promoted for *that*?'

He licked the side of the cigarette paper, stuck it down and poked the protruding strands of tobacco into one end with a matchstick. Despite there being not a breath of wind, out of habit he lit his smoke while shielding the match flame with cupped hands.

'I didn't see it coming, either. I found myself sitting up straight on my best behaviour, as if I'd been a bit naughty in class and hoping to avoid the strap. Towards the end I was nodding along with everything I heard, just like Len Kelly does all the time. He said the promotion had immediate effect. I should've realised from the start no-one gets pulled into the RMO's quarters to have a friendly chat about the weather.'

'It still beats me why you're only finding out about this t'day?'

'Beats me, too. Maybe they need a driver at short notice, someone who has experience on rough roads? It seems my father knows the major, who's a senior medical officer attached to the 22nd Brigade. He's still based in Malacca where we were, but I think he's come over to Mersing for briefings with the colonel for a week or so? My old man contacted him after we finished our final training at Redbank. I've now been made the major's assistant, a junior orderly or something? The colonel's already approved the whole thing … and get this! It's worth more dough too, no questions asked … and, by the way, I'm not supposed to be tellin' you any of this.'

'Well, you know what *any of this* probably means. If you're going to be a medical orderly, you'll be cleanin' blood off the floor more often than polishin' the major's boots. I bet he didn't say too much about swappin' a bayonet for a pair of scissors, did he?'

'No, but he did say I'll be getting some basic training in the army clinic next week. And he'll arrange my transfer to the hospital staff of Australian Army Medical Corps. I'll be learnin' on the job, he said.'

'You'd bedda be a fast learner, Sandy. I wouldn't mind bettin' orderlies will be the first ones runnin' round like headless chooks whenever enemy shells start landin'. Being an officer's glorified lackey might not work out so well for your personal safety, either, when we finally start firin' at the Nips … and they start firin' back. You can't drive an ambulance and still aim a rifle, and as far as I know, a Red Cross brassard has never stopped a bullet. Did that ever enter ya head?'

'Don't worry, *Gunner* Walls. You've obviously been hanging round Cobra Snake far too long … you're even starting to sound like 'im. For a bloke with your sense of decency, I can't work out why you continue to have anything to do with 'im, an' always seem to be quietly taking in his nasty cock-and-bull stories.'

Tassie made no attempt to answer and looked a bit sheepish.

'Anyhow, the major talked about me helping set up an advanced dressing station that deals with serious casualties. He said I might end up attached to one of the brigade's field ambulance units, the 2/9th, maybe? He didn't mention carrying a rifle, infantry duty or stuff like that. I guess that means he'll want me around mainly for dressing wounds, driving the injured, as well as keeping records. But that can't be too bad can it, if it lessens the chance of getting me head blown off on the frontline? Dad'll be pleased about that!'

'I wouldn't be so sure. If ya think about it, you'll probably be closer to the action than any of us on the big guns. We'll be firin' howitzer shells at enemy targets from *at least* a couple of miles away. You might be pickin' up wounded blokes on stretchers, close to wherever a front-line is formed. Funny thing,' said Tassie, still more unsettled than over-joyed by the news, 'I overheard a couple of the rough nuts on board ship back in February talkin' about you before we got here. They were sayin' you're a strange fella, and might be coverin' up a few secrets? Sayin' that despite ya build, deep down you might be a bit of a sheila, even a muscle-bound pansy? That was a new one on me! And I don't think they were talkin' about you strugglin' with seasickness, either.'

'I don't care what they said, and if I hadn't been so crook, I'd have soon flattened all ov 'em if I'd heard that.'

'I don't doubt you could've handled yourself very well. But when they get wind of this transfer and promotion, what they fancy they already know about your background will now be taken as dead-set certain – that you're the officers' white-haired boy, not only the mummy's boy Merv Nethercote already calls you behind ya back. They'll say you've been playin' your cards close to your chest all along – been bankin' on your sweet looks an' family connections to get transferred to ambulance duties.'

'Look, I didn't ask for this transfer. It was approved by the battalion commander! So, if those two shifty bastards Leffler and Nethers, your nasty little mate Cobra Snake, or any of those other useless dipsticks like Stiffy don't believe it, you can tell 'em *all* to go and get stuffed. Or they can go talk to Nobby about it.'

'I'll be sure to pass on your advice,' replied Tassie, extending his hand and realising he'd probably gone in a little too hard. 'I suppose old-fashioned congratulations are in order, then. You won't be gettin' too many handshakes or slaps on the back from any of those names you just rattled off – that's for sure.'

Although still perplexed and a little disappointed by the news, Tassie quickly decided not to try and push his luck. It was confidential, after all, and he was no dipstick.

'Good onya, mate … or is it *Bomber* Campbell from now on?' he said, trying to conceal the lingering tinge of regret in his voice. 'You've gotta laugh. While I'm rollin' a smoke with the makins, you'll probably be rollin' a bandage with the major,' he added dryly. He then went off to prepare for afternoon drill, not all that happy with his crude attempt at half-rhyming doggerel.

———

Campbell's rudimentary medical training touched on the treatment of malaria, basic anatomy, the vascular system and an accelerated acquisi-

tion of an equivalent Level One Red Cross Certificate covering infection and open-wound dressings. With all the talk of mosquitos in the
air and hookworms in the soil, there wouldn't be many opportunities
for soldiers to spend any part of the night or day without their shirt
and socks on. It all started to sink in for the first time.

He also had to get his head around the meaning of terms like
antibacterial sulphonamides, mercurochrome, neuritic beriberi,
atabrine, amoebic dysentery and niacin deficiency, well before he could
spell them. Despite only a very brief introduction to medical care,
Campbell embraced his new role with all the enthusiasm, application
and sense of purpose of those described as answering a calling.

At the end of his first week absorbing his new responsibilities, he
was told to have his kitbag packed and be ready to go on a two-day
furlough. He would be driving the major and two other senior officers
from Mersing to Johore Bahru at the tip of the Malay Peninsula, and
then over the Causeway to Singapore Island. All told, it wasn't much
more than 90 miles or so, barely three inches on one of the major's
heavily creased wall maps, but he'd been forewarned that the substan-
dard road and foot traffic around Kota Tinggi at the halfway stage
often made for heavy-going and unavoidable delays.

CHAPTER
TWELVE

MERSING–KOTA TINGGI ROAD, OCTOBER 1941

WHILE CAMPBELL WAS ASSEMBLING the luggage, the major introduced him to Lieutenant Colonel Thomas Manning and his adjutant, Captain David Peters. The three officers went on talking together as the reinforced trunk was being loaded and then securely fastened with enormous leather straps. It seemed the officers were arguing with one another, but Campbell was later informed it was simply a robust exchange of ideas. He'd soon discover this so-called exchange would last the entire journey.

As commander of the 2/18th Infantry Battalion sharing the defence of the southernmost part of the Malay Peninsula, Manning had accepted an invitation to a formal reception to welcome the recent arrival in Singapore of the British government's emissary and former first lord of the Admiralty, Sir Jeremy Pym, and his wife, Lady Celia Dalrymple.

The couple and their daughter Georgina had arrived in early September via Hawaii, so it was quite preposterous that the visit would mark the third occasion on which such a welcoming celebration had taken place. It wasn't fully explained in advance, but Pym had been eager to invite a high-ranking Australian officer with whom he could openly discuss his frustrations in dealing with the British armed services chiefs he was obliged to cooperate with. The meeting hadn't been easy to arrange. Major General Charles Dalziel, Head of the 8th Division, and Brigadier Harold Vernon, Commander of the 22nd Brigade, had both declined an invitation to attend. In private, each had considered the minister's approach as a friendly but essentially pointless and deeply uninteresting gesture.

In General Dalziel's case, an unstated contributory reason was his dreading the thought of spending even one evening engaged in forced bonhomie with a clique of civil service grandees – the type who still dressed for dinner at home. He knew he'd probably dislike them at first sight, and they wouldn't take long to reciprocate the displeasure. Although he'd only seen Jeremy Pym once before, and from a distance, Dalziel had peremptorily dismissed him as just another self-important civilian toff. He feared the air at his reception would be thick with the sound of those who might address him as old bean, then assail him with several volleys of those clipped vowels he'd sometimes compared to a scented fart.

Manning was a shade more open-minded than Dalziel and a stickler for observing correct form. He considered it rather unmannerly, even a bit churlish, that the Australian Army's two most senior officers in Malaya should have turned up their noses at such an invitation – especially one from such a well-connected British parliamentarian who'd been dispatched to Singapore as personal envoy to the British prime minister himself, Winston Churchill. He'd developed his own thoughts on how haphazardly things were being organised militarily in Malaya. Nevertheless, he'd told Dalziel he thought the meeting would be worthwhile, if only to get the strength of what was really going on within the British Far East High Command. 'I doubt whether we'll get a second invitation, so we might as well seize the opportunity to gauge the current state of play from the horse's mouth, rather than its arse,' he'd said.

The party's accommodation would be paid for out of a ministerial allowance, and Manning was pleased that reservations had been arranged by Pym's personal secretary to stay for one night, perhaps two, at the Adelphi, the secretary's highly recommended landmark hotel at the intersection of Coleman Street and North Bridge Road. The freshly promoted Lance Bombardier Alexander Campbell would be driving Wake, Manning and Captain Peters to the hotel.

The colonel had deliberately requested that the party not be accommodated at Raffles Hotel, commonly referred to as the Savoy of Singapore and extolled by his adjutant as the finest caravanserai east of Suez. The colonel believed he'd be unable to avoid being trapped at its celebrated Long Bar where, going by what he experienced during an earlier visit, many invitees to the official reception could probably be found lounging and lying in wait for prominent military figures at any hour of the day.

There was also something that grated with him when any establishment advertised on its handbills that it was the hotel preferred by 'some of the most distinguished royalty and European personages while sojourning in Singapore.' Although he gave the appearance of a rather courtly and urbane senior officer, Manning was wary of appearing to subscribe to the myth of exclusivity it dedicated to itself. Nor could he stomach the thought that he might be seen as fawning before members of a largely effete and moribund European aristocracy.

This prejudice might have been viewed as somewhat of a contradiction from someone who'd claimed that his favourite smell was that released whenever he opened the bound volumes of the King's Bench Reports in Sydney's Phillip Street law library. In common with its contents, it was an aroma to savour, he liked to say, replete with precedents and musty propositions of law – an unlaundered Tory Party smell that demanded your close attention by asserting its authoritative voice from the first page to the last. According to Manning, the smell's persistence was easily explained; undergraduate students seldom opened the reports, and if they did, generally ventured no further than reading the *ratio decidendi*, conveniently located in the headnotes to a decision.

Raffles Long Bar shared its renown as a haven for expatriates and the business elite – the *tuan besar* – with the prestigious Singapore

Club. However, membership of the club, which occupied several floors of the neoclassical-style Fullerton Building, was only open to the right sort of chap – those whom Westchester Country Club members might have said were long off the tee. The colonel had heard that certain members of these exclusive establishments reputedly wouldn't have a bar of welcoming Australians of any rank into their midst. In short, distinguished arrivals from the Dominions were sometimes considered by the colonial upper crust to be only one rung above the blackballed employees of the Singapore Harbour Board in respectability. It didn't matter to the colonel if he were not invited into that sort of environment. Neither Wake nor himself were particularly clubbable, and they hadn't made the trip to talk rubber, tin, the stock exchange or the isolation of plantation life on the estates. Least of all, they had no intention of being pumped for confidential military intelligence on the war in Europe over several gin and bitters.

Major Wake was overall a more affable character than either Dalziel or Manning, less disputatious and rather untroubled by any of their social hierarchy fixations. A man of simple virtues, he was grateful that at whichever first-class establishment he stayed, it offered a rare chance to get an added feel for the sort of place the 8th Division had travelled all this way to defend.

A further side benefit for the major was his temporary respite from supervising his battalion's instructional sessions primarily focused upon personal hygiene, the danger of contracting malaria, and the prevention, control and management of venereal disease. The brief stay might also provide a unique opportunity to experience firsthand some of the romanticised charms of Singapore's environs, renowned throughout the English-speaking world as the Gateway of the East. *Why make a fuss about things you can't control? Encountering a few bumptious silvertails along the way surely wouldn't spoil things greatly,* he reckoned.

Campbell soon understood the reason for Wake's insisting on his getting fitted out with formal dress kit, which had been quickly arranged at the same time he was appointed to his new position. He already had some inkling of the comfortable and cosseted way of life enjoyed by the Oriental Raj, even if stories of its opulence and extravagance were largely apocryphal. There was nothing to suggest that his attendance at the proposed reception would in any way diminish those alluring misconceptions.

What he *did* know was that Singapore had a large naval base near Sembawang in the north, as well as several RAF airfields scattered across the Malay Peninsula and on Singapore Island itself. He was aware of some fixed-gun batteries strategically located along the southern shoreline equipped with armour-piercing shells designed to disable, if not sink, an approaching enemy fleet. He also knew the British maintained such a large garrison of troops at Fort Canning that it encouraged everyone to think of the whole island as an invulnerable fortress.

What he didn't know beforehand was the desperate condition of the RAF capabilities in Malaya. Manning had likened what remained as serviceable aircraft to the inevitable fate of an injured antelope being stalked by a pride of hungry lions. In fact, Manning's conversation with Major Wake on this matter, went much further. 'I couldn't believe the air defence of Singapore was being left to a couple of squadrons of Vickers Vildebeest torpedo bombers backed up by the promised delivery of more Brewster Buffalo fighters from America. There's only a squadron or two of combat-ready Hurricanes as well. Our intelligence suggests the first two are well-named; lumbering bovines, presenting an easy target for more agile predators, which in this case might happen to be Japanese big-game hunters,' he'd quipped.

Campbell couldn't help but remember that only a few weeks ago seasickness had made him as woozy as a patient under the first whiff of chloroform on the operating table. He'd now awoken to find himself chauffeur to the top brass, heading for the Padang and the bustling quays of the great port city with all the flourish of an imaginary, jewel-encrusted nawab being transported in a motorised palanquin.

The staff car was, of course, totally out of place in the tropics, for which the first signs of rust around the door hinges provided ample evidence. It was a cream and brown Mark IV Bentley saloon, its interior fascia embellished by burr walnut panelling. The creases in the deep chestnut-coloured leather upholstery were beginning to take on the distinctive patina of age, despite the vehicle's relatively limited mileage. 'This'd be quite the thing for motoring to Henley-on-Thames to attend the Royal Regatta,' Wake had commented on first sighting it.

When shipped out to Georgetown, Penang, in the late-thirties, it had been the motor manufacturer's latest model, powered by a four-litre Rolls-Royce engine. Manning had acquired it by negotiating a legally obscure bailment arrangement at minimal expense. Wake's estimation of Manning's astuteness had significantly increased when he heard the background to the Bentley's acquisition. All that *he'd* been able to successfully requisition was a bulky teak dining table from the Malacca High School's refectory, which he made sure was immediately shifted to his office in the 2/10th Australian General Hospital located nearby.

'They tell me, Campbell, that you can handle any type of motorised contraption,' Manning said to the novice driver who was carefully readjusting the layout of the luggage inside the trunk.

'Yes, sir, and I can usually fix 'em up too … with the right tools.'

'If that's the case, and the major determines you're not up to scratch as his medical assistant, you might find yourself at the wheel of a Bren Gun Carrier before you know it.'

'That'd be fine too, sir. I'll give anything a go, at least once.'

'That's my soldier! I must say, I was impressed with your standing-to when we arrived a few minutes ago. It tells me you're respectful, and grateful for your recent promotion and reassignment of duties?'

'More than grateful, sir. Both of those sure came out of the blue! But being singled out to drive this monster around will top that for me. As my dad would say, it's the cat's whiskers!'

'Maybe so,' Manning replied, 'but you had more than a driver's licence, your sporting attainments and your musical studies to recommend you. When the major went in to bat on your behalf, he told me you received what they used to call a gentleman's pass in your final examinations, eligible for matriculation, the world at your feet. But for all that, you preferred to remain on the land to help the family, even though you'd completed five years of secondary education at boarding school. Is that the story?'

'Not the whole story, colonel. My father said he'd cut off my allowance if I refused to leave the house I was sharing in the city and move back to the bush. My older brother, Dougal, had married a girl from Clayfield in Brisbane, and couldn't talk her into settling down in Dalby. She called it a one-horse town. Dougal didn't agree, but eventually gave in. His mates said it was the power of the pussy that did it. I wasn't about to leave my ol' dad to run the place by himself, helped only by my younger brother and the jackaroo. And you don't disobey your father do you, whatever his demands? When Dougal chucked it in, I remember dad saying, 'One sissy in the family is enough.' I always hoped he was referring to Dougie and not me. As for boarding school, did the major tell you that both of us had the same Scotsman as history master at St Andrew's?'

Almost immediately, he regretted bringing up anything to do with college life uninvited.

'Well, I'll be blowed … you must've been *decades* apart? As a matter of fact, no. Bernard barely mentioned anything about the staff at his old school. Your father told him a little about your good marks, captain of the First XI, some college plays, musical ensembles, that sort of thing. Those accomplishments alone were rather impressive to my way of thinking. I mentioned to Bernard that you're plainly officer class material. I've always maintained one should never be surprised by the leadership qualities of those who hail from the back of beyond. It brings to mind some of those Old Testament stories, where all the prophets seem to come from the desert. West of Dalby's probably a lot greener, but I may seek your prophecies on our future military success given you've come from that relatively dry, unpromising landscape.'

Despite the colonel's unexpected jest at his expense, Campbell was pleased to hear all this, although he found it hard to imagine Manning was unaware of most, if not all of the sordid details of his final year, which Wake was undoubtedly privy to. Then again, maybe the major could also keep a confidence and adhered to whatever he'd said about honour and integrity?

'All this says to me that you've not only shown commendable loyalty to your family, but also being a scholarship boy, so Bernard tells me, you must be able to read, write and add up better than most of the other men in your regiment. Come to think of it, your level of literacy is probably better than that of the NCOs from the permanent army as well? Not many are able to string two sentences together, and often their meaning would be clearer with a different word order. However, I don't know whether we can put your piano lessons to much use over here.'

'Well, I'm not that good, though they did get me to play at the amateur concerts on the *Queen Mary* coming over.'

'That comment reveals a lot to me about your character. It's a sad truth Campbell, but many of our other ranks simply enlisted to get a full-time, permanent job for the first time in their lives. For a lot of them the Depression never ended, and as to be expected, we've been landed with our fair share of unemployable troublemakers. In fact, a young gunner from your former artillery unit has recently been brought to my attention for repeated insubordination. He went AWOL twice in Malacca and apparently thinks nothing of directing obscene language towards his superior officers. I've ordered Sergeant Major Cruickshank to quietly bring him down a peg or two and have approved a short stay for this disreputable character in our new lockup. He'll be one of the first guests in the huts recently built by Brigadier Vernon's company of engineers, to serve as camps for any future enemy captives. Perhaps being pulled out of his unit and deprived of his freedom for a few weeks, will be enough to get him to wake up to himself? Clarence Roberts is his name, and Nobby tells me he's a bit of a strange cove – what do *you* make of him?'

'Can't really tell, colonel, he keeps pretty much to himself. They call him Cobra Snake. He's a sort of misfit according to his only mate in the regiment. He said Roberts was beaten by his ol' man as a kid and hasn't gotten over it. Must've been a pig of a man. Roberts never experienced any love in his family life, I'd say, and says he only misses his old dog, called Dusty. He doesn't seem to like other people either. Most of the blokes tend to give him a wide berth. I think he tries to attract attention by deliberately fart-arsing around.'

'That's a shame! Sounds like he's straining for importance, covering up a sense of inferiority with his rebellious streak and appalling conduct. 'Whatsoever a man soweth, that shall he also reap,' comes to mind. When you're struggling to explain things, I've found it hard to go past a biblical saying. You've probably been given many a scripture lesson by your college chaplain, and hopefully you'll be able to draw upon the nuggets of wisdom he would've imparted to cope with the bloodshed over the horizon. I suspect quite a number of those who've recently signed up, like that Roberts fellow, are only nominally Christian, much preferring excerpts from whatever illicit publication falls into their hands to a reading from the Gospels. That'll change on the battlefield. You might recall, Bernard, General Monash saying there were no atheists in the trenches at Passchendaele?'

'Ha, I remember it well. No doubt he was fortified by his Jewish faith.'

'I assume so. I'm pretty sure those lacking *any* type of faith in a supernatural, imagined God will be totally unprepared for the testing times that lie ahead.'

'I met quite a few on board the *Queen Mary* who fit that description, colonel. It wasn't hard to recognise ignorance of the scriptures in that place. Like you said, it was mostly the book of lewd jokes they seemed to be familiar with. One night I heard that same Gunner Roberts recite whole passages of 'Eskimo Nell' off by heart – he probably knew it far better than the Lord's Prayer. He said he didn't want to forget the lines, so practised them night and day in the pubs he'd visited. But it'll be a lot harder for me to forget the things a couple of the rough-heads said about *me* on that ship, that's for sure. I heard they ridiculed me behind my back. And it wasn't because I was seasick, either. As for passing all my final exams, I don't think it'll be much use for the type of work the major has in store for me. I enlisted because it was the right thing to do, and my father encouraged it – said it would toughen me up and keep me out of mischief.' Wake gave him a subtle wink.

'I like your attitude Campbell, but what I find most refreshing is your plain-speaking. It reveals lots of common sense mixed with a touch of humility.' Then, glancing at his adjutant, he added, 'These are qualities definitely in short supply over here, as I'm discovering on a daily basis.'

Campbell was suitably chuffed by everything the colonel had said and thought his father would've been proud. 'I can hardly believe my new duties today, colonel. The only thing missing is those gilt-buttoned uniforms worn by the chauffeurs of wealthy Americans you see in the newsreels. My khaki shirt might be less impressive, but I guess it's a good deal more comfortable.'

'Spoken like a true syce – you know, those Indian grooms renowned for handling the maharajah's ceremonial carriages. You'll see plenty of uniformed drivers where we're going, ferrying all the prosperous *tuans* around. Some even wear the traditional chauffeur's soft cap for good measure! But you can dispense with the slouch hat for the drive today, and leather gloves won't be required either,' he said drolly.

'I've already had a little test drive along the main road, colonel, and I've gotta say, unlike the tractor back home, the Bentley doesn't have a mind of its own.'

'Well, lance bombardier, I like your initiative. You're obviously familiar with the way out of town, so let's head off … on the double,' said the colonel, thrusting his peaked cap firmly down upon his head, leaving only a few tufts of his salt and pepper hair visible around his temple and ears.

'It's pretty muggy already, Bernard,' Manning said, his hand lazily resting on the top of the open door. Then, looking sternly at the sky before settling in alongside the major in the back seat, he added, 'I hope we're spared from more of the heavy rain that pelted down overnight, at least until *after* we arrive in Singapore.'

———

Upon discharge from active service at the end of the Great War, Thomas Manning had joined a firm of solicitors in Bligh Street, Sydney, where he'd started his civilian career as an articled clerk. It took only seven years post-admission before he'd been invited to become a partner. During this time, he continued to serve part-time in the peacetime militia, rapidly advancing to the rank of major. He'd been called to the New South Wales Bar in 1928, at the age of 35.

By 1937, Major Manning had been promoted to Acting Lieutenant Colonel. With the outbreak of war, it was a point of contention among some senior officers in the regular Staff Corps that he seemed to have been given preferment over what they believed to be their own, more legitimate claims. Permanent staff officers treated with suspicion and growing resentment any rapid career advancement that was not substantially based upon longevity in the regular armed services.

But unofficially, when it came to senior appointments, the Military Board took into consideration a host of relevant criteria and recommendations. Despite their natural bias towards selecting from among their own, occasionally an application for officer promotion based substantially on merit outweighed continuous service as the determining factor.

In Manning's case, promotion was clearly justified because he was an officer who possessed what was favourably looked upon as the common touch, a quality that was in reality not that common at all. His ability to inspire confidence and proven disregard for personal safety were seen as pre-eminent qualities for the role of battlefield commander. Fellow officers routinely referred to Manning as a soldier's soldier. In no time at all he was transferred from the Citizen Army straight into active service in the 2nd AIF.

Manning's bearing was rigid and disciplined, and the attention he paid to his starched uniform was meticulous. Although it was still early morning and he was freshly shaven, his profile was already distinguished by the faint charcoal outline of his permanent five o'clock shadow. By midday, the stubble around his jawline had taken on the quality of emery paper, so it would have been more accurate to say his shadow was fully developed by half-past two. Manning's forthright, positive disposition had set Campbell at ease from the word go, such that he quickly felt at liberty to openly express his feelings without fearing a schoolmasterly rebuke.

'If the governor's given this up, then what remains in his garage in Penang must be an eyeful, sir?' he'd said excitedly through the side window of the car.

'I suspect Sir Percy's routine visits to the various states in Malaya have been curtailed over the past year or so,' Manning muttered, though not in direct response to the driver's uninvited remarks. 'He appears to have become increasingly preoccupied with military matters nowadays, especially since Martindale's appointment in May. I don't know about you, Bernard, but I believe it can cause no end of problems when civilians, however exulted their status, feel they have a right to start meddling in military affairs. Perhaps it's time the generals got together and advised the governor about the proper way to run the civil administration over here.'

'You're a bit hard on him, Tom. It may be that he's become increasingly worried about the current military situation in Indochina and wants a box seat in the deliberations of those proposing to deal with it?'

'And, rightly so; but in Charles's opinion we can do without his undue interference in tactical discussions. What was it the Irish poet Yeats said – when civilians start suggesting military strategies to generals, a terrible bullshit is born? Something along those lines, wasn't it?'

The major acknowledged the hugely disfigured literary allusion with a broad smile, a simple nod of the head and his characteristic stroking of his moustache thrust up in a pout by his bottom lip.

After making one final inspection of the tyres and checking that the trunk's lashings were absolutely secure, Campbell took control of the steering wheel while the adjutant moved into the front passenger seat alongside him. A compact metal medicine chest lay on the floor between them. The party then set off along the Mersing–Kota Tinggi Road, which was eerily deserted at that hour of the morning.

———

After crossing the rickety wooden bridge over the Mersing River, the vehicle finally gathered enough speed for those inside to appreciate the smooth purring of its six-cylinder motor. The loud squelching of the tyres passing through pools of rainwater soon gave way to the gentler swishing sound of rubber over evaporating wetness.

As they passed the Nithsdale and Joo Lye Estates, everyone noticed groups of villagers squatting not far off the side of the road. Campbell secretly yearned to try out one of those quaint, regal flutters of the hand he'd seen in the Movietone newsreels on board HMT *Queen Mary*; the rigid, mechanical ones favoured by His Royal Highness to acknowledge his loyal subjects lining The Mall. During those ceremonial processions, children would continue to wave their little toy flags in such concentration that they took on the appearance of suspended confetti, well after the Sovereign's carriage had receded from view.

This morning, by way of contrast, His Majesty's native subjects seemed totally uninterested and, if anything, looked the other way as the limousine rolled by. This evidently wasn't a royal procession, with thousands of loyal citizens milling around the gates of Buckingham Palace. The natives' apparent indifference and perhaps silent contempt directed towards the European intruders would be unlikely to trail off and disappear like the misty tyre tracks left in the passing.

The party soon hit the Jemaluang village intersection and the Bentley started wending its way past terraced hillsides covered in palm oil and rubber plantations interspersed with clusters of pineapple trees. Huge numbers of wretched-looking Malays were already toiling away in vegetable plots that surrounded their *kampungs*. None of the passengers was more alive to the quiet hostility on their faces than Peters.

'It's the calm before the storm, the early stages of a rural uprising,' he declared, never failing to share his bleak, Nostradamus-like prophecies in relation to the imminence of war. There was no way of determining whether the adjutant's predictions were justified or not. Reliable news of the magnitude and regularity of the recent strikes in the mines and on the rubber plantations was sporadic, and any sketchy details that emerged appeared to be swiftly suppressed by the colonial authorities. Peters understood he was probably the sole occupant of the vehicle who thought of the current situation in terms of the post-colonial governance realities, irrespective of the British Empire's survival.

After they'd travelled several miles down this only unbroken east-coast road in southern Johore, the party came across groups of agrarian workers who were balancing poles bent almost to breaking point by the panniers at either end. The women, although skinny as a rake, balanced enormous baskets of produce on their heads, walking with surprising poise and agility along the shoulders of the road. Chinese–Malay workers in conical hats intermingled with the rag-tag Tamils employed to tap the rubber trees. The former were transporting vegetables, livestock, chickens and baskets of rambutan to the local bazaar, or to the larger markets on Singapore Island itself.

For Peters, the proliferation of rubber plantations in northern Johore and the tin mines of Selangor had presented a textbook example of Empire built on the flagrant exploitation of native lands. This rapacious conduct throughout the Malay Archipelago was evidence of a recurring colonial legacy; the extraction of minerals and other raw materials for boundless profit, accumulated on the back of indigenous starvelings. Peters' extensive book-learning placed what he currently saw within the context of centuries of relentlessly brutal economic enslavement by European colonising powers. Allied with successful gunboat diplomacy, it had guaranteed a permanent state of enrichment for the few, built upon the immiseration of the many.

'What we're seeing, gentlemen,' said Peters, 'is similar to rural life in late Tsarist Russia, where the first stirrings of insurrection were fuelled by the depredations of serfdom. The peasants were a potent vehicle for providing momentum for the proletarian revolution beyond the urban areas,' he confidently asserted. Whether the Marxist–Leninist state had improved the lot of the peasant or the proletariat by creating soviet collectives and communal workshops was something that far exceeded his powers of observation or analysis, he confessed. Nor did he say much about the dialectical arguments of the comrades who'd recently planted an ice pick into the back of Leon Trotsky's skull in Mexico.

Campbell's thoughts had already drifted elsewhere. He was not in the slightest bit interested in Peters's political discourse but was obliged to take it all in, regardless. He was simply overwhelmed by the exoticism of everything he saw. As far as he could make out from the limited confines of the Bentley, further inland there was more in the way of impenetrable jungle covering the landscape than the rubber-tree plantings and undergrowth they were presently passing by. It certainly fell short of the lush tropical imagery routinely depicted in the *Boys' Own Annuals* he'd leaf through after evening prep at boarding school.

'You'd have thought with all these coolies around, the governor could've prevailed upon the sultan to improve the roads a wee bit?'

Manning casually remarked. 'I might have a word to Brigadier Cadwallader to get to the bottom of it.'

'I don't know how you'll find the time to negotiate what that might entail?' Wake said in a dispirited fashion.

'Well, that's part of the chief engineer's job. The Brigadier has to liaise with both the military and the civil authorities. It may turn out that the traditional clout of his office in getting things done has been downgraded under his predecessor, for all I know.' Whatever the colonel said was delivered in such a deep mahogany voice that even his casual observations were imbued with the arresting sound of authority.

———

Manning's adjutant, Captain David Peters, had not long graduated from the Royal Military College at Duntroon in Canberra, where he'd excelled in military history. His largely self-taught speciality included not only the formation of the British and Dutch dependencies, in what the British Colonial Office called Far East Asia, but also the French Indochina protectorates of Annam, Tonkin and Laos. As a result of Japan's growing influence in the region, he'd decided to undertake an intensive introductory course in Japanese culture and language prior to his graduation.

Peters was only in his late twenties, but his ideas and eccentricities had already ripened into those more commonly shared by much longer-serving officers. Being slightly older than the usual graduate was an advantage, and his first-class academic attainments had soon brought him to the attention of not only the commanding officer of Duntroon, but also experts from within the East Asia branch of the Department of External Affairs.

Following the outbreak of war in Europe in September 1939, Peters had been rapidly promoted to the rank of captain and subsequently appointed to Manning's battalion staff upon the raising of the 8th Division in May 1940. This was fully three months before Major General Charles Dalziel assumed overall command of the division. The role of military adjutant was a position he'd coveted for years, but far from being elated, he gave the impression of being no more than mildly satisfied when his appointment was formalised. In deference to his expertise, Peters was afforded unrestricted licence that morning to impart his considerable knowledge of the workings of the British colonial economies and the complex sociopolitical culture of the region.

For all his dispassionate erudition, Peters wore his political heart on his sleeve. He found it difficult to disguise his distaste for the way in which the native populations were treated by their traditional rulers, aided and abetted by their colonial overlords. Yet it was difficult to say whether his sworn loyalty to the Crown or his exposure to crypto Marxist ideology informed the greater part of his sometimes contrasting opinions.

Manning came to feel that everything Peters said sounded politically doctrinaire, but he'd be blowed if he could tell what his adjutant *actually* stood for. He gave very little away. The colonel had given no indication that he privately held quite dissimilar sociopolitical views to those of his adjutant. He would have been reviled by the suggestion that his own beliefs incorporated any elements of the traditional Marxist–Leninist critique of society, such as the dictatorship of the proletariat and the collectivist ideology. He had trouble with the word dictatorship, for a start.

Manning would probably have described his own political viewpoint as being derived from a sense of fairness, not privilege. It was informed by a belief in robust individualism, economic advancement based on merit, and capitalist free enterprise. These values were enlivened by what he accepted as the eternal verities of Protestantism. None of the enduring Christian values, he believed, were compromised by the United Kingdom's colonial rule, however deeply exploitative and paternalistic it had become. More good than harm had flowed to those living under the British flag was his overly simplistic though steadfast belief.

As a consequence, Manning found his adjutant to be someone who was not just socially indignant, but often tiresomely so. He wasn't altogether certain that Peters fully appreciated the threat to liberal democracy in the dismantling of colonial regimes. He considered those regimes, ruled by the British, had not proven to be bereft of benevolence towards its colonised peoples. Not that the colonel had ever had a lengthy conversation on this matter with an innocent victim of the coloniser, let alone those who'd been enslaved and might've begged to differ. For Manning, respect for the freedoms guaranteed by parliamentary sovereignty, capitalist free trade and the rule of law underpinned the commercial if not the moral justification for colonial expansion. He much preferred it to rule by fiat, the autocratic decree, or the diktat of a Central Committee and its unelected commissars.

'Sometimes, Peters gets so carried away it can appear as though he's talking to himself, giving voice to an interior monologue,' Manning had said to the major prior to departure. 'Dalziel thinks he may have issued from dour Scottish Calvinist stock and can't abide his sanctimonious, holier-than-thou attitude. In less guarded moments, he refers to David as an insufferable, natural-born dissenter – someone who has no difficulty providing both halves of a conversation simultaneously.'

The reason why the Chief of the Army Corps in Canberra had pressed so hard for Peters to be appointed to his staff remained a mystery to the colonel. Someone who seems to have risen without trace was the gently sardonic way in which he described his adjutant's unheralded promotion. Before Peters had joined them that morning, Wake questioned Manning once more about his adjutant's character.

'I was going to ask you Tom, whether Peters was religious, but from the way you've described him, the obvious answer is yes. It sounds as if he's quite used to both sermonising and dispensing his nostrums with God-like authority.'

'I'm not so sure about the depth of his Christian beliefs, Bernard. Sometimes he gives the impression that the only heaven he can imagine is the one supposedly enjoyed by the workers in Soviet Russia. You could call it a socialist theocracy, perhaps? If you *could* compare it to a religion, it's one whose priests, as far as I can gather, firmly believe in the equal distribution of misery.'

'Yes, and *Das Kapital* is their Holy Bible,' Wake had felt obliged to say in an attempt to disguise his almost complete disinterest in political ideology.

'To be more to the point, Bernard, I doubt whether David prays as any reasonable conversation with the Almighty might necessitate a grudging acceptance of a dissenting opinion from a higher authority. His display of immodesty in the presence of an audience is boundless. I've concluded that he's what we lawyers refer to as *sui generis*, one of a kind. However, unless it's well-concealed, he doesn't appear to possess the necessary fanaticism to participate in the various national-istic insurgencies he imagines are just around the corner.'

'Hopefully, he's not too irritating on the trip down to Singapore.'

'We can only hope for the best, Bernard, but I guess I'll have to grin and bear it.'

'I can understand your misgivings about his appointment to your staff, Tom, but coping with unavoidable setbacks is part and parcel of the compromises we all must make in life. I'd much prefer a vase of highly perfumed freesias in the surgery but am resigned to the fact that I'll have to put up with the unpleasant smell of disinfectant forever.'

Captain Peters was a little under average height and quite sickly looking. His shiny brown hair was meticulously parted and neatly brushed back from the middle of his forehead. However fastidious this grooming had become, it failed to disguise a scalp partially invaded by psoriasis. A set of loose-fitting, rimless spectacles edged down the bridge of his nose, giving him a distinctly ascetic appearance. Although his rank encompassed the role of overseeing the battalion's preparations for battle, if he were fortunate, his short-sightedness would probably relieve him from regular engagement in frontline combatant duties. This fact and Peters's conspicuous lack of athleti-cism led Manning to wonder how his adjutant had ever managed to pass the physical examination at the recruitment stage. He'd neverthe-less determined that Peters would be the official chronicler of the battalion and record, among other things, the details of each regiment's hostile engagements, decorations for valour, and list of casualties.

On a personal level, and rare among those who joined the military, Peters felt comfortable telling anyone – whether they were interested or not – that he was teetotal and a devout bachelor. All his candid admissions were unaccompanied by the slightest trace of levity. He was certainly not one who enjoyed the knockabout, bawdy humour to which Campbell and the other ranks had been exposed on board the *Queen Mary*. Peters wasted no time with small talk and readied himself to break into a commentary on the present situation in Malaya at the first lull in the conversation. And that came shortly after Manning's simple query as to the state of the road leading to Johore Bahru.

'From what I've gathered, colonel, the sultanates have left road construction and maintenance entirely to the British engineers and the exchequer. It's not as if they can't access the capital to finance some of these works themselves. A couple of the Federated Malay States have encouraged the mining and export of vast quantities of manganese, iron ore and wolfram deposits to the Japanese for decades. But, by the look of it, not a great deal of the royalties has been funnelled back into improving the roads, or the communal amenities in the villages we've passed, you might have noticed?'

'Yes, but I dare say there's little hope of your nationalists and militant socialists getting a foothold in this predominantly agrarian countryside,' Manning sarcastically remarked. 'You'd be flat out finding a decent hammer and even fewer rusty sickles lying anywhere around here.'

'You're quite right. Colonel. There are very few light or heavy industries, and no fields of wheat or barley. What they term in Europe the *lumpenproletariat*, if it exists at all in Malaya, is likely to be wearing sandals and a conical hat.'. Neither officer in the back seat of the car had ever heard the word before. 'And it wouldn't surprise me, either, if certain of these rulers have already struck a political deal with the Japanese by secretly bartering their neutrality in exchange for a guarantee of conserving their economic power should war break out.'

Encouraged by what he took to be the silent assent of his audience, Peters went on and expanded a little upon his largely censorious assumptions about the current geo-political situation in British Malaya. 'Sultan Ibrahim of Johore, in particular, is a well-known Japanophile. He's benefited from lucrative investment by Japanese commercial interests in his state, which goes all the way back to his grandfather's time. It would be a mistake to believe the protected status his family has enjoyed under British rule over all these years will deter his willingness to sup with the Nipponese devil, should the occasion arise. I strongly suspect the outward respect for the civilising influence of the British among these Far Eastern potentates has all but run its course.'

Manning was less put off by the uncertain validity of the adjutant's opinions than the didactic tone in which they were delivered.

'Apart from communist cadres in the jungle,' Peters went on, sensing there'd be no attempt at this stage to interrupt his discourse, 'there are known to exist all sorts of Malay, Indian and Chinese nationalist cells and fellow travellers throughout the region. I believe the Americans are also doing everything in their power to maintain the supply route through Burma for the benefit of the Chinese nationalists in Chungking. But, beyond that, it's hard to know *what* they're up to.'

'All of that may be true, David. Really, I don't know how you came by all that information, but I imagine none of those nationalists you appear to support would be particularly upset by the prospect of colonial rulers being expelled by an Asian power. As the Russian communists have already shown, the leaders of anti-imperialist movements are practised opportunists. So-called nationalists are probably no different? The rise of the Bolsheviks during the last war demonstrated how revolutionaries can simultaneously exploit both the workers' domestic grievances and their dormant nationalist sentiment.'

'Yes, I agree, you've hit the nail on the head there, colonel. The local Malay insurgents could certainly be tempted to ally themselves with the Japanese in their anti-colonial enterprise. If they do, then like Sultan Ibrahim, they'll need to sup with a very long spoon.' Manning still wondered how his adjutant could possibly know so much about the local nationalist cadres.

'You're aware, aren't you, David, that General Dalziel finds the Sultan congenial company and claims he's a dyed-in-the-wool anglophile?'

'Yes, that may be so, colonel. However, if history tells us anything, it's that these indigenous chieftains will compromise their integrity any time of the day if it means conserving, as I've already said, their status, power and political influence. Sultan Ibrahim is exactly the type of autocratic ruler who doesn't need to put a wet finger in the air to detect which way the wind's blowing. He may get a surprise if he thinks he'll be better off swapping one imperialist regime for another.'

'Yes, that's right. Like you, I don't trust any patrimonial ruler who runs with the hares and hunts with the hounds. When it all boils down, the sultan may aspire to possess the trappings of British culture, but I suspect he doesn't give two hoots for the robust principles of democratic rule that underpin that culture.'

Major Wake was not prepared nor particularly qualified to interrupt this robust exchange of bald assertions and sweeping generalisations.

'As you've mentioned the influence of the Nips, let me add this, David. From all accounts the Imperial Japanese Army is an unyielding and merciless foe. They consider their emperor to be God incarnate, a figurehead they worship and who seems to inspire in his subjects a war-like spirit they call *bushidō*. Indeed, Emperor Hirohito is believed to issue orders directly to the nation's military commanders, which means it would amount to a damnable sacrilege, not simply an act of treason, to disobey them.'

'Yes, I share your insight regarding the Japanese psyche. I've heard it said that Hirohito's embodiment of the divine rivals that of Jesus Christ himself –they're the only two religious figures who *knew* they were God. It's a pity the emperor's instructions don't extend to observing Christian compassion and the moral conventions of Western warfare. The treatment of civilians during the occupation of Nanking a few years ago was reportedly brutal. I think the word atrocity has been bandied about in relation to what occurred in that engagement.'

'That appears to be the case,' said the colonel, 'but it's hardly surprising. The nationalists have denied them total victory by retreating to Chungking in the mountainous southwest, as you've already pointed out. The Japanese military can't get to them without compromising their control over the coastal cities. Nanking was left defenceless. To me, that outcome again demonstrates how retreat and capitulation can lead to ruthless reprisals by the victors.'

———

Even the car hitting several rain-filled potholes failed to interrupt Manning's verbal jousting with his adjutant. 'Where's the justification for Japanese aggression? I can't see how they have suffered any intolerable injustice or moral iniquity they needed to redress since they were opened up to the West over seventy years ago. So far, militarily, they've looked indomitable.'

'I agree,' Peters said. 'They want to advance their imperial interests, to be considered as successful as British colonisers, without sharing our values. But there's an important difference in their tactics. Based on past conduct, they're the masters of deception. They're prone to strike their enemy unawares, and it's clear their military leaders have never spotted an opportunity for a surprise attack that was unappealing. They've found a natural ally in joining the Nazis, who've recent experience in employing the same tactic. Imperial Japan is also adopting something like the Nazi policy of *Lebensraum* to spuriously justify the annexation of neighbouring countries. Western nations have collectively underestimated Japan's policy of territorial expansionism, and it's been to our peril.'

The colonel then brought the conversation back to the realm of the mundane by surprisingly floating an open-ended question. As a barrister, he would've known that you never pose a question to which you don't already hold the most persuasive answer.

'I've often wondered what type of fellow this Sultan of Johore is. They tell me he's extremely wealthy and was the first owner of an automobile in the whole of Malaya.'

Such an invitation fell into Peters's lap.

'I've not actually seen him in the flesh, colonel, but I believe there's plenty of him,' replied Peters, whose voice stepped up a gear before launching into what his colleagues feared might be another extended polemic.

He quickly confirmed their expectations.

'If *The Times of London* is anything to go by, Sultan Ibrahim seems to spend a good part of the year travelling and dining in luxurious surroundings throughout the gaming casinos, spa stations and rivieras of Europe. Journalists report his main passions to be tiger-shooting, horse riding and younger women ... and not necessarily in that order.'

'Well, I suppose you can do all that when the British exercise indirect rule over your personal fiefdom.'

'That's a significant factor, colonel. No hereditary ruler not forcibly in exile appears as comfortable being so seldom at home. I even saw him in a photo taken at the Grosvenor House Hotel in Park Lane in one of last year's editions of the *Illustrated London News*. There appears to be no limit to his social climbing and extravagant tastes. I'm sure he would've been upset that the races at Royal Ascot were called off last summer. He made an appearance in '39, and there's an old photograph of him in the Royal Enclosure, top hat, puffy cheeks and bursting out of his morning suit like all the other overfed interlopers aspiring to be knights of the realm. When it comes to mixing pleasure with matters of state, his timing is impeccable.'

No-one argued the point with Peters's self-confident analysis of the situation, which was delivered with his customary tinge of bitterness and envy. His colleagues had no idea that Peters's eclectic knowledge extended to familiarity with the more gossipy content in the British newspapers. But, like most people, they were not averse to savouring a bit of low-level slander from time to time.

'I certainly don't follow the scandal sheets as closely as you obviously do, David, but I'm not unaware of his political influence and connections. It's well-known he always manages to drop in on the civil service mandarins in Whitehall upon an annual basis, and it's not for old times' sake. I suspect his motives may extend beyond a selfless desire for an unbroken military alliance with Britain. Perhaps that's the reason why the Colonial Office still doesn't have a single active field officer stationed anywhere in Johore. As I've said, General Dalziel seems to quite like him and was even invited to the sultan's palace earlier in the year, along with his aide-de-camp and some of Brigadier Vernon's staff officers.'

Peters responded by making it clear that he had no time for *any* of the other sultans, tunkus, chieftains and potentates spread across Malaya, the East Indies and the South China Sea. He referred to many of those who were Western educated as *ideological cross-dressers*. Those who mistakenly thought they knew him might be excused from thinking that Peters was the person you'd least suspect of being familiar with the practice.

———

Although a little short on generosity of spirit and lacking Colonel Manning's natural gravitas, Peters's observations on political issues were generally cogent, and never simply a matter of dismal, uninformed speculation. Manning believed them to be based, at the very least, upon a coherent and reasoned set of prejudices. Rather than continuing to exhaustively discuss which indigenous Malay rulers appeared to be the most ambivalent towards Japanese aggression, the officers turned their attention towards the commotion that was going on, either side of the Bentley.

As they craned their necks to witness the kerfuffle, they were quietly impressed by their chauffeur's evasive driving skills. He narrowly avoided skittling clusters of bicycles, many laden with live chickens, their legs tied and their wings flapping in obvious distress. Other riders were burdened by large hessian bags bursting with rice and tapioca precariously balanced across the handlebars. Campbell's frequent recourse to the car's klaxon, intended to scatter the throng, only succeeded in drawing their haphazard meanderings ever closer. All around, the bicycles jostled for space, interfering with the car's progress by darting across its path as if their riders were seized by a sudden impulse to invite collision.

It wasn't long before one of the half-naked cyclists untroubled by all the honking, was finally knocked over. Campbell immediately stopped and jumped out of the driver's seat to render assistance to the injured victim.

'He's putting himself in a bit of danger doing that, don't you think, Bernard?'

'No doubt about it, Tom … rather overzealous in lending a hand, without weighing the consequences. Fortunately, I've got a Webley pistol under the seat. He may have taken the Hippocratic oath I told him about a little too literally.'

Campbell managed to give first aid to the fallen cyclist, who nonetheless appeared ungrateful for the attention. He'd quickly retrieved his damaged bicycle, gathered up his scattered produce and pedalled away despite a wobbly wheel and multiple abrasions to his arms and legs.

'Tough little bugger. I don't think any bones were broken – but if I hadn't stopped, I reckon he'd've been left sprawling there,' he said, as he jumped back into the driver's seat. 'It was the charitable thing to do. All the others just kept going – they seemed happy to abandon him. Thanks for handing me the medical kit, captain.'

Progress slowed again whenever buffalo carts emerged from the side to join the main road. Their wheels had caused deep ruts to develop on the road's surface. In fact, the car had been unavoidably drawn into a place where motorised vehicles of any description were easily outmanoeuvred by more primitive forms of transport. The Bentley's progress was reduced to a type of jolting movement, drawing heavily upon the quick reflexes, concentration and patience of the driver.

'One good thing about this rabble,' said Wake, 'is they don't seem the slightest bit interested in who we are. If we were travelling anywhere in India or the Middle East, I'm sure there'd be beggars everywhere, taking advantage of the stop-start progress we're making. They'd be banging on the side of the doors and the windows, demanding any token offering they could get.'

He'd no sooner said that when the back window became heavily smeared with grime from open-handed pounding. Following these acts of spitefulness and aggression, Wake was obliged to retract his previous generalisation.

'In situations like this, I'd like to get out and give those little devils a bloody good walloping; take up the cudgels like Squire Western did with those ruffians he encountered on the King's Highway,' Manning spat out angrily.

'You'd never recognise which ones did it, Tom, they all look alike,' said Wake, slightly amused by the old-fashioned mention of squires and cudgels. 'I wouldn't get out of the car again, Campbell,' he cautioned. 'Last time, you may not have noticed how many were carrying those *parang* machetes in their waistbands. Try to make sure you don't knock another one of them over, even if he deliberately asks for trouble. We were lucky earlier on … I've heard if you do accidentally collect a native, others will sometimes surround your vehicle until you cough up and pay the injured person some monetary compensation. It's even worse if you collide with their livestock.'

Campbell's earlier feeling of exhilaration behind the wheel had now given way to one of dogged determination to avoid *any* possibility of imminent collision with a moving object. With this renewed incentive to maintain awareness, he had to emulate all the guile and instinct displayed by his working kelpies, yapping a mob of sheep towards the shearing sheds back home. Such was the intensity of his grip on the steering wheel that the blood was starting to drain from around his knuckles. But it was soon apparent that this particular mob remained unresponsive to the large and noisy black object nipping at its heels. He realised they couldn't be effectively mustered or easily penned in. In the rear-vision mirror, bobbing heads continued to look into the car, their hands pressed hard against the rear window above the trunk. They reminded Manning of a bunch of impoverished street urchins licking the windows at Mark Foy's in Sydney, desiring objects they could only ever dream of possessing.

Like their fellow travellers, the Bentley had become an inseparable part of the rudderless surge to sell or barter produce at the market in the shortest time possible. Taking up Manning's earlier remarks in relation to the state of the roads, Wake eventually offered his own view of the slow progress, in his characteristically measured way. 'Look on the bright side, Tom, it's hard to imagine the Japanese Imperial Army contemplating any sudden, land-based attack on Singapore over this narrow road and the mud-filled culverts we've had to navigate. In fact, all the maps show there's only swamp and mangroves between here and the eastern coastline. I imagine all this will turn into a quagmire and be nigh on impassable for heavy vehicles and tanks once we're hit with the worst of the north-east monsoon. That'll come in a matter of weeks, if not days.'

'Funny you should mention tanks, Bernard. The Japs have already used them to great effect in Manchuria. We don't have *any*. To my mind, that's even more of a reason to pull back from our forward positions in the north-east, along coastal Pahang and Johore. Our lorries and artillery would surely get bogged around here once the monsoon starts. I've already recommended to Dalziel that he try to convince British Command to gradually redeploy the greater part of our infantry, and the 2/10th's old 18-pounders and howitzers, to north-western Johore. Your artillery mates might be involved in hostilities earlier than expected, if my recommendations are taken up, lance bombardier.'

'Let's hope so, sir. The gunners still can't understand why they're not stationed where they might back up those British and Indian battalions already there.'

'Unfortunately, we don't have overall command,' Manning grudgingly admitted. 'To me the justification for our redeployment in that location is compelling. If the enemy were to land in Northern Malaya or southern Siam, I anticipate they'll advance along the better trunk roads on the west coast, ending with a major infantry assault on Singapore Island itself via Johore Bahru.'

———

What Manning was wary of commenting upon was Dalziel's poor relationship with the leaders of the British Malaya High Command. Lieutenant General Martindale, the GOC, and the resident chiefs of the separate armed services all considered Major General Dalziel to be somewhat of a martinet, heavily armed with an irascible temperament. 'That bumptious little Australian commander,' they'd laugh, 'behaves as if he were constantly beset by a bad case of haemorrhoids!'

They'd heard that Dalziel had already attracted a solid reputation in Australia for undermining his superiors. It was rumoured he'd also recently experienced personality clashes with his own brigade commanders in the 8th Division at Kuala Lumpur headquarters. Manning had weighed all this up before arriving at his own conclusion. He saw the wisdom in the adage that you can often judge a man not so much by the company he keeps, but by the quality of his enemies. He already knew Dalziel had managed to collect quite a few enemies of unquestionable integrity and distinction.

General Dalziel's prior conduct had strongly indicated that he was in fact contemptuous of the leadership credentials of *any* senior officer who'd never pursued a vocation on civvy street, but had chosen to settle permanently into a military career in the Staff Corps. Such publicly stated opinions had annoyed federal politicians, the adjutant general and senior officers of the Military Board in Australia, who, as a consequence, had deliberately delayed Dalziel's appointment as commander of the 8th Division until late September 1940. This occurred despite his legitimate claim to the vacant position as early as May on the basis of seniority alone.

In Dalziel's opinion, Lieutenant Colonel Manning's impressive combination of the successful civilian, combined with his redoubtable military pedigree, made for the ideal commander, much like himself. It came as no surprise therefore that the newly appointed General Officer Commanding (GOC) Malaya, Lieutenant General Horace Martindale, who'd spent most of his recent years as a staff officer at Aldershot in England, fell squarely within Dalziel's category of the ineffectual armchair general. It didn't take long for Dalziel to privately refer to him as General Complacency.

His fear of the new GOC's creeping ineptitude was not alleviated by the sight of Martindale inspecting his troops in a Wolseley pith helmet from the Boer War era. Having to defer to Martindale, whose orders he could not countermand, exacerbated his strained relations with the British High Command at a time when the military situation demanded greater cooperation and common resolve between allied forces.

Manning was also privy to another of Dalziel's reported weaknesses, which stemmed from his overly friendly relationship with the Sultan of Johore's young Romanian wife, Marcella Mendl. Campbell took in these gossipy revelations, despite the hushed tone in which they were spoken. 'In her presence,' Manning confided, 'Charles's frequent detachment and natural aptitude for displaying all the emotional sensitivity of a pachyderm tends to mellow appreciably, it's said.'

Upon learning of this unwise liaison, Manning thought such a relationship had probably compromised Dalziel's objectivity in dealing with the Sultan's ambivalent though outwardly apolitical stance towards the Japanese. The fact that the general had decided to establish his own HQ near the Sultan's palace, the Istana Bukit Serene at Johore Bahru, only deepened Manning's serious misgivings about this highly questionable entente cordiale that had developed with a dubious ally.

Lance Bombardier Campbell was neither expected nor invited to be part of the conversation and maintained his unobtrusiveness with the same intense concentration with which he'd maintained his grip on the steering wheel. The only memorable things he'd picked up about Horace Martindale were that he was as lean as a whippet, spoke in a fluty voice, and his protruding teeth were so prominent that they could probably be used to peel an orange through the strings of a tennis racquet.

Otherwise, from what he'd pieced together, there was an absence of any compelling military argument for embarking upon this seemingly pointless furlough while the enemy's presence was expanding throughout Indochina faster than the Sultan's waistline. According to what he'd overheard, Japanese military forces already posed an imminent threat to the Malay states of Kelantan and Pahang, to the north of Johore. Somewhere along the journey, Manning mentioned the Japanese Navy had established bases in Haiphong and Cam Ranh Bay in French Indochina, well before last Christmas.

Therefore, *what sort of polite campaign are we involved in,* was a question Campbell not unreasonably asked himself at various intervals. He'd picked up that the politicians' denial of reality in the face of aggression had clearly encouraged the Japanese to advance unopposed throughout the French colonies by the end of 1940, spurred on by the precipitous fall of metropolitan France during the northern summer.

It seemed to him that spending a relaxing couple of days in Old Singapore was not something he would necessarily skite about when he returned to barracks. In fact, *any* talk of a pleasurable time on leave, might not be advisable. Word had come through that back in Brisbane, everyone thought the 8th Division was living the life of Riley, and the girls were chasing the recently arrived Yankie sailors, seeking more than silk stockings, flowers and perfume. Whether the stories were true or not, most of the blokes who came from around Brisbane were not happy at all with what they imagined was going on.

The Bentley made a brief stopover in Kota Tinggi to enable Major Wake to inspect preparations for a casualty clearing station. Although not yet officially informed of the decision, this was where Campbell would soon be based, as part of the 2/9th Field Ambulance.

CHAPTER
THIRTEEN

SINGAPORE ISLAND, OCTOBER 1941

AFTER LEAVING KOTA TINGGI, it wasn't long before the car whisked over the Causeway at Johore Bahru and onto Singapore Island. There was a noticeable absence of fortified gun turrets, anchored barbed wire or defensive slit-trenches anywhere in sight. Manning was not impressed, as this type of basic deterrent had already been installed on his orders near the coast at Mersing, thanks to the round-the-clock effort from the 22nd Brigade. Earlier in the month these men had also built a rudimentary POW camp to house all the Japanese soldiers they imagined might be captured.

'If the Japs ever get this far, they won't find much in the way of serious obstacles,' said the major. 'Not one strategically positioned pillbox or even a bamboo *basha* on stilts is visible on the horizon.'

'Yes, don't worry, Bernard. I've noted all that.'

'What I suppose is commendable, Tom, are the fewer potholes filled with rainwater, like the ones we've had to plough through back there. At least someone's been busy excavating the earth to create monsoon drains on either side of the road.'

'Yes, I agree, but it's a pity they're much too wide and too shallow to be of any use as foxholes. If the Japs do invade, I'd be more worried about being hit by mortars and heavy ordnance than disturbing a squadron of mosquitoes in stagnant water.' While there seemed to be an even greater concentration of human activity than on the chaotic roads of the Malay Peninsula they'd left behind, they hadn't come across a single military vehicle.

'I thought we might have run into some British units from Fort Canning or Kranji barracks by now,' Manning commented. 'If they *are* stationed around here, I'll be sure to commend their commander for the quality of their camouflage. They must all be lying in wait in the lalang grass,' he said sarcastically.

'They've got to be here somewhere, because since crossing the Causeway, the road resembles a smooth tarmac, a foot soldier's delight. I bet your old artillery unit wouldn't mind going out on manoeuvres around here, eh Campbell? Even that ill-disciplined gunner the colonel mentioned earlier might discover some enthusiasm for the training.'

The Bentley was now able to approach top speed as it cruised south along Woodlands Road. The proliferation of *kampungs* soon became a blur of ramshackle, split bamboo houses on stilts, topped with attap roofs. They were generally bordered by coconut palm trees, offering protection to the adjacent, small ponds set up for farming fish. The full gamut of village life remained half-hidden behind the papaya trees and pineapple fronds. Narrow jungle pathways seemed to lead nowhere, as though defined by the directionless meanderings of strutting chickens and the packs of scrawny pye-dogs.

The closer they got to the old colonial precinct towards the southern end of Bukit Timah Road, north-west of the city, the greater the number of small commercial premises run by Chinese shopkeepers started to dominate the streetscape. Before long, they gave way to the first glimpses of elevated villas and Palladian-style mansions along Orchard Road. These were owned by wealthy Peranakan, the locally born descendants of older immigrant Chinese from Melaka and Penang, referred to as baba Malay. The more successful had profited over the years from extensive concessions of land from the sultans, some of which they'd turned into gambier and pepper plantations for the burgeoning export market to Europe. Their garden pavilions and the distinctive, raised black-and-white bunga-lows, with their wide porches and deep verandahs shaded by over-hanging eaves and lush vegetation, were set back from the road. As a result, the bungalows' roofline met the eye from the moving vehicle only in patches.

Signs pointing to the nearby racecourse and golf course would normally have rendered further commentary superfluous. However, Manning couldn't let the opportunity slip to suggest that the golf course was probably the only site on the island, apart from Fort Canning, equipped with decent bunkers.

As the lush vegetation dropped away, the road gradually widened into a broad boulevard fringed by magnificent flame trees. The Bentley soon found itself merging into a steady stream of motor cars, trolley buses, rickshaws, bullock carts, trishaws, and even the occasional Ford Yellow Top taxi. Despite the Bentley's path being no longer clogged with wandering animals and cyclists, the tide of converging motorised traffic behaved in roughly the same manner.

'Looks as though your past has caught up with you, Campbell,' the major cheekily remarked as he pointed out the distinctive spire of St Andrew's Cathedral looming in the distance.

Campbell froze for an instant and then swallowed deeply, dreading the possible mention of some unwelcome, old-boy reminiscence. But the major, clearly honouring his undertakings in relation to confiden-tiality, quickly changed the subject. He was no doubt wary of offering Peters the slightest opportunity to provide background to the colony's ecclesiastical history.

With glimpses of Keppel Harbour now more regular, travel along North Bridge Road gradually became choked with coolies loaded down with oversized bundles of goods. The staff car had finally arrived in the central core of the colonial precinct, and their vehicle was the only thing capable of movement that seemed hesitant and uncertain of its destination.

The whistling Sikh policemen doing point duty with a set of wooden directional wings attached to their back, performed this activity with great flourish. However, their earnest gesticulations and alternating foot and arm movements at the few major intersections were mostly ignored, as all the traffic chose to independently go about their business in a strangely ordered form of chaos.

All the while, the visiting party was not so much concerned by the bedlam outside as with promptly reaching the hotel, with its promise of relief from the searing tropical heat that was now blanketing the entire city. By late morning, the humidity had insinuated itself into every aspect of daily life. Despite the vehicle's canopy shielding the soldiers from the glare of direct sunlight, the backs of their shirts had become soaked in sweat, and the bottoms of their khaki drill shorts clung to the upholstery. Even Manning's starched pleats had merged into the rest of his now sodden apparel. His elasticised sock garters were starting to slide down his calves as the first signs of prickly heat emerged in tiny red blotches on the skin.

Meanwhile, after a bit of desperate map-reading, and before the car pulled up at the final intersection, Peters managed to summon another unsolicited observation. It seemed to come out of nowhere, much like the fully laden, bullock carts through which they'd earlier tried to navigate a pathway. The crucial difference in this instance was that Peters's intrusion allowed no time for evasive action, nor promised even the slightest frisson of excitement.

'Listen to all that jabbering going on out there,' he exclaimed. 'I can't make head nor tail of whatever it is they're saying.'

Everyone was mildly surprised at this rare admission of fallibility.

'You know, someone told me that around thirty different languages and dialects can be heard conducting business on the streets of Singapore at any one time. Well, all of them were possibly being used at the last couple of intersections, from what I've managed to pick up. And, by the way,' he said, raising his voice in emphasis, 'several are *untranslatable*.'

Although everyone suspected Peters's anonymous informant was actually Peters himself, the statement sounded perfectly reasonable and disclosed nothing sufficiently controversial to attract further comment. The colonel felt like saying he knew that Peters was not a polyglot but was happy enough having this fact confirmed out of his own mouth. Unlike his adjutant, Manning wore his learning lightly and had a more complete education than Peters could ever aspire to achieve. At sixteen, he'd been dux of Fort Street Boys' High in Sydney, an impossible achievement at the time unless you were athletic, could accurately conjugate Latin verbs, master calculus and easily digest *Bleak House.*

At least David had acknowledged the linguistic pluralism of Singapore by referring to the existence of discrete dialects, Manning silently conceded. He understood the less familiar, minority tongues of Singapore were as mutually unintelligible as the Cantonese spoken on the Pearl River Delta was from the Chinese patois unique to the island of Hainan.

Peters's declarations about the difficulty in transcribing this cacophony of foreign tongues were greeted by the others with blithe indifference. It was as though no native-born English-speaker need be troubled by such matters. This was unsurprising, since it reflected the entrenched attitude of most resident Europeans, who insisted on conducting their business affairs almost exclusively in English.

———

As they drew up in front of the Adelphi, Campbell snapped out of his trance-like participation in the imagined pageantry of it all. 'Well, blow me down, take a look at that,' he exclaimed as he brought the Bentley to heel. 'That's not a pub, that's a fair-dinkum palace!'

All the passengers sensed a speech coming on, based upon the hotel's status and architectural grandeur. But, to their relief, Peters decided to allow his fellow passengers to take it all in, uninterrupted. What they saw was a neo-classical facade decked out with striped awnings and heavy-duty rattan blinds, which overhung timber-louvred plantation shutters on the upper floors. At street level, stuccoed plaster arches created what resembled a terrace on the Boulevard des Capucines, except for the fact that the Adelphi's colonnade was possibly 150 yards in length. But, despite the brightly coloured awnings, this was not Paris. For one thing, the terrace had no outdoor cane chairs huddled around wobbly, marble-topped tables. If by chance there had been, it would've been far too steamy to even order a *Marie Brizard aux glaçons* from one of those sniffy garçons de café who always seem to be occupied at other tables. Neither was there anyone sitting around who might have passed for a smarmy boulevardier, pretending to read *Le Figaro* while surreptitiously casting a lascivious eye over the chic clientele.

Peters had never previously stayed at the Adelphi, but not long after his arrival in Malacca in late February, he'd made a point of perusing the descriptive illustrations in all the glossy catalogues he could lay his hands on. Foremost among those was *The Gate of the Far East* travel booklet. This highlighted landmark buildings and exoti-cized sites of interest to foreigners visiting Singapura, the Lion City, for the first time.

'Once you see the interiors,' said Peters, unable to resist a further opportunity to parade his superficial learning in these matters, 'you'll get an idea of the prosperity in this city.'

'I don't feel we need any convincing about *that* David. The splendour of its many opulent Victorian-era buildings is already apparent,' replied the colonel in a tiresome voice.

'Agreed,' said the adjutant, undeterred by Manning's subtle rebuke. 'But beyond these exterior colonnades, you're about to see the most luxurious furnishings that you'll ever come across in any comparable hostelry outside Europe. I've seen photographs of the lobby. Its ceiling is fitted out with the most exquisite electric fans east of Suez. You won't find any Bengali punkah-wallahs sitting around inside, like they do at Raffles,' he concluded with the self-satisfied smugness of someone imparting the type of bloated descriptions that were only acquired courtesy of a travel brochure.

Peters had already compiled a brief inventory of the Adelphi's notable amenities for the colonel's benefit prior to leaving the barracks at Mersing. Perhaps he was eager to display his photographic memory by reciting what he'd already gleaned from the facts in his well-thumbed travel booklet. At any rate, he saw no reason *not* to repeat the same facts, which by now he'd honed into something akin to an advertising spiel for the edification of a slightly larger audience. The pity was, he lacked the true salesman's acumen in pulling back before over-egging the pudding. Campbell's immediate thoughts confirmed the failing. *How will someone who's swallowed a whole flamin' almanac as well as a dictionary, still have enough breath left in 'im to get out of the car?*

It seemed that even before the Bentley had come to a complete halt, the doors had been opened, the luggage removed from the trunk and taken inside with a minimum of fuss by a large team of liveried porters. They were following the directions of a tall, turban-wearing doorman, whose face was plastered with an inscrutable, business-like smile throughout.

Stepping beyond the revolving door at the front entrance to the hotel, it was difficult for any of the travellers to disagree with Peters's effusive endorsement of the Adelphi's splendour. The foyer presented a dazzling combination of lacquered teak and black and white, diamond-patterned marble flooring. The presence of several huge, potted palms gave the impression, at least, that they had a cooling effect on the surroundings. Manning was happy *not* to see any black and white stills of Mary Pickford, Douglas Fairbanks or Charlie Chaplin adorning the walls. There were none of those conspicuous reminders of a close association with celebrated film stars, which Raffles constantly sought to promote through the names of its most expensive suites.

A solid brass stand carried a large photograph of Harry Mackmire's Band with Lisette and Popular Radio Vocalists, who were listed for today's tea dance entertainment. Prominently displayed at the reception counter, the advertising handbills indicated that the Adelphi had over 100 bedrooms offering 'Every Comfort, and Perfect Hygienic Arrangements'.

The reception desk was presided over by the same tall Sikh who'd greeted them at the door. He was sporting a very thick, neatly trimmed beard, and wore a *kirpan* fastened at the waist. He issued directions to the assembled porters concerning the destination of each guest's luggage, addressing them in an officious tone in what appeared to be a fair sprinkling of Peters's list of exotic tongues.

From all the deference and catering to the comfort of the over-privileged white man in the colony, a casual visitor would be entitled to believe that indigenous self-rule would be anything other than aeons away. Whereas greater Malaya might have developed into a linguistically pluralist society, at the Adelphi's reception desk it was apparent that only the word European was both a proper noun and a distinguished adjective.

As befitting their status, the officers were accorded individual, deluxe suites on the first floor overlooking a modestly proportioned courtyard bordered by a garden packed with rhododendrons. The whole area below was tended to throughout the day by two Indian *berkebuns*. When not pruning or weeding, these garden workers would busy themselves by noiselessly sweeping and raking up any chance leaves that might have made the mistake of landing within the hotel's perimeter. The whole garden was built around a small, rectangular kikuyu lawn so closely manicured that from a distance it resembled the green baize of an oversized billiard table.

The party was escorted to the lifts by the ever-attentive Sikh, except for the colonel, who'd stayed behind to speak to a well-turned-out gentleman in the foyer. Campbell was consigned to a less spacious room than the others, which gave over the busy thoroughfare and colonnade below. The double bed was certainly better than the Indian *charpoy* he'd had to get used to on his first bivouac in Malacca. If he'd earlier imagined his status was equivalent to that of a trusted equerry, lodged in commodious quarters adjoining those of his royal patron, his distinctly inferior Adelphi room at the far end of the corridor soon shattered the illusion.

Before Campbell went off to his steerage-class room, Peters gave him a nudge and repeated his earlier reference to one of the hotel's lesser-known amenities – the presence of a Dutch wife in *every* bed, and in *every* room. He'd laughingly explained to his fellow officers in the Bentley that this was a local expression imported from the Dutch East Indies. It referred to a long bolster filled with kapok placed that was across the bed to enable a guest's tired legs to be supported during sleep and reduce the likelihood of chafing.

The expression was reputed to have arisen because not many *actual* Dutch colonial wives were prepared to swap the salubrious comforts of The Hague or Amsterdam, for the malaria and rampant dysentery of Batavia. At any rate, their distanced husbands were often accused of being married to the company, so if they needed a spouse to embrace during the night, the bolster would at least prove to be a reliably discreet and quietly submissive alternative.

'I'll leave you now, Campbell, but you'd do well to remember what I said earlier about the bed. Don't get *too* excited by the Dutch wife lying around, and the promise of connubial pleasures,' Peters reminded him.

'Connubial pleasures, what's he on about?' mumbled Campbell under his breath as the adjutant moved briskly down the corridor towards his room. He could tell when he was spoken down to, treated as though he were a country bumpkin chewing on a stalk of paspalum. But then again, he told himself he ought not be greatly offended, as Peters succeeded in giving the impression to almost everyone he met that he thought them not very bright. Ultimately, he was comforted by the thought that for a few hours at least, he'd have time by himself to briefly explore the less refined quarters of the city. He was hoping for a taste of the local Chinese culture, as it was euphemistically called, without the experience being constantly mediated by one of Captain Peters's historical disquisitions.

They'd been informed that they were not expected at the reception until seven o'clock that evening. The minister's secretary had conveyed this to Manning in the foyer on their arrival. An official limousine would pick them up from the hotel, around thirty minutes beforehand.

'Before you head off to your room, be aware of the time you're to be ready for the trip to this evening's reception,' the major had warned him in the lift. 'We won't wait for you, so if you're not here by six-thirty sharp, you'll have to make your own way to Jervois Road.'

'Yes, sir, understood. I'll take that rickshaw for a tour of Chinatown and skip the curry tiffin lunch in the dining room, if you don't mind. I'll go and change into my civvies straight away.'

Jeremy Pym's secretary had already arranged for Manning's party to visit the Singapore Cricket Club later that day. They were to be the guests of a former MCC office bearer who now worked as an agent for a large rubber-exporting house. Prior to his agreeing to the visit, Manning had been told of the club's obnoxious attitude towards racial identity, but not the extent of the prejudice. Alone among all the

European clubs in Singapore, the Cricket Club on the Padang excluded not only non-Europeans from membership, but even disallowed entry to members' guests who were not of the pure white race. It maintained the sort of exclusive social atmosphere in which both the disgraced Duke of Windsor and the German Reich ambassador to the Court of St James's might have felt totally comfortable.

Peters abhorred the endemic racial prejudice of most Europeans towards Asiatics, however it was going to take some time to expunge the premise of superiority from within the minds of even the most socially enlightened humanitarians with whom he identified. Although taking on different forms, the unwillingness to recognise bigotry by self-accusation was an attitude sometimes shared in equal measure by the grandees, the educated and the riffraff in all colonial societies. However, he accepted the invitation without demur, despite earlier expressing an intention to hire a rickshaw driver for the afternoon. Peters was genuinely interested in being introduced to the remarkable collection of historical cricketing paraphernalia said to line the walls of the club's dozen rooms and spacious hallways. At the very least, the visit might serve to replenish his already burgeoning store of boring facts and anecdotes.

Campbell would have expressed no view either way. Nevertheless, the prospect of his tagging along to a club possibly full of bigoted gentlemen with personalities in the mould of Captain Peters was an invitation he found easy to decline. He no longer liked cricket anyway and agreed with Rudyard Kipling, who delighted in deriding the chaps who did play as 'a flock of flannelled fools'.

CHAPTER
FOURTEEN

CHINATOWN, SINGAPORE, OCTOBER 1941

'MEESTAA CAMPBELL, OBER HERE,' a strange voice rang out from a distance as Bomber Campbell left through the hotel's revolving door. 'Ober here!'

He was met at the roadside by his designated trishaw rider, a small, gaunt but nevertheless well-proportioned package of muscle and bone named Lim. The name struck him as highly appropriate, as he'd be relying upon at least two of those appendages to pedal him around throughout the afternoon. The positive impression he made was helped by the fact that he was shod with a new-ish pair of rubber-soled canvas shoes and wearing reasonably clean, bleached blue clothing. *This bloke's conical-shaped straw hat was also in pretty good nick,* he noted approvingly, *and his neck doesn't have one of those dirty cloths wrapped around it like most other sweaty jinrikisha.*

Lim had been lined up by the head doorman Manjit Singh, the extremely tall and well-dressed Sikh who'd worked previously at the Hôtel Métropole in Hanoi for over a decade. As a result of this prior experience, Manjit became moderately offended if he wasn't properly acknowledged by the staff and all-comers as Concierge. Eventually, he arranged for the fashioning of a small wooden plaque bearing this title and had it installed adjacent to his station at the reception desk. The word itself was capitalised and embellished with gold-leaf lettering. Management went along with this ostentatious – though essentially harmless – display of self-importance which was, after all, a defining characteristic shared by all the carpet-crawling managers of luxury hotels.

Lim had been instructed to provide a guest named Alexander Campbell with a brief tour of the port's bustling quays and its China-town. He was told that the soldier was a last-minute replacement for Captain David Peters, who'd decided to accompany the other officers to the Singapore Cricket Club instead. If time were limited, Lim was to focus upon some of the more distinctive cultural features on the chosen itinerary.

Lim had a commercial arrangement with the Adelphi, largely due to the fact that he was reputedly one of only a handful of trishaw riders who understood English and, more surprisingly, wasn't leasing his vehicle from a wealthy Chinese owner. The reasoning was that because independent owner–riders got to keep their earnings, this would encourage them to provide a higher level of service.

Campbell's strong streak of egalitarianism meant he initially had serious misgivings about hiring a human being to drag him around, even if he were a self-made man. But, as he thought more about it, he satisfied himself that Lim's investment in his own trishaw meant that he was probably a cut above the more servile jinrikisha coolies he'd already seen hobbling along the thoroughfares, some in bare feet, their necks bent down like two-legged donkeys. He also assumed Lim had arrived at this relatively privileged situation through old-fashioned thriftiness, hard work and enterprise, his modest earnings no doubt supplemented by the patronage of the hotel's well-heeled, European clientele.

'Hurro, meestaa Campbell, where you rike go?' Lim wheezed through a withered set of slate-coloured teeth. The incisors were so worn down they would have been flat out making an impression on wet blotting paper. The rather haughty doorman had alerted Campbell that, as a rule, this particular trishaw rider spoke only broken, unpol-ished English. But he'd also confided that Lim's limited fluency was known to become more lustrous should you happen to apply the right amount of silver to the palm of his hand. He also said Lim was known to be well-connected within the Teochew community in Singapore, information that was totally meaningless to a visiting soldier like Campbell.

'You can call me Sandy, mate,' he urged, slowly enunciating the syllables while pointing his index finger back towards his chest at the same time. This was a gesture back home that was normally reserved for unlettered foreigners, very small children and the hearing impaired.

'I'm out of my uniform now, so what's say we head towards the Chinese quarter ... on the other side of the river. I'll leave it to you, Mr Lim, to stop at any inviting places along the way. I can only hang around until four o'clock.' Feeling the need once more to point things out, he splayed the four fingers on his right hand and then placed them against the glass face of his wristwatch. As soon as he had finished giving these directions, he realised how condescending he'd been in telling a local Chinaman where Chinatown was located. *Better to shut up and be thought a fool than open your mouth and remove all doubt,* he recalled being one of his schoolmaster's more telling reprimands.

'Okay, no more Meestaa Campbell ... Rim unerstan. We go to Tua Poh.' His words were accompanied by a broad smile, parting the few sparse and wayward strands of greyish hair that formed the goatee hanging from his chin. Whenever he smiled in this way, his eyelids contracted to become no more than slits above his surprisingly unwrinkled but leathery cheeks. 'Cost is one dorrar but vely srow tlip, many tongkang boat unroading near blidge an quays ... an some vely dar praces.'

Mindful of the doorman's advice, Campbell winked as he slipped his guide an extra dollar. Lim's face lit up almost immediately, disclosing his fine set of gums, and he even stroked his sparse goatee in registering his good fortune. Soon he was brim full of more appealing suggestions. 'You wan whisky? beer? raydies? ... nice tayra suit? ... smoke chandu?'

After reaching into his pocket for a small packet that he waved in his passenger's face, Lim clenched his fist and, moving his elbow in a levering motion, said, 'You rike *len-shen*?'

Campbell had about as much need of a translation as he had for this Chinese medicinal form of aphrodisiac. He responded with a look that said, *you've gotta be jokin' mate* in just about any language under the sun. 'I'll settle for a stop along the way for a beer or two, if that's ok?'

'That fine … we go Pagoda Sleet … beer shrop ebrywhere,' Lim said obligingly.

He now realised why this driver was chosen by the doorman. Not only did he speak enough broken *ingreesh* to engender trust, but it was obviously not the first time he'd taken entertainment-deprived soldiers on his rather loosely defined but no doubt broadly appealing cultural tour.

For his part, Lim noticed from the glint in his passenger's eye as he handed over the fare that today's client might have a taste for *all* of his suggested menu of the day. He might even chase the dragon on impulse. On the other hand, Campbell made it clear that the time restriction meant the opportunity to try out that newfangled jitterbug at The New World amusement park would not occur. And taking in a film at the air-conditioned picture theatre inside the new Cathay Building, was definitely *not* on the cards.

As the trishaw's oversized wheels trembled over the rutted, laterite roadway, Sandy was overwhelmed by the sight of commercial activity rubbing shoulders everywhere with abject poverty. Close to the river-bank, bumboats – the small *twakow* barges powered by men pushing down on the riverbed with long bamboo punting poles – were coasting into the quays. Countless boats were so closely moored that they provided convenient pathways to the wharves. From a distance they resembled schools of oversized sardines gently bobbing on the shim-mering surface of the water. Many provided the only accommodation available to the immigrant population.

In the distance were larger vessels with sails, the *tongkangs*, which sported a huge eye painted on the side of the bow, acting as a protec-tive talisman for the superstitious Tamil seafarers who plied their trade on the open sea. They were surrounded by a variety of smaller, motorised craft chugging along at the mouth of the Singapore River.

At Boat Quay, sacks of nutmeg and rice, as well as chests of commodities of unknown provenance, were being unloaded from lighters by swarms of bare-footed coolies. They broke into a half jog along a series of unstable gangplanks no more than two-foot wide, linking the boats to their landing berths. The coolies, or *sinkhehs*, came from the southern Chinese coastal ports of Swatow and Amoy, and wore their hair in pigtails. The now wealthy, previous immigrant Chinese called them *cheena-gerk* – low-class Chinese, in Baba Malay. These men endured backbreaking manual labour from sunrise to sunset, put to work like expendable slaves, no less recognisable as such for the absence of manacles or tattooed numbers scored into their flesh.

———

Over decades, thousands of coolies had landed as deck cargo, without savings and in such desperation that they were ready prey for commercial exploitation. Barely considered human by their masters, they were dealt with in much the same way as the commodities they shouldered. In the evenings, crammed together into pokey tenement cubicles, they fed their addiction to opium and its derivatives, which acted as a supplementary, albeit disguised form of permanent indenture. While the opiates eased the pain of relentless toil that soon took root in every fibre of their body, it also served to deplete their health and meagre wages with equal speed and certainty. Once brought on shore, the bundles they carried were then transferred to waiting bullock carts and small lorries or trundled by pushcarts directly into the godowns situated only a few yards from the boat moorings. Many of these warehouses were routinely filled to the roof with bales of rubber and sacks of copra.

Leaving the port vicinity, Lim's trishaw dawdled in random zigzags across Elgin Bridge, down South Bridge Road before turning into Temple Street. On the way, they passed rows of shophouses on each side of the road, where stiff, distressed-looking laundry was strung-up on poles across narrow balconies. Pools of fetid, russet-coloured water stagnated in the late-morning heat.

Campbell sighted more Hokchiu barbers, as Lim mysteriously described them, than you could poke a razor at. Splattered globs of betel-nut juice were coagulating on the side of the road, competing in number, if not volume, with the dispersed puddles of muddied rain-water. It was difficult to detect the entrances to the shops for all the ragged hawkers with their wicker baskets. Sitting around on low stools, they spilled out from the shop facades onto the edge of the road. As they made their way towards Pagoda Street, wherever Campbell looked his senses were assailed by a range of exotic sights and smells, as well as discordant voices entwined within the sounds of commerce. The scene was so crowded and volatile, he imagined that if one stray firecracker were to go off, it might result in mass panic.

Cooking was conducted in the open, the most impoverished-looking food hawkers forced to use coconut husks and broken-up pieces of cardboard as fuel for their braziers, rather than the more expensive charcoal. Behind small shopfronts, all manner of basted poultry and partially moulted wildlife was strung up in rows across the windows. It didn't pay to dwell too long upon the likely species.

A pervasive odour of frying oil, charcoal burners, garlic, spices and joss sticks filled the air, excreted from every tenement building and remotely habitable location. The smell was inescapable, which along with the squalor and unsanitary surroundings was only remarkable if you were a stranger to Chinatown. For a country boy, it recalled the stench of fly-blown, reasty carcasses of dead livestock, days after the dingoes and the crows had scavenged their entrails. It slowly dawned upon him that the rare space of unencumbered land across the road served as a communal cesspit.

With wretched-looking individuals crouching in dimly lit door-ways, it wasn't hard to spot several of Lim's colloquial dark places. And, no matter how dark, someone always emerged who seemed to be on speaking terms with his trishaw guide. Witnessing this familiarity, Campbell was suddenly grateful to have an apparently well-known local identity negotiate a pathway through this vibrant, slightly dangerous and densely settled quarter of the city. He reckoned there might not be a better opportunity to sample some of the unique oriental pleasures he'd heard about, even if today there wouldn't be time to go the whole hog.

———

Lim had already decided that the first stop would be halfway along Pagoda Street. A couple of paces from where he pulled up, an old man was squatting over a stool, flanked by a compact, portable easel. When not spitting a gobful of sluiced betel nut on the pavement, he appeared to be writing Chinese characters on a scroll.

Lim noticed Campbell's interest and anticipated the probable question by saying, 'He rite retters back home China, send monies to famry.' Campbell put two and two together and had already come to the correct conclusion; the queue of people surrounding the man were probably illiterate, reliant upon the services of a professional scribe to transfer modest amounts of money to relatives in southern China.

'Him money render too,' Lim added, before letting his passenger off. He then peddled his trishaw towards the relative isolation of the rickshaw station in nearby Sago Lane. This was the suggested second stop; a narrow laneway where Lim indicated there were many brothels, as well as the place where the homeless poor came alone to die in cheap funeral parlours. Upon hearing this last piece of information, Campbell was starting to feel that the proposed next stop in the itinerary wasn't looking too promising for a lively session of sex.

After parking the trishaw, Lim rejoined Campbell, who was led towards a quieter section of the street to a tailor's shophouse, where there were relatively fewer people and sensory distractions. By now his thirst was so strong, he'd even settle for some of the rot-gut arrack he'd been dared to drink in Malacca. *Lim's a bit slow finding those beer shops he said were all over the place,* he silently moaned.

The shophouse facade advertised the name of the premises in oversized, faded red Chinese characters, embossed in peeling gold leaf. In response to Campbell's vague details regarding his interests, Lim thought for starters, his passenger might be happy to get some form of apparel for himself, or perhaps something a little fancier to send back home. He knew that upstairs on the first floor was a small opium den, and a space where the *raydies* slept, sometimes three to a cubicle. With Campbell not having much time on his hands, Lim had decided to head directly to the type of establishment that might serve as a potential one-stop shop.

'What's this place?' Campbell enquired excitedly. There was no indication of the type of business it was as he stood just beyond the five-foot way. The pavement either side of the entrance was cluttered with stick-like hawkers selling bundles of dried fish, shrivelled mangosteen, baskets of plump champedak and other less recognisably digestible produce.

'Chan Kai Kah bizness inside, meesta Sandy. He can make shirt by end of day, all blight carours … many design … tlouser his speciality, with nice shilk pocket. He deribber to hotel, or soldier ballik if you rike?'

'Sounds pretty good, I'm game. Let's go in,' Campbell said, not so naive as to believe that this stop on the itinerary wasn't prearranged, so the tailor might have his own pockets nicely lined as well. *I know what he's up to, but so what*, he thought. *I'll fall in with Lim's choice of shop so long as everything's cheap and they don't try to take me for a mug.*

He already pictured himself in a heavily embroidered silk shirt with a raised mandarin collar, nattily attired for an important occasion. The extreme unlikelihood of such an occasion ever arising in Mersing never entered his mind. He hadn't yet received official confirmation of his increased pay, but the mere thought of it was already burning a hole in his pocket.

As Lim walked in front to push apart a pair of half-length, *pintu pagar* doors at the entrance, the lingering pungency of the pavement smells, if not the full intensity of the stifling heat, accompanied them inside. Within a few feet, Campbell noticed an assortment of partitioned, confined spaces on the ground floor. There was also the muffled sound of footsteps on the wooden flooring above to add to his sense of curiosity. None of this internal activity could be detected from the modestly proportioned shopfront at street level.

The interior was windowless but had a glassed-in light well situated towards the back. The walled area at the rear was reserved for a toilet and laundry, with a charcoal-fired cooking area to one side, where fortunately, all smells coalesced. There was water all over the floor, requiring wooden clogs to be worn by those busy washing the utensils and preparing the food. Reliable plumbing, like dentistry, was still in its infancy in Pagoda Street.

Lim introduced his foreign visitor to the tailor, Mr Chan, who lived with his family of six on the top floor. He was presently engaged in overseeing the seamstresses, both of whom were hunched over their sewing machines. Neither made any effort to look up from their job for a single moment. Alongside one of the workers a baby was swinging gently in an improvised fabric sling that acted as a cradle. It was fastened between two posts. The sling was strung up on cords attached to a large spring in the centre, which in turn was tied to a ceiling joist.

For young Chinese women, even unskilled jobs were hard to come by, and if you'd arrived in Singapore from the mainland without your mother or extended family, there was no alternative but to bring your dependent child to the workplace. Apart from menial tasks in the hundreds of kitchens, the only other choice of labour for these immigrant women in urbanised areas was in building construction – working as female coolies, the *samsui*. These women soon became prone to serious bouts of lumbago and dislocated joints, against which even their red headdress, worn for good luck, proved an ineffective safeguard.

The truly desperate could spread their thighs and put their vaginal muscles to work in Bugis, Lavender and Hailam streets. Civic-minded administrators took the view that while prostitution tended to corrupt public morals and caused the spread of venereal disease of near epidemic proportions, there were benefits in restricting its location. They were satisfied that the flesh trade was contained in and around Chinatown, where previous attempts to shut it down had proven unsuccessful. On the other hand, if you'd taken a vow to keep your thighs closed for business, you might be fortunate enough to secure employment as an amah, a valued childminder cum domestic servant, preferably in a wealthy European or towkay household.

'I reave you for rittle while, meesta Sandy. Chan will fit you up and raydies, maybe sreeping? Onry two on firs froor ... one Nipponese *kalayuki san* from irand ov Kyūshū. Cheapa dan Chan's crothes,' he said with a lecherous smile, as if somehow equating these two distinct forms of personal service. 'Hoshiko san bin here ober twenny year, but now a bit ol an bent ober. She rast *kalayuki san* who still work for Chan but she speak bery good ingreesh ... and use muscle ... favoulite of Blitish soldier.'

Campbell had trouble taking in all the details. 'Or we go to Sago Rane? Many young Guandong raydies ... tiny feet no ronger raced up, but other parts vely roose,' which he imagined must have been Lim's attempt to transmit some form of gynaecological information.

The thought of dropping his strides in an upstairs cubicle in this place didn't excite him that much. Soldiers from his regiment who were more knowledgeable in these matters recommended visiting the higher-class ladies in Malabar Street, who advertised rooms the size of six tatami mats in which to disrobe and fornicate.

Lim had no sooner left the premises than he was drawn into an animated conversation with a group of gesticulating individuals who'd been waiting for him outside. One of the men stood out. His head was completely shaven, and although possessing a rather jovial face, it was disfigured by a prominent scar across his forehead and temple. Campbell glimpsed a surreptitious exchange of papers among the group, but although curious, thought nothing more of it.

Further inside Chan's workshop, was a makeshift, curtained-off area that separated the sewing activity. Two juvenile apprentices were hand-stitching buttonholes. They both looked no more than ten years of age. Within minutes, after all the pointing, grunting and instructions in Singlish had been exhausted, he'd been measured up, and the shirt fabric selected from a pile of bolts stacked against a wall. Finally, the whole transaction was costed to the rapid-fire clicking of a well-worn abacus before the precise details were recorded in a gigantic ledger. Chan promised a speedy completion time for the following day.

Campbell looked around for Lim at the doorway but he was nowhere to be seen. Rather than step out onto the street to investigate, he decided to venture further in along the shadowy, airless corridor of

Chan's shop. He slid a tentative hand into his pocket and his fingers detected more Frenchies than loose change. The major's repeated warnings about VD had paid off. It'd always been his intention to explore the upstairs sections of the building for at least a sight of the raydies, whether they were open for business or not. But the pungent smell of dried fish from the food hawker's stall outside the entrance soon quelled his carnal desires.

Upstairs wasn't an established brothel as such but part of a small, exploitative side business run by Mr Chan and a part-time madam, one of his concubines. If nothing else, Campbell thought he might take a puff of the *chandu* pipe with the Boat Quay coolies who, along with several *jinrikisha*, were renting the hutch-like cubicles on the floors above. He'd progressed no further than the light well and the beginning of the kitchen area when he saw a scantily clad woman squatting alongside the sink, alone. She looked like the wreck of the *Hesperus*, bruised on both arms, sipping water from a small wooden cup. She was the *karayuki san* Lim had spoken about earlier. As it looked like the promise of some Tiger Ale had all but evaporated, he approached her to ask for a drink.

'I'll have some of that water, please,' he said, accompanied by several demeaning hand movements, before remembering she spoke English. 'I'm as thirsty as an outback camel! Can I borrow that bowl of yours?'

'You asked Chan for his Kyūshū whore, didn't you?' she replied. 'Why are you, maybe a British soldier, asking *me* for water? Chan's usual customers treat me very rough, even more after Japanese soldiers raped women in Nanjing. You see me as an enemy person too, don't you? Just take the water and push me up the stairs, if that's why you're here?'

'I'm not British. My name's Sandy, from Australia, and I'm no longer sure *why* I'm here. I know what you work as ... there's no need to explain. By the look of you, some of those customers must be brutal, and don't only push you up the stairs either. Don't be afraid, I want nothing from you except a drink from that bowl you're holding.'

Before she could respond, a high-pitched shriek echoed from the floor above. Campbell was about to climb the precipitous, wooden stairs to investigate when a large metal pan came tumbling down. It spilled its faecal contents all over the steps as it rolled and pitched, hitting both the railings and wall with ever-increasing clangs. Scrambling down the stairs behind it came the distressed toilet-pan remover, who was as embarrassed as could be imagined at something that had literally gotten out of hand. After moving from one job to another, he'd forgotten to properly refasten his trousers, and at the top of the stairs they'd dropped to his ankles, causing him to trip.

The commotion sent all the occupants in the shophouse kitchen area into a frenzy. Campbell's pants had missed a soaking by a matter of inches, but the cuffs and his footwear had not escaped a minor splattering. Before coming to rest, the can gave him a slight nick on the ankle. As he turned around, he saw the *karayuki san* still cowering in the kitchen area, deserted by the other women who'd been working there. He encouraged her to stand up and helped her navigate an escape path amid the surrounding turmoil.

Later that day, he polished his boots with a degree of fastidiousness that even Cruikshank would have begrudgingly commended. Thereafter, he spent considerable time in the bathtub in his room, *to be on the safe side*. If the rest of the party had already departed for the reception, Lim promised to hang around to pick him up, should the cleansing process take too long.

It did.

Amid the disarray, Campbell hadn't immediately rushed to the front of the shophouse like everyone else but volunteered a bit of crowd control. As well as ushering the *karayuki san* to safety, he could be seen from outside the premises shouldering both child apprentices above the crowd. His dominant physique also allowed for the tiny seamstress clutching her crying infant to move forward in his wake and reach the outside unimpeded.

The narrow doorway and the shop's threshold had quickly become impassable. Within minutes bells were ringing to announce the frenetic arrival of the local clean-up brigade, while Campbell waited beside the swinging doors at the entrance. The state of his apparel had put a definite end to his intention to do a bit of lurking around in some other dark places, and any remaining thoughts of going upstairs for a puff of opium or exploring the charnel delights of Sago Lane had receded even further. Once he got outside, to his dismay he discovered that every Chinaman in the street started to look like Mr Lim.

CHAPTER
FIFTEEN

THE RESIDENCE, JERVOIS ROAD, TANGLIN, SINGAPORE, OCTOBER 1941

THAT EVENING, the three officers left the hotel for the minister's residence, a fifteen-minute ride away. Pym had insisted on sending his personal driver to pick them up from the front door. Before their departure, Lim had told Major Wake that Meestaa Sandy had probably dozed off in the bath and would see to it that he arrived at the reception in good time.

The Residence was situated within a large compound, the main house surrounded by smaller staff dwellings set among tropical gardens. Jervois Road was located in a hilly area of the city that had become a designated enclave for Europeans, as well as a significant proportion of the colony's prosperous and influential Chinese business leaders, the towkay.

The latter included naturalised British subjects, sometimes referred to as the King's Chinese. Yet, despite having lived here for many decades, they would never have referred to themselves as Singaporeans. Their principal allegiance was to their family's ethnic background, language and cultural traditions.

If you closed your eyes, when they conversed with their British acquaintances, it was in the type of Received Pronunciation that was spoken by the educated classes in southeast England. Their fluency in English belied their ethnicity, and approached that of their native Hokkien or Teochew, the *langue maternelle* of their forebears from the Fukien and Guangdong provinces in southern China. Their total embrace of the outward trappings of European refinement might even have enabled them to fit quite easily into the rarefied conversations conducted at the almost exclusively British Tanglin Club, from which all Asiatics, bar the Sultan of Johore, were refused membership.

This ingrained racial prejudice mattered little to the wealthiest Straits Chinese businessmen, who had their own millionaires' club, the Ee Hoe Hean Club on Bukit Pasoh Road. This was a club where fellowship, philanthropy and financial support for the Chinese nationalist movement, the Kuomintang, were privileged over the more hedonistic preoccupations of the various sporting and social clubs to which their colonial masters belonged. When it came to political engagement, their caustic opinion of the Japanese rivalled the virulent strain of racism directed towards their own countrymen by the Japanese army in occupied mainland China.

Notions of relative power, wealth, status and the maintenance of one's unique cultural identity informed the behaviours of all ethnicities cohabiting in Singapore and across the Malay States. The social cleavage along Chinese sub-ethnic lines was integral to the maintenance of the political status quo cherished by the colonial authorities. The towkays did not need any convincing that the revolutionary strictures of the most fervent communist sympathisers in their midst, were inimical to the continued enjoyment of that political reality.

In this regard, it was financially rewarding to have active membership within the complex network of traditional clans, the Huay Kuan. These lay at the core of interdependent commercial relationships built up over successive generations throughout the colony. One of the oldest and most prominent of these clans was the Hokkien Huay Kuan, located in Telok Ayer Street. Among its earliest presidents was Tan Kah Kee, a rubber tycoon and founder of the colony's most influential Chinese newspaper, the *Nanyang Siang Pau*.

The British admired the business acumen and industry of the Overseas and Straits Chinese, and the wealthy Eurasian families domiciled elsewhere throughout the Malay Peninsula. Their presence had led to the flourishing of government-licensed enterprises, all of which were duly taxed, enabling a good proportion of the profits to be regularly remitted to the Office of the Exchequer in Westminster.

This was a complex arrangement from which all parties benefited. For the non-British, a degree of subservience and permanent detachment from direct political power in the colony was an acceptable price to pay for the British rule of law and the financial dividends that accrued through its guarantee of administrative, political and economic stability.

Leaving to one side this economic reality, the British had otherwise failed to colonise their minds. Accordingly, His Majesty's colonial subjects were more partial to assimilating the putative *decency of purpose* claimed to underpin the notion of British dominion, if in fact they materially benefited from its implementation.

The Straits Chinese were justifiably unimpressed by the Japanese promise of a co-prosperity zone for Asians. The towkays had financially prospered for generations under British rule, and they knew for certain that upon the Japanese invasion of Manchuria in 1931 and events in Nanking in 1937, the only thing that prospered on those occasions was the Imperial Army's indiscriminate pillaging, violence and unbridled indulgence in sexual gratification. This depraved conduct was more egregiously racist than being knocked back for membership of the Tanglin or Singapore Clubs.

———

The minister's residence was a spacious two-storey bungalow commanding a panoramic view over the city and onwards to the sea. Its aspect was surpassed only by that enjoyed by Governor Sir Percival Townshend, who occupied the Istana, a palatial building that had served as the official Government House Domain for several decades. If one were important enough to be invited there to celebrate the King's birthday, a full military band would have played as you were escorted into the drawing room and then processed into the sumptuous banquet hall. Once seated, you would be served by Hindu waiters dressed in scarlet and gold coats with matching hats.

A markedly less formal approach was adopted by the Pyms at Jervois Road, though it too was not lacking in ceremonial pretentions. But, compared to the governor's entertainments, while there might have been less pomp and circumstance, there was certainly a good deal more food and alcohol.

Once you passed through the wrought-iron entrance gates to the compound, your eyes were met by spectacular, flame-red poinciana trees. They soon gave way to flowering hibiscus and the scent of white frangipanis, which drifted across the lawns on either side of a semi-circular driveway. The whole length of the entrance path was lined with majestic palm trees from the gatehouse to the impressively proportioned *porte-cochère*, where guests alighted from their various modes of transport.

A huge canvas marquee had been erected adjacent to the portico. It had been deliberately positioned in such a way as to be framed by the native white-blossomed tembusu trees in the background, which provided a natural arbour throughout the grounds. The interior of the marquee was furnished with white linen-covered tables and chairs; floral arrangements and coloured streamers were woven around the tent poles. It would not have been out of place to see a troupe of Morris dancers jigging around a maypole. But what was truly remarkable was the fact that there was not a single person to be seen anywhere in the grounds. The marquee seemed to have been installed for appearance purposes only.

As the printed invitations had stated, the lady of the household had originally intended to hold the early stage of the reception alfresco, mimicking the type of English-style garden party she often attended before her arrival in Singapore. For a while, Lady Celia even toyed with the idea of offering games like croquet on the lawn, as well as the novelty of French boules, using one of the wider gravel pathways bordering the garden. In view of the muggy climate, both were deemed to be less sweat-inducing alternatives to a few sets of hit-and-giggle badminton, an energetic pastime she'd adored since childhood.

The athletic-looking Mr Junichirō Taguchi, impeccably dressed in white linen suit, Panama hat and red tie, was Celia's special guest, despite husband Jeremy's disapproval at his being invited at all. He was a long-term resident who ran the photography shop on the ground floor of the Raffles Hotel. She'd already engaged his services to compile an album of picturesque snapshots of colonial Singapore, in which she insisted her presence was necessary in order to endow the photos with a suitably photogenic and recognisable foreground for her society friends in London.

Taguchi san had been primarily invited by the hostess to demonstrate the time-honoured martial art of *Kyūdō*, a samurai-era archery skill, in which he claimed some expertise. He enjoyed a virtual monopoly of the family portraiture business in the colony, and Lady Celia was not the only one surprised to learn that he was currently in the process of selling his lucrative business lock, stock and *yazutsu* quivers. He was planning to return to Tokyo the following month but declined to provide anyone with a specific reason for his unexpected departure.

Suffice to say that all the proposed activities had to be abandoned at the last moment due to her ladyship's disbelief in the almost certain prospect of inclement weather at this time of year. She'd been clearly misinformed by her husband's spurious claim that early October was as close as Singapore ever came to experiencing a dry season. In fact, there *was* no dry season.

Fortunately, when it came to the selection, purchase and preparation of food, Celia paid greater attention to the more reliable knowledge provided by her domestic servants. While traditional western cuisine might be regularly served in the dining rooms of private clubs and hotels in Singapore, she was having little of it. It seemed to her that everyone except her husband's private secretary, Robbie Bosanquet knew the food was not very good in those establishments, although its highly stylised description in French did its best to pretend otherwise.

Even before she landed, Celia was aware that food was perhaps the most important aspect of Singaporean life apart from the accumulation of wealth and influence. In her kitchen, she'd decided to adopt a consultative rather than domineering role in her relationship with the

Hainanese cook and his Teochew and Tamil assistants. That day, there would be a balance between her favourite spiced dishes recommended by the cook, and those bland dishes she might have served for Sunday lunch in London.

She increasingly drew upon her amah's understanding of the rich culinary history of Baba Nyonya cuisine from Melaka and Penang. Indeed, that particular attribute had proved decisive in the retention of Tan Quan Neo in the household above all other considerations, apart from her proficiency in English and her physical attractiveness. Celia had made it plain to secretary Bosanquet, that her social gatherings *must* showcase an array of dishes and ingredients demonstrating the reach of Britain's Far East Imperial possessions. Bosanquet was unimpressed. His body might be in Singapore but his appetite dwelt elsewhere. It ran to *Tournedos Parisienne,* prepared in the kitchens of the great London hotels to the recipe of Auguste Escoffier. Still, he didn't press the point, as he knew which side his bread was buttered on.

Since the reception would now take place wholly inside the Residence, a larger than usual retinue of servants had been quickly convened to prepare savoury hors d'oeuvres, known as *makan kechil.* These included spiced chicken and potato curry puffs, *babi pongteh* pork, *ah bo ling* rice balls with red bean and sesame paste, *udang garam assam,* prawns in a spiced tamarind sauce, and *soon kueh,* dim sum dumplings. It would be served as a stand-up, buffet-style meal supplemented by waiters circling the rooms with large platters. Cookie had been dispatched earlier in the day to the street market along Serangoon Road to purchase the spices, vegetables and fresh fruit that were brought in daily from the *kampungs* in the north of the island and southern Johore.

As a concession to the more conservative tastes of her husband, his secretary and the clusters of overfed but under-nourished civil servants, she'd instructed Cookie to also purchase prime saddles of Australian mutton from the Cold Storage Co. in Orchard Road. The experienced cook could not be counted upon, however, to satisfy Robbie's nostalgic yearning for a bowl of spotted dick. The more flavoursome sago pudding, *gula melaka,* would have to do as a substitute. Celia requested a small bowl of the dessert be prepared and set aside solely for the secretary's consumption. She thought it to be the only foreign food *not* on the evening's menu that would be to Mr Bosanquet's taste.

He could count himself lucky. Cookie struggled to conceal his sense of shame at being addressed as Ping Pong on every occasion they met. Demeaning verbal slights and gratuitous ridicule provide the manure in which the seeds of racial stereotyping are encouraged to thrive. Bosanquet so seldom looked directly at the servants that he was completely oblivious to the look of scorn in Cookie's eyes whenever they crossed paths.

The relationship had become so bad that Quek Shin, which was his family name in Hainanese, would try to make himself scarce whenever Bosanquet appeared in the kitchen. This was difficult to arrange at any time, but especially whenever the secretary dropped in around mealtimes unannounced, in order to exchange pleasantries with Bhadrang, the younger of the two Tamil houseboys. It was noticeable that he was one of the few servants Bosanquet deigned to address in a civil tongue.

Cookie was not deficient in self-esteem but all the same felt deeply humiliated. As he secretly harboured support for the nationalist, anti-imperialist cause advanced by the local partisans of the Kuomintang, he was acutely sensitive. From the nationalists' point of view, whereas patriotism required deep conviction, nationalism simply needed enemies, and there were plenty to choose from apart from the marauding Japanese. Although as suspicious of the motives of the mainland warlords as those of the local communists, Quek Shin was not alone among the Hainanese community in Singapore, in believing the foremost imperialist enemy were those who enforced local decisions from abroad and often wore a bowler hat.

Revenge was said to take many forms, but Cookie had heard it could taste sweet, was best served cold, and quite effective in small helpings. Lady Celia's earlier request had given him an idea. An especially aberrant mix of ingredients, no suet but with a passable substitute for currants, might render the rather sugary *gula melaka* less likely to settle on the stomach as well as might be expected later in the evening.

———

A visiting jazz orchestra and piano recitalist had been separately engaged to provide the evening's light entertainment. The piano music was filtering through the voices of the guests upon their arrival. Before the small group of instrumentalists had set themselves up in the main room, a diminutive, wizened man with a shock of dishevelled white hair had already started to perform, largely unobserved, on a surprisingly well-maintained grand piano. His name was Joshua Eidelman, and the piano was a Bechstein on loan from the nearby governor's residence. It was one of only three shipped from London after the war to politically favoured British dignitaries in the Far East.

Eidelman needed little monetary enticement to accept this evening's engagement once he'd discovered the host's piano wouldn't be one of the usual untuned, weather-affected uprights upon which he was routinely obliged to conduct his private tuition sessions in the colony. He'd agreed to play some unremarkable background music, but it appeared Lady Celia had interpreted the undertaking literally, because both he and the pianoforte were trundled away to a secluded recess at the far end of an adjoining room. It was if she'd decided that if there were to be any rhapsodies performed this evening, it would be she and not a musician who'd provide them.

For those who noticed, Eidelman played with a lightness of touch and with such colour and tone that it would have rendered even a rendition of Franz Liszt's Sonata in B Minor reasonably accessible. He'd trained at the Vienna Conservatory around the turn of the century and, in common with his near contemporary Gustav Mahler, had personally experienced some virulent antisemitism in his daily life. But, unlike the more illustrious pianist and composer, over the years Eidelman received few orchestral engagements and attracted none of the prosperous and well-connected patrons essential to nurturing a successful career as a soloist or conductor.

By the thirties, the vitality and influence of that once great cultural and artistic centre was in decline. The isolated instances of discrimination to which he had grown accustomed under the remnants of the Habsburg Empire had insidiously become state sanctioned. His wife and large numbers among their extended family in Leopoldstadt had convinced him of the imminent danger to their community's physical safety. Therefore, and in common with many of his colleagues, he'd left Vienna prior to Kristallnacht, which swept through the capital on 9 November 1938. By then both he and his wife had already fled Austria and sought sanctuary in Belgium. He cursed the fact that the Anschluss instigated by the Germans that March had not aroused his fears of a catastrophe for Jewish citizens much earlier.

As a committed Sinophile, Eidelman had always dreamt of spending a portion of his later years exploring the Far East before heading to New York. He'd managed to visit Shanghai and Peking, fortuitously avoiding the worst of the destruction caused by the Japanese invasion throughout mainland China. Yet, for all their racist attitudes towards Manchurians and the Chinese, Japanese imperialists did not appear to share the Nazis' visceral hatred of the Jews.

In Europe, he had never imagined he'd be obliged to bring his retirement travel plans forward and flee his home country as an émigré. He and his wife had intended to be ultimately reunited with other members of his family already domiciled in Washington Heights, Manhattan. However, the opportunity to earn a living in Singapore meant the trip had been postponed. Practically, the whole of his own and his wife's former possessions were shipped to Singapore in two large trunks, within which he managed to cram his large portfolio of sheet music manuscripts. Their home and furniture had been confiscated not long after their departure, and he'd not acquired much in the way of the readily transportable gold and jewellery that some in his persecuted community had managed to take with them. He'd partially remedied that situation after drawing upon his brother's beneficence in Antwerp.

Once settled in Singapore, he found work easily as music tutor to the sons and daughters of wealthy Peranakan families eager for their children to be schooled in the Western classical music tradition. The teaching sessions paid well, but it tested his patience to endure the daily repetitions of Dmitry Kabalevsky's excruciatingly pedestrian piano pieces, hammered away by children who were clearly more endowed with money than musical talent. Within weeks of his arrival in the island city, he realised that his exile in this reputedly invulnerable fortress was now no longer the haven it had once appeared. One thing was for certain – he wouldn't be waiting for signs of a comparable Japanese Anschluss in Singapore before departing for America.

———

As they stepped out of the limousine, the three Australian officers were met at the bottom of the steps by Pym's personal secretary, Robbie Bosanquet. He was holding a half-unfurled umbrella dripping with rainwater. Thirty minutes later, Campbell arrived in Lim's trishaw. He was still straightening his bow tie as he tail-ended the other stragglers beside the portico. While he stood at the foot of the stairs, he delicately dressed to the left, trying to leave his crown jewels undisturbed. He then ran his fingers through sprigs of closely cropped blond hair, the last sprinkles of rain helping to give his distinctive cowlick less prominence.

Campbell's late arrival required a brief explanation and an apology. He'd introduced himself first as Alexander, then said he preferred Sandy. The secretary responded with a rather disarming and elongated, 'The pleasure's all mine ... Sandy,' slightly tilting his head forward in the process. In the circumstances, Campbell couldn't help admiring the secretary's wavy locks. They looked as if they'd been styled by a proper hairdresser, not one of the 8th Division's military barbers. The latter presumably owed their current occupation solely to the fact they'd mentioned a short stint of sheep-shearing on their enlistment form.

After telling Campbell in a lush baritone that he preferred to be called Robbie, Bosanquet assured him that the hosts would be unconcerned by his delayed arrival, dismissing it as a mere peccadillo.

The secretary's suave appearance and polished manners suggested he was the type of person upon whom the post-nominal esquire would sit quite comfortably. In fact, the word itself was embossed in its abbreviated form, along with his full name and official title, on all his stationery. He appeared younger than his years, was floppy-haired, tall and slender, and looked spiffy in an embroidered silk waistcoat under his smartly pressed, white dinner jacket. A vermilion-coloured handkerchief peeped out just so from one corner of the breast pocket.

'Top shelf,' the major had earlier muttered on arrival, turning his head towards the colonel in undisguised admiration.

Despite his being trussed up in formal dress, there was only the tiniest trace of perspiration on the secretary's brow. His lack of susceptibility to the heat seemed to run counter to that experienced by ordinary mortals, as if he had refrigerant coursing through his veins. In comparison, those around him gave the impression that they were in the process of melting, their shirts already polka-dotted with sweat. Some of the more heavily upholstered male guests lining the steps were constantly wiping their foreheads with the back of their hands or, in exasperation, using the cuffed end of their coat sleeves to mop up the perspiration. This led them to curse under their breath at the abrasiveness of the row of buttons on the side of the cuff, deliberately designed by military officialdom, it's alleged, to discourage the very practice.

Robbie Bosanquet had read modern languages and history at Balliol College, Oxford, and had proven to be a loyal civil servant of the Crown in the chillier climes of London for nearly a decade. It therefore came as a surprise to his closest colleagues that he'd forsaken almost certain career advancement to the top echelons of Whitehall to take on the role of personal private secretary when Jeremy Pym's star was on the ascendant in 1937.

Few were aware that both he and the minister had known one another since Bosanquet's accelerated promotion to the Remove in preparatory school. Although they were more than twelve months apart in age, the personal relationship grew close during their subsequent school days while boarding together once more, this time at Charterhouse. Perhaps that was the reason why people who met them for the first time mistakenly believed them to be the younger and elder brother. They'd started to sound and even look like one another. Boarding together from an early age can do that to public school boys.

Everyone remarked upon Robbie's radiant smile. Its effect had certainly been totted up as a political asset, a vote-winning complement to his dignified bearing and effortless charm, should he ever decide to follow Jeremy Pym's example on the hustings. Yet he was obliged to concede when looking upon the sunken faces of the present-day cabinet ministers, that a beaming smile was apparently of no further use beyond being elected to parliament. This realisation alone had proven a significant disincentive to his joining their ranks.

While Robbie was viewed favourably in certain circles as the minister's talented protégé, others dismissed him as a foppish dilettante, who'd probably fagged for Pym in the sixth form. There were all the usual scurrilous rumours of a fondness for boys, but it never went any further than suspicions. On the other hand, it was a well-established fact that he regularly passed his vacations at either his father's residence in the huitième arrondissement, or at a secluded fishing village on the French Atlantic seaboard. This privileged opportunity for leisure went a long way to explaining how he'd managed to cultivate a life of dissipation and what his detractors described as his affected Parisian mannerisms.

Despite Bosanquet's scholastic achievements, the party grandees considered him to be of limited intellectual substance, which reflected their innate distrust of *cleverness*. They also mistakenly considered him a little too Whiggish in his sociopolitical views, offering no greater promise in bolstering the electoral fortunes of the Conservative Party than his ill-fated patron. Indeed, Jeremy Pym's well-publicised resignation from the cabinet over a matter of principle was seen by his political enemies as clear proof that both he and his protégé would never amount to much more than rank amateurs in the dark arts of political intrigue. Despite briefly holding a cabinet portfolio and being supported by Churchill, Pym was the type of MP they were prone to priggishly dismiss as natural backbench material. This rendered him of limited value to those adept at plotting to undermine whomever the current Tory Party leader happened to be.

While it may have seemed like a bit of a setback for both Bosanquet and the minister to have wound up together in Singapore, there were some potential career-enhancing benefits for both. Given the relative anonymity to be enjoyed in the absence of scrutiny of pressing matters of state in the Far East, one's social proclivities were able to be handled in much the same way. In Westminster, any unbecoming secrets in your private life would eventually become publicly exposed in the newspapers – your promising career swiftly undone in the morning's lurid headlines delivering the punchy scoop of the day.

In Singapore, on the other hand, it was said that you could mysteriously guard your secrets and secretly reveal your mysteries untroubled by the potential scandal promoted by the sensationalist, rumour-mongering hacks on the *Daily Mail*. It was not so much that racy gossip was unknown, but that it was seldom, if ever, published. Even Chamberlain's 'Peace for our time' proclamation garnered no more than two inches of bolded headline in *The Straits Times*.

———

On reaching the vestibule, the whole party, apart from Sandy Campbell, had been officially welcomed by Sir Jeremy Pym's wife, Lady Celia Dalrymple, in her husband's absence. Her appearance coincided with yet another of the intermittent torrential downpours they'd encountered throughout the day. No sooner would the rain end than a flurry of servants would emerge from the rear of the bungalow brandishing very long barge poles designed to release the rainwater that had collected in the rolled-up sides of the marquee's canopy.

'I'd prefer you didn't have a whisky in your hand all night,' Celia said in a bitter aside to her husband as he unexpectedly joined her at the door. 'And try not to upset those Australian officers over there, who you insisted on dragging all the way down here, for whatever purpose you had in mind.'

'Well, for a start, they weren't *dragged* down here, my darling. They gratefully accepted the invitation, and the purpose is to discuss the current military situation in an informal, social setting. That's one of the reasons why I was posted to the Far East as an emissary, unless you've already forgotten?'

'No, I'm reminded of it every day,' she hissed. 'In your absence, I told the gentlemen to relax, have something to nibble, and you'd join them in a minute or two. That was ten minutes ago! It was a little bit rude of you not to welcome them personally at the door, don't you think?'

'Please don't trouble yourself with such matters. Robbie welcomed them all on my behalf earlier today at their hotel. Allow yourself to focus upon the flight to Hong Kong we're taking together next week. You'll be pleased to hear Robbie isn't coming along. He's probably a little put off by my decision, so bear that in mind.'

'Good gracious, I wouldn't like to think I've come between you two anymore than usual? I can assure you; he's not really put off. Your absence just gives him greater licence to offend the servants. Haven't you done enough for him already – rescuing him once more from possible press exposure over his latest episode of dissipation, and even getting him out of London well before we left?'

'Well, it seems to me that because you're an actress, you fail to understand that *true* friendship is neither staged nor a matter of rehearsed performance.'

'Well, it's *not* Robbie being a bit put off that *you* fail to understand – it's me! I'm terribly bored, and so is your daughter,' she said as her voice started to quaver. 'I never considered Singapore a proper diplomatic posting in the first place. It was an appointment set up as a political, face-saving exercise, solely for Winston's benefit. You and I both know that for a fact. I don't mind being pampered by all these servants, but everything else seems so frightfully … *Edwardian,* and exceedingly hot.'

'Well, you can think what you like about your imagined misfortune, but please choose another evening to discuss it, if you don't mind.'

With those few sharp words, he drifted off into the formal reception room to renew his acquaintance with another large whisky and tonight's delightfully impressionable female company.

———

Lady Celia's notoriety in London as a vivacious society hostess and sometime stage and screen actress had preceded her arrival in Singapore. Her goings-on were often reported in *The Daily Sketch* tabloid newspaper, as well as *Tatler* magazine. Long out-dated editions of these publications reached the colony at bimonthly intervals, along with the diminishing number of world-weary passengers disembarking at Clifford Pier on Collyer Quay.

Celia was quite tall, poised and graceful, but it would do her an injustice if she were to be simply described as statuesque. Although no longer a spring chicken, she looked stunning in a salmon-pink evening dress that clung to her body in such a way as to leave little to the imagination. The absence of sleeves served to accentuate the ostentatious cluster of bracelets that threatened at any moment to slide from her slender wrists.

Like all newly arrived European visitors, she was informed that to cope with the relentless humidity throughout the night, one should sleep on a hard mattress that rested on a well-ventilated bed base. So far as the type of bedlinen was concerned, the advice was to let your body come into contact with as little as possible. It was apparent to everyone in the room that the latter recommendation had also been enthusiastically embraced by her ladyship when it came to her choice of evening wear.

Perhaps she'd overcompensated for the oppressive tropical heat, but her décolletage was quite revealing and highlighted by a longish pearl necklace she tended to clutch while speaking. The immediate effect was that it made some of the other ladies' prim attire appear as if it were a parting gift from the recent postulants in the nearby Convent of the Holy Infant Jesus. However, judging by the snorting and the ungracious content of their conversation, the same ladies had declined to follow any of the spiritually uplifting and contemplative practices of that religious order.

From her high cheekbones, clear blue eyes and burnt honey-coloured bob right down to her uncorseted, svelte figure, everything about Lady Celia screamed English blue blood. So far as Wake was concerned, she reminded him of his erstwhile infatuation with the curvaceous Carole Lombard, an American goddess of the silver screen. He found Celia equally beguiling and simply couldn't take his eyes off her. Manning lightheartedly put Wake's penetrating gaze down to a probable consequence of the major's specialist training in ophthalmology.

For the colonel, the immediate comparison she evoked was decidedly less contemporary but no less apposite for all its mythic status. His earlier, though limited, schooling in the classics suggested a different cast of deified womanhood. It was more in the mould of Aphrodite, who according to ancient myth emerged from the sea and rode upon the tumescent foam amid the severed genitalia of the god Uranus.

For his part, despite being turned out like a swell from the Home Counties, Lance Bombardier Alexander Campbell felt decidedly uncomfortable, once he eventually came in close proximity to such an uncommonly attractive woman – especially one who bore a title and, if he were not seriously mistaken, had clearly acknowledged his late arrival with an approving gaze.

Anticipating an imminent opportunity to speak directly to her, Campbell began to lightly brush his shoulders, even though it had been years since he had been alerted to the presence of dandruff on his clothes. This evening it was simply a nervous, reflex action, intuitively honouring his promise to the major to remain spick and span and as inoffensive as possible. 'Make sure you leave the scallywag at the door,' were the major's parting words.

Campbell was temporarily denied Celia's undivided attention when she was diverted by some remarks she'd picked up elsewhere in the room and moved away. Had the dignified nature of the evening been less forbidding, he might've addressed the major with a good-natured, though mildly offensive, 'You can't be court-martialled for mentally undressing a civilian, can you, sir?

If Campbell had in fact aired his speculations, the major might've readily conceded that the somewhat indecent enquiry needed very little time and even less imagination to be satisfactorily performed. He couldn't help but be affected by a nostalgia for his own gallivanting post-graduate years in Edinburgh, when most of his crucial appendages were much firmer than his present appearance would suggest they'd ever been.

While he might have successfully camouflaged his broad accent and stifled his inclination to offer an ill-advised, indecorous comment, Campbell's broad-shouldered and healthy good looks did not go unnoticed as he decided to thread a path through the multi-ethnic elite drawn together that evening. He felt decidedly out of place clutching a funny-coloured drink in a fragile cocktail glass with his rough and rather large, agricultural hands. Although he'd made hard work of his first sip of gin, he soon discovered that subsequent ones went down quite smoothly. Once he'd become more relaxed, he cheekily remarked to the major that there seemed to be lots of smallish, chubby and elderly men in the room, and they outnumbered the women of any shape or age by a considerable margin.

Not to be outdone, the major concurred, by adding, 'I suppose from your elevated point of view, Sandy, youngish, shapely females are very thin on the ground?' He was rather pleased with what he believed to be a witty observation in rounding off the conversation.

———

The main room was quite spacious compared to the several smaller rooms where the food was being served. The ceiling in the principal reception area rose to around fifteen feet above the tiled flooring. Large fans gently whirred, positioned where the chandeliers they had possibly replaced would have looked completely at home. Openings in the walls on three sides separated the room from the verandahs. If protection from the harsher elements were required, these openings could be secured with the shuttered wooden doors, which tonight had been pushed to one side.

'I say, you must be one of those lifeguards they're all talking about at the swimming club,' a young, waif-like woman casually remarked over her shoulder as Campbell was weaving his way through the main room. Then, moving a little closer, she said: 'I'm told a whole team from a lifesaving club in that wonderfully named Queensland, had volunteered as soon as a regiment had been formed? If that's twue, then it's no wonder you *Aw*stralians have a reputation for being so frightfully bwave.'

Her comment came across as both a snooty enquiry and an inviting tease. It almost managed to conceal her slight and not unattractive lisp. For a few moments, he could not have felt more tongue-tied than if he'd been addressed in Buginese, one of Peters's allegedly untranslatable languages, its usage confined to the southernmost parts of Sulawesi in the Dutch East Indies. He gingerly clasped her outstretched hand, its softness indicating it may have normally been gloved, and had rarely encountered any form of household cleaning utensil in its life. He nervously replied in a tight voice he scarcely recognised as his own, 'Well, yes … miss?'

'Georgina,' she interrupted.

'Some of those rumours are possibly true, Miss Georgina … but I'm no lifesaver. My name's Alexander, and I'm a lance bombardier assigned to the medical corps.' Although tempted, he thought it'd be risky to bring up his recent rescue of the victims of toilet pandemonium in Chinatown. That might be something a Sandy, rather than an Alexander, would have let slip.

'My mates will tell you I'm not too keen on the ocean waves. I'd be useless rescuing people in the surf at Tugun, or anywhere else … and I've decided to put off travelling on boats. I'm more suited to working on dry land, doing a bit of carpentry, slapping up a tin shed – that sort of thing. Just a simple country bloke, happiest when I've got my two feet firmly on the ground.'

'How modest you are, Alexander,' she replied with a languid bat of her eyelashes. 'All I can say is … should the enemy arrive over land or sea, it would be awfully nays if you promised to become my very own, *personal* lifesaver?' she lied.

Georgina's sense of self-possession and poise suggested she was every bit her mother's daughter. However, the short blond ringlets dangling either side of her cheekbones gave her more the appearance of a wistful ingenue than the femme fatale allure of Lady Celia, whose glamour she rather transparently sought to emulate.

Campbell had been taken unawares by her impish forwardness and was mildly surprised by the fact that the bush telegraph seemed to be operating with remarkable speed and accuracy in the tropics. At the same time, he could tell that her fleeting smile and limited conversation was something reserved for those who were fascinated by her, but to whom she would offer no further encouragement. She'd learnt that intriguing pose from her mother at an early age.

As she started to move away, she stopped fidgeting with her necklace and lightly ran her fingertips across his sleeve. If the purpose of her provocative gesture was intended to sexually arouse the unsuspecting recipient, it struggled for success. He'd been rebuffed by sexually precocious young women before, but never with such elegance and aplomb. He knew there'd be no romantic tryst later that evening, or indeed on any other occasion. That much was conveyed in the unambiguous message relayed by her abrupt averting of any semblance of a backward gaze, which in Campbell's case followed her closely around the room. He eventually realised he'd just been sent back, below stairs.

CHAPTER
SIXTEEN

GEORGINA PYM HAD JUST TURNED twenty and her immersion in the full panoply of the 1939 London season still strongly resonated in her consciousness. She'd emerged with a newly acquired independence and feistiness, embracing some rebellious ideas on social and religious matters. She'd recently discovered like company among a type of demi-monde, whose assertiveness and values were disturbingly at variance with what her parents had expected of her. They wondered what aspect of instruction in the ways of the leisured class they'd failed to impart thus far in their daughter's educational formation. She seemed to be dabbling in whatever esoteric cults were fashionable at the time. Most alarmingly, she was known to have attended meetings of the Theosophical Society and professed an interest in the heretical cult of Rosicrucianism. Both parents were quietly despondent at how these late-Victorian influences were playing out. They now deeply regretted their delay in not enrolling her in a reputable finishing school in Lausanne before the outbreak of war.

In an effort to reimpose their outwardly conservative views on these developments, and even though the worst of the Luftwaffe raids over London had subsided by mid-May 1941, the Pyms had insisted that Georgina accompany them to Singapore in September. They needed her to make a clean break from her newly acquired *spiritual friends*, with the promise of what Celia portrayed as *terribly exciting* side trips to other reasonably accessible, exotic locations. To partially legitimise their decision, they dressed it up as a self-styled Far Eastern Grand Tour, a relatively modest though much safer alternative to the traditional European version, which was no longer possible for well-bred young ladies to safely negotiate, anywhere on the continent.

In London, Georgina had attempted to adopt a variant of her mother's persona, but she'd struggled to achieve even an approximation of its intended effect. Although barely beyond adolescence, she desperately sought recognition as a mature adult, attracted to the capricious notion of becoming a seductive woman. Since there were even fewer dashing, young Englishmen than single, white females in the colony, within no time she had become despairing of the lack of opportunity to practise her flirtations. Nor did she find suitable companionship by participating in the many sporting pastimes available to her in the late afternoon. Moreover, the absence of any of her erstwhile social-climbing diversions, such as the musical soirées conducted in the salons of southwest London, had rendered the twilight hours and late evenings equally uneventful.

Georgina felt that with each passing day the likelihood of her ever satisfying her mother's expectations by marrying well was also steadily diminishing. With the outbreak of war, Celia likewise realised that if her daughter remained out of the country for an extended period, on her return the field of eligible suitors would be even further reduced. She would inevitably be obliged to choose between an assortment of spendthrift, middle-aged philanderers and an endless file of shell-shocked, infirm ex-servicemen, abandoned by the government and repatriated to equally disabled marriages and shattered careers. In other words, a situation not dissimilar to that faced by single women and widows in the aftermath of the Great War.

Consequently, Georgina's normal state of mind since arriving in Singapore had fluctuated between bouts of petulance and idleness. This inevitably gave rise to a life untethered to reality, her moods as unshakeable as an unwanted, overly solicitous chaperone.

Fortunately, her relationship with her mother's new amah, Tan Quan Neo, had gradually developed into a close personal friendship.

Within days of their first introduction to one another, Georgina had seen to it that Tan should occupy the most private and well-appointed room inside the servants' quarters, situated within the grounds of the minister's official residence. She'd also persuaded her mother that Tan should be permitted to wear clothing other than the distinctive white blouse and black trousers by which these Chinese nannies were traditionally recognised in the street.

This dispensation caused little consternation with Tan, who'd long ago decided to walk a path less trodden. Fortunately, she'd had the foresight to bring with her some stylish *banju shanghai* ensembles and several lace-embroidered *nonya kebaya* blouses. All these traditional items of clothing had been chosen and purchased at great expense by her parents to underscore the physically and financially attractive proposition their only daughter presented to prospective marriage partners. These bespoke items were made from imported silk, damask and the finest Chinese linen. Most of the blouses had high collars and the typical asymmetrical side-fastening, secured by floral buttons and contrasting embroidery. Georgina often remarked how beautifully Tan filled out her clothes.

'Lately I've been thinking, Tan,' Georgina cooed, 'that since you've become more than a household amah to me, I no longer wish anyone to tweat you like any of our other servants. As you've become almost *femly*, it doesn't sound right to simply refer to you as our amah? If you agree, then I might decide to introduce you, whenever the occasion arises, as *my confidante*, or *my twusted companion?*'

Tan was disinclined to ask whether her assigned duties would be altered, as both forms of address sounded more intimate and way beyond the accepted description of the duties her traditional domestic role entailed. But she felt obliged to satisfy her mistress's flights of fancy in the absence of any direction to the contrary by Lady Celia herself. 'That's good,' Tan replied with the faintest of blushes. 'If Miss Georgina uses those words, I will love them.' Although she realised that what she'd said sounded rather precious, it was the very least she could say or do that gave practical effect to her acquisition of amiability in which she had received instruction in her formative years.

'Very well, let's speak no more of it,' Georgina replied. 'I'll try it out when we go to Robinson's tomorrow morning. You'll accompany me as a *fwend*, and not as a servant to the mistress of the house.' Then, almost as an afterthought, she whispered: 'When we're alone, and especially when my parents are not around, I'd like you to call me ... *George*.'

Slightly bewildered, Tan nodded her approval with a weak smile that scarcely masked her dismay. She was uncertain whether this unusual request would prove to be more of a burden than an agreeable departure from formality. After a few days play-acting, she thought that what memsahib had proposed was simply impulsive, if not frivolous, but she had little choice but to go along with it.

Tan had initially come to the departing Donald Travers' household with a unique set of credentials for the job. In the first place, she was of Straits Chinese extraction, not much over thirty years of age, although she looked much younger. This contrasted with the majority of amahs, who were more elderly and had migrated almost exclusively from Hainan Island during the 1930s. Tan nevertheless adhered to the amah's customary tradition of celibacy.

One came across the conventional amah in their distinctive apparel almost everywhere on the streets of Singapore. On Sundays especially, they could be seen at the swimming pool, supervising the children of those mems who preferred to cultivate their close relationships with a few gimlets and a curry tiffin while gossiping on the club verandahs. While it was a welcome break from their daily routine, in no time this weekend pastime also became little more than pleasantly monotonous.

Tan Quan Neo, the only daughter of a third-generation Peranakan family, had been enrolled in Sophia Blackmore's Methodist Girls' School in the late-twenties. The eponymous Sophia, who had long since retired, was a widely respected Australian educator and evangelising Christian. Besides Bible study, her school aimed to instil the highest standards in elocution, good manners and grooming in all the young girls who passed through its doors. Miss Blackmore's decision to leave Sydney and travel overseas had been a boon to her career and her feeling of self-worth. At home she would have become conditioned to the life of an intelligent, slightly eccentric but socially invisible maiden aunt; just another nice person titivating around the house in a well-worn cardigan pinned with costume jewellery. By contrast, in Singapore, there was no shortage of demand for her services, especially from those parents whose upward social mobility seemed incomplete in the absence of the type of education and deportment classes she offered their daughters.

At some point in late adolescence, well after finishing at Miss Blackmore's, Tan had decided to summon the courage to resist the clumsy and insensitive matchmaker stratagems repeatedly forced upon her by her parents. She respected the traditions and culture of her Peranakan heritage and its adherence to a solidifying endogamy, and accepted that her father was only acting in conformity with the mores that informed his community's cultural identity. However, life for her now meant far more than fulfilling the requirements of child-bearing domesticity, being satisfied with the perfectly enunciated English, the plain and fancy needlework that, among other things, had been required to receive Miss Blackmore's Amiability and Accomplishments Certificate.

From her parents' perspective, the ultimate purpose of her education was somewhat narrower. Possessing the admittedly desirable refinements of an English lady was decidedly less important than marrying and producing a line of healthy male progeny who would be worthy recipients of the family's patrimony. It was never viewed as a means to broker their daughter's lifelong happiness.

Tan managed to hold off a succession of eligible suitors proposed by the *meiren* matchmaker engaged by her parents well into her early twenties. Eventually there was one refusal too many on her part before she was effectively disowned by her father, Tan Keong Saik. He was co-founder of the Straits Steamship Company and resided in the Tanjong Pajar district near Chinatown. He found it impossible to reconcile his daughter's instruction in morality and religion with her failure to obey his insistence on an arranged marriage to a boy from a family of similar status to his own.

He told her that her unwillingness to accede to his paternal demands had caused him to lose face within his Hokkien Huay Kuan and had brought permanent dishonour to his family's reputation. In the circumstances, Tan was left with few other options than to seek employment as an amah in an established European household.

———

Were it not for Tan's companionship, Georgina would've thought she'd become a sort of shipwrecked castaway, sharing a longboat with a bunch of ne'er-do-wells. Her behaviour had become increasingly erratic and snobbish. Whoever unwittingly incurred Georgina's displeasure was routinely referred to as *wather beastly*, and their ignorance of what correct form dictated in particular social settings was described as *howwid*.

To dispel her growing sense of ennui, she would spend prolonged periods in front of the full-length English oak cheval mirror left in place by the previous residents. She would adjust her stance to assess the degree to which various items of apparel managed to mask her flat-chested silhouette. Whatever her facial contortions, and no matter the level of deliberately exposed flesh, the mirror refused to reflect the desired resemblance to her mother's bodily curves and smouldering good looks. In moments of pique, she had the occasional doubt about whether Celia was really her mother at all but understandably never voiced her suspicions to anyone.

Perhaps this ruby-encrusted amulet laced by a gold chain? Should it be a little further up? What if I pull it tighter? she would mumble self-consciously. As she screwed up her nose pondering these weighty concerns, she began to delight in the touch of Tan's fingers as they delicately fastened and adjusted the length of the necklaces to best advantage around her neckline. 'If only the clothing I'm forced to wear could go with some of the jewellery I brought with me,' she lamented.

Tan's untiring attention to her mistress's dressing aroused more positive feelings between them than whether any chosen item of jewellery managed to complement her attire. She would solicit an impromptu opinion on these matters whenever their hands met in the process. Whether the answers were satisfying or not, she eventually understood that the pouting, po-faced reflection in the glass would likely be the only lasting friendship – other than that of her amah – she would ever strike up in her present surroundings. Episodes of this nature often ended in tantrums and tears. And, no matter how many ensembles met Tan's approval, Georgina inevitably came to accept that her charming confidante could never be trusted to advance an entirely disinterested opinion.

Eventually, her former self-indulgent pastime of dressing up as though she'd never left her pretentious Bloomsbury set fell away. Things had reached the stage where she soon preferred to dispatch Tan to John Little & Co.'s emporium to place an order for the latest imports of French lingerie advertised in their catalogue. Desperate to overcome her contrived misfortune, she began a brief affair with a romanticised alter ego. More out of vanity than artistic affinity, she felt impelled to embrace the slightly wistful, nymph-like look depicted in some of her favourite paintings from the Pre-Raphaelite school. Their mood did not speak of domesticity and childbearing. On the contrary, it was as though the reproductive role of a woman was somehow viewed as *unproductive*, not simply less appealing than the sexual ambiguity of the artist's muse.

Tan was sent to procure a suitable array of loose-fitting casual clothes to closely reflect the stylistic milieu she conjured from the paintings of the era – perhaps something that *la belle dame sans merci* might feel comfortable wearing. In Singapore, it was a task that could only be discharged by visiting the silk merchants on South Bridge Road, as she wanted to avoid any resemblance to the inexpensive, baggy clothes worn by the low-caste Samsui women in the streets.

Her new fetish promised a world where the female gender could embrace aesthetic notions of leisure, sensual allure and mystery. She'd observed her mother clothed in so many roles that she was convinced she'd be good at it too. The opportunity, however illusory, of imitating the insouciance conveyed by the recumbent female in *Dolce Far Niente* by John Waterhouse became increasingly appealing. Perhaps one of the artistic movement's more prominent motifs, the depiction of the young woman's sweet idleness suggested female agency and independence, combined with the sort of erotic fantasies associated with *Psyche and Cupid*, which she now manifestly coveted. *Would a deeper attachment to those languid free spirits rub off on her,* she wondered.

However, such was the transient nature of her whimsy that well before that night's reception, she had grown as tired of the glamourous affectation of loosely flowing hair as she had of her previous dabbling in the occult. She had cast all aside with the same air of nonchalance in which she'd taken them up in the first place. At a stroke, she bid farewell to the oversized silken blouses and billowing, gossamer-like pantaloons that had swamped her red mules whenever she arose to place her teacup and late-morning reading on the low table beside her velvet divan.

Tan was grateful that Georgina's infatuation with rejecting social conformity didn't last more than a week or so. She was especially relieved to be able to resume wearing the amah's white sampoo top and the black satin trousers she'd arrived in on her first day. Her mistress insisted upon supervising the redressing and softly patted down all the folds and crinkles in the fabric – and, in fact, anywhere on Tan's body that was agreeable to her touch.

I can do it by myself, Miss Georgina, she wanted to say, but the relationship between them hadn't yet reached that level of forwardness. Besides, Tan was still so enamoured by the idea of what it meant to be an English lady that she dared not jeopardise the opportunity of perhaps accompanying Georgina back to London, whenever that might be. However, her mistress gave little indication that Tan's optimism in this regard was only ever wishful thinking.

By the time she'd changed upstairs into tonight's performance, Georgina had completely abandoned her trousered tomboy look and replaced it with the studied aloofness of feminine disappointment she'd practised for hours in front of the mirror. Gone were the unbound tresses of hair – she now emerged with fashionably cropped natural curls, a flouncy patterned cotton dress and sensible shoes, yet still resistant to conforming to her mother's unimaginative idea of love.

Lance Bombardier Campbell had been immediately spotted as her first flirtatious engagement of the evening, with all its projected sexual ambiguities and cultivated deceptions.

CHAPTER
SEVENTEEN

ALL THE WHILE, the horde of flush-faced estate managers was gradually filing in from the vestibule. They tended to mill around for ages at the entrance, acknowledging certain guests with wordless half smiles or by waggling their fingers, simultaneously tilting their double chins slightly to one side for the benefit of those furthest away. Despite living in such an insular environment, it appeared that many were known to one another only on nodding terms.

Most were sloppily dressed in off-white, unpressed cotton suits, the status-neutral get-up favoured by European gentlemen in the tropics. Prominent members of the Asiatic bourgeoisie also adopted the same loose-fitting suit as a means of advertising their economic success and claim to greater social standing.

Even newish-looking outfits were as crumpled or creased as those that had been clearly subjected to repeated wearing. The worst were slightly blemished by food stains around the midriff. The more corpulent among the gathering were mopping their brows with folded handkerchiefs grasped in the one hand, while on the other their pudgy fingers lunged for their favourite tipple, or grasped several titbits from the passing cornucopia of hors d'oeuvres. The salty perspiration that continued to drip into their eyes was no deterrent to their gluttonous behaviour. Both food and drinks were being ushered around on large salvers, rather too slowly for their liking, by a succession of sarong-clad servants.

Some of the latecomers were still in the process of negotiating a convenient place to deposit their sweat-stained topis. The few planters from upcountry Johore were easily recognisable by their broad-brimmed, double-terai hats. They were noticeably reluctant to hand them over for safe keeping to the unfamiliar, hesitant lackeys who'd been assigned to perform the task for the first time that evening. It took several of the gentlemen quite a while to locate –unaided and through clenched teeth – the designated nook in the corridor off the foyer that served as a makeshift cloakroom not only for their hats, but for the ladies' parasols as well. It didn't help that the space was almost completely concealed by huge, potted palms, alongside which waiters stood at the ready, as if reporting for sentry duty. Not surprisingly, this whole rigmarole caused some displeasure to those men standing around, who were used to simply signing a chit for even the most modest commercial transaction, and accustomed to discharging every menial task around their estate from the depths of a rattan armchair. At the sight of all the rather rumpled garb, Campbell sensed he was comparatively overdressed for the occasion, a bit too *pukka*, he feared, even to British eyes.

This was a sentiment no doubt shared by the various contingents of senior officers in the room, clad in their laundered cutaway red jackets, for whom regimental protocol demanded the wearing of armed-services attire for all social engagements, whatever the climate. This dress regulation had the added disadvantage of eliminating any possi- bility of their anonymously booking a taxi girl in one of the city's famed dance venues later that evening.

Although large numbers of regular soldiers on staggered leave frequented them, Singapore's large-scale entertainment districts gener-ally catered for all respectable civilian gentlemen as well as the hoi polloi. Captain Peters had already informed the other officers that at both the New World and the Great World amusement parks, anyone could hire a lady to partner them in a dance for a mere sixpence a throw. But, he emphasised, he was not just anyone and wouldn't be seen dead in either place.

———

To say that Celia Dalrymple enjoyed being the centre of attention was an understatement. Whenever she swept across the room that evening, she was invariably surrounded by a crowd of preening, middle-aged men. They were essentially the same cohort of thick-jowled government officials and military officers who made it their business to attend every social function of note in the colony. For tonight's performance, Celia assumed the starring role and that of the supporting cast, as well as providing the theatrical effects. In her presence, the audience was only required to bring along obsequious conversation and an overweening display of self-importance.

Unfortunately for Celia, by her own assessment, most of these gentlemen would not have appeared out of place alongside the scabrous caricatures depicted by William Hogarth in eighteenth-century London. Several believed they still cut a dashing figure despite their receding hairlines, and possessing the type of paunch that meant there were significant parts of their anatomy that they and their most intimate companions hadn't laid eyes upon for quite some time.

'Crumbs thrown at starving town-hall pigeons,' the adjutant commented sardonically. Captain Peters had long developed an irritatingly puritanical attitude towards uniquely feminine charms. It was as cold-hearted and austere as it was unoriginal. His fellow officers detected a degree of Victorian-era prurience in his dismal moralising on matters of personal taste and sexuality. The quality and depth of an individual's knowledge, their scholastic accomplishments and literary sensibilities ought to be privileged over everything else by his reckoning. The ideal person he had in mind was perhaps someone very much like himself.

Within minutes of conversing with Lady Celia, he'd unfairly formed the view that possibly the only book the minister's wife had ever peeked into was *Debrett's Peerage*. In fact, she had read widely, was renowned for her eloquence on stage, and had benefited from all the educational advantages bestowed upon the English aristocracy. There certainly was no library at ground-floor level, and any stray books laying around were significantly outnumbered by servants, but this was not of her choosing.

The adjutant also dismissed her ladyship's robust sexuality and its predictable adulation by the strutting peacocks in the room as rather distasteful, her elegant attire mere frippery. He likened the display of ineffectual fawning to the sight of white-hot ingots being quenched one by one in a blacksmith's water tub. Despite her near-flawless beauty, all he saw was someone jaded and permanently dissatisfied – romantically inaccessible. That evening, he tried to bring the major around to his point of view.

'Lady Celia probably spends most of her free time organising garden parties and flaunting her extravagance,' he said to the major. 'Watching her behaviour, I believe I'm witnessing some of the symptoms of the inevitable decline of European colonial power in the Far East.'

Wake made it abundantly clear he didn't share the adjutant's opinion of tonight's hostess, especially the implication that her type of conduct was some sort of blight on the health of the British Empire. In fact, he was quite smitten by her genteel projection of disdain.

'So, David, you don't only take exception to the sultan's appearances in the social pages of the *Illustrated News*,' he pointedly remarked. 'This is not the occasion to indulge in such negative commentary, and I won't be providing you with any encouragement on that score.'

Wake decided he was having nothing more to do with the captain's moralistic sneering and recommended he enjoy the evening's harmless distractions while the going was good. He'd never encountered any soldier of rank so remorselessly unforgiving as Peters once he'd got a set against someone or something. 'Look at Campbell over there,' he said, adopting a more jovial tone. 'He was a bit put out when I told him he'd never find Bulimba Ale being served anywhere in the Far East. He assured me it's on tap in every pub in Toowoomba and thought some bottled supplies ought to have accompanied the 8th Division upon embarkation!'

'Now I know you're joking,' Peters finally bit back.

'All the same, he seemed to believe me when I said with a straight face that I'd heard the quartermaster had issued orders for its delivery to Singapore, and the brewers of the local Tiger brand were quite disturbed when they heard the news. Whether he believed me or not, what I like about Campbell is his natural good cheer. However, beneath that meek and mild demeanour lies a steely resolve, which I believe we both witnessed during that trip today.'

Peters looked askance but remained as hard-boiled as ever.

'As I predicted, Campbell appears to have forgotten all about beer and is having little trouble swallowing those gins Mr Bosanquet's been thrusting into his mitt. He's clearly intent on having a good time tonight. I'd promised to keep a close eye on him, but Tom said to let him off the leash – this might be the last chance he gets to let his hair down, so to speak.'

'Aren't you a little worried he might have one too many of those gins, major? Loose lips sink ships and all that,' he sniffed.

'I wouldn't concern yourself too much about that. You and I both know there aren't any capital ships docked in Singapore at the moment. But, to be honest, even though our Sandy seems to be getting on rather well with the debonaire Mr Bosanquet, he's not privy to any meaningful intelligence. He doesn't know how much he doesn't know. And if I were to say that to him directly, I'm sure he'd accept the comment with good grace and humour. In any case, I wager the secretary knows a good deal more than Campbell about the way things are going militarily. By all accounts, most of the shipping news is routinely printed in *The Straits Times* anyhow, so I'm not concerned about what he may say to the British officers here tonight, or to anyone else for that matter.'

Even though Wake knew the adjutant to be something of a wet blanket socially, he nevertheless optimistically suggested, 'Why don't you go and join him, David? You might even hit the town together later. I'm sure you can both meet up with some attractive ladies elsewhere whose faces aren't as sad as some of those sitting around here tonight, fanning themselves like swooning maidens.'

Peters offered no reply to the major's ludicrous suggestion before giving a polite nod and sauntering off. He was more than content to simply skulk around the room, picking up only what he wanted to hear from those breathless conversations into which he knew he'd never be invited.

———

A month before the Pyms's arrival, Bosanquet had personally interviewed and finalised all the staffing at Jervois Road. This included two smooth-skinned Tamil houseboys, an experienced cook and, most notably, a youngish-looking amah, who though petite possessed a body that was perfectly formed. What was particularly striking was her glossy black hair cut short like that of a boy. She'd already been employed in the households of several departing civil servants, including the former residents of Jervois Road, and if anything seemed over-qualified for the position. Her proven experience with English-speaking mistresses convinced the secretary she'd be more than capable of attending to all of Georgina's unnecessary needs and capricious desires.

Every one of Tan Quan Neo's applications for placement as an amah came with a letter of recommendation from the rubber tycoon Lee Choon Guan, who like her father, traced his family origins back to Melaka. He'd been a leading figure among the Straits Chinese business community for many years, and besides receiving a vernacular education, he'd also attended the prestigious Raffles Institution on Bras Basah Road. Lee's testimonial vouched for the high moral and economic status of the Tan family within the broader Peranakan community.

Discovering that all the staffing arrangements had been settled prior to her arrival had greatly pleased Lady Celia. She'd urged Bosanquet to make sure the amah had experience in preparing Peranakan cuisine. It helped enormously that her present household was paid for out of an overseas ministerial purse, and its largesse was swiftly disbursed with all the enthusiasm that invariably accompanies the spending of other people's money. It allowed her to employ a *dhobi* to do the laundry, as well as the two Indian–Malay house servants, both of whom were attractively Eurasian. One was quickly trained to be on hand, to graciously perform every menial task short of blowing a cooling breath over her hot cup of tea. Besides the amah, the much-prized Hainanese cook, who had also served the previous occupants, was kept on to manage the kitchen.

The new, well-groomed and rather handsome houseboys both possessed slick-backed hair and teeth whiter than the ivories on her borrowed piano. It was difficult to tell their age, and they'd be the last ones to tell you. Their blemish-free skin endowed them with the slightly effeminate appearance she found alluring in young Eurasian men. Robbie's hand in the selection process was obvious. He often admitted to being attracted to what he termed their *métis Portugais* complexion.

That such an array of highly presentable servants was hired at no personal expense helped temper Celia's barely concealed desire to secure passage back home on the next available tramp steamer bound for Suez. Like her daughter, she longed for engaging female companions in whom to confide her constant misgivings about agreeing to accompany her husband to Singapore. There was really no-one here with whom she shared an affinity, and certainly no-one at this evening's reception, apart from her daughter, who possessed the pouting, rosebud lips and pencil-thin eyebrows favoured by the women in her social milieu in southwest London.

Celia could never be accused of inhabiting a world of ideas. In common with most of the colonial civil service and planters' wives, she preferred to remain ignorant of the jingoistic maelstrom that had developed in the Far East. There were enough problems, she thought, with the scourge of Nazism throughout Europe, which had led to the blitz over London and soon extended to England's major industrial cities in the Midlands.

The most *ghastly* consequence for her had been the indefinite postponement of the grouse-shooting season on her father Lord Alfred Dalrymple's country estate on the Yorkshire moors. She missed the unbridled enthusiasm of the pack of lurchers more than the hunting itself. Her moodiness was not due to any misgivings that such activities ought not continue in time of war, but the fact that almost every one of the regular beaters, including Lord Alfred's trusted ghillie, had wasted no time enlisting in various branches of the armed services.

They doubtless saw greater merit in returning home with a brace of plump Nazis under their belts than a clutch of undersized gamebirds. She pretended to ignore the fact that warfare was likely viewed by experienced hunters as the pinnacle of blood sports.

Lady Celia was nevertheless grateful for the fact that temporarily living in a remote and sparsely industrialised northern county had sheltered her from the smell of cordite, the fires, the rubble and stepping through human carnage among the demolished buildings of inner London. The militaristic ascendency within the Japanese government, which had ultimately led in 1938 to its proclamation of a Greater East Asia Co-Prosperity Sphere, was not a subject of interest to her. Her husband may have mentioned such matters over breakfast, but to her it remained little more than unintelligible officialese. It was among any number of things she dismissed as best left to the men to discuss, along with hounds, horses and hospitality.

Yet it was precisely these geopolitical developments that impinged directly upon the continued existence of her privileged way of life. The proclamation document of the Japanese militarists was in fact nothing short of a policy manifesto designed to reorder Asian society and eliminate all European colonial power and influence in the Far East. This would occur by the enforcement and consolidation of an Imperial Japanese hegemony throughout the region. Once endorsed by their deified emperor, the policy would remain politically sacrosanct forever.

It wasn't as if Celia hadn't heard from her husband that the small enclave of resident Japanese nationals in the colony was not to be trusted. Large-scale internment of those suspected of sedition, however, was discouraged by Whitehall. They believed the profitable receipts from Japanese traders might seriously decline if harsh retaliatory measures were adopted. Nor after reading *The Straits Times* was Celia unaware of the Sultan of Johore's visit to Tokyo, and his recent meeting with Reich Chancellor Hitler in Berlin. She also realised it was no coincidence that over the past few months, the non-commercial activities of the Japanese firm of freelance photographers in Hailam Road, called Nakajima & Co., had come under even closer surveillance by Special Branch. The need for multiple cameras to accompany

234 E. J. JOHNSON

visiting fishermen along the coastline not surprisingly aroused alarm about the true nature of their activities.

Despite being aware of all this talk of sedition by Japanese operatives, and even rumours of Taguchi's possible complicity, her ladyship remained untroubled by the sultan's welcoming gift to her of a pet parrot that squawked in Japanese.

CHAPTER
EIGHTEEN

THE PYMS'S zest for entertaining and their relative informality soon made an invitation to their parties among the most sought-after in the colony. Such functions served to break the monotony of the gin rummy, mahjong and bridge sessions at the club, where female players were expected to indulge in the customary gin and lime juice gimlets before, during and after play. It was as if talk of the very real threat of war seemed to have been permanently banished.

Manning had already conceded that it had been worth travelling the 100 miles at not much more than strolling pace through inhospitable, steamy villages to savour tonight's proceedings. He was greatly entertained observing the comical deportment and status anxieties of all the pinch-faced memsahibs dolled-up in their patterned dinner frocks. To his untutored eye, some of the garments looked as if they'd long ago lost their flounce and had only mothballs for regular company until that evening.

Within minutes of arrival, most of the women had gravitated towards the long rattan settees scattered around the main room. Once seated, they wasted no time in setting to gossip, accompanied by the peal of social laughter which resonated with the unmistakable gusto of those who are seldom entertained. Some had travelled from as far as

Pahang in central Malaya, the wives of tea planters from the cooler climate hill stations in the Cameron Highlands. By and large they were comfortably ensconced in their Tudor Revival cottages and bungalows surrounded by mountain greenery, fruit gardens and even a nine-hole golf course. Tonight, they welcomed the opportunity to interrupt the prolonged social isolation they experienced, living within the confines of their sequestered plantations.

Most of these women had arrived friendless in Malaya and had largely remained so. The Australian officers had never seen so many fans waving in such a relatively confined space. The way they were being used bore no resemblance to the mildly erotic purpose to which they were put in the more traditional forms of oriental theatrical performance.

'I can see what you meant, Bernard, when you talked about the peculiar set of behaviours displayed by English women in the colony, especially among these tallow-faced planters' wives,' Manning felt compelled to comment. 'It seems to me it partly stems from their natural feeling of displacement from the familiar, something I struggle to come to terms with myself. Maybe the ladies' lethargic behaviour is also due to their failure to acclimatise to the tropical environment, as well as the constant threat of disease. Everyone has to worry about contracting malaria. Isn't that what you were saying, Bernard?'

'Yes, you've managed to put your finger on two of the biggest problems they're faced with – idleness and tropical disease. But it's not all bad. While our men have to rely on medication, the ladies at least seem to be getting their regular dose of quinine from all those gin pahits they're swallowing.'

After Manning failed to acknowledge this embarrassingly feeble joke, Wake invaded the silence and continued, 'But seriously, Tom, given the swarms of mosquitoes breeding in the swamps around here, I can well understand why those mems who do succumb to boredom might have reason to seek their medication in the alcohol cabinet. The sun is always over the yardarm well before breakfast in Singapore, so who can blame them for getting in early?'

'That's what I was thinking. Though you can bet your life back home they wouldn't't've indulged in anything stronger than a tired, old sweet sherry before dinner.'

'Yes, and it would've been poured from a dust-laden crystal decanter that spent most of its life standing to attention on the sideboard in a darkened parlour,' joked the major. 'Though it's not that different in Australia, where foreign visitors say the men talk dry and the women drink sweet.'

'Yes, I've heard that comment more than once. Yet I'd be surprised if the arrival of the Pyms in Singapore hasn't had something to do with their bittersweet appearance tonight; it may've thrown them off guard? Did you notice how they couldn't stop craning their necks when Lady Celia swept into the room? She's much more than a novelty for those who don't read the social pages as avidly as Captain Peters apparently does.'

'I must admit I found it difficult to look elsewhere myself, but hopefully I exercised a little more discretion. Even your adjutant was not unaffected by her charms, although typically dismissive, as you'd have come to expect. David seems to be not just socially awkward, but also devoid of what may be termed, the natural human appetites. Certainly not the large ones I had when I was his age.'

'Yes, Dalziel may not have been joking when he said the reason socially reserved and prudish bachelors like Peters probably abstain from sex, is because it could lead to ballroom dancing.'

'Hahaa, perhaps the general's right? David was standing right next to me when Celia passed by, but all he could say upon sighting her ladyship's cleavage was she must have been poured into that dress! Sounded like something his mother might say. I've only seen Celia sipping once from that small cocktail glass she's holding, but he almost described her as a promiscuous *lush*! I couldn't help thinking that this was perhaps his rather offhand way of acknowledging her undeniable capacity for sexual arousal.'

'Yes, you may be on to something there. I can't imagine young Campbell coming out with that sort of comment.'

'Hopefully not! I've coached him about what he should and shouldn't say in tonight's company. David was also brutal when he described, rather sniffingly, some of the men's undignified behaviour in Celia's presence. He likened it to a flock of pigeons fighting over a crust of bread on the pavement. That was a rather apt comparison, though moths attracted to a streetlamp would've been closer to the mark. I told him his analogy lacked the poetic flourish of Shakespeare's description of Cleopatra, which I long ago committed to memory for a school examination: 'Age cannot wither her, nor custom stale her infinite variety: other women cloy the appetites they feed, but she makes hungry where most she satisfies ...'

'That's quite impressive, Bernard! I now see what you meant by natural appetites. I took you for someone more interested in memorising mathematical theorems than quoting the Bard.'

'Well, both are aesthetically pleasing. Though I must say, while it takes a little time to appreciate the beauty in methodically proving a complex equation, when it comes to Lady Celia's physical beauty, the proof is immediate.'

'Your point's well taken. Speaking of appetites, did you notice the way her ladyship nibbled at the hors d'oeuvres?'

'No, should I have?'

'Well, she might not possess the false piety of Chaucer's nun, but she appears to share some of her affectations. I noticed she tasted only morsels of food and scrupulously avoided dropping the tiniest amount by delicately dabbing her lips with a napkin.'

'That's very observant of you, Tom, but why are you telling me all this? I'm well aware your eyesight is perfect.'

'I found it a revealing insight into her character,' he said, indirectly acknowledging the potency of Wake's quotation from Shakespeare.

'By the way, while I already know David's a bit of a sourpuss when it comes to admiring women, I couldn't help but notice *your* ogling the lady's finer points on several occasions,' Manning cheekily remarked.

'Well, I wouldn't put it quite that way, and I certainly wasn't studying her eating habits,' Wake responded.

'If that's the case, then at the very least you must've got a load of some of the sour looks those older women gave her? That's to be expected, I suppose. Honestly, if one were to form the most charitable assessment of their appearance, very few could even be described as interestingly plain. Not one good sort among the whole lot of them!'

'A little unkind, Tom, but quite accurate nonetheless. As I was saying to you earlier, we shouldn't assume their behaviour is not shared by the long-term permanent residents as well. The Malays have a phrase for it – *Tida' apa* – a condition of chronic physical and mental fatigue and episodes of depression. It's a sickness and wasting disease unlike any other. One of the wags at the hospital refers to it as *tidapathy*. Quite amusing, don't you think?'

'Hmmm. That might help explain Molyneux's total lack of any sense of urgency' was Manning's retort.

Without offering any response to his friend's sarcastic remark, Wake amplified what he meant in a more serious tone. 'For what it's worth, Tom, the clinical term for this condition is called neurasthenia. It seems to be as contagious as the common cold and as widespread as malaria, though obviously more difficult than either to shake off. In some ways, it resembles the insidious fungi and bacteria which infect the leaves and the roots of potato plants in cooler countries. Like those poor buggers we passed on the road this morning, neurasthenia's something that'll always find work in this type of climate, I'm afraid.'

Surveying the room once more, both officers recognised various indicators of depressive illness in those ladies with the longest faces. They were all creatures of a transported class system, which had not been entirely successful in imposing its social mores in an environment way beyond the green and pleasant land of England. But neither dwelt upon this psychological phenomenon for too long, pretty sure any derisive comments would be exhaustively provided by the adjutant during their return trip to Mersing.

———

'Jerry *daarling*, over here,' Celia impatiently urged. 'Colonel Manning and his colleagues are finally together in the one spot.'

Despite his failing to respond, she did not press the matter any further. While Pym had moved his head slightly in her direction, Celia knew she would exert more influence once the female guests orbiting around him lost their gravitational pull and started to peel away.

Campbell was rather chuffed at being referred to in the same breath as the three officers whom he'd accompanied this evening. But he was less pleased when Bosanquet took her ladyship aside and announced, not quite *sotto voce*, 'Finally, allow me to personally provide the answer to your earlier question, "Who is that devilishly handsome young man who's arrived unaccompanied, and a little late?" *Alors, le voici* – let me formally introduce you to Lance Bombardier Alexander Campbell. But I already know him as Sandy.'

Robbie then quickly stepped aside in order to practise his charm on the three waiting Australian officers, leaving the present conversation somewhat up in the air. Campbell had remained discomfited by Robbie's provocative remarks and felt more awkward and ill at ease than ever.

'Pay little regard to what Robbie comes out with at times – Lance Bombardier Sandy, is it? He loves being a tease. He has a scathing wit and his words can be either wounding, or rather amusing if taken in small doses. He told me he'd already met you on arrival and found you quite dashing – "possessing a certain boyish charm" is how he put it. I imagine he said your late arrival was a mere bagatelle, or some such phrase?'

Upon hearing this, Campbell still didn't know whether he'd been praised or patronised.

'As I said,' Celia continued, 'don't be greatly put out by what he says; he's always complimenting me on my appearance as well, which I don't mind by the way. But then he tends to overdo it by occasionally calling me a gorgeous *allumeuse,* or even more rudely, *la dame aux belles fesses.'*

'I'm sorry, but I don't know what any of that means, your lady-ship,' Campbell said, more out of politeness than pure innocence. He was pretty sure part of it was the same as gorgeous cockteaser, though the French sounded infinitely more refined than his Australo–English rendering.

'Well, he thinks *I* don't know what he means, but I play along with it and won't be drawn into his addiction to clever word games and kindergarten French. The one exception I made was when I enquired whether his favourite street address in Paris still remained the Rue de Remarque. He was taken aback for a few seconds, but my attempted witticism was so weak he just laughed it off and walked away, visibly unscathed. In London, he has a reputation for being a first-class rotter with exquisite manners, a description that needs no further explanation within *my* circle of friends.'

'I think I can guess what that means, but I might not describe it the same way.'

'I suspect not. You must find it quite odd that despite his sauciness, I still find his presence a welcome distraction.'

'No, I hadn't thought about it.'

She knew from observing her own husband that when a man says he's not thinking about anything, he generally is.

'Apart from the constant threat of bombing, I'm missing London *terribly*, so I'm rather grateful he's duchessing me around this ghastly Singapore whenever he has the time or inclination. I'm treating his flattering attentions as a harmless pastime in which I'm free to indulge – with Jeremy's explicit approval, I hasten to add.'

'I'm also very new to Singapore, so maybe Mr Bosanquet can lighten things up for me too? I'm not that interested in discussing politics or the scary lack of planning for war in Singapore. That's something my senior officers are always going on about.'

'Well, that'll suit Robbie. The only skirmishes he likes to get involved in are with me, and unfortunately, my daughter – although Georgina's current hostilities are more with what to wear in this stifling climate. As you've already discovered, Robbie can say things that are intentionally hurtful or in poor taste, and when it comes to slanderous gossip and political intrigue, he's something of an expert. Another thing to remember – he never apologises for whatever he says or does, no matter how outrageous. I'm sure he'll engage you in a wicked conversation about something or other before long,' she said with an air of foreboding in her voice.

Up close, he found Celia slightly less beautiful than his first sighting of her from the bottom of the steps. The lines on the face of a fading beauty are always difficult to detect from a distance. Nonetheless, his conversational skills remained sorely tested in her presence. He was not having much luck summoning up anything interesting to say that didn't involve the peculiar mating habits of feral soldiers or domesticated livestock. But simply talking to Celia meant he was less unsettled by the secretary's remarks. As for her ladyship? Well, his laconic utterances and stony silences didn't really matter. She was quite used to the inhibiting effect she had upon even the most extrovert of males, so she continued her breezy conversation where she'd left off.

'As you can see, I'm not having much success attracting my husband's attention. Unfortunately, in his eyes, Robbie can do no wrong, even if he disapproves of some of his frequent lapses in propriety.'

Campbell felt that as long as he kept smiling, she would continue the conversation, and despite his noticing the first signs of smile lines at the corners of her mouth, she remained easy on the eye.

'Jerry considers himself broad-minded and claims that his personal disapproval of certain aspects of Robbie's unconventional conduct doesn't have to be expressed as a condemnation. All of it is part and parcel of a gentleman's foibles and passing vanities, he likes to say. Both spent most of their adolescence being told what to do by people other than their parents. Parental absence – and being monitored in the communal bathrooms by leering boarding masters –has its long-term troubling effects, I've since come to realise.'

The more Celia surprisingly revealed about Robbie's character, the greater the level his curiosity rose. She was very obliging in maintaining his interest. 'I used to say, God only knows what they got up to during their college days and half terms together, but I'm equally sure only God knows how to maintain a confidence. It wouldn't surprise me if quite a few members at their club in Piccadilly have been entertained on more than one occasion by exaggerated tales of their misbehaviour upsetting the beaks.'

'I suppose I shouldn't ask, Lady Celia, but what are some of those unconventional things you referred to?'

'Well, yes, you *are* forward in asking, so let me put it this way. Robbie calls himself a libertarian. I don't suppose there are that many of those in the army,' she smiled, looking directly at Campbell, who was more than a little nonplussed.

'Judging by his past conduct, I gather it entails a disinhibited, devil-may-care attitude towards life, an instinctive desire to do – and some-times say – whatever one likes, so long as it's lawful. Although I'm not altogether sure he strictly adheres to *that* requirement.'

'It sounds like what a lot of us in the army would like to get up to, if we weren't so worried about doing it in uniform. Maybe Robbie behaves like any other soldier on the loose – when no-one's lookin', we're all pretty much up for anything.'

'Well, it's not *anything* with me! He obviously believes giving it a fancy name lends an air of respectability and moral legitimacy to activ-ities that might otherwise be considered deliberately risqué.'

Then, further sharpening her claws, she continued, 'How he recon-ciled his former role of administering conventional government regula-tions with his unconventional personal beliefs and conduct, is anyone's guess. I don't know how all that sits comfortably with his so-called libertarianism.'

She also wanted to say that he was racially prejudiced and could be frightfully intolerant and vindictive, especially towards the Asian servants. While she realised the strands of his antagonism were often superficial, she sensed the perverse attitudes ran deep.

'It was rather sweet of you to enquire, but without going into further details, I don't know whether I can express it any more discreetly than that,' she finished off in an airy-fairy sort of manner.

Reflecting upon what she'd said, she decided to curtail the young soldier's growing infatuation. It had slowly dawned upon her that she'd already given him way too much of her time. And, more to the point, she'd unaccountably been more than a trifle gossipy, even slightly waspish in what she'd disclosed about her husband's child-hood friend. She hadn't intended the conversation to stray so much into the personal, and thought, *why didn't I simply say, Robbie can be a bit of a stinker at times, and leave it at that?*

Under the guise of attempting to attract her husband's attention once more, she ended the conversation with a turn of the head that could not have been more abrupt had Campbell broken wind in her presence. Agitatedly running her fingers along her string of opera-length pearls in what appeared to Sandy to have been a family trait, she took a few steps in her husband's direction. Celia would make sure this time he'd finally engage with the patiently waiting Australian guests.

———

The minister was certainly within earshot of his wife's conversation but was possibly distracted, well-primed by the warming effects of his third stengah of the evening. 'Nothing wrong with a glass of water that a dash of whisky won't improve,' he liked to say, unconcerned he might've said it way too often.

Tonight, he insisted on a three-finger nip served neat – soda water was only ever something for the day after. His stengah was served on an ebony-handled silver tray, his glass replenished at increasingly shorter intervals by his white-gloved house servant. Although this servant supported a young family, he was still referred to as *the boy*. Tonight, he appeared to be solely employed in shadowing his bibulous master's every move, pandering to his frequent requests. In fact, at whatever function he attended, Sir Jeremy made sure he was never more than five paces away from a whisky. He liked a drink, and it *wasn't* a Pimm's No. 1 Cup, he would quip, as if anyone needed a reminder.

Having become used to her husband being plied with alcohol in this way at all their at-home functions, Celia understood within a very short time that little could be done to restrain him from attempting to ingratiate himself with every passably attractive female in the room. The longer he drank the more attractive they all became, even the matronly ones who'd turned up tonight with too much foundation caked on.

Celia was obliged to engage in a fair bit of eyeballing to divert the minister from his seamless flow of small talk with some of the more flirtation-deprived females with whom he was holding court. She had long tolerated her husband's addiction to strong drink and weak women but was a little astonished that prising him away wasn't easier this evening, given the elderly composition of the guest list. This task was slightly irritating for her since elsewhere, as a rule, he reacted to her demands more dutifully than those of the chief whip whenever a division was called for in the House of Commons.

Pym's campaigning experience for his Westminster St George's London Borough meant he had become quite adept at working the room, whatever the location or occasion. In common with many other ambitious politicians, he'd trained himself to deftly move away from those with whom he was conversing if he spied someone more attractive or influential unattended. Mastering the art of conviviality while subtly extracting oneself from uncongenial company, saying hello and goodbye in the same handshake, were social strategies he'd long perfected. It was deceptively simple but no less skilful than his practice of joining a private conversation uninvited.

The seemingly concentrated, though fleeting attention he lavished on those in his orbit, only served to reinforce his well-earned reputation for laying on the charm with all the unattached ladies in his parliamentary constituency. This was especially the case on those carefully scheduled occasions when Celia was visiting the Yorkshire grouse moors, touring with her repertory company, had been *called away unexpectedly*, or was otherwise *indisposed*. In each of those circumstances, you could be assured the honourable member would lay it on with a trowel.

His adulterous affairs perhaps failed to rival in number – though exceeded in concealment – those of the first and last Edwardian monarch, the libidinous Dirty Bertie, heir to the throne under Queen Victoria. Consistent with the mores of the socially privileged, Jeremy Pym had also managed to emulate the monarch's sense of duty in refusing to leave his wife despite a loveless marriage. A peculiar facet of this selective amorality made it equally inconceivable to ever contemplate the giving up of a mistress. On either side of his deathbed, it was reported that King Edward VII was attended by his consort, Queen Alexandra, *and* his favourite mistress, Alice Keppel. In fact, the royal prerogative was regularly invoked to set aside the seventh commandment. Forgiveness of sin apparently came easily to those who wielded enough power and influence to secure it until the hereafter.

———

Although she pretended otherwise, Celia desperately wished to be called away – *permanently* – to any posting that offered regular exposure to a range of entertainments patronised by civilised Europeans and conducted in a reasonably temperate climate. More particularly, at this time of year, she longed to slip back into her Harris tweed skirt, ribbed woollen stockings, shooting jacket and the smart feathered hat she wore during the autumn hunting season in West Yorkshire.

She'd recently returned from official trips on what seemed to her to be pointless sightseeing visits by boat to Port Sweetenham, Georgetown and Rangoon. The lashing rain of a tropical storm while on board was not something she ever wanted to experience again. Until this year, her idea of an uncomfortable sea journey had involved nothing more arduous than a bit of a squall and choppy transit on a yacht across the Solent to attend a garden party at Cowes on the Isle of Wight. Her recent travel experience of sleeping in cramped conditions aboard an ageing steamer had done nothing to diminish her antipathy towards the tropics. Not even the bracing sea breeze on deck of an evening could compensate for the tedium of official duties during the sweltering daylight hours. In a week's time, she would again officially accompany her husband, this time to assess the situation in the Crown colony of Hong Kong. At least for this visit, she'd made sure they'd be travelling in a relatively comfortable RAF Catalina flying boat.

On the brighter side, Celia was comforted that her husband's official tenure was never expected to be anything other than temporary, and she was determined to do everything in her power to realise that expectation. In the meantime, it was still reassuring for her to know that she already possessed three of life's most desirable blessings – wealth, talent and beauty. To which she might've added a fourth – the fact that she was English – were it not for the war, which had rendered this a less desirable attribute than her perfect teeth.

With a sense of entitlement by birth always to the forefront of her mind, she decided that evening she would once again inhabit her well-rehearsed identity as the charming society hostess. She would continue to dissemble the unpalatable fact that she was stuck in an increasingly suffocating colonial backwater. Accordingly, she would drown any dispirited feelings by bathing in the self-affirming cool waters of her own narcissism. For Celia, the sometime leading actress, this type of pretence was a role she had sedulously developed into a finely honed, elaborate conceit. At the same time, she knew she was not the only lady at the reception that evening whose smile and outward composure served to conceal a medically untreatable, life-threatening despair.

———

There came a point at which Pym could no longer ignore his wife's entreaties. Once he'd drained his whisky glass, which his boy had obligingly whisked away in a flash, he was free to glad-hand the waiting party of Australian officers. He was the only person they would meet that evening who joined their company already talking.

The handshake Pym decided to adopt was a practised variant of the exuberant Texan habit of hand-pumping, which he'd first encountered at embassy parties in London. Over the years, he'd been introduced to quite a few who hailed from the Lone Star State – they seemed to address both individuals and groups of people, whether they were coming or going, with a democratic, 'Y'all.' Some were all hat and no cattle, while others happily described themselves against interest as cornballs, but every one of them possessed a bone-crushing handshake.

Since their arrival, Manning's party had moved around the rooms surveying the broad array of guests chattering away in unmistakably, gin-soaked voices. Campbell had strayed a little and had to be summoned from a side room where he and the guest pianist were engaged in deep conversation.

'Thank you for the invitation, minister,' Manning said. 'The trip down the east coast was very instructive. Young Lance Bombardier Campbell over there chauffeured us with remarkable ability for someone more used to driving a mob of sheep. He showed a lot of skill in dodging the endless procession of coolies we encountered on that narrow stretch of road. He was what you English might describe as unflappable.'

'Good to see y'all arrived in one piece,' Pym smiled at his own private joke. 'In a few weeks' time, they tell me those same roads will be all churned up and probably impassable. You'd be better off travelling with those bullock drivers you were no doubt introduced to on the way, when you least expected it. Nothing like it if you want a very slow unofficial escort, is there?' he said, with all the sincerity of someone who'd never actually experienced what they'd attempted to describe.

'Yes, I believe that's exactly what we encountered today between Kota Tinggi and Johore Baru.'

'Anyone would think they own the road,' Pym said with an unconvincing tone of disapproval.

'Yes, we came to the same conclusion.'

'It's not really a laughing matter, but if those drivers selfishly refuse to give way, and look Chinese, the governor is fond of naming them On Lee Mee. Not bad as far as lame jokes go, I suppose, but in the governor's case, they tend to go nowhere – about as fresh as last year's news.'

Within a matter of moments, the others might have attested to Pym's own expertise in eliciting forced hilarity. Perhaps in the interests of conviviality, or simply not to be outdone by the governor, Pym proceeded to make an equally tasteless joke himself. It involved the examination of testicles, a procedure by which a suspected Chinese insurgent called Wan Hung Lo was conclusively identified. Pym never seemed to tire of retelling this schoolboy joke, but the same could not be said for those who'd heard it more than once. There were never any of the thigh-slapping, side-splitting reactions he might otherwise have expected.

Hearing this for the first time, Peters recognised more than a tinge of the untroubled acceptance by privileged Europeans of their claim to racial superiority – wrapped up in the so-called civilising mission for which the British Raj provided the colonial model. Pym reinforced the perception of his unconscious arrogance by abruptly snapping his fingers in the direction of his boy, who was standing to attention beside a drinks tray. This behaviour was in stark contrast to the relaxed level of civility he extended towards the visiting Antipodeans.

'Gentlemen, may I offer you a whisky? Only the very best I might add – not the run-of-the-mill White Horse anyone can purchase over the counter at Robinson's.'

Pym liked to break the ice with a surfeit of information. 'The previous occupant here was Donald Travers from the Surveyor's Office. He managed to secure possibly the last case of The Macallan to be dispatched to Singapore before the blasted outbreak of war in Europe put an end to regular shipments. Thank God it's still served at the Fullerton! Mind you, even there, if supplies get any worse, they'll soon be cutting it with a lot more water. On New Year's Eve, I'll be surprised if we'll still be able to "tak a right gude-willie waught, for auld lang syne,"' he said with a huge smile. 'Instead, we'll probably all be drinking arrack along with the sepoys.'

The small party was amazed at hearing someone run off at the mouth for so long without appearing to draw breath. It couldn't have been solely due to the number of stengahs he'd consumed, they all thought.

At first, everyone politely shook their head at the offer of a whisky, save the major, who immediately broke ranks and made a point of attesting to the spirit's medicinal and legendary restorative qualities. The acceptance was sealed when he came out with something that perhaps no native Scot would ever say: 'Reet … joost a wee dram or two afore ye go.'

While Wake's eyes lit up at the generous pour, he told Pym he'd had a pleasurable experience touring the best distilleries in the Highlands during his medical residency in Edinburgh – researching the provenance, as he phrased it, of his preferred single malts. He and the minister clinked glasses, first fingers raised in an ironically light-hearted toast to the doctor's plausible, if largely unscientific reasoning about the health benefits that would accrue. At the sight of this time-honoured ritual, Manning belatedly decided that he too would join in the toast with a robust clink of his own. Campbell indicated his preference by drawing his glass of gin to his chest, while Peters remained silent and aloof, cynically observing that to see, smell and taste whisky was presumably not enough – you had to hear it as well?

Following General Dalziel's declining to attend the reception, Pym had personally extended the invitation to Lieutenant Colonel Manning, known to be a distinguished battalion commander with the 8th Division, 2nd AIF. Pym had heard he was a no-nonsense sort of chap, and for that reason alone, someone well worth sounding out on the current military situation. But the minister's delay in personally welcoming the Australians suggested the sounding-out was hardly treated as a matter of urgency.

He'd been told that the colonel's military bearing was so bolt upright that subordinates joked he must have been issued with a special set of cast-iron underwear. It wasn't surprising he'd been given the nickname Starchy by his battalion cohorts either, since by all accounts, even the pleats of his shorts looked as if they'd been starched and pressed. It conformed with his personal reputation for being as straight as a die. Pym would soon discover that all the rumours turned out to be true, and the colonel's opinions were no less rigid. Knowledge of this parody of the colonel's demeanour had more than prepared him for the vice-like handshake the colonel dutifully administered when they'd exchanged introductions. Employing the Texan howdy-pardner grip had proven a wise decision.

For all his wariness around officers from the Dominions, Pym preferred the notoriously bluff opinions of an Australian colonel any day, over those of the atrophied hierarchy of the British High Command in Malaya with whom he had to deal on a regular basis. It was their unacceptable tardiness in prosecuting war readiness that had prompted Churchill to pluck Pym from the political sidelines and dispatch him to Singapore to give the service chiefs a little nudge along. He was afforded Cabinet status but without portfolio, a special minister.

Pym was aware that the Australian contingent was slotted to play a subordinate role to that of the much larger British and Indian forces. However, the brief history of their infantry's engagements in conflicts since the Boer War, indicated the Australian forces would not be lacking in either effectiveness or valour on the battlefield. He was also aware of the fact that unlike the situation in Britain, the Australian government didn't have a Foreign Office to impose the bureaucratic secrecy and obfuscation with which he'd had to contend since his arrival. This meeting with Manning would also hopefully provide some useful background before the Pyms' scheduled visit to Canberra, Sydney and Melbourne in late November.

Before taking Manning and the other officers aside for the confidential tête-à-tête, Pym ushered the doctor's assistant away from the front of the spacious drawing room where the jazz band was warming up for the long night ahead. In common with the hotel orchestras at the other regular dinner dance venues, the Seaview and Raffles, the musicians were mostly European-looking. Accordingly, their repertoire did not noticeably depart from the popular American jazz-swing dance music of the era, and as is the nature of certain people on these occasions, a few of the sprightlier couples were already practising their dip-and-sway dance moves. They were jockeying for prime positions in front of the musicians, waiting to publicly display their razzamatazz in performing the latest variation of the foxtrot and jitterbug. A few of the female dancers were not averse to showing a bit of leg in their swirling, even if those appendages were often less attractive than those supporting the Bechstein.

'Listen, lance bombardier,' the minister enthused. 'If you prefer a less formal turnout than what you've been landed with this evening, it might be a jolly good idea to take in the cabaret with the Goan and Filipino musicians at the New World Amusement Park. I've dropped in a couple of times myself. I wouldn't call their act particularly *new*, but there's also Asian-style vaudeville troupes, plenty of Tiger beer stands and striptease performers that I dare say you might consider a novelty. If you time it right, you may even get to see Hasnah and Moona, the touring Ronggeng Sisters and their erotic dancing.'

'I can't say I've seen much of that type of entertainment in Dalby, sir.'

'That's understandable. They haven't visited Timbuktu either, I'm told. For a young off-duty soldier like yourself, it's just the bee's knees, as they say. It's located around Serangoon Road in the Hindu quarter. If you're not in any recognisable sort of uniform, there'll be no recriminations if you're tempted, shall we say, to get involved in a bit of late-night high jinks,' he added with transparent insincerity.

'Why would a gentleman like yourself want to be entertained at that type of place, with someone like Lady Celia at home?'

Pym was surprised by the naivety of the question and chose not to respond directly. 'Look, I decided to go there to become familiar with the local culture, to see things for myself. I can assure you it's quite an experience. The amusement park's more than a brisk stroll away, but there's any number of rickshaw-wallahs waiting downstairs alongside the portico who'll take you there at the drop of a hat. Or you can ring through in the foyer for a motor taxi, if you prefer?'

'Thank you, sir,' he replied, momentarily forgetful of any of the minister's array of titles. 'It sounds like you expect me to get up to mischief?'

'No, not at all. Your commanding officer's already spoken highly of your skill behind the wheel, so I don't think he'd be overly pleased if for any reason you're unable to fulfil that same duty for the return trip.'

'Well, I know that place is off limits to officers, and I didn't have time to go there this afternoon, so tonight might be as good a time as any to have a close look at those taxi girls, hey? As things have turned out, the major's already given me an unofficial ticket-of-leave for the rest of the evening. I think he's more worried about what I'll say to some of your guests if I stay here too long, than wherever I end up for the rest of the night.'

'That's splendid. Allow me to check once more with the major before you go. I'm sure there won't be a problem,' he said while walking away. Pym seemed unconcerned by the prospect of Campbell mixing with the military personnel, much less the Peranakan trading magnates chatting nearby. Nor would he be likely to seek company at the far end of the room, where small cliques of long-term Japanese residents stood apart, huddled in whispers.

Each group adhered to the unspoken observance of the colony's rigid social demarcations. No amount of casual intermingling among the ethnically diverse guests could disguise an underlying tension – and the fact that all the groupings would demonstrate an increasing preference for self-segregation – as the evening wore on.

Now free to wander around the rooms, Campbell unexpectedly

found himself amid a heated exchange of angry voices. What had started as barbed words and simple jostling looked like developing into a physical altercation of potentially more serious consequences.

'What's goin' on?' he innocently said, before several closed fists threatened to answer his enquiry. Without hesitation, he grabbed two of the lightly framed antagonists by the scruff of the neck, his strength sufficient to lift them up and place them both down at a distance that discouraged further aggression. There was only a hushed reaction from the nearby onlookers to his display of physical prowess, seemingly happy enough that order had been restored and the music had remained uninterrupted.

The Japanese invited to the evening ran commercial activities associated with import and export businesses. The majority did not trade in espionage, but in drapery and haberdashery, enterprises that were centred around the Echigoya company's shophouses in Middle Road. The fact that they invariably switched from Japanese to English as soon as Europeans approached did little to allay the unfavourable impression their muffled words conveyed.

Anti-Japanese sentiment among the local Chinese importers of fabric, predominantly the Cantonese in South Bridge Road, made for extremely chilly relationships in sections of the room. It hadn't taken long for the simmering ill will to reach boiling point that evening. Pym hadn't been around long enough to understand the degree of mutual enmity. He was certainly aware there'd been concerted pressure on the British to impose an anti-Japanese boycott of cheap imports. However, unlike the Japanese boat-owning fishermen, surveyors and photographers, the long-term Japanese traders and entrepreneurs in cotton piece goods and textiles were not yet under regular police surveillance.

Compared to the transient British and Japanese residents and sojourners, the locally born Straits Chinese had longstanding and extensive commercial ties throughout the region. Accordingly, they were not in the business of downplaying the alarming threat posed by the inexorable advance of the Japanese Imperial Army from Manchuria to the littoral regions of the Chinese mainland, and now further south into French Indochina. Reports of atrocities committed by the Japanese in Nanking were widespread and highly credible, and if tonight they spoke to one another more often in Hokkien, Teochew and Cantonese than in English, this was likely *all* they were talking about.

The old Empire upon which the sun never set, and to which they'd long sworn fealty, was now being challenged by one whose sun, the Hinomaru, was conspicuously on the rise. They feared this might be the end of benign colonial rule, which would irreversibly destroy their entrenched commercial power and transform their settled way of life forever.

CHAPTER
NINETEEN

'COME ALONG GENTLEMEN, we need a little privacy,' the minister said, at last stirred into action, unaware of the brief altercation at the far end of the room. 'I've told young Campbell you wouldn't have any objection if he toddles off to one of our amusement parks later on. I've recommended the place to go if he's at a loose end,' he said, with a touch of condescension.

'That's fine, minister,' said Wake. 'I've already granted him that dispensation. He's earned a bit of time off duty after his chauffeuring today and might relish kicking up his heels in town. He's aware we've got some important matters to discuss, and the fewer involved the better.'

'Yes, less noise, more privacy, that's a good idea,' the colonel said. 'There seem to be a few Japs invited here tonight, and I bet they've all got big ears. I also don't fancy competing with that drummer either, once he really starts thumping the tom-toms.'

'I don't know about the travelling musicians, but Special Branch has recently started to keep closer tabs on the Japanese. This evening, contrary to my wishes, we've had to invite a handful of the long-term residents, who'd lose face if we neglected to do so.'

'That's a wise decision, minister. I imagine the only reason for your inviting *us* to visit Singapore at this juncture is to enable a frank

exchange of views on the imminent prospect of war with their compatriots – not to provide us with the opportunity to practise our twostep
on your dance floor.'

'Hahaa! That's true, there's no skirting around the central issue, if
you'll pardon my jest. Please, call me *Jerry*,' Pym continued, lightly
placing his hand on the colonel's shoulder in what was meant to be a
tentative sign of comradeship. For Manning, it was an uninvited touch
of familiarity that had yet to be earned.

'Well, that suits us … *Jerry*,' Manning cheerily replied, though not
altogether at ease with being invited to use a word that closely rivalled
kraut as a derogatory term for those serving in the German
Wehrmacht.

'I'm sure Bernard and my adjutant David Peters will both be glad
to dispense with formality. You're probably aware that we colonials
have a well-deserved reputation for not standing on ceremony, nor
taking ourselves too seriously – our former prime minister Billy
Hughes being a notable exception,' he added facetiously.

Captain Peters was a little more reluctant to accept the notion of
informality despite the unofficial duties involved in the visit. Although
not unsympathetic to a certain levelling in society, there was no possibility of his ever addressing his colonel as Tom, even at a relaxed social
gathering.

'That's excellent,' Pym said. 'Let's get a wiggle on, and take in one
of the glorious sunsets best seen from the verandah around this time of
day, shall we?' He half-closed the shuttered doors behind him as they
all moved outside. Peters couldn't help thinking that there was no
need to enjoy such a view from the verandah – the encroaching sunset
of Empire was everywhere on display, inside.

Lance Bombardier Campbell was unsurprised that he'd been
discreetly sidelined from joining the officers on the verandah. He had
only to look at the single chevron on his sleeve, compared to the officers' pips, to confirm that his place was unquestionably elsewhere. He
was comforted by the thought he'd at least be rid of the irritating presence of Captain Peters. Pym had steered him towards the younger
women in the room, though they were few and far between. Both had
noticed Robbie Bosanquet roaming around, looking for somewhere to

dispose of what Pym believed to be his secretary's specially prepared bowl of pudding.

The air was cooler on this more sheltered side of the residence, the eaves still dripping after the last burst of rain. The verandah's massive white stone pillars were set off by clusters of fuchsia-coloured bougainvillea flowers, and the delicate fronds of a Persian silk tree. Both species had been pruned and trained to climb only so far from the wide garden beds beneath. This allowed the fragrant star jasmine that threaded its way through a broad trellis fastened to the wall to grow in profusion in the afternoon sun.

'I'll come to the point straight away gentlemen,' Pym said as he handed out enormous cigars to his guests. Peters alone declined the offer. Once they were finally lit, they all puffed away, frequently taking them out to inspect their dimensions in quiet appreciation. Pym had offered the type of fat Habanas normally favoured by successful deal-making robber barons, banking magnates and gaudily dressed impresarios. The evening's cigars were even more savoured as they were a parting gift from Churchill himself, which Pym was not backward in advertising. 'The prime minister included a bulbous humidor commensurate in relative size and shape to its donor,' he joked. This ceremonial inspection certainly delayed his coming to the point straight away.

'Since my arrival in Singapore, I've been at odds with Governor Townshend, and increasingly the Far East General Officer in Command, Air Chief Marshal Sir Henry Molyneux. Both have refused to admit any personal shortcomings in relation to planning for the civil and military defence of Malaya,' he openly confessed. It was as though the wafting smoke, once lifted, had served as both a sufficient and necessary curtain-raiser to what he was about to say.

'That doesn't come as any great surprise to me, Jerry,' Manning broke in early.

'Yes, word spreads quickly, but lately everything's become much worse. The recent appointment of Lieutenant General Martindale as the army's own general officer in command Malaya, has unfortunately now made it a threesome of competing decision-makers with whom I'm obliged to cooperate. The trouble is, in varying degrees, all three are ditherers. *None* of them, especially Sir Henry, strikes me as the sort of forthright leader that the present situation demands and the PM expects, quite frankly.'

'I believe neither of those two senior military officers has any recent field command experience, though I'm aware of their commendable bravery while on active service *almost a quarter of a century ago.*' Manning cuttingly remarked. The conversation was interrupted while the minister gave his houseboy a welcome reprieve from duties on the verandah. His final task had been to place a large ashtray, cigar piercer, matches, a half-full decanter and extra whisky glasses on an oversized rattan table he'd drawn close to the balustrade.

Pym had been conscious of the fact that deep within the Australian psyche was a certain distaste for authority, a peculiar aversion to the thought of being bossed around by descendants of their erstwhile British gaolers. He realised they often failed to appreciate the difference between someone diligently performing a service, and a display of servility. He suspected this stemmed from the innate desire of the emancipated and the free-born currency lad alike, to have the stain of convict heritage permanently erased. Pym therefore thought it preferable to dismiss his boy early, rather than be thought of as someone who insisted upon being plied with alcohol by his native servant all evening. Topping up his own and the officers' glasses with another generous pour, Pym had become suitably fortified and ready to fire off another salvo of complaint.

'Those three gentlemen, together with the other armed services chiefs, I tell you, Tom, have effectively thwarted my attempts to set up an integrated War Council with a Far East military governor at its head. They scoffed at the suggestion. I told them Winston considers this recasting of operations to be a priority and believes there cannot be any further procrastination. My job is to monitor the situation and advise the War Cabinet in Westminster as to what is required to make cooperation to achieve this objective more effective.'

'How did they react to that idea, Jerry? And if you'll excuse me for saying so, your monitoring and advisory role seems to lack the neces-sary teeth to change anything?'

'Well, to be honest, progress is rather crab-like, and the PM's wish for change will remain just that – wishful thinking – unless there's unanimity of purpose following a bit of compromise. Regrettably, as you've implied, I have received somewhat vague instructions with respect to making any enforceable recommendations directly concerning military matters or strategic planning. However, my appointment alone tells you that Winston is not entirely convinced that Sir Henry has the Far East situation sufficiently in hand.'

Manning nodded a few times, and his taking longer than normal puffs on his cigar reflected his growing consternation. Wake and Captain Peters hovered nearby but implicitly understood it wouldn't be long before Manning adopted a more adversarial approach towards the minister's bleatings. If previous conduct were any indication, it would be a full-frontal indomitable attack, undeterred by the prospect of glancing verbal blows in retaliation.

'One of the intractable problems, of course,' Pym continued, 'is the governor himself. He's a jealous protector of his vice-regal status and the administrative power that attaches to the office. He hasn't said as much, but I believe he sees me as a direct threat to his position. As you are aware, not only is he the King's representative in Singapore and the other Straits Settlements, but he also acts as High Commissioner of both the Federated and Unfederated States of Malaya.'

If he knew I was fully aware of all this, why labour the point, Manning thought.

'Townshend clearly resents someone in my official capacity being foisted upon him from Westminster and possibly subverting the almost complete administrative autonomy he has enjoyed for years. He sees himself as a Victorian-era Viceroy, done up to the nines, who insists on being addressed as Your Excellency, even when Celia and I are invited to his private luncheons. Rather than being accepted as trusted friends, it's as if he believes we ought to feel graced by his vice-regal presence. This expectation also seems to apply on other occasions that neither of us can avoid attending at the same time, in our official capacities?'

Manning already understood the conundrum and didn't waste any time gauging the direction in which he'd steer the conversation. He was in no need of further and better particulars. 'Yes, I grant you this is a fundamental handicap in turning the present military situation around, Jerry,' he confidently weighed in. 'Yet, for all the governor's real or implied executive powers in civil matters, any crucial military decision-making is essentially up to the GOC and the separate chiefs of the armed services acting in situ, as I understand it. It's not so much Townshend, but the chiefs of the armed services who've lost their way. Might that be the situation?'

'Yes, I'm afraid you're largely right,' the minister replied with a noticeable reluctance in his voice.

'And I'd imagine those very same officers are ultimately accountable to the general staff at the War Office in London. Isn't that the sorry predicament you've flown into?'

'Unfortunately, that's also a significant stumbling block. You're probably aware there are plans to mount an offensive operation over the Siamese border, code-named Matador, should the Japanese make an unmistakably aggressive advance towards Siam or Malaya. However, neither Sir Henry nor General Martindale seem to have much enthusiasm for discussing these contingency plans before the operation being fully approved by the War Office. Perhaps they fear they lack the authority to even implement the strategy without receiving London's prior imprimatur?'

'Good God,' declared the colonel, 'if that's the case, it confirms my preference for field commanders on the ground having the power to direct operations immediately. I doubt whether Rommel ever sought advice on tactics for his Africa Korps from that little *gefreiter* in Berlin?'

And speaking as though it were Dalziel himself doing the talking, he added, 'Nothing's changed. It seems there's never any shortage of half-pay, senior officers still fighting their previous wars in retirement. We're certainly not unaware of the Matador proposal, but my fear is it might be on a par with the policy surrounding the Munich agreement, which demonstrated no appetite for direct confrontation with the Führer. In hindsight, that appeasement policy was clearly based on an overoptimistic, naive appraisal of his bellicose intentions.'

'Beyond doubt, Tom. A similar imbroglio surrounds the administration's inability to recruit a decent labour force for civil defence purposes. The hiring of native labourers at a reasonable hourly rate is something the Exchequer and the Colonial Office have consistently obstructed. They obviously see the pressing need for defence expenditure over here but claim they can't afford it! They insist that diverting the workforce in this way would put a huge dent in receipts from our lucrative tin and rubber exports.'

'They can't *afford* it. The argument against greater expenditure on defensive measures cannot withstand intelligent scrutiny. That must be the reason why there were *no* fortifications to speak of around that Causeway area?'

'Yes, I'd like to pretend the defensive barriers are well-concealed, but it turns out you're right again. I can see you fully appreciate my dilemma. Nevertheless, despite recognising all the impediments to interservice cooperation, and the paltry sum set aside to train and enlarge the local volunteer defence forces, I lack the authority to implement the radical changes required. I'd like to have been given the same powers those European plenipotentiaries exercised earlier this century.'

'That may be the case,' said Manning, 'but diplomacy can only go so far.'

'Yes. It didn't seem to have much effect on the Kaiser's timetable, did it? I think you should also know that Sir Henry has privately expressed his personal dismay at the lack of security intelligence backup he's getting from London. Apparently, our naval radio operatives seem to be tracking Japanese shipping movements effectively, but there's next to nothing being done in relation to aerial reconnaissance of their troop and air force concentrations.'

'That's not good news, Jerry. Early warning around the mobilisation of their infantry is of critical importance, and as for our *own* air force capability? Well, … I'll come to that in a minute.'

At the same time, Manning gave his adjutant a withering side glance. This had the desired effect of deterring Peters from adding his own tuppence worth by way of an opinion, *before* being expressly invited to do so. Major Wake all the while looked uncomfortable puffing half-heartedly on his cigar. He missed the dried-out nicotine taste of his pipe, even when unlit. He said nothing other than emitting the occasional grunt to indicate he was still alive and probably listening. He knew where the conversation was headed. Wake's reluctance to go in full bore was not a characteristic that Manning noticeably shared.

'My current apprehension,' Pym resumed, 'springs from previous experience. You might recall I resigned from Cabinet a few years ago – in October '38 to be exact.'

'Yes, your reputation's definitely preceded you,' Manning said through a broad smile.

'That decision followed most of my colleagues' obstinate refusal to jettison the policy of appeasement. They fell for the Nazi leader's Big Lie – that colossal deception in Munich. I'd already foreseen Hitler's continued military aggression beyond his reclaiming the Sudetenland. My stance has since been totally vindicated.'

'Yes, and that's to your eternal credit,' Manning responded. 'But as it's turned out, Chamberlain's policy of maintaining the peace at least gave your government some breathing space for rearmament, before the Nazi invasion of Poland eleven months later?'

'Yes, I guess that was something of a bonus.'

'But it pains me to admit, Jerry, that when it comes to our handling of the Japanese, we've acted little differently to Chamberlain. Until recently, we've been selling the Japs pig-iron out of Port Kembla. There's even been talk of a secret deal to dissuade or at least constrain their military leaders from further aggressive acts in the Far East. Like Adolf Hitler's gradual ascendancy in the Reichstag, civilian government in Japan has succumbed to the military ambition of General Hideki Tojo. It wasn't surprising to see the Japs fall in with the Führer and il Duce last September. The position we've adopted towards the Japs is clearly another form of appeasement inviting a similar calamitous outcome, however politicians might choose to dress it up.'

'Well, Tom. I can tell you that unfortunately, I remain one of only a handful of dissenting voices among the many who don't want to openly admit the similarities. Half the Foreign Office seems to believe Hitler's claim to the Sudetenland is legitimate – they even gave it an obscure name – referring to him as an irredentist, a once-was-mine, always-mine justification for his subjugation of the Czechs.'

'What a woeful line of reasoning. That type of moral and political weakness simply gives succour to the blatant aggression of dictatorial regimes, wherever they seize power. That's why it's good to have an envoy to Singapore of your standing at this crucial juncture, Jerry. We all know you're someone who recognises bare-faced aggression when he sees it and won't quail when under attack from the apologists and fence-sitters popping up all over the place.'

'Thank you, Tom. Even though I don't go around boastfully saying, I told you so, it's a matter of record that I'd forewarned Cabinet that Hitler's favourite victims would be the unprepared, the neutrals and especially the advocates of indifference or laissez-faire. And there were plenty of those sitting around the Cabinet table in the autumn of '38, I can assure you.'

'And not just in Westminster, I can assure you, Jerry.'

'As I said, I don't want to make a song and dance about it but look where sticking to that policy failure has landed us today. The Foreign Office has finally realised the folly of conflating a prolonged armistice with changeless peace. One doesn't need a crystal ball to realise we're revisiting the same sort of thing in the Far East.'

'We're at one with you there. As I mentioned, General Dalziel and I are hopeful that your presence will finally turn things round and maybe bring some sorely needed political heft to policy deliberations – give the service chiefs a bit of a kick up the backside, if you like.'

Pym made no attempt to respond directly to this comment, and perhaps out of a sense of false modesty preferred to change the focus of the conversation. He reached for The Macallan and topped up all the glasses once more, save the one abstention, who was left chafing at the bit – a silent participant in a dry argument, his muted frustrations as slow-burning as the cigars.

––––––––

After a short break to sample the hors-d'oeuvres, Pym's conversation became less terse and more anecdotal. 'You're no doubt aware of Sir

Henry's previous background,' he said, swallowing a *soon kueh* dumpling. 'He's turned sixty-three only recently and unexpectedly called out of retirement from his east African diplomatic posting. I'd welcome your opinion on the way he should be handling things,' Pym rounded off in a surprisingly chipper fashion.

This was exactly the type of open invitation the colonel was waiting for, and he soon jumped in, all guns ablaze. 'I'm not all that interested in his past experience or his somewhat advanced age,' Manning said, ashing his cigar and then moistening his lips with the tip of his tongue. 'While I've no real quarrel with the man personally, I'm unconvinced about his suitability for a role that demands proven experience in military tactics, and what I like to call soldier management. He might've flown those Sopwith Camel biplanes with distinction during the last war, but that's no substitute for recent infantry field command. I realise he's only been here since last November, but it took only a few briefings this March for Charles to label him an absolute model of indecisiveness. He said he was irresolute to a fault, and someone who appeared to keep counsel exclusively with his own fears. He even went so far as to say, there are only two perfectly useless things in the world – one is an appendix, and the other is Sir Henry Molyneux.'

Pym tried hard to mask his amusement at what was said, however, he thought the criticisms might've sounded less vitriolic had Dr Wake expressed them.

'On the next occasion we met, his face was permanently creased with pessimism, a beleaguered individual if ever I saw one. The last thing needed at this time, Jerry, is a Far East commander who seems eminently qualified to oversee the ceremonial management of decline he apparently performed in the Kenya Colony, but precious little else.'

'If I may roughly paraphrase what Sir Henry came out with, he claimed we can't afford to upset the Siamese desire for neutrality ... and the American embargo on exports of oil and scrap metal to Japan is starting to bite, but you know, gentlemen, we're unable to properly mobilise when we're several battalions short. And, can I tell you what he finally said to General Dalziel, after lowering his voice to project reassurance? "In the end, Charles, I believe we're pretty safe here in Singapore." I tell you, the way Molyneux droned on, if he were a clergyman the pews would have emptied well before the first plate had been passed around.'

Major Wake had trouble stifling a laugh and thought it an appropriate point at which to break his silence. He sought to pick up on one of the reasons for *not* maintaining the status quo, without resorting to the colonel's more provocative assertions. 'I believe, Jerry, the embargo on the procurement of American goods has indeed started to bite, as Sir Henry suggested. How could it be otherwise, when I've heard they furnish around three-quarters of Japan's oil imports? However, common sense tells me that being denied access to American markets will more likely encourage the military elements in the Japanese cabinet to increase their sabre-rattling, rather than lead to an outbreak of pacifism.'

'That may be all well and good, Bernard,' Pym replied, 'but we can't do much more on the diplomatic side of things. Our Washington embassy is constantly on Roosevelt's back to persuade Congress to abandon its policy of isolationism. Let's not forget, they set up the League of Nations but then showed no interest in joining it. Until they see America's business and territorial interests being adversely affected in the Pacific to an *intolerable* degree, they'll probably leave Malaya in the lurch. Economic institutions like their Federal Reserve, Wall Street banking and brokerage firms, along with the so-called barons of industry, hold enormous sway in their polity. The American ambassador in London once said to me with some justification, that *business* is America's *only* business.'

'Or else they continue their business of coming in late, claim the glory of victory, recast dismembered states in their own economic interests, and withdraw into splendid isolation as they did after Versailles.' Manning ruefully added.

'Yes, but we'll always need them, Tom – they're indispensable. With their economic power and military reach, they'll remain a bulwark of democracy in the world for as long as I can foresee. I've got the feeling, gentlemen, that the real reason for American equivocation runs much deeper. It's not just the pervasive influence of Charles Lindberg's opposition to anti-German sentiment; it's got a lot more to do with the continued existence of colonial rule across Asia and the growing impetus for self-determination by historically disenfranchised peoples. Such a policy stance is likely to be at odds with that of Churchill's closest advisors, and perhaps his own world view. It's not an unreasonable assumption that the bitter lessons of America's War of Independence from British colonial rule still resonate strongly in their collective political memory.'

'I accept the political realities operating in America, Jerry,' the colonel interrupted, 'but Bernard's observation remains pertinent. We all know the Japanese Imperial Diet is dominated by a war-mongering clique. I'm therefore aghast that both Churchill *and* Roosevelt seem to have downgraded the direct Japanese threat to both the British and America's strategic and commercial interests in the Western Pacific, as well as the increased danger to Australia's own security. The Japs would have recognised this weakness long ago. I know Menzies, the UAP and the Labor Party leader John Curtin have been sounding alarm bells about this dire situation for quite a while. Whoever wins the next election in Australia, you can bet your life any new AIF battalions will *not* be sailing towards the Middle East!'

The special minister let him run.

'The Japanese have been emboldened by decades of successful military engagements in the region. Like the major, I believe their hostility will only increase as a result of their territorial ambitions being held in check for the first time by the American trade embargo. With respect to effective *British* action, it seems Molyneux is keeping his diary closed until he arranges a suitable date for an appointment with inglorious defeat. It's probably kept in the same drawer where he's filed away a blank, single sheet of paper entitled, Strategic Plans for the Defence of Malaya: Awaiting Further Investigation. When we first raised this issue with him a couple of months ago, rather than dwelling upon the likelihood of a Japanese invasion, Sir Henry seemed preoccupied with domestic surveillance. He spent most of the time lauding the efforts of the police Special Branch in arresting a Japanese spy called Shinozaki.'

'Not so fast, Tom. I for one have been quite impressed with the police crackdown on suspected foreign operatives.'

'Yes, and I wouldn't deprive them of the praise they're rightfully getting for those arrests. They're also to be commended for identifying and clamping down on communist cells, agents provocateurs and the like. But this type of operation is only a sideshow. Its importance pales in significance when compared to the real danger of underpreparing for a full-scale Japanese mobilisation. Until recently, I believe local Japanese nationals have been able to come and go as they please all over Singapore. They would have spotted the strategic weaknesses I've drawn attention to, rendering the current situation no longer ripe for sedition, as it's already occurred.'

Captain Peters's forced reserve was sorely tested as he appeared to know more than any of those present about the operation of activists and subversive cadres throughout the Far East. Much to Manning's silent approval, his adjutant continued to bite his bottom lip.

'I agree, Tom. This lax stance is entirely a product of everyone's misplaced reliance upon the enemy falling for the illusion of a fortress Singapore. The Foreign Office even has a so-called Singapore Strategy, an out-dated doctrine of war based on the presumption that if we're invaded, the fortress can comfortably hang on for months while awaiting the arrival of the Royal Navy.'

'And pigs might fly as well!' said Wake, unable to maintain his usual reticence.

'I'm afraid you're right, major, but unfortunately the strategy remains the cornerstone of British Far East policy, and there's sweet Fanny Adams either you or I can do about it!'

'Incredible!' said Manning. 'If this island is still considered to be an impregnable fortress, then I'm a monkey's uncle. It's essentially a convenient political contrivance based on a doctrinal error, if you like. The very concept is an anachronism derived from feudal times. The Causeway's the only thing resembling a drawbridge over a moat, but it's forty miles away and can't be lifted by chains. And, while I'm at it, why can't we even talk to civilians about a possible siege? Isn't that the *very thing* a fortress was designed to withstand? The mere mention of the word, I'm told, has been officially proscribed. Talk about turning a blind eye. Motoring down from Woodlands and Mandai this morning was as carefree as I imagine it would be in the Lake District at this time of year. Even coming across a couple of foxholes, surrounded by coils of Dannert wire laid either end of the Causeway, would've been mildly reassuring.'

Pym took a deep breath and cleared his throat as if he were about to defend the indefensible, but his prolonged silence confirmed he lacked the conviction to go through with it. Either way, Manning now had the bit between his teeth.

'Charles tells me Martindale delights in referring to this place as the Gibraltar of the Orient. It's as if the mere recital of this phrase acted as some sort of iron-clad guarantee of security. At least he isn't as deluded as Molyneux, who said those little yellow men wouldn't dare attack this bastion of the British Empire. I couldn't get over it!'

'I believe I've already indicated my disappointment with Sir Henry's complacency,' Pym tetchily interjected.

'Yes, but will it take an enemy bombing raid over his headquarters at the naval dockyard to finally encourage him to change tack?'

At this juncture, Pym excused himself, promising to bring back a fresh bottle of The Macallan. He was hoping his brief absence might quell the dispiriting effect of Manning's cutting observations. He'd been unsurprised but intrigued all the same by the candidness of what he'd heard. After he returned, he remained largely expressionless, except for the occasional *hmmm* – his way of communicating dissent without moving his lips.

———

'I respect your view about this invidious situation, Tom, but as I've already outlined, it's ultimately a question of unifying the decision-making process of which, as you've already recognised, Sir Henry Molyneux forms only one part.'

'Actions speak louder than words, and last a lot longer,' said Manning before adding, 'I can't help feeling Sir Henry, Martindale and the service chiefs have all lost that old fighting spirit that played out on the fields of Agincourt. We need to be as determined to give the Japs as strong a taste of cold steel as the English king gave to the dauphin's forces. Hal's resolve on that Saint Crispin's Day victory was also reflected in the valour shown centuries later by regiments of the British Raj on the Northwest Frontier, David's reminded me.'

'Yes, Tom, your courageous Light Horse Brigade at Beersheba, and our 21st lancers in Khartoum, are fine examples of the bravery and derring-do displayed by cavalry from a bygone era. But let's not over-sentimentalise things, shall we. Neither of those regiments had to face the advance of seasoned infantry over tropical terrain, supported by armoured vehicles and a modern air force. There's no room for imag-ined heroes to emerge, as the French recently discovered, when your troops are being strafed by the Luftwaffe. There's a world of difference between bravery and rashness. Military history tells us,' said Pym, applying his own ironic slant on an imagined glorious past, 'that for every victorious Duke of Wellington historians might point to, there's always a half-dozen erratic Lord Raglans hiding up their sleeves.'

Manning thought there was some merit in Pym's recommendation of restraint. After all, the ill-fated decision to launch the Dardanelles campaign in 1915 had provided a more recent ignominious precedent for a misconceived military engagement. In this, Churchill himself, as First Lord of the Admiralty, had played a not insignificant role. Colonel Manning remembered a colleague in the citizens' militia sardonically calling the needless sacrifice of thousands of troops under the overall direction of British commanders, as an act of pomicide. Therefore, he reflected, who could blame Churchill, of all people, for his hesitancy in allowing his generals to give a pre-emptive order to invade Siam.

For his part, Pym was inclined to think that when it came to imperial nostalgia, perhaps high-ranking officers from the Dominions had become more British than the British themselves? But in the end, he was forced to recognise that Australia was only forty years old as a federation of former colonial states and, compared to grown-up nations, was still in short pants.

And what was that ranting about King Henry? Does he want to equip the infantry with the Excalibur swords and longbows of a Merrie England? The only steel that troops are tasting in the Middle East is boiling hot and meted out from the muzzle of a tank. Pym regretted he didn't come out and say all this and more. He'd invited someone to speak his mind, and that's exactly what was happening. He excused himself once more from their company to answer the call of nature. But it wasn't only his bladder that sought relief. He promised to return, after directing the servants to bring more food to the verandah during his temporary absence. Normally he would have found this an ideal opportunity to vanish *permanently* from uncongenial company.

———

Among the many admirable qualities that Manning brought to his arguments, legal or military, concision was not one of them. His experience in advocacy enabled him to sense when the accumulated force of his contentions was gradually wearing down an adversary. For him, relentless interrogation was second nature. Once Pym returned, Manning quickly decided to continue in the same vein as he left off, as though re-engaging in a lengthy cross-examination after a brief adjournment in proceedings.

'As I was saying, Jeremy, all this vacillation is rationally indefensible to any soldier worth his salt. The armed forces chiefs need to stop their internal bickering, or to be less polite – their straight-out *whingeing.*'

Without looking at the colonel, Pym poured out the whisky less generously and glowered as though bracing himself against a further bout of criticism.

'I see it this way,' Manning resumed. 'You may claim to be at loggerheads with them, but more crucially, they appear to be at odds with *each other*. They seem more interested in trying not to encroach upon each other's bailiwick, than forging a joint initiative.'

'Well, with the greatest respect, colonel, that's precisely what I've been tasked to overcome, and I believe I said that at the outset,' Pym replied with surliness.

'I'm not denying your own efforts,' Manning continued, 'but the turnaround in their lack of resolve needs to happen soon, if not yesterday. It's beyond me how Martindale can endure their constant havering. As one of those ancient Greek philosophers probably never said, *the only man to learn from history is the Unknown Soldier.* And no-one ever talks about the spoils of defeat, as far as I know.'

Pym was confused by the comments and their relevance to the discussion.

'They ought to roll up their sleeves and make do with what they've got,' Manning pressed on. 'This type of response has a certain nobility in its simplicity. I wouldn't be relying on the Japanese fear of American naval intervention or the promise of infantry reinforcements that may never arrive. Good workmen never quarrel with their tools is a time-honoured maxim, which for my money still holds true.'

'I'm broadly in agreement with your recognition of the vacillating leadership group we have over here at the moment,' Pym eventually replied. 'What you've highlighted unfortunately provides the corner-stone of the military orthodoxy to which a broad cross-section of our political leaders stubbornly adheres. My attempts to convince Cabinet it should abandon the policy of appeasement have taught me this: it's sometimes useless to reason with those who arrive at steadfast opinions that were never acquired through the process of reasoning in the first place.'

'That's well put, Jeremy.'

'A case in point is the recent briefing I've received for the conference of Far East ambassadors, which I'm about to attend in Hong Kong. The consensus seems to believe that the Japanese won't *dare* attack the Crown colony. This defies reason. Yet my repeated warnings about the colony's chronic unpreparedness and inability to repel a full-scale seaborne invasion by the Japanese, based only a stone's throw away from Singapore, are deemed to be unduly alarmist! I've already expressed my view on the current state of disrepair of our aerodromes, and the lack of readiness of our air force across Malaya. Sir Henry described this whole schemozzle as nothing more serious than a bit of a sticky wicket. Presumably the situation will eventually be ironed out with the heavy roller. In other words, it's just a spot of bother we'll fix when we get the contraption out of the shed, so to speak. That's something I thought I might toss around at the Cricket Club next time I visit.

'Hahaa! An excellent suggestion ... so long as it's not a full toss, something even those retired players at the club will be able to comfortably put away.'

'That's a well-bowled yorker, Tom. I'd say middle peg, though if Robbie were batting, he'd claim it was a *chinaman*. Whenever I seek to raise the urgency of this matter with Molyneux he says very little and defers to the advice of Air Vice-Marshal Stretton. This gentleman will then abruptly curtail the conversation with a comment that goes something like, I admit it's a bit of a rum show, but steady on old chap, you of all people understand it ultimately comes down to wartime budgetary restraints signed off by Churchill's Cabinet. And aren't you part of Churchill's Cabinet?'

'Let me say, Jerry, I sympathise with your predicament, but he does have a point. Japanese intelligence would know that Britain has been financially crippled by the repayment of its war loans to America, and its current shouldering of the armaments burden to repel the Nazis in North Africa. It's understandable that the War Office and Treasury in London are placing much less importance on Singapore's needs compared to those of the military operations already on foot in the Mediterranean. This means we can't afford to wait for reinforcements. In failing to adjust their thinking to this reality, I believe that both Stretton and Molyneux are completely misguided. With that in mind,' Manning added, 'if either disagrees with my assessment, you should ask them whether the Luftwaffe or the Wehrmacht's panzer divisions sought any beg pardons as they launched their surprise attacks by circumventing the supposedly impregnable Maginot Line?'

Pym was uncharacteristically reserved for a politician used to holding the floor and responded with no more than his familiar, guttural *hmmm*, accompanied by an ever-deepening frown.

'In the few briefings to which we've been invited,' Manning continued, 'I've also noticed that Sir Henry inevitably allows the service chiefs to take over. Molyneux may be a man of very few words, but it soon struck me they were enough to express the full range of his ideas.'

The minister offered a wry smile in response and, having witnessed Bradman's celebrated Test innings at the Oval a few years before, realised Australians didn't like to muck around *or* mince their words. With the Don at the crease, it was sometimes a rare and unappetising duck in the second over, but more often than not a century, followed by a deliciously glazed *canard à l'orange* at lunch on the first day.

CHAPTER
TWENTY

PYM WOULD HAVE SHOWN GREATER appreciation for Manning's portentous advice had he himself not been so notably unsuccessful in convincing Malaya Command and the Far East GOC to get off their backsides. The colonel, of course, was not unjustified in arriving at his rather uncharitable character assessment of Sir Henry Molyneux. He'd heard rumours it was most probably this retired aviator who'd disparaged the 2,300 soldiers from the 2/26th and 2/29th battalions that had recently disembarked from the Dutch steamer *Marnix van Sint Aldegonde*. They'd been immediately branded as the latest sweepings from Australian gaols. They might've been a bit rough round the edges and short on intensive training, but so were the 1st AIF volunteers who landed at Gallipoli, Manning would have submitted in their defence. To denigrate them in this way implied they were mostly a bunch of lags, no better than those nineteenth-century felons transported to the Australian colonies from those prison hulks anchored in the Thames.

'I wasn't overly surprised to learn,' the colonel resumed, 'that no matter how often the service chiefs meet, they invariably fail to agree on a concerted plan of action. I hear they're not short of ideas, but almost all of them are bad.'

'If that's the case, and your informant was not exaggerating, then I fail to see what the air chief marshal or anyone else can do about it at this late stage,' Pym replied, clearly exasperated.

'They might well heed some of the things I've mentioned so far this evening, for a start. Remind me, David ... what was that high-falutin' term you used to describe the frame of mind General Dalziel was alluding to? Pusi ...'

'*Pusillanimous,*' the adjutant replied with his usual alacrity in these matters.

'I wouldn't necessarily put it that way, Captain Peters,' the minister caustically interjected. 'It's more like pussyfooting around, indecisiveness, rather than any inherent lack of fortitude that your word selection seems to suggest. It smacks of dishonour and even cowardice. You need to give Sir Henry some credit. His principal concern seems to be the negative effect it would have on morale if large-scale defensive preparations were seen to be suddenly put in place by the military. He believes such action would inevitably set in train a siege mentality, akin to a virulent infection that would quickly take hold throughout the entire civilian population.'

Pym's last statement was clearly directed towards Dr Wake, whose attention to the proceedings had noticeably wandered off.

'This analogy has some merit, I would've thought, major? I might add however, that Sir Henry's opinion around this question of morale is not shared by General Martindale.'

Wake offered no answer.

'Well, that's something, I suppose?' Manning cautiously responded on his behalf.

'In my experience, the thing about morale is this: it will quickly fall apart if it's shown that military leaders have failed to take adequate steps to counter a surprise attack that's not surprising at all, because it's been entirely predictable. I don't claim any searing insight into the likelihood of further Japanese aggression ... it's as clear as the nose on your face. The evidence pointing to an imminent invasion is incontrovertible, not merely circumstantial. A failure to provide basic countermeasures, such as fixed defences and anti-tank weapons, will be viewed as an obvious act of negligence – rather more serious than allowing the sale of a bottle of ginger beer with a snail inside.'

No-one knew what to make of the strange comparison Manning had drawn, which their silence confirmed. Pym was quick to regain the floor, attempting to reassert what he still believed to be his pivotal role in the discussion.

'I trust I'm not evading the issue, gentlemen, but I'll share with you something one of the departing civil servants said to me upon my arrival. The sentiment has apparently enjoyed widespread currency here for ages. He said the exponent of any idea that, however well-known elsewhere, is new to Singapore, has first to get across three fences; and they are marked respectively, it can't be done, it has never been done before, and now is not the time to do it. I didn't think much of it at the time and bid him safe passage. I thought his criticisms may have simply issued from a deep dislike of his office superiors for perhaps ignoring his day-to-day recommendations. On the other hand, his bitterness may have stemmed from the fact that he was unable to bring his wife to Singapore, whereas I'd insisted Celia accompany me before I accepted my appointment.'

'Well, with the greatest respect, what your returning servant of Empire said to you on that occasion sums up precisely what I've being saying to you all evening. Though I'm sure you'll agree, it's a pity I couldn't't've said it in fewer words.' Pym was certainly aware the colonel did not subscribe to the adage that brevity is the soul of wit, but was otherwise unmoved by this rare instance of self-deprecation.

'It's clear to me,' Manning went on, 'the type of inertia that civil servant spoke about is most pronounced nowadays around the non-provision of bomb shelters or blast walls to protect the civilian population. But there we are. Unfortunately, the need for these cannot be just waved away, like that repatriated official. We made a brief tour this afternoon around Beach Road, Connaught Drive and the Esplanade. While those thoroughfares rival some of the grandest boulevards of Europe, I couldn't help feeling that it's all rather deceptive. Despite the frequent downpours of rain, the atmosphere was highly combustible and beneath everything lay the smell of complacency and slow decay. It filled the air as much as the fragrance of the frangipani.'

As a sign of his frustration, Pym topped up his own glass but conspicuously failed to replenish the others. Pretending to ignore this petulance, the colonel was unrelenting in his criticisms.

'We also noticed,' said the minister, 'that while Singapore has many impressive stone buildings, there are remarkably few statues in the colony. Apart from the Cenotaph, the most prominent pedestals appear to have been reserved for colonial administrators and men of commerce. There's not so much as a bust of a warrior anywhere; no trace of anyone's involvement in warfare, or even a distant reminder of it, apart from the large number of troops at Fort Canning and those big guns pointing out to sea.'

'That's quite observant of you, colonel, but you must remember, people like Stanford Raffles and Governor Coleman operated when the only threat to British naval superiority was the Dutch East Indies' fleet, which had been effectively neutralised by Napoleon's invasion of the Netherlands. Apart from the mutinous German sympathisers at the outbreak of the Great War, Singapore has enjoyed well over a century of relative peace. And the prosperity we've enjoyed is due in no small measure to the commercial acumen of successive governors ... not the armed forces.'

'Granted, but that's not the situation now with the navy's capability severely stretched,' Manning replied. 'I was appalled by the relative paucity of military fortifications anywhere to the north of the island. Precisely nothing offering real deterrence appears to have been constructed there. It wouldn't take that long to build some decent tank traps, surely?'

'I 've no idea how Brigadier Cadwallader currently fits into the scheme of things,' Pym replied, now clearly incensed by the extent to which the conversation had degenerated into sustained accusation. 'But I suspect it's beyond the gift of any civil administrator or ambitious warrior for that matter, to turn things round. One matter we seem to be in fierce agreement about, colonel, is that decision-making concerning civil defence appears to be a low priority. And, if it does exist, it seems to take longer than receiving a credible cable on the war's progress from Herr Goebbels in Berlin.'

Manning's look remained downcast, but his log of criticisms was far from exhausted. 'I think you've gathered General Dalziel didn't take long to have a few run-ins with *all* the service chiefs, including the air vice-marshal, around these very concerns. He was particularly disappointed to learn that anti-tank defences have not been put in place on the north-west roadways, apparently because the local planters didn't take too kindly to their private property being adversely affected? For God's sake, who are they to be interfering with strategic military decisions, was the gist of what he said. He believes supporting these fossilised arguments about losing markets and not upsetting civilian morale are about as useful as pockets in a pair of long johns – and I'm of the same opinion.'

At this point, Pym felt that if at any stage he'd had a tenuous control of the conversation, it had by now completely slipped away. While he appeared unruffled, he certainly hadn't anticipated the degree of rancour that lay at the heart of everything Manning had said.

'To be fair, minister, on another occasion,' Manning added in a more conciliatory tone, 'I heard General Dalziel point out that before Sir Henry's arrival, he'd already been dealt a losing hand from a stacked deck of cards. By that he meant that the air chief marshal would've only realised the under-resourced situation he'd inherited well *after* his posting here last October.'

'I'm pleased you've finally found something positive to say, colonel.'

Manning took that slightly acerbic comment on the chin and came back stronger. 'I don't know if you've ever played rugby, minister, but I believe in accepting the appointment, Sir Henry's been thrown what's known among players as a hospital pass.'

'Not rugger, but I received a blue when selected for the First VIII at Oxford.'

'Congratulations – then you'll certainly know how difficult it is going against the tide!'

By the tone of Manning's voice, Pym could've been excused for thinking the colonel considered him someone who rested on his oars, the weakest member of a coxless four.

'It must've been quite distressing for Sir Henry to learn he's been denied the funds to secure the latest fighters needed to protect multiple airfields,' Manning continued. 'I've recently spoken to Wing

Commander Curly Davis at the RAAF base at Kota Bahru, and he said they weren't joking when his pilots referred to the old Brewster Buffaloes as flying coffins.'

'Yes, I've heard that invidious comparison as well. I can't do much about aircraft procurement, but rest assured I'll put your views to the air vice-marshal at the earliest opportunity.'

Manning paused only long enough to nod his acknowledgement of Pym's unconvincing promise, before continuing to twist the knife. 'As for those Hawker Hurricanes soon arriving in crates from Britain, so they tell me ... well, that name may turn out to be another ironic misnomer. If you set aside our official propaganda, their operational success against the Messerschmitts over the Channel indicates they can barely whip up a stiff breeze. They're not in the same class as the Spitfire, but they'll have to do in the present circumstances, won't they?'

In the absence of any further comment by the minister, who by now seemed content to take a back seat, the harangue became even more trenchant.

'There's no doubt Air Vice-Marshal Stretton had already faced difficulties getting his hands on any new fighter planes. If it were otherwise, there'd be no insistence that artillery units with Bofors guns remain stationed around airfields across Malaya to protect the few squadrons we do have. Am I right about this as well?'

'Yes, I'm not going to deny the bleeding obvious.'

'Well, that brings me to another point. You've said there were worries about undermining the morale of the local population. To our way of thinking, that's a specious argument for doing nothing. The type of morale *we're* most concerned about is the declining morale of the Australian field artillery units. They've been training as part of the 22nd Brigade in jungle areas in central Johore since late March. There are only so many times they can be ordered to service the guns or practise military raids in the heat, to pass the time of day.'

'That may be the situation, but you know I can't do anything about the deployment of the armed forces.'

'Yes, I know, but this issue remains one of our major concerns. If chronic boredom and lack of purpose were desirable qualities, I would've arranged for my men to become honorary members of the Singapore Cricket Club.'

'That's a little unkind, colonel,' said Pym, 'though I must admit several of the members there look like they might derive as much pleasure from a drawn test as an Australian XI's unexpected batting collapse.'

'Precisely. I don't know whether General Dalziel has pressed the matter, but fortunately it's Australian government policy that no division under the control of an Australian commander is to be broken up by Malaya Command without his say so.'

'Well, that's probably the reason you've been held back to defend Johore,' said Pym. 'Surely, not being stationed further north and spared significant casualties is also a morale booster?'

'That's true up to a point, but most of our troops were not long out of school when they enlisted in droves after the fall of France. They signed up thinking they were reinforcements for the 6th Division and headed for action in the Middle East like the original Anzacs. Their lack of real action since arriving here makes them feel like garrison troops, condemned to endless parade drills and marching on the spot.'

'I'll tell you once more, minister, the decision to deploy our mobile field artillery around poorly defended aerodromes is a regular source of discontent among our officers. If an attack occurs, it won't only be the pilots who'll be scrambling.'

'Well, colonel, maybe those officers should take a leaf out of your book and stop their whingeing,' replied the minister, a gentle scowl indicating he had clearly taken umbrage at a number, if not the entirety of Manning's corrosive remarks.

'I don't believe it's a matter of whingeing about things at all,' Manning dryly answered, seemingly unfazed by Pym's newly discovered tetchiness. 'Both General Dalziel and I believe the field regiments should be concentrated where the enemy's most likely to launch a land-based assault on Singapore. And that's to the north-west of Johore Bahru, well beyond the Causeway. Our battalions in eastern Johore have been compass reading, laying mines, crossing rivers at night and having mock attacks and reconnaissance practice in the jungle near Jemaluang for several weeks. But none of this has apparently been replicated by those British-led battalions in the more vulnerable north-west.'

'I appreciate your telling me all this, but I'll repeat – it's not part of my role to recommend the deployment of those British battalions, nor am I an apologist for the unfortunate deficiencies of our air force. It's not what I'm here to do. Correct me if I'm wrong, but it's also beyond the power of Major General Dalziel to interfere with the GOC's decisions.'

'Unfortunately, you're correct. But the general's not going to fall in forever with the prevailing assumptions as to the best strategic location for all our currently dispersed forces, if I may dignify their deployment in this way.'

———

Pym was ropeable with Manning's endless string of criticisms but realised it was too late to effectively muzzle him. What annoyed him most was the thinly veiled depiction of his own role in the current planning fiasco as befitting that of a lapdog. But rather than advancing a contrasting and equally partisan view, the minister maintained his sangfroid – that stiff-upper-lip Englishness for which his compatriots were renowned.

'And, added to that,' the colonel resumed, 'apart from having little say in the governor's civil defence arrangements, neither Sir Henry nor General Martindale exercise any authority whatsoever over the navy. In any event, where's the value in building the Far East's most expensive graving dock if it's flat out welcoming the Royal Navy only once in a blue moon? The interminable delay in its construction has been a blight on strategic planning for maritime war readiness since its inception.'

Manning's opinion was stated as though it was something upon which no reasonably intelligent person could possibly differ. Then, adding the finishing touch to what he considered his unassailable arguments, the colonel said forcefully, 'It's still not clear to us which outfit is running the show over here in Malaya. We'd like more appreciation of the opinions of those sweating away in the jungle in their slouch hats, than communiqués from those chinless civil servants strutting around Whitehall in their homburgs.'

'Jolly good … that's settled then,' said the minister with a snippiness in his voice that effectively foreclosed any further discussion of the matter. 'It would seem to me that we're *all* under no illusions as to the seriousness of the external threat to our security.' He gave one of those pained, insincere smiles that end almost before they begin. After anxiously looking around for his boy, Pym concluded the proceedings by adding, 'I'll keep you informed gentlemen, in due course, of any steps I've taken to overcome the impediments we've all recognised and thoroughly discussed this evening.'

He had absolutely no intention of doing anything of the sort.

With those totally disingenuous words, Pym shepherded the officers back into the main reception room where the jazz musicians were now starting to hit their straps. Before wandering off once more to the lavatory, he'd paused to introduce the men to other guests, who were all obliged to raise their voices to be heard above the rising cacophony on the dance floor. It didn't really matter as no amount of pointless small talk, which was now mercifully inaudible, could lighten the mood of despondency that had descended upon the Australian officers after the minister's departure.

CHAPTER
TWENTY-ONE

'I COULD SEE where all that was going to end up twenty minutes ago,' the colonel huffed before leading his colleagues further away from the annoyingly cheerful Latin rhythms that were interrupting his train of thought. It struck him that there was something about watching couples happily dancing that seemed sadly out of place. Or, maybe because of the mood he was in, he missed his wife's company, recalling her floral skirt flaring out as he swept her around the dance floor years ago at the Trocadero in George Street, Sydney.

'Nothing was settled at all, gentlemen,' he said despondently. 'Pym managed to trot out all the familiar platitudes I've come to expect from civilians in his position. His smarmy, *please call me Jerry* air of familiarity was simply part of the affected charm that comes naturally to most politicians.' Manning was now surer than ever that political life was an occupation where honesty and personal integrity were routinely traded at a deep discount.

'Bugger it,' he said. 'I guess that's that! I thought a bit of plain-speaking would've been welcomed. But seemingly, all I've managed to do is to put him further offside by repeating some of our longstanding grievances.'

'Yes, but at least he heard them from you, and not General Dalziel. Charles might've been a lot briefer, but certainly way less civil.'

'All the same, Bernard, I don't seem to have achieved anything positive by travelling all this way in the interests of civility. It's turned out to be just another elaborate social gathering, on this occasion orchestrated by a pompous ladies' man, a manicured dandy and a fading socialite dripping with jewellery. Perhaps that's exactly what Charles suspected when he declined the invitation in the first place.'

'I imagine so. Pym seemed to be quite taken aback when you chose to use a bit of sharp language. He clearly bristled at being assailed by – what did you call them – *your undisclosed interrogatories*?' From then on, his initial display of ebullience started to noticeably wane.'

'I can't say I took much notice of his demeanour, Bernard, though I admit my tone of voice could've been unhelpful. My honest intention was to forcefully argue for the truth, not win some sort of debating competition. Perhaps I came across a little too truculent?'

'I don't want to sound overly critical,' Wake said, clearing his throat, 'but yes, Tom, you *were* a little longwinded and overbearing at times, as if attempting to play him at his own game. I thought you got to the crux of the matter on several occasions, but perhaps its constant reiteration wasn't all that necessary. Your repeated warnings about the chronic unpreparedness for war might've had greater effect if you'd simply said our deepest fears should not be communicated in polite whispers, and battles are not won by issuing Quakers with a uniform. Something along those lines and left it at that. Your opinions might've hit home earlier had they not sounded like well-rehearsed courtroom pleadings.'

'That's quite observant, Bernard. I always value your objective viewpoint. But, if I repeated myself, it's because I imagined he'd been quite used to having his bottom routinely thrashed at his public school, and any verbal sting I administered was probably the best way to make him sit up uncomfortably and take notice. However, his failure to concede very few personal shortcomings in discharging his *own* role would suggest I wasn't that effective in forensically examining him at all.'

'I'd say he wasn't expecting to be put through the wringer at his own function. You certainly managed to get his dander up. Perhaps in your examination you sounded a little too cross,' he couldn't resist saying, trying to make light of the situation.

'To tell the truth, Bernard, I didn't imagine he'd be tickled pink with everything I said, but I expected him to be a bit more assertive in rebutting my arguments. After all, wasn't he someone who'd made quite a name for himself, blowing his own trumpet, you could say, by fearlessly opposing the appeasers in Chamberlain's cabinet? Despite that, Dalziel still has reservations about his aptitude for political life. There are many like Pym, he said, who quite like the idea of becoming a member of the mother of parliaments, but who quickly reveal themselves to be politically inept and end up warming the backbenches. And I don't think he'd learnt much from all the cricketing analogies he was rather fond of. It wouldn't be far from the truth to call him a wrong 'un. Which reminds me, speaking of cricketing terms, I'd almost forgotten what Dalziel let slip – that despite landing a prize catch in marrying the glamorous Celia Dalrymple, he wouldn't be surprised if Pym batted for the other side.'

Wake allowed himself a half-smothered smile before Manning went on talking. 'As I've said, all I seem to have achieved has been to put him on notice at the dispatch box, so to speak, much as any opposition member in Westminster might do on the floor of the house. You heard him, he even indicated he would table his response to my express warnings, *in due course.* That empty phrase allows him to indefinitely delay addressing any of the matters I've raised.'

'He certainly gave me the impression he understood the consequences of inaction and accepted your highly persuasive analysis of the current situation,' Wake said. 'Had it been otherwise, I'm sure being one of those rare individuals who's paid to hear himself talk, he would've tried to bluster his way out of it. I've never encountered a politician who doesn't like to think overly well of themselves, and Jeremy Pym would appear to be no exception. Yet I was still left with the feeling he's genuinely disillusioned by what he's been confronted with since his arrival.'

'He may indeed be frustrated by the task,' Manning replied, 'but surely he has the prime minister's ear?'

'That's undeniable, but Churchill has a lot on his plate at the moment. Pym's likely been thrust into a position where he's been forced into being a reluctant apologist for the poor decisions of those more highly placed in the scheme of things. And I'm sure he's struggling to come to terms with the fact that his whole mission might be ultimately seen as a failure. I suppose it's excusable if he was a little touchy and may have taken your criticisms personally.'

'As usual, Bernard, you're way too magnanimous, but I take your point. He was sent here to be Churchill's eyes and ears in *all* of Britain's Far East spheres of influence, not exclusively focused on Singapore. He at least seems to be aware of the widespread shortage of whisky supplies at the moment.'

'Yes, he was drinking like there was no tomorrow. But I was more interested in what he left unsaid than his lukewarm acceptance of your judgment and opinions.'

'That may be so. Although he was certainly critical of the indecision of the local troika, if I may label them as such. He expressed no determination to mount a significant challenge to their cloth-eared resistance to uncomfortable ideas. Repeated tut-tutting in disapproval is a poor substitute for decisive action. Situation hopeless, but not serious, seems to be the prevailing attitude.'

'You've been rather quiet, David,' said the colonel, cocking his head to one side. 'Not so much as a squeak? I dare say you've an opinion on what's been discussed.' And, for the sake of amusement, he added, 'Come on, captain, don't be coy – or should I say, *pusillanimous*?'

'As a matter of fact, colonel, I do,' he replied, announcing the seriousness of what was to follow by slowly removing his spectacles and giving them a brisk polish on his jacket's lapels. No matter how long he rubbed, there was never any risk those glasses would turn out to be rose-coloured.

'Like the major, I was put off as much by Pym's general demeanour as by his ill-disguised fence-sitting. Even that shady character Wally Leffler said at this late stage you can't lay an each-way bet with him on the likelihood of war – it's odds on. He claims jokingly that the Japs come from a winning stable, have recent form, lightweight jockeys, and aren't carrying lead in their saddles – that's reserved solely for ammunition! And, speaking of horse flesh – Pym was a bit too full of himself for my liking. What I'd call a show pony. He said he didn't like to say, I told you so, but that can't be right because he said it *twice*.'

'Yes, I picked that up as well.'

'I don't know whether you also noticed, colonel, but he was a little unsteady on his feet and appeared glassy-eyed? He's probably not the only chap here tonight who likes to hit the bottle, though no-one else had a servant at hand to ask whether sir would like a top-up. By the time he finally got around to seeing us, he already seemed half-cut, as I believe seasoned drinkers choose to describe it. That might have been attractive to those powdered matrons who were swooning in his presence, but I found him utterly charmless.'

'Don't hold back, David, tell us what you *really* think,' Manning couldn't resist saying. He remained unsure whether his adjutant was also having a subtle dig at the amount of whisky both he and the major had consumed.

'I kept asking myself, what was his purpose in seeking your counsel in the first place if he was powerless to effect any change? He seemed unaware of the nationalist sentiment that's taken root right across the Far East, which along with the Japanese aggression might make the collapse of European colonial rule somewhat inevitable.'

'Yes, please go on,' Manning replied, knowing full well that Peters was only warming up.

'Despite all the huffing and puffing, he seemed to be going to great lengths to say practically nothing of any significance – though I thought he did *that* very well. I realise he brings with him a reputation as an unflinching operator within the Tory Cabinet, but I feel he's been comprehensively out-gunned over here. For all his supposed political clout in Westminster, his influence over the service chiefs in Singapore has proven to be as insipid as his jokes. He's obviously turned out to be a bit of a dud, a well-credentialled lackey, not the astute and experienced diplomat the situation requires. Maybe it's the heat?'

Encouraged by the fact that both Wake and Manning were smiling broadly, he went on. 'It may be drawing a long bow, colonel, but this vacuum in collective decision-making is possibly due to the fact that none of those senior officers wants to end up being singled out as a scapegoat. This will assuredly be someone's fate, should a Japanese invasion ultimately lead to the fall of Singapore. I imagine that the service chiefs might take some comfort in the fact that since biblical times, history has rarely recorded the word scapegoat being used in the plural.'

'That's fair comment, David,' said Manning, 'unless you exclude the persecution of the Jewish tribes, way beyond the biblical era. It's not just for the killing of the Christ, but collectively they always seem to cop the blame for all types of perceived deceptions and unscrupulous financial transactions, even in today's society.'

'Yes, reports from Europe of life under the Third Reich seem to confirm what you've just said. But to get back to the point, I cannot see how the service chiefs can hope to escape the ignominy of such a disastrous outcome as the possible Japanese occupation of Malaya. This will be their fate if they're all found to have been sitting on their hands for months, if not years.'

'I agree. Perhaps General Martindale will bear the brunt of it? But he's unlikely to fall on his sword, is he? That's something his Japanese counterpart would no doubt literally perform, if he found himself in a similar humiliating situation. It's well-known that the Japanese have a spiritual addiction to ritual suicide. I believe it's called *seppuku*, part of their military cult of *bushidō*? At the moment, the service chiefs are not so much acting like samurai warriors as behaving like a bunch of peevish school prefects, intent on denying any one of their peers the opportunity to become head boy. But it's a little more serious than that of course; they appear to be sleep-walking into disaster and taking us along with them.'

'I agree with your analysis entirely, David, and can see your personal dislike of Pym has not stopped you from apportioning the greater measure of blame for the present situation to his superiors. While I was a little sceptical at first, I think the major's onto something as well. Perhaps our ruddy-faced minister has become infected by the widespread torpor you've previously identified, Bernard?'

'Yes, since my arrival, I've noticed a certain listlessness that's ingrained almost everywhere. A type of mental sclerosis may have slowly set in – allied to that curious form of neurasthenia I've already referred to?'

'If that's the case, then it's surely a condition from which the senior British officers, and the ineffectual envoy with whom we've been dealing, could've scarcely remained immune.' Manning's stern pronouncements had now reached the stage where nodding agreement was the only advisable reaction.

'It's almost as if those senior officers view the running of Malaya command in much the same way the *tuans* probably conduct their affairs at the Tanglin Club, only a mile or so up the road. Can't you imagine it gentlemen? The committee-men passing the port around at the end of a meal, exchanging the same old anecdotes, ensconced in their very own members-only fortress. Collectively, I feel they'd be as useful in battle as that Society of Friends you mentioned earlier, Bernard. If the Japs get beyond the Causeway, they won't be carrying a polite letter of introduction, humbly submitting a proposal for club membership in the hope of enjoying a spot of tennis in the late afternoons.'

The Australians were left with nothing more to say to one another but did not intend to allow Pym to put a complete dampener on the evening. Joining Campbell once more, they soon set about mingling with those same middle-ranked officers and wearisome civil servants for whom the pall of tidapathy had long since become an accepted facet of life.

CHAPTER
TWENTY-TWO

WAKE HAD no interest in feeding his despondency over the outcome of the briefing with Pym. He quickly decided to make a beeline for Lady Celia, whom he'd spotted unattended for the first time that evening. He took a moment to adjust his coat-tails and breathed in heavily, hoping to revive memories of the chivalrous charm of a much younger doctor in Edinburgh. In those fanciful days, he'd believed he simply had to curl-the-mo before confidently approaching an attractive female.

Realising his medical assistant might be feeling a bit like a shag on a rock among such an elderly array of guests, before departing he said: 'Why don't you try your chances again with Georgina over there? She looks as if she's trying to get out of being lumbered all evening with the minister's secretary.'

Campbell dutifully obliged and strode purposefully into their company.

Lady Celia had already alerted Campbell to Bosanquet's reputation as a rather louche character, very entertaining but notoriously secretive when it came to his libertarian pastimes and relationships. This had made him even more appealing to someone like Campbell who, since being excluded from the officers' discussions on the verandah, had found himself in the company of unexciting middle-aged army officers and disaffected planters' wives. His opinions on most matters, however topical, were afforded little weight, and he noticed how their voices seemed to fall away whenever he strolled by, threatening to engage them in conversation.

In the welcome absence of his superiors, he decided to spice up the small talk he'd had to restrict himself to up to now, with his own candid observations on the port city. He started to recount his recent experiences in the less salubrious locations he'd visited, but in deference to Georgina's presence, certain details were discreetly abridged.

Georgina initially feigned interest in his novelty effect, but in fact, he'd said nothing much of interest to her at all. As was her mother's custom, she soon began fidgeting with her pearls while looking around the room. Whether planned or not, within a few minutes she'd drifted out of the conversation, leaving Campbell by himself in Bosanquet's company, who broke the ice by offering him a cigarette, which he initially declined.

'I noticed Jerry had your colleagues puffing away on those large Habanas on the verandah. It surprised me you weren't invited into their company to share the pleasure.'

'Obviously, some promotions can only take you so far,' he replied, still disappointed by the inferior status of his allotted hotel room.

'That's unfortunately true. Be that as it may, I was impressed by the unflurried way in which you defused that minor disturbance over there a little while ago. It could never have been done from the verandah. I thought, if only the Japanese military had a peacemaker of your stature. It was a bit dishonourable that none of those scheming Orientals nearby stepped in to help you. But I suppose their inaction was hardly surprising given the current level of interracial animosity in Singapore. To celebrate your selfless conduct, perhaps I can again tempt you? They're not Cuban cigars I'm afraid, but Senior Service unfiltered, and according to the publicity, *they satisfy*.'

'All right then. I'm only a social smoker – that annoys the hell out of the blokes in my regiment. They can't put the bite on me for a smoke, like they do with everyone else. As for that row over there, I didn't think twice about the action required to handle the situation. I remembered what the colonel mentioned during our trip here today –

the only way to effectively deal with a breach of the peace is through the timely and judicious intervention of superior force. You can tell he's a fighting soldier, and used to be a top lawyer in Sydney, coming out with something like that, can't you?'

'I was unaware of his professional background. I hope he gets the opportunity to apply those steadfast principles against any invading enemy.'

All the while, Campbell couldn't help admiring the secretary's long pincer-like fingers and manicured nails, as he delicately opened his silver-filigreed cigarette case that he'd deftly removed from his waistcoat pocket. It was held open just long enough for those nearby to see its top, etched with the initials, R. B. Esq. He finally attached his cigarette to a short bakelite cigarette-holder, as though it were the culmination of a performance – which it was, and carried off with panache. For Campbell, social smoking had never seemed more elaborate or inviting. He started to think there wasn't too much about Robbie Bosanquet that wasn't sleek, mysterious and quietly seductive. A cigarette lighter then appeared as if it too had been conjured out of thin air. He was half-expecting the sleight of hand action to be accompanied by the magician's click of the fingers, followed closely by an abracadabra.'

'What's that?' Campbell enquired, as Robbie had obviously anticipated given the promptness of his explanation.

'It's a relatively recent American invention, called the Zippo lighter. It opens and closes on tiny hinges, with a closing sound that's like the release of a small, steel trap. It keeps the moisture out and never fails to ignite. It beats striking those wax safety matches in the vesta box, hands down! Listen again to the crisp sound of it closing. Nothing like a bit of old-fashioned style I say, even when it comes to the simplest of things.' And, looking directly at Campbell, an eyebrow roused, he added in a hushed tone, 'I like the way it snuffs out the wick in one go, choked of air.'

As Robbie cupped his sinewy fingers around the sides of the lighter, Campbell noticed a chunky gold dress ring with an emerald setting worn unconventionally on the secretary's right-hand index finger. The band itself was so broad it all but covered the space between the knuckle and the finger's primary articulation point. He then proceeded to perform the open-close action of the lighter on two further occasions, the last time seemingly for the sole benefit of Georgina, who'd casually drifted back into their company.

'Not that again! How boring,' she sighed as she rolled her eyes. 'I'll leave you two gentlemen to get to know one another better,' she said through pursed lips almost as soon as she arrived.

One look at her busy eyes suggested she was already distracted, thinking about something, somewhere or someone else? As she slowly edged away, she added with a slight tilt of her head, 'I wish you good luck, Lance Bombardier Alexander, trying to discover more about Robbie than I've managed to prise out of him over the past few years. But be aware, around Westminster he had a reputation as the most mischievous *under*secretary one could ever hope to find,' she said in the voice of someone who might have preferred to be called *George*.

Campbell had little time to digest her cryptic warning. His thoughts were also elsewhere, and his gaze tended to bounce along with the spring of Georgina's corkscrew curls as she flitted to the top of the staircase leading to her bedroom on the first floor. He gently smiled when it appeared as if she'd fallen into the arms of someone standing beyond the threshold. Robbie had also cast a fugitive glance at Georgina's destination but made no direct comment on what he knew had occurred.

'Georgina's trying awfully hard to grow out of her mother's shadow, don't you think?' Robbie finally said, exhaling a deep draw-back of smoke through his nostrils. 'Let me assure you, you're not by any means the only infatuated fellow here tonight, who's been dangled a line, fancied a nibble, and then been helplessly drawn along in her undertow, to rather strain the metaphor. I'm certain she practises the dreamy voice and that come-hither look for hours in front of her mirror. I imagine she's already touched you on the sleeve at least once this evening. She's gradually come to realise that well-bred gentlemen callers upon whom to cultivate that enticement are an extinct species in Singapore, if they were ever here at all.'

Campbell was a little discomforted by the gossipy conversation into which he had been inadvertently drawn. And hadn't the secretary just implied an Australian soldier couldn't possibly be a well-bred gentleman?

'I've seen her play badminton with her mother, and that elderly chap over there talking to Colonel Manning, but not anyone younger. There's faint hope of her meeting a beau courtesy of a game of mixed doubles lawn tennis here in Singapore. In any case, it's way too humid here to indulge in that venerable courtship ritual, certainly of the kind wonderfully depicted by the artist John Lavery. I suppose I'm partly to blame for her delusions as I've encouraged her to persevere. It won't be too long, I assured her, before she's pursued by some worthy fellow who thinks all she wants is an innocent frolic but ends up becoming ensnared in a more permanent relationship. *Chassez l'amour et cela revient au galop* – that's how the French put it. Chaste no more, you might say?'

Robbie was pleasantly surprised by his companion's close interest in whatever he said, but knew it didn't necessarily extend to appreciating Scottish Impressionist art or the flavour of his bons mots? It was clear Georgina had made such a lasting impression on Campbell, that he decided to continue an exposé of her character, seemingly for their mutual gratification.

'It might come as a surprise to you, given her flirtatiousness, but there's only one thing Georgina finds more *howwid* than an unwise, premature marriage followed by a homemaker's life of endless child-bearing – and that's spinsterhood. I would just *squeam* and *squeam* if I ended up like that, I've overheard her say. She no doubt had in mind some of Celia's sour-faced artistic friends in London who were in their thirties before realising they'd neglected to get married. By then, of course, they'd run out of eligible suitors capable of breeding.'

'You must've made some contacts over here to set her up with a bloke?'

'Not really. She's quite fussy about the type of *bloke*, as you put it, she considers eligible. No soldiers, no civil servants, and no Eurasians for starters.'

I'm in that excluded group, Sandy now realised.

'It's a long list. When I told her on arrival that I enjoy being husband and wife in bachelorhood, she didn't know how to take it. But

I notice recently, I've got her thinking. Then again, who am I to criticise her need for idle distractions?'

Bosanquet was clearly loath to interrupt his having a jolly good time at another's expense, living up to his reputation as a first-class rotter.

'In her favour, I must say the return of her ringlets and curls is a vast improvement upon the wild hair tied back with a decorative band she recently jettisoned. She was trying to emulate the pining look of *Flora and the Zephyrs*, I'm told. The climate here tends to turn women's hair curly as well as addling their brains, so in the end I think she gave up trying to do much about either.'

'I wonder if her mother ever needs to change her hairdo?' said Campbell, clumsily trying to contribute to the conversation.

'You've got to be pulling my leg, Sandy? Most men fall for Celia's natural projection of sexuality on the spot. The last thing they're looking at when she's up close is the lustre and arrangement of her hair, I'd have thought. I've noticed that women only change their hairstyle when they desire to be more sexually appealing to a prospective partner. That's not a problem Celia has ever had to worry about. As for Georgina? I'm not altogether certain her dalliance with fashionable hairstyles is designed to highlight her physical attractiveness to the opposite sex at all. She's not unaware of the advantages of being unmarried and attractive, which I like to remind her about.'

Campbell wondered how an ageing bachelor like Robbie could speak with any authority on married life.

'Whenever Georgina attempts to play-act her mother, unfortunately she can come across as rather skittish – all sighs, purring and bedroom eyes. I was invited for dinner a few weeks ago and caught sight of a creature wearing a gorgeous silk turban, swanning around the living room and wielding an oversized cigarette-holder. It was Georgina. She reminded me of Pola Negri in one of those early silent films hoping to seduce Ramon Navarro.'

'You mean Rudolph Valentino, don't you?'

'Whomever. Those oily Mediterranean-types all look alike, don't they? In any case, Georgina's histrionics didn't seem to help greatly, as smoking only succeeded in making her cough uncontrollably. Whatever means she imagines might sexually arouse her immediate target still needs a lot of work. When I pulled her up about the purpose of her dressing up in this silly fashion she put that fantasy back in her wardrobe. She tries terribly hard to play the temptress but can't really pull it off.'

'That's true, Robbie. Like you said, she tried that sleeve-touching routine on me earlier, but she would have worked out quickly that I wasn't much interested. It'd crossed my mind that if she saw me in the street, she'd probably look the other way and cut me dead. Now I know I'm one of those ineligible *soldiers*, that'd be certain. On the other hand, if a few of the galoots from my artillery regiment were given the same come-on as I got, they'd be into her quick as a shot.'

'Well, that's refreshingly honest,' said Robbie, who was quite amused at hearing such inelegant comments.

'I dare say for those willing galoots in the artillery, most of their serious thinking about women starts and ends a few inches below the navel. You could probably blame it on all those long barrels they hand polish, load and are ready to fire off once they set their sights on something, I suppose. But I can assure you, Georgina's no *hussy*. She's quite a different proposition to the garish trollops those soldiers probably seek out while reeling around the alleyways of Malacca.'

Campbell was untroubled by the last remark, though he thought he should've been, had Robbie's observations not been so unerringly accurate. The secretary was quite unlike anyone he'd ever met. Increasingly, he realised there was something about Robbie's suggestive comments that had caused him to jettison his vow to the major to watch his p's and q's.

'Don't be so sure about us knocking off those tarts in Malacca. In the first few weeks stationed there, the medical officers, under directions from the major, handed out more French letters than real ones from back home on mail day. After their warnings, everyone's become shit-scared of getting gonorrhoea. But a proper lady's not going to give you the clap, and as you say, Georgina's no cheap bit of fluff, is she?'

Robbie continued to be amused by his new acquaintance's undignified sense of humour, and it only served to encourage his own unsavoury comments and the salacious nature of the conversation.

'No, Mr Campbell, she's hardly what the Americans call a *floozie*. I've tried to tease her by exaggerating aspects of what her mother refers to as my dissipated life. I can't say it's unexpected, but she runs a mile whenever I deliberately raise what Celia likes to call my moral indecencies. I rather enjoy exploiting Georgina's emotional frailty and delicate sensibilities by insisting that whatever I say about carnal delights is simply tongue-in-cheek, as it were.'

By now, both had become instrumental in pushing the conversation in only one direction – downhill.

'She flinches when I explain she's much too young to have learnt anything about the sensual art of lovemaking. This entails not allowing one's emotional desire to compromise one's physical performance. From my point of view, it's the physical aspect of rogering that really matters, and which ultimately comes out on top. That's why I tell her I like to assume the dominant, strategic position of divide and rule. I don't know *why* she gets so offended?'

'Well, you certainly like geeing her up with all that cheeky talk!'

'Good gracious, I do like your wordplay. And yes, if I'm a bit of a tease, I seek forgiveness *m' lord!* Incidentally, I've recently noticed the only occasions on which she appears happy are when she's in the company of her amah, whom I recently overheard calling her mistress, *George!* That says everything to me. Tan was my choice for the role, and she's exceeded expectations. She's not the conventional pandering lady friend she's used to in London, and Georgina's less highly strung whenever she's around. I've asked her whether she's thinking of taking her amah back to England, and she said while they have *a mutual affection*, such action would be a step too far. I took that as a definite no. At least she appears to have fallen into comfort and happiness at the top of the stairs tonight, as you've probably noticed?'

'I think I know what you're getting at Robbie, but maybe with women it's different, more about feelings than the need to physically dominate? She's already inherited her mother's good looks and won't ever be short of blokes falling over each other to take her out. She doesn't light up the room like lady Celia does, but she's still only a young filly,' he casually asserted, and immediately thought, *I can't believe what I've just said*. He was startled by his boldness in venturing what he feared were extremely naive opinions, which had come out of nowhere. Perhaps his prolonged exposure to Captain Peters's judgmental attitude was contagious. Or what was more likely, the endless supply of gin had gone to his head and was making itself at home.

———

'I know you're all booked in at the Adelphi, so how do you find the sleeping arrangements?' Robbie resumed, keen to finally deflect the conversation away from Georgina.

'Yeah, it's all hunky-dory. Except I thought I'd be given a room near the others, not plonked down the end of the corridor close to the back stairs. How did you know we're at the Adelphi ... Georgina must have told you? She already knew about the surf lifesavers from Queensland in our regiment.'

'No, not at all. I personally arrange all the minister's appointments. In fact, I organised a proposed itinerary several weeks ago before General Dalziel and Brigadier Vernon unexpectedly declined his invitation. There wasn't much I could do about the individual allocation of rooms. That sort of thing is handled by the reservation clerk. You wouldn't have been aware, but had the general accepted the invitation, you *all* might've been the guests of Governor Townshend himself at the Istana mansion. That's if you'd been included among the guests at that stage.'

'I'm impressed with our hotel, I've gotta tell you. You might ask Captain Peters to get the full story on our digs?' he sarcastically added.

'I can assure you he'd be unaware of the Adelphi's *full* story. You might inform him the splendour of Government House makes the Adelphi look decidedly run-down. The floor of the entrance hall up there is a brilliant white marble imported from Java. Within its extensive surrounds there's a private swimming pool and a stone chapel worthy of a bishop. There are no second-class rooms tucked out of the way down the corridor at the Istana.'

'You sound like you've been taking notes from the captain anyhow, with that description?' he replied. Then, subtly changing the focus of the conversation once more, Robbie commented, 'You were obviously taken by the elderly piano player who was here earlier this evening. He was invited to the Istana two weeks ago to give a private recital for the governor, which we all attended. Afterwards, Celia invited him to play some cocktail music for us this evening.'

'Yeah. I had a bit of a yarn with Mr Eidelman. From a distance he sounded very good, not someone just tickling the ivories as my mum describes my playing. I eventually found him at the back of that side room over there. He called it a *withdrawing* room, with a twinkle in his eye.'

'Delightful! He's quite cosmopolitan, and it shows in his wit.'

'Sure does! It didn't take me long to see he was sharp as a tack. He interrupted his playing to tell me about the dangerous roundabout journey he'd been forced to undertake getting to Singapore. He said he'd left Austria with his wife and travelled across Europe about three years ago, when it was still safe to leave by train. He finally left for Singapore out of some port called Antwerp, where he'd been staying with his brother-in-law. Since then, he said he'd been to China to study artwork from the Ming dynasty era. He had a contact in Shanghai, which is now overrun by the Japs.'

'Well, that's entirely understandable … they *do* have a reputation for wandering, don't they?' said Robbie, astounded by Campbell's impressive recall of spoken details.

'"It seems the wolves are coming for me again," Eidelman said when I mentioned the Japs are now likely headed here. Then he said something strange: "I've seen what the Japanese are capable of doing in China, and if they land in Malaya, the battle will not be won on the playing fields of the Singapore Cricket Club."'

'That's a shrewd observation and typical of him.'

'I wonder what he meant by that. He must be worried, because before I was called away, he told me he and his wife had decided to leave Singapore before the end of November. When he saw the major trying to get my attention, he said something like *gayt gezunt*, which sounded optimistic. I took it to mean he'd see me later.'

'It might be *a lot* later. He mentioned he was anxious to depart for America when I first met him, so his comment doesn't surprise me. The last time we spoke, he said that for a trained musician like himself, it was disappointing his decision to come to Singapore had demon-strated such poor timing. His alluding to Eton's cricket fields was made by someone with a reasonably good understanding of British military history – even its celebrated myths. I'm glad you noticed the quality of his playing. When he first played for me, it didn't take me long to realise he was a true maestro. Whether in a ruminative mood or simply improvising, he could transpose anything, be it a sonata, fugue or part of a concerto, into any key and carry it off with freshness and bravura. He's what people call a virtuoso, a musician with God at their fingertips, so they say, whereby a soaring performance is best under-stood as an act of prayer.'

'Too right! I'll go along with that. How did you bump into him?'

'Hahaa. You rarely bump into people like him in this town,' said Robbie. 'I tracked him down even before the governor did. I'd already got a tip-off soon after my arrival. Evidently, he was seen wearing several gold rings with precious stones when he reserved a table in the Adelphi's dining room. My search didn't prove that difficult – there aren't too many elderly Europeans here with his distinctive appear-ance who speak English with a thick German accent. He mistakenly believed he and his wife Esther could live anonymously in a rented terrace house in Joo Chiat, not far from the beach at Katong.'

'No-one can safely hide when you're around, that's for sure,' said Sandy.

'Yes, it pays to keep my informers on the alert. When Eidelman described his predicament in having to flee Austria, it helped that I could readily sympathise with his status as a persecuted émigré. I told him my forebears were Protestant Huguenots, who fled to England centuries ago in order to escape persecution from the Catholics in the French seaside town of La Rochelle. Adherence to a minority faith never ceases to arouse animosity, especially when authoritarian rulers get into bed with the dominant clerics ... or so it seems? My father kept in contact with his relatives on the nearby Île de Ré and took me back there several times during my term breaks, or *exeats* as we used to sometimes call them.'

'I went to boarding school as well, Robbie. That's what we called them *all the time*,' said Campbell, almost swallowing his gin in one gulp and noticeably warming to the conversation.

'How fascinating! I dare say we might have other things in common. As I was about to say, Herr Eidelman reluctantly agreed to play for Lady Celia this evening, but only after I informed him that he'd be playing once more on the governor's Bechstein. This was despite realising in advance that his classical repertoire would likely be greatly under-appreciated by those more interested in jumping around to what's called hot jazz later on. "At least Singapore is zee ideal place to put zee *hot* into jazz," he joked.'

Campbell was more than happy to allow his garrulous companion to monopolise the conversation, something Robbie showed no inclination for doing otherwise.

'Believe me Sandy, a skilled private secretary has to demonstrate a certain talent for tracking things down, besides gifted pianists. One learns to spread one's tentacles over the landscape, so to speak, disinterring as one goes. Above all, one needs to lay one's hands on the type of information that will likely be of some immediate value to one's lord and master.'

Campbell was relieved when Robbie finally reverted to using the first-person singular pronoun.

'Inhabiting the corridors of Westminster, I quickly discovered the only thing honourable members liked more than facing one another while delivering their puffed-up orations, is speaking behind their backs. It's a world in which deception and betrayal are encouraged to prosper. Jerry used to reward me handsomely for sharing some of the tittle-tattle I unearthed.'

'You must miss that type of life, being stuck here in Singapore?'

'Not really. None of us can truthfully say we belong here. It took only a few weeks before I'd met everyone worth knowing. Jerry's posting has a finite duration, and Celia loathes the climate, so none of us will be returning. In the meantime, you shouldn't be surprised that I continue to keep an ear close to the ground. Wherever you are, there's still an art in assaying a pile of scuttlebutt and determining whether there's anything of value rotting away within. I recently uncovered a good deal about the amorous behaviour of your General Dalziel, for example.'

'I bet it's got something to do with the sultan's wife?'

'I couldn't possibly comment,' Bosanquet replied, flabbergasted by Campbell's apparent familiarity with such rumours.

'But surely you can't ignore the fact there's a war going on, Robbie? Wouldn't it be more useful preparing to fight a real enemy than digging up the latest gossip no-one cares about?'

'There are many ways one can contribute to the war effort without being a moveable target wearing khaki. I like to think I'm doing my bit, greasing the axle while others do the pushing. Do you think I'd be here at this time if my responsibility extended no further than attending to Jerry's correspondence, organising his daily appointments and settling the dinner invitations? At these types of functions, for instance, if you see me kowtowing to any of those slant-eyed monkeys over there, it's for reasons other than being convivial, I can assure you.'

Bosanquet didn't reveal the precise nature of his contributions to the war effort but clearly bristled at the imputation he led a feckless, unpatriotic life, and was little more than a gentleman's valet. He paused to see if what he'd said had produced its intended effect.

It had.

For Campbell, it was like receiving an unexpected clip around the ears. He looked away, and was left to ponder the paucity of his own life experiences once the sting of the secretary's words had fully sunk in. Life was much simpler back on the farm. He was left alone with his thoughts for several minutes while Bosanquet trotted off in search of a drinks tray to call his own.

———

Robbie announced his return by saying, 'I've brought you back a gin sling – well, close enough to one. I'm feeling rather queasy, so the major advised me to load the gin and lime juice with a healthy dash of Angostura. It's evidently the naval officer's remedy for an upset stomach, and less intoxicating than their customary tot of rum. I thought I'd introduce you to the mixture as well. I hope you don't mind the slightly bitter taste?'

'That's all the same to me. What do you say, bottoms up?'

Robbie smiled at Campbell's choice of words for the toast and took their meaning in the only way he found promising at this stage of the evening.

'As I was saying, I soon discovered you don't have to dig very far in the tropics to get more dirt than you're accustomed to around London. Here, simple snippets of information can become the whole narrative in no time. I suppose that's to be expected when the soil's moist, fertile and largely untended.' By employing this clumsy metaphor, he was trying to dispel the impression that he was no more than an ordinary, old nosy parker. Then, bringing his appreciative audience back into the conversation, he said, 'No doubt you've already met my good friend Manjit Singh, the willowy Sikh resplendent in his sapphire blue turban? I'm sure you would've had dealings with him soon after your arrival at the Adelphi?'

'Yeah, he was all over us like a rash at the reception desk. He struck me as being overly friendly but certainly produced the goods when it came to choosing a trishaw-driver who spoke reasonably good English.'

'That would've been the Chinaman who sometimes goes by the name of Lim Chi Cheng, most likely?'

'Yeah, Mr Lim.'

'Manjit informs me that Lim's a person with multiple skills, which he can selectively employ for the right price. He apparently has a vast array of contacts within the Teochew Kongsi, his clan association. Manjit let slip that Lim was also acquainted with Lee Choon Seng, the President of the Singapore Chinese Chamber of Commerce, no less! You wouldn't have thought he holds much sway within that rather influential group, given his lowly occupation and his somewhat murky past, I'm led to believe?'

'Is that right? Now you say that, Mr Lim did seem to be recognised in some murky places around Chinatown, to use your word. He turned out to be good value for the tour I had there today. It was a real pity I had to cut it short, but I suppose you already know about that too?'

'Well, you may not have noticed, but I was sitting on one of those leather chesterfields in the reading area adjoining the lobby when your little entourage arrived this morning. So, I certainly know where you're staying and Lim's availability for your tour. I spoke briefly to your colonel in the foyer while Manjit escorted you and the others to the lift. He told me your name and decided to dispense with any formal introduction at the time. He knew we'd meet this evening.'

'I've only known that Sikh doorman for a few months, but he gives me plenty of information, like Eidelman's arrival at the Adelphi's dining room wearing a dazzling set of rings. With my encouragement, he's taken it upon himself to especially look after the English-speaking guests. I also benefit from his close connections with compatriots in the local police. He meets up with them after prayers at one of the nearby gurdwaras. Manjit would've contacted Lim in anticipation of one or other in your party requesting a brief tour. He's provided me with some very worthwhile information, especially when it comes to foreign visitors he considers I might find, let's say, *interesting*. He may even arrange an introduction if he detects the person in question is clearly at a loose end in Singapore and may require my services.'

What type of services is he referring to, Campbell pondered, not daring to ask.

'As for your party's arrival ... well, I contacted your colonel weeks ago. I hadn't met him before, but he wasn't hard to recognise after my contacts had spoken about his unmistakable physical appearance. He entrusted me with all the necessary arrangements for your stay. I appreciated his courtesy in acknowledging my efforts to facilitate a tight schedule of visits on his behalf.'

'I suppose, when you spotted me, you could see that I'd most likely be the one looking for company, at a loose end as you say, unlike the group of officers I turned up with.'

'Perhaps so, but not immediately. From a distance, you certainly looked out of place alongside that rather squat officer with the rimless spectacles. I couldn't believe my eyes when I saw him looking around, scribbling things down in a little notebook when he ought to have been filling out the register, attending to his luggage or … heading for the bar? He looked like the type of humourless soul who'd find it hard being off duty, even in his own bedroom.'

'Hahaa, that's Captain Peters, for sure! He loves his military history books and, now you mention it, he probably sleeps with them as well. *He* might be at a loose end too, for all I know. He told me before we left our base in Mersing that he likes being a bachelor, and you won't find him at the bar because he doesn't touch alcohol. I'm always a bit suspicious when a bloke speaks like that. He might only be attempting to hide his real cravings. It's hard to get close to a prissy, dyed-in-the-wool wowser and know for sure.'

'I'm inclined to agree with you there,' Robbie added, pretty certain he understood the scope of the pejorative expression. 'He sounds a bit like one of those sexually inhibited monk-like characters eager to foist their understanding of morality and the numinous on their unsuspecting victims. I find they're often emotionally stunted, ideally suited to the celibate priesthood and the practice of self-mortification.'

'You've lost me a bit there, but I've heard some of those priests and monks don't mind a drink, and can be a bit naughty too? So that rules out Captain Peters, doesn't it?'

'I'm not sure. One never knows what that type of person gets up to in private. They might be unmarried, but whether that entails abstaining from the pleasures of the flesh is perhaps another matter. I believe the granting of papal indulgences to the less contemplative religious sisters was not that uncommon, and several of those old popes are known to have regularly conducted private communion with multiple mistresses, as you've implied.'

'I'll take your word on that, but every Tom, Dick and Harry knows about their love of wine.'

'How amusing. Talking of wine, I notice your abstemious captain is sticking to the soda water and seems more interested in conversing with a few of the influential Chinese nationalists here tonight than almost anyone else, male or female. I find *that* a bit unusual.'

'How do you know who's a nationalist? You've not been in Singapore very long yourself.'

'That's true, but Jerry made a point of meeting all the leaders of the

China Relief campaign on his arrival. Captain Peters has been speaking with a couple of the more prominent ones, like the Teochew patriarch Lee Wee Nam, and the businessman Tay Koh Yat. He's the one at the back of the room waving his arms about.'

'Hang on a minute. Who's that bald man with him? I'm sure he's the same bloke who bailed up Mr Lim in Chinatown today.'

'That's Teo Eng Hock. He's an intriguing character, but I find his nationalist politics as indigestible as the desserts prepared by his friend Ping Pong in the kitchen. Do you want me to ask your captain for an introduction?'

'No, thanks. I don't care who Captain Peters is talking to, so long as it's not me. I was going to ask you about the name you used for that bloke in the kitchen, but don't worry. What were you saying earlier about morality, sexless monks and a numerous life, was it?'

'Well, if I can put it this way, I once *adored* a well-to-do chap who had rooms in my college in Oxford. He was a bit older than the rest of us, called himself a *bon viveur*, and displayed all their usual appetites for French-inspired cuisine, vintage claret and excessive flattery. He would regale us of an evening with stories of all the carousing and pleasurable distractions he pursued. There seemed to be no end to his first nights at the opera and parties at Claridge's with bright young things – a self-professed habitué at the best tables in Soho and The Strand.'

Campbell kept nodding, as it seemed the only polite thing to do when you understood practically nothing about what was being said.

'Eventually, after a night on the tiles, he admitted his stories of evenings spent in fabled restaurants, the soirées and spanking good times among the smart female set of Mayfair and Knightsbridge, was all an elaborate fiction. I can remember he ended up saying to me, despite the presence of his regular group of muckers, "Bosie, dear boy, take my word for it. I've discovered the best number for a dinner party is two – myself and a damn good head waiter."'

'At first, I felt he was either owning up to his well-concealed romantic void or had not yet resolved his sexuality and was possibly indifferent to the usual display of feminine charms. I helped him resolve some of his doubts later that evening. His confession taught me

that people are not always what we assume them to be; that we regularly form our views on what we see, not necessarily on what we
understand. He'd realised he was an impostor, someone who no longer
had much in common with all the poseurs and self-styled indulgent
gourmands with whom he might've once consorted. Thereafter, he
chose to live out what he called his authentic identity over that which
others found comforting and had been led to believe was the reality.'

'For the life of me, Robbie, I can't see what that story's got to do
with Captain Peters? He hasn't fessed up to anything like that to me,
and doesn't give much away, especially about his love life. By the time
we'd reached the hotel this morning, I was convinced the only thing
he's ever thrown his leg over would've been his childhood rocking
horse, or a broken-down Shetland pony!'

'How deliciously vulgar! That confirms your *low* opinion of him.
That's the sort of saucy comment I'm used to dropping into polite
conversation myself. May I borrow it?'

'Sure, there's plenty more where that came from. You don't get to
spend three weeks locked up with five or six thousand randy men on
the *Queen Mary* without remembering lots of lewd stories and obscenities. I didn't go along with all their blue jokes and prejudices, but in
that sort of company it's better to keep your opinions to yourself. Even
when I was seasick, one of the rough nuts always tried to bait me
because of my looks and my parents' background. I suppose you could
say he too formed his opinions on what he saw, not what he
understood.'

'Well, whatever your captain's or your own hidden desires, it's
unlikely Manjit will be in the slightest bit interested in satisfying them.
He shies away from having much to do with men in uniform. I
presume this stems from his family's unhappy experiences with
martial law and *disorder* in the Punjab. While he might steer clear of
the military, I'm impressed by his ability to gain the confidence of the
civilian, the man-about-town and the occasional self-important
literary figure. Some of the more prominent scribblers pretend to be
travelling incognito, despite loudly presenting their visiting cards at
the reception desk upon arrival. It's always a bit trickier to amuse
them, especially if they're accompanied by a male companion who's

referred to as their *amanuensis*. I'd never heard the relationship called *that* before.'

Listening to Robbie, he realised there appeared to be no shortage of exotic guests at a loose end who'd made a habit of staying at the Adelphi. Robbie continued to extol Manjit's ability to slot the peculiar array of guests into their appropriate categories.

'He can also spot the jaded theatre types from the West End – the ones whose curtain calls have become few and far between. One dotty old thespian, he told me, even made an appearance in the foyer wearing plus fours with diamond-patterned hose, topped by a Tattersall check shirt. He seemed blissfully unaware of what passes for comfortable golfing attire in the tropics.'

'There mustn't be many of that type of traveller since the war started?'

'Yes, I'm certain of that. But from time to time, you can still be surprised to see retired ex-military types, their heads buried in the English newspapers in the Reading Room. Some emerge in tailored tweed, holding an ivory-handled walking stick as though setting off for a bracing walk in Kensington Gardens in the gleaming autumnal light. But not all of them arrive well-dressed or in a Bentley, if you know what I mean?'

'Where do we Aussie soldiers fit into that list? We're not at all famous, and certainly not in disguise. I've seen our regimental sergeant major with a stick under his arm on parade, but it wasn't ivory-handled.'

Bosanquet smiled at the retort, and the innocence from which it sprang.

'None of us could ever afford the Bentley we pulled up in,' Sandy explained. 'It's owned by the governor, and only temporarily in the safe custody of the army according to Colonel Manning. But that's not to say an ordinary soldier like me wouldn't be interested in some of those diversions you said Manjit can arrange. I'm not one to knock back a dare. But I don't have a lot of time. I won't even find out until breakfast whether we're staying here for another day.'

'Well, Manjit tells me there's been a substantial drop-off in interesting guests from *any* walk of life visiting Singapore; certainly, since the start of the German blitzkrieg across Western Europe almost two years ago. It seems the number of visiting dignitaries pursuing their orientalist fantasies, who usually make their reservations at Raffles, has also dried up? You'd have noticed the team of lackeys falling over themselves to carry your luggage into the hotel?'

'Sure did. They were swarming around the car like flies, even before we finally pulled up.'

'That's entirely due to the decline in arrivals. The Adelphi, like all the grand hotels, has found itself seriously over-staffed.'

Campbell remained cautious of engaging in topics that might again disclose his narrow range of life experiences and remained dazzled by the glow of Robbie's conversation. There was communication enough in their prolonged eye contact to suggest they'd already formed a more than favourable opinion of one another. And it'd happened more quickly than either had anticipated.

For his part, Robbie was happy to titillate Bomber Campbell with his racy innuendos and droll turn of phrase. He sensed his novelty hadn't worn off, and his captive audience seemed to derive a certain pleasure in being entertained in this way. He was rather glad he'd not turned out to be anywhere near as boorish as those Australian troops often seen staggering throughout the streets at night. Indeed, *The Straits Times* had only recently reported on a small contingent of Australian NCOs on leave, who overplayed the larrikin role in a brawl with a few of the 2nd Argyll and Sutherland Highlanders at the Union Jack Club on Anson Road. *At least Sandy's the first regular soldier I've encountered in Singapore who appears comfortable using a subordinate clause*, he snobbishly conceded.

It wasn't long before the conversation reverted to the unique character of the Sikh doorman at the Adelphi.

'As I mentioned before, Manjit's quite adorable, although his attachment to the title of *concierge* can be a tad annoying. He seems to think because it was used at his former French hotel in Hanoi it's better than any ordinary English word to describe his role. He's really only a glorified clerk if truth be told. Should you really wish to upset him, just call him *durwan*, which apparently denotes a humble porter in most Indian dialects.'

'Yes, he came across as someone who likes to be in charge, and I reckon he doesn't think of himself as *just* a doorman?'

'That's right. He aspires to an importance that far exceeds that to which his lowly station in life would normally allow. What I find amusing is that he is completely unaware that in Paris the word concierge is commonly associated with the bothersome sticky-beak old hags employed in apartment buildings who collect and closely examine all the tenants' letters. Those women are notorious for reporting to the police the comings and goings of all the occupants living in the lodgings above.'

'They're just ordinary busybodies, aren't they?'

'Not quite, Sandy. Being resident caretakers living near the stairs on the ground floor, concierges are well placed to keep an eye peeled for the regular, and most importantly, the *irregular* visitors. I hope they're not collaborating these days with the Nazis, that's all I can say. In peacetime, those women are reliable informants, to whom the gendarmes are permanently indebted in apprehending all manner of villain. Let's hope nowadays they inform for the Resistance, and not the Gestapo?'

'Well, when you think about it, Robbie, that's pretty much what Manjit does for you here?' he said, giving Robbie's elbow a gentle nudge in the process.

Robbie paused for a moment, gave a deep belly laugh, and offered a slight bow in mock deference.

'It seems you're not only a handsome lad, but a clever one to boot. But don't get me wrong, Manjit's no interfering *pipelette*, to use the slang. He's the model of discretion, never opens the mail and doesn't pry into anyone's private business, unless I request it, of course. And most of his services require only a reasonably modest baksheesh in consideration. For my purposes, he's simply *first rate*.'

'That's good to know, I suppose, but he gives me the creeps all the same. There's something about him that's not quite right? He comes across as the type of bloke who might even betray his own mother, for the right price.'

'I find your immediate impression completely understandable, especially if you haven't encountered Sikhs before. Quite a few of his Punjabi Jat Sikh community are in fact moneylenders and reviled locally as much as the Tamil Chettiars. I haven't asked him how he got into the hotel business. With his imposing physique, his contacts and command of English and Punjabi, he could've strolled into the Police Special Branch here in Singapore.'

'Maybe he *is* in the Special Branch, but you don't know it?'

'I've never thought of that as a possibility. He's certainly well-placed to provide useful intelligence to the local authorities, and perhaps gets a fee for services rendered? Yet, underneath all the hauteur, I find he's quite the regular chap. He just puts it on to impress the European guests and his craven underlings, so his posturing and often justifiable rudeness towards the menial hotel staff doesn't worry me in the slightest. More to the point, he's put in place a mutually beneficial arrangement with the French bar manager, Régis, to take care of the chits I have a habit of running up in the Adelphi's billiards room most weekends.'

'Funny you should mention running up bills, Robbie,' said Campbell, welcoming a rare opportunity to enter the conversation. A group of us from the artillery spent three or four nights on leave in the rundown bars of Malacca. On one of those nights, the total bill was forwarded next day to the battalion's quartermaster. He naturally hit the roof when he discovered the bar owner accepted us putting all the grog we ordered *on the slate*, as we call it. One of the blokes, called Wally, had smooth-talked the barman into believing the payment would be honoured, fair and square.'

'How did he manage to pull that off?' Robbie only half-heartedly enquired.

'Well, it seems Wally had somehow gotten hold of an official-looking requisition form. I suppose he convinced the barman it operated a bit like the chit you were talking about? He must've figured out the Malay behind the bar with his broken English was a bit of a soft touch to start with. He'd already doctored the form, so it had a stamp, a signature and bore an AIF regimental letterhead. Trust Wally to pull that off! After the brass got wind of what'd happened, leave was withdrawn, our pay docked, and they imposed strict curfews on *all* the men in my unit.'

'You don't say,' said Robbie, pretending to be mildly startled while noticing his companion's terrible addiction to spouting clichés and a distinctive vernacular. It didn't stop, as the gins were working overtime, causing Robbie to frown ever more deeply.

'Yeah. It's caused all types of strife. When I get back, they'll probably be real dirty if I tell 'em what I've been gettin' up to? It might've turned out for the best that I've been transferred to the medical corps. One of the hopeless gunners in the 2/10th, a bloke they call Cobra Snake, if they ever let him out of the lock up, will be furious if I decide to tell his mate Tassie about my time here. He'll be mad as a cut snake, sure to live up to his nickname.'

'I see the comparison in your story, up to a point. But when a *gentleman* accrues a debt, puts it on the slate, as you say, it would be nothing short of dishonourable to avoid payment through a deliberate deception. Your Wally sounds like nothing more than an old-fashioned swindler, what they call a *fakir* on the streets of Singapore. There's always a reckoning in commerce, as much as in life. I may be a little extravagant in my spending habits, but I always settle my debts one way or the other, by the end of the month.'

Campbell had not forgotten Robbie's earlier admission to some sort of payment arrangement with Manjit and the bar manager but chose not to bring it up. *Words are cheap,* he thought, not entirely convinced by Robbie's professed distaste for deception and the late payment of debt.

By now, he'd become very pleased that someone apart from the piano player seemed to be taking him seriously. He passed on a few more bawdy anecdotes he'd picked up on the *Queen Mary*, to which Robbie continued to respond with his distinctive bursts of operatic laughter. However, by the secretary's pained look, he was fast becoming worn out by the need to maintain that theatrical level of hilarity.

CHAPTER
TWENTY-THREE

'I SAY, I'VE GOT AN IDEA,' Robbie said rather excitedly, once his interest in hearing about the drunken antics of artillerymen had started to wane. 'Why don't we take the opportunity in a little while to slip away to the Adelphi's bar?' Campbell thought the suggestion sounded more like a dare than an invitation. So far as Bosanquet was concerned, the stories weren't that funny, and even the military version of three men walk into a bar type jokes sounded stale and contrived. In any case, nothing was more disappointing to him than the number of uninteresting men who'd gone into those bars. There was only so long he could convincingly throw his head back in laughter or bring himself to say the words, 'That sounds quite fascinating, Sandy.' Bomber Campbell's new liking for gin slings was fast approaching that dangerous, let's have one more stage on the slippery slope towards intoxication. His earlier determination to watch his p's and q's had long since stumbled out the door, and the remainder of the alphabet meandered not far behind.

'They've recently employed a new bar manager at the Adelphi, a Frenchman called Régis Dufresne, whom I mentioned earlier. Régis ran the bar at The Continental in Saigon and left once the Vichy collaborators took over the city. The other day he eventually got word from a sous-chef still working in the kitchens that the hotel had been requisitioned by the Japanese military. The few remaining bar staff are now having to serve rice wine from tiny earthenware flasks rather than grands crus classés by the bottle.'

'*Jeeez*, Colonel Manning won't like hearing *thaat!*'

'Which one, the occupation by the Japanese, or the disappearance of Château Haut-Brion?'

'Don't muck around Robbie, you know what I mean.'

'Yes, only joking. But I can assure you, no-one in the officers' mess would like to hear the Japanese Army has not only seized control of virtually the whole of French Indochina but has also withdrawn access to the finest part of the Gironde. Régis said he can't think of anything more demeaning than being forced to bow and scrape before a bandy-legged Japanese soldier who's wielding a rifle with fixed bayonet. That's exactly what his friend was recently put through, and apparently what most Europeans are randomly bludgeoned into performing nowadays in the streets of Saigon.'

'You oughta be worried a lot more about what's happening so close to Singapore,' he slurred. 'I've gotta tell ya, Robbie, we Aussies are. The officers I travelled down here with didn't much talk about anything else. They had no doubts the Japs'll invade Malaya from their naval bases near Saigon.'

'I've already noticed you're a good listener and seem to be blessed with an exceptional memory. I'll have to watch what I say!'

'It's not like I was eavesdropping in the car, but they also weren't too confident the locals would put up any sort of resistance either, once they got to Malaya. They said the way things are goin', a full-scale landin' will happen sooner rather than later.'

'Well, if that's their informed opinion, maybe they'll succeed in putting a flea in Jeremy's ear after he's spent the best part of the evening in their company, I've noticed. Not that he'll need much convincing. I know he's having ongoing problems with the service chiefs around that very likelihood. He feels they're in denial, avoiding realistic discussion of the invasion issue in his presence.'

'Yeah, I picked up the fact there's no love lost between our General Dalziel and those service chiefs either.'

'Anyhow, while that's Jerry's problem to sort out, I don't think

Churchill has invested him with the power to do very much about it. The way he's been treated recalls what he experienced at the hands of Neville Chamberlain. He now tends to keep his nose clean and finds his principal solace in searching out interesting female company, whisky glass in hand.'

'Sounds as if you both need a bit of a relaxing experience, like I've been having?'

'Not really. Where would we go? Apart from having to deal with the military, Jerry's life is seldom monotonous. He's already visited a few trading ports in the region on board the old steamship *Kedah*. Unfortunately, I'm requested to stay behind on some of those trips. I miss his company, but quite like the added freedom his absence affords, all the same. Celia is only taken along for the favourable impression she creates with the local dignitaries, and I must concede, there's only room for one dazzling ornament when he travels.'

Campbell knew that comment was said for his benefit, but his tongue was too slow to deliver a timely riposte.

'Régis has been my personal saviour in that regard. I've spent many hours chatting with him while Jerry's been gallivanting around. He says I'm good at the *badinage*, so to get me on the go, the first one's always on the house. He's got a cache of The Macallan concealed behind the bar.'

'I can't handle spirits, Robbie, or the prices they charge for the thimbleful they dribble into those stumpy glasses they're served in. I guess I liked the pink gins tonight, mainly because I didn't have to pay for 'em? I've managed to knock back quite a few, but I still wouldn't trade a dozen of 'em for one pot of cold Bulimba Lager.'

'I'd be surprised if you could find any of *that* in the Far East.'

'You're damn right, Robbie. The bars around Malacca really slug you for anything that's not the local bottled beer. On one of those nights, I spoke about, one of the NCOs decided to lash out and order a brandy and then went crook at being charged almost ten bob for somethin' that hardly touched the sides. He was a croweater from Millicent in South Australia and was put out when the barman hadn't heard of his favourite, Gramp's Pre-War Strength brandy. The confused geezer behind the bar said all he had was a twenty-year-old cognac, kept under lock and key. The sergeant had never heard of it, but said it'd have to do. After it had been poured, he then added, quick as a flash, 'Well, whatever you call it, mate, it's rather small for its age, isn't it?'

'Apart from hearing the cost of that single shot of brandy, that was the best joke of the night. I mean, I don't know about an NCO, but for me that was a few days' pay. I think I only get about five bob a day. Luckily Wally Leffler's counterfeit chit came to the rescue.'

'In that case, I'd advise your disappointed sergeant *not* to develop a taste for whisky either, if he or that Wally fellow ever drop into the bar at the Adelphi. And make sure to warn them, that crow's not on the menu there, either! Unless you're on familiar terms with Régis, at this time of night you'll more likely to end up with a whisky that's already been cut. It'll still cost more than that peg of French brandy served in Malacca.'

'How can they allow that to happen?'

'It's the underhand trick played by the Bengali bar boys, normally reserved for the late-night drinkers already three sheets to the wind. They often pay in cash and are easily taken in. Those scoundrels pocket the difference and deny all knowledge of the practice. They're compulsive liars.'

Robbie made no secret of the fact he held immigrant sojourners, the servant class and in fact all minority groups in equal contempt. Like his favourite vegetables, he liked to see them turn colour when left in hot water, but as a rule he preferred them soft on the inside and diminished in size after being well-roasted. With the rare exception – most notably the boy, Bhadrang – Bosanquet's unfeeling treatment of the household servants was indistinguishable from the scorn directed towards the hunched-over beggars who impeded his progress along the five-foot way in Chinatown. If they failed to move, he wouldn't think twice about kicking them out of his path. He saw it as a birthright, a privilege of his class that placed more emphasis on parading superiority and enforcing obedience than in garnering respect. It was nothing less than racialised arrogance, a distorted view of the white man's burden.

'It took Régis a while to wake up to their canny little game,' he resumed. 'That's why he now keeps The Macallan in a secure spot.

He's become meticulous in maintaining an inventory of the spirits and the measures they pour, and he never allows empty bottles to fall into their grubby little hands.'

'You're a bit tough on 'em, aren't you Robbie? They wouldn't earn a lot of dough behind the bar. Isn't what they're doing, only what the Americans call free enterprise?'

'Their racket is certainly enterprising, and they engage in it freely, I'll give you that! But I don't trust them as far as I can throw them. And if Régis hears of anyone starting to excuse their corrupt behaviour, he immediately cuts them short – a response quite in keeping with his countrymen's deep attachment to the guillotine, don't you think?'

'Hahaa. You'd better not tell him my opinion then.'

'I won't be doing that. He's overheard them calling me *pukka sahib* in a sarcastic tone of voice. You've lost the lower classes when they don't seem to care anymore if their master picks up in public what they may once have only dared to say in private. In a similar vein to what happens to the whisky, if you don't keep a close eye on things, respect for the natural authority of the white race itself will be gradually watered down.'

Campbell was discomforted by the depth of Robbie's racial prejudice but felt ill-equipped to debate the matter in a sober fashion.

'My sources have led me to believe that many of those Indian devils are what's loosely termed *fifth columnists*, secretly supportive of the Japs, and promoting the fall of the British here, as well as in Burma and Bengal.'

'Funny thing, I think Captain Peters was saying the same sort of thing in the Bentley, but I'm not quite sure he's dead set against the natives eventually running their own show, rather than the British.'

'That's a growing feeling, I must admit, and I've heard it referred to as the spirit of the times. But I ask you, would the new native leaders find decent positions for the Europeans who wish to stay on in the Far East, if there's an end to our imperial presence? Would you be able to make the same trip you made today without having to hand over a wad of banknotes to a venal police force to guarantee safe passage? I seriously doubt it. The natives might retain some residual bitterness towards the former British authorities to start with, but without our military presence to keep the peace, our incorruptible civil administration and highly reputable institutions, things will inevitably change for the worse. Native factional leaders will soon impose prolonged curfews and martial law. They'll plunder the state coffers, promote a bunch of cronies, followed by a ruthless purge of political opponents of a different religious or racial background. It's happened throughout history. Once they institute their version of self-determination, those out of favour will come to realise what political repression and inequality *really* means.'

'That's a bit of a mouthful, Robbie, but I think that's the sort of thing the officers were talking about non-stop on the trip down here. The colonel was suspicious of the Japanese links with the wealthy Sultan of Johore, as I remember it?'

'And rightly so. You've only got to look at what the Japanese have done since their modernisation. They embraced everything from Europe in an attempt to rival our imperial status, but they know nothing of our successful civilising mission wherever we've set foot. We respect the ballot box to maintain stability and improve society. Elsewhere, military dictators and states under hereditary rule decide elections, if they have them at all, before any votes are cast.

Now that's *real* class hatred.

'You're really starting to sound like Captain Peters now.'

'Yes, well, he probably knows his history too.'

'I tell you, Sandy, the Japanese are *Asian* imperialists, belligerent oppressors with no genuine understanding of parliamentary democracy, nor respect for any other race, language, religion or the rich cultural heritage of this region.'

It was obvious that Robbie accorded the Japanese race no more than qualified, zoological status.

'Régis also has his suspicions about those bar wallahs' loyalty to the Crown, and talks to me in the same breath about the Vichy betrayal in France. Manjit is a little more direct and uncompromising when it comes to disloyalty. He says the separatist Sikhs like nothing better than bashing Hindus and Muslims – only the fanatics, he insists – whenever each of their mutually hostile religious followers are demonstrating for independence in the Punjab. It's all about the assertion of power and promoting self-interest he says, and I suspect Manjit Singh himself is no stranger to that motivation.'

'Now that you've said that it helps explain why he seemed quite happy ticking off all the other Indian-looking porters in the foyer when we arrived.'

'Yes, behind it all is his self-identification within a caste system that's more rigid than the class barriers commonly encountered in Britain. I'd be surprised if Manjit doesn't struggle to conceal his contempt for British rule as well? It's a matter of historical record that our military killed hundreds of Sikhs in Amritsar twenty years ago during what was essentially a peaceful demonstration.'

'I haven't a clue about Manjit's India, and Régis might be good for a yarn but I'm not in the mood to talk about politics, war or religion, especially with a Frenchman who's down in the dumps.'

'She'll be right, mate – that's a saying I hear your fellow soldiers come out with all the time. He can teach you a few words of French, perhaps?'

'It's my English that seems to be letting me down at the moment.'

'Hahaa! You can just listen then. Normally, we simply reminisce about how free and easy life must have been in Paris during the *Belle Epoque*. There were a handful of violent anarchists at that time, but they would've had trouble overthrowing the local prefecture. It must've been a paradise compared with what's going on there right now under the Nazi gauleiters?'

To cope with this current dose of unknowable history, Sandy resorted to his usual rescue nod, but even more slowly.

'Anyhow, you can bet your life Régis will want to talk about old Paris again, but maybe since hearing of Saigon's occupation, he'll be ready to recall better times there as well?'

Then, slowly looking around the dance floor, he said rather irritably, 'It's time to go. I feel if I stay at this reception any longer, there's no telling which obnoxious planter I'll get tied up with. Much worse, one of their tightly girdled wives over there might even seem a mildly attractive proposition to get to know better as the night wears on. Looking at all the plump old boilers cackling around the room,' he winced. 'I can't believe I just said that. I now regret advising Georgina that if she wants to become more sexually appealing, she needs to *fill out* a bit.'

'Fair crack of the whip, Robbie, that might be someone's mother you're on about?' he chimed in before sculling another gin. He did so with such speed it seemed as if he were protecting the honour of his mates in a drinking competition called the regimental boat race.

'Well, I'd be surprised if you're attracted to mother superior over there, spread across the settee – the one with the fuller figure hiding behind the green fan? You could call her the mother load, I suppose?' Robbie quipped.

'Yeah, she looks like she's been dressed by Wirth's Circus.'

Robbie couldn't withhold a child-like snigger as he unbuttoned his collar and unfurled his bow tie, allowing the ends to dangle rakishly over his lapels.

'Or else,' Campbell cruelly added, 'what about those two heifers attempting the light fantastic close to the stage? Their big jacksies are moving around like a couple of frightened possums trapped inside a sugar bag. One's got a face like a twisted sandshoe.'

Campbell's tongue had by now become totally disengaged from his brain.

'Haa … haa! Why are people so terribly cruel? You've been reading my mind, even if what *I've* been imagining doesn't have as much wildlife involved. After your pointing that out, it's made me even more eager to sign a few chits at the Adelphi. Come to think of it, I need Monsieur Dufresne to top up my first-aid kit while I'm at it,' he smiled, giving the slight bulge inside the breast pocket of his jacket a reassuring pat. 'Make sure your major issues you with one of these Sandy. You mightn't have developed a taste for it yet, but a few swigs will prove to be of greater recuperative power than the flask of anti-septic you'll no doubt be issued with in your medical kit. Pour it into your khaki water flask – it'll make the world of difference.'

At the sound of the word khaki, for a fleeting moment Campbell envisaged the days ahead and the bleak reality of the preparations for war that would be sure to set in on his return to Mersing. Robbie's real-ity, on the other hand, seemed securely anchored in an unending, hedonistic present.

'There's bound to be much more agreeable company in the bar at this time of the night. What say we join them?' He then strode away without waiting for any verbal acceptance, clearly indicating he had no further interest in extending the conversation.

Campbell had simply responded with another mechanical nod, which finally sealed what had become an unspoken compact between them during the evening. Within minutes, Robbie had melted into a sea of bewhiskered men, totally immersed in their lubricated guffaws and boisterous opinions. By this stage Campbell was partial to joining *any* social gathering where he didn't feel so out of place – any venue where there'd be fewer of those toffee-nosed pensionable officers who'd given him the unsubtle brush-off all evening. His liberal consumption of pink gins was now starting to kick in quite alarmingly, and in this frame of mind he'd needed little urging to take up Robbie's proposal. Whether or not he suspected he was being taken advantage of by an older and more worldly man was of insufficient deterrence to the excitement of being led astray.

As he threaded his way through the crowd towards the foyer, Campbell signalled his departure to Major Wake, whose increasingly flushed appearance confirmed the minister's undiluted single malt was having the anticipated medicinal effect. Peters was holding what looked like a glass of flat soda water, and the chat he was having with two Chinese towkay appeared even less effervescent.

Campbell was not remiss in loudly expressing his gratitude to the Pyms themselves, accompanied by an unsteady and wildly exaggerated farewell wave. They both nodded politely – no hearty cheerio or pleasant toodle-oo – just a stiff and perfunctory movement of the chin. As he slowly edged towards the exit, he could tell Lady Celia had given him the type of parting look that said he'd never be invited back.

Outside, Robbie was already seated in a rickshaw lined up at the portico ready to go. Once Campbell jumped inside, Robbie placed his hand on his thigh, which he gently squeezed while issuing directions to the rickshaw-puller in a bastardised form of Singlish. Perhaps too engaged in settling back in the cabin while unfurling his own bow tie, Campbell failed to notice the partially obscured solitary figure of

David Peters, who pretended to be taking the air just out of sight behind one of the pillars at the top of the stairs.

As the rickshaw cantered off along the driveway, the adjutant darted down the steps and proceeded to hail a single-seated trishaw, which promptly emerged from the midst of the queue. There appeared to be no protest from those rickshaw coolies closest to the steps, who might normally have been expected to become animated, if not enraged, by this clear breach of the universal cab-rank rule.

'I expect we're headed towards the Adelphi, Lim,' said Peters a little breathlessly. 'Follow that rickshaw ahead and make sure you don't overtake it. You might have to go slowly, as I'm sure you've noticed, it contains two rather large, long-legged men, one of whom you're already acquainted with, I believe?'

'Actually, I know both of them, Mr Dabid. The brond one is called Meesta Sandy. He bisited Chinatown today with me, after you cancelled our meeting. He paid me extra to bling him here this eebening. He's a good man. There won't be a probrem, Lim will peddle nice and srow.'

Compared to earlier in the day, Lim spoke English with a strange hybrid accent, the words delivered with a level of fluency Campbell would not have recognised. It had long been Lim's practice to adopt a tone of voice that modulated according to the company it kept.

CHAPTER
TWENTY-FOUR

CAMPBELL AWOKE as the first shafts of sunlight penetrated the shutters and fell obliquely onto the base of the bed. He was soon conscious he was in a place where daybreak didn't slowly seep in but quickly burnt its way across the room. The sun had already stoked the now-familiar cauldron of tropical heat that would intensify throughout the day.

The air was so heavy he couldn't see any dust motes floating in the early morning light. He rubbed his forehead and then tried to pick the sleep from his eyelashes. Through half-closed eyes, he noticed thumb prints smudged on the sides of two undrained whisky glasses resting precariously on the edge of the bedside table. The cause of the nauseous feeling he'd awoken to set in train a succession of diffused recollections.

When he finally emerged from his half-slumber, he attempted to extract his foot from a coiled section of mosquito netting that had been serrated here and there by flailing toenails during the night. He slowly sat up, stretched his arms and arched his shoulder blades, admiring the silhouette of his muscular torso projected onto the wall on the opposite side of the room. His formal attire lay misshapen on the floor, discarded in a distinctly unmilitary fashion. Close to the bedpost lay an empty hipflask and Robbie's embossed cigarette case. 'God, he must've left in a hurry?'

As he massaged his throbbing head, burnt smells from the hotel's ground floor kitchen invaded the room. Street sounds became increasingly clothed in disembodied voices rising from the colonnades directly below his open window. This was nothing like his usual start to the day. He dropped back then buried his head in a pillow, still unable to fully extract his big toe from the torn netting wrapped around the bedpost. He wanted to go back to sleep but his head was reeling. The wobbly blades of the wooden ceiling fan were rotating with the strangely hypnotic slow-tapping rhythm that had successfully induced sleep during the night. The downward movement of air caused the netting over the top of the bed to sag inwards from the bedposts, as if weighed down by an invisible load at the centre.

As is the custom of most men post-coital, he instinctively sought to lift his sticky ol' fella away from his scrotum. To perform this delicate task, he had to carefully disentangle the sheet from around his buttocks and groin. It was only then that he discovered the cause of the stinging sensation he'd become aware of even before he'd opened his eyes. There was a large friction burn at the base of his penis, caused by its robust contact with his sexual partner's hand jewellery. His nether regions were smarting like hell. He'd once heard someone refer to such a condition as a scotch burn, but couldn't understand why, as there was very little Presbyterian about it to distinguish it in that way.

He asked himself how he'd allowed it to happen, but like Peters's wowserism, it was pointless to explain the compulsion. The inflammation of the skin was not going to heal any time soon. The discomfort was almost as acute as when Lim applied his cure-all, Haw Par Tiger Balm, to a small cut on the ankle he'd received the previous afternoon in Chinatown. *No salving effect there,* he recalled.

Had he not been complicit in the cause of the irritation, he might've found his injury somewhat repugnant, but the feeling stopped well short of that, and he remained ambivalent about the pleasure and pain induced by his partner's frenetic hand movements. He fell back on following the bushman's only available two-step remedy – trust in one's immune system and the passage of time, which had generally proven superior to any ointment.

Nevertheless, he knew that if any of his mates got wind of his evening with Bosanquet, he'd be pinned against the nearest wall and buggered shitless with the closest thing to a roughened-up waddy they could lay their hands on. You could guarantee it'd be less gentle than the polished wooden baton ol' Pudding Face had occasionally used to sodomise his current favourite weakling, rather than simply fondling his genitals, as he allegedly did with Carstairs many years before?

Campbell's head continued to thump and his tongue felt fur-lined with the stale taste of alcohol reflux and God knows what else. Overindulging in those gin slings had been a serious mistake, as the way he felt when he'd surfaced this morning evoked unwanted memories of heaving his guts out on the *Queen Mary*. Once disentangled from the net, he shuffled into the bathroom and tried to put his head under the tap. The basin was too shallow to allow it, as the inverted j-shaped spout almost reached the plughole. All he could manage was a few flicks of water, which quickly drained through his cupped hands, dribbled down his chest and onto his thighs. His head emerged with not much more than a set of wet ears. He dried his face with a bath towel that seemed no larger than a handtowel. On closer inspection, it indeed turned out to be one of the hotel's monogrammed handtowels. A proper bath towel lay on the floor, crumpled and slightly soiled. Robbie had been unwell.

After Campbell edged his naked body towards the window, he peered through the slats to the streetscape below. In the distance a limp Union Jack draped the top of Fort Canning's flagpole. The flag couldn't have looked more mournful if it had been drooping at half-mast on a ship in the doldrums. There'd been no opportunity for that nostalgic chat with Régis Dufresne; no reminiscing about his time as sommelier at Chez Maxim's amid spirited conversation and magnums of Perrier-Jouët. There'd scarcely been time for Robbie to replenish his hip flask.

While he successfully resisted the urge to vomit, he soon realised he couldn't stand for more than a minute or so in the one spot. As he dropped back onto the bed, he closed his eyes and reimagined the sensation of Robbie's long fingers skimming over his sweaty skin. He felt once more the bite of fingernails in flesh and the pressing of bony ankles locked over either side of his spine. What lingered most was the slapping sound of clammy flesh. Their initial tentative movements hadn't taken long to be transformed into an almost comedic no-holds-barred assertion of primal masculinity. They'd both gone for it, hammer and tongs.

But whatever Robbie had said earlier about domination, the previous night's experience had turned out to be a bit of an anticlimax. He'd surrendered without much resistance while Campbell had managed to bring him to his knees more often than pious Sicilian pilgrims genuflect on the Via Dolorosa during Holy Week. Moreover, in frequently asserting this superior position, he'd indirectly acknowledged their charitable Christian credo that it was far better to give than receive.

If that encounter could be described as a conquest, then it would remain largely hollow and uncelebrated. This was partly due to the delayed realisation that Robbie had been more than a little off-colour and had left the room without a word. The echo of their feverish writhing was already starting to fade, reduced to a sort of emotional tinnitus. What he was left with was a sense of mild disbelief at his having indulged in a satisfying taboo, even if the sting around his genitals would do little to encourage its repetition.

Robbie had indeed taken ill in the early hours of the morning, but he'd managed to throw up without disturbing his partner's sleep. Fortunately for him, whatever Cookie had dished up as an emetic produced only the mildest of purgative reactions. The more lasting effects of his concoction would be felt later in the day.

———

After his visit to the bathroom, Robbie had quickly dressed and departed the hotel in semi-darkness through the kitchen's service entrance close to an alleyway. He'd be sure to tip Manjit for once again arranging a room that was readily accessible to the stairwell at the end of the corridor. On these types of occasions, Robbie aimed to return to his bungalow well before sunrise, but this morning he was running late. Any later and his arrival might have been noticed by the servants who resided close by in separate lodgings within the grounds of the minister's residence. Punctuality was strictly observed, as his personal houseboy was under specific instructions to wake him at six every morning. An abundance of caution had informed Robbie that it was unwise to presume a vow of confidence shared with even the most loyal of staff would remain unbroken. Consequently, apart from a very select few, he unfailingly consigned his evening whereabouts to the realm of mystery. Should anyone else enquire about his unexplained absence, there was no unopened store of plausible excuses to which he didn't already hold the key.

At first, he thought he could never love Alexander Campbell in the commonly understood, sentimentalised meaning of the word. Nor would he ever be a former lover, but at most a person whom he'd once held in some affection. The word love implied a form of possession he considered inimical to his sense of independence. While in Singapore, his casual liaisons were never considered anything more than that. They were generally conducted in the borrowed intimacy of a darkened hotel room ideally suited to such encounters. Essentially transactional in nature and obligation-free, this was the level at which Robbie preferred to operate. Sex was one thing, love, quite another. But this encounter was altogether different – not quite love, but something deeper than infatuation or mere dalliance.

He never had any gnawing doubt about whether his conduct was based solely upon lust and the exercise of power. It was viewed as a pleasurable service offered or taken, and Campbell was, after all, just another serviceman, wasn't he? Yet, last evening's experience remained distinctly unsatisfying. He'd surrendered to illness and had performed inadequately. He deeply regretted not saying goodbye and vowed to make amends should they ever meet again.

Despite a lingering nauseous feeling while settling back in his pre-dawn rickshaw ride to his bungalow, Robbie remained unconcerned about having revisited what Lady Celia referred to as his moral indecencies. He always considered his own conduct, his untrammelled licence to be himself, to be devoid of the hypocrisy with which her ladyship pretended to ignore her own and her husband's marital infidelities. This was compounded by the way she attempted to sublimate her own sexual frustrations by playing the field at her society functions, then invariably rebuffing all-comers like some coquettish debutante at a society ball.

The Pyms had both sought their version of love in extramarital affairs, an elaborate masquerade that neither could ever bring themselves to relinquish. Robbie considered it appalling that their type of private conduct was never referred to in public as gross indecency. Compared to his own predilections, *why was it that the amoral behaviour of the society couple attracted the lesser degree of public opprobrium,* he not unreasonably objected.

After undressing, he quickly bathed, dried off and untied the mosquito net from around the bed posts. He swallowed a small glassful of liver salts before slipping under the crisp white top sheet that was turned down every evening by Bhadrang. The fresh linen was tightly tucked in hospital-style around the base of the mattress, awaiting his naked body to be inserted into what resembled a close-fitting sheath. None of the servants was as yet astir. Before he closed his eyes, he'd worked things out. He gave a mocking smile, quietly determined that if he had anything to do with it, Quek Shin would soon be welcoming his last day in the minister's kitchen.

He slept through the usual wake-up call of his boy – an obligingly restrained tap on the door. This gentle sound was a pleasing substitute for the muted chimes of the old tortoiseshell clock he'd brought from England, set to Greenwich Mean Time. It had wound down long ago and was now banished to the top of the dresser at the far end of the room. The clock's face was turned to the wall, as if no longer in good working order. The air of confidence and reliability once imparted by the sound of its ticking, which had regulated the timetable of Empire, had been set aside and consciously neglected, as if time itself had lost its meaning. Instead, at this hour of the morning, the room was filled with the sound of a deceptively comforting, balmy peace. He'd been lulled into slumber by schoolboy memories of choral evensong in the chapel, alive to its reassuring harmonies but deaf to its religious undertones.

As a rule, Robbie's sleep would be disturbed by the piercing rasp of the migratory Javan myna birds, which echoed from their shadowy perches within the surrounding tropical gardens. But this morning, their plangent heralding of the day, sweetened by Bhadrang's docile tap on the door, were met with no response.

After seeing the back of Quek Shin earlier in the day, in the late afternoon he fatefully decided to notify the YMCA of an unscheduled visit. He continued to tell his closest acquaintances that he occasionally fancied attending the organisation's devotional meetings and its promotion of muscular Christianity, despite their justifiable disbelief in his embrace of any form of piety or athleticism.

Although he was an infrequent visitor during the daytime, his sexual incontinence was routinely accommodated after hours, usually by appointment. Around sunset, Quek Shin and several of his militant associates happened to be in the vicinity of Orchard Road and had no problem recognising the much-despised incarnation of colonial entitlement swaggering towards them along the pavement. Immediately set upon, thrown to the ground and repeatedly kicked in the face, groin and abdomen, Robbie sustained the type of injuries from which he would never fully recover.

He'd regularly claimed there was always more than one way for a gentleman to settle a debt, and today he'd paid his outstanding dues well before the end of the month.

————

Campbell had learnt a fair bit about Robbie Bosanquet, both before and after they had individually departed at that discreet interval from Pym's reception. Foremost was the realisation that sexual gratification and gender attraction were not always the same. He'd spent only one day and one night so far in Singapore, but his current wooziness made it feel like a week. As his thoughts wandered in this way, he noticed the heavy kapok bolster on the floor and entertained the devilish idea that if Captain Peters were to turn up, he'd make sure to tell him that the Dutch wife was extremely supportive and comforting throughout the night. He might even add, in a voice that mimicked the adjutant's trademark pomposity, *you'll be pleased to know captain, she was irreplace-*

able when employed in several positions. He smiled as he rehearsed these juvenile but all the same pleasurably mischievous thoughts. It didn't come naturally to someone unpractised in the art of deception.

He didn't have long to wait, however, as a forceful knock on the door was immediately followed by Peters's sharpish direction, 'Wakey, wakey – hands off snakey!'

The adjutant paused momentarily to enjoy this uncharacteristic lapse into his very own piece of barracks' humour before concluding in his usual officious voice, 'The major's expecting you to join him in the dining room in twenty minutes. The colonel's decided we'll be leaving the hotel shortly after breakfast.'

'Good heavens, what's the time? I'm still exhausted, captain. I didn't get much sleep ... I'll be there in a jiffy,' he shouted with mock weariness through the door. 'You still listening, captain?'

There was just dead silence, not even the anticipated sound of footsteps moving away in a huff in response to his impudence. Campbell had to be content with imagining the sour look darkening the usual pallor of the adjutant's face as he fumed in the corridor. But in fact, this hadn't been the case at all. Peters knew for certain there'd been no participation by Campbell in any New World-designated amusements; nor did the evening culminate in a bout of horizontal dancing with a Javanese taxi girl. Both men knew the only taxis ridden the night before had Robbie Bosanquet on board.

Resisting the temptation to have the last say, Peters had simply smiled in the supercilious, humourless way of someone who's never been exposed to moral ambiguity. He'd been disappointed he hadn't caught Campbell *en flagrant délit*; that he hadn't detected the voice of anyone else in the room while resting his ear to the door on arrival. After delivering the major's command, he'd turned on his heels and briskly strolled away. He decided he'd keep the previous night's observations to himself until the ideal occasion arose when the salacious details might be more profitably exposed.

TWENTY-FIVE

SOUTHERN JOHORE AND SINGAPORE, JANUARY 1942

AS LANCE BOMBARDIER CAMPBELL HAD ANTICIPATED, the return to Johore had all but erased his memories of the furlough in Singapore. All he could now see and smell were formations of men in sweaty khaki. Since the start of November, he'd been transferred to the 2/9th Field Ambulance based at the casualty clearing station at Kota Tinggi.

In late August, his former artillery regiment had moved to the Mersing–Endau region on the east coast, which had been identified as a possible landing site for a Japanese invasion. By mid-December 1941, the Japanese had already struck decisive blows against the British and Indian forces in the north of Malaya, close to the Siamese border. The west coast was soon overrun.

There was an air of dread and repressed excitement as word had filtered through that the entire 2/18th Battalion would soon confront the rapidly advancing enemy along the east coast. After some initial success ambushing a battalion of Japanese infantry to the north of Mersing, the 2/10th Field Artillery Regiment, part of Manning's 2/18th Battalion, was ordered to withdraw in late January 1942. The speed, precision and concentration of the enemy forces was over-whelming, and their advance effectively unstoppable.

Tassie used this brief respite from engagement with the enemy to write an unaccustomed, longish letter to Florence Burns, the widow of his deceased uncle Keith.

28 January, Jemaluang Road, Johore, Malaya

Dear Florence

I wanted to write to you again before the fightin gets any worse. I haven't got much time to put this together. If you open up that rough map I sent you'll see where I'm writin from. My regiment is attached to 2/18th Battalion as you know and we've been defendin the east coast of Johore. I'm tellin you all this cause I know our letters take weeks to get back home if at all.

We had to blow up the bridge at Mersing 3 days ago and until recently seemed to be holdin up pretty well. My artillery battery has been practisin dry runs in the jungle around Mersing for months on end and the blokes are now glad to be shellin enemy positions for a change. The Japs bombed Singapore and landed in Kota Bahru on the north-east coast of Malaya early December. You would've read about them sinkin those two British battleships around the same time. From the tiny bits of news we're getting they've already been pretty successful along the west coast and now they're finally comin down the east coast.

The Pommie battalions and the 3rd India Corps have all been ordered to pull back. There was a big retreat earlier this month from Kuala Lumpur and then the Slim River area. It's no secret our colonel was right when he warned it'd be the west coast and not around Mersing where we would've been most effective in stopping them gettin this far. Last night we got orders to abandon our positions along this main road and in the morning we're headin south towards Johore Bahru only a stone's throw from Singapore Island. That place looks like bein our next stop.

We don't seem to have any air cover and the Jap planes make sorties over our heads every few hours. There's no resistance from what remains of the RAF and those two British warships sunk before Xmas must've been the only naval defence we had. And talkin about the Navy it's the generals who are now all at sea if you don't mind my joke. I guess that's why we're retreatin when the boys simply want to stand our ground and get stuck into the enemy. It's all a bit grim.

I've been keepin an eye on Clarrie as promised. He hasn't yet buckled down to the job of firin the new 25-pounders. He was locked up for about 10 days recently for his poor attitude. I've managed to keep up to date that big journal I took with me when I finished up at the printers. It's already full of Clarrie's hard-luck stories on the road before arriving in Wynnum. I'm havin a few problems cartin it around. I don't think Clarrie's spotted it yet or worked out why I'm the only close listener to whatever he raves on about in his past. I haven't let on that you and I are related. That's been tough goin. He still thinks I befriended him out of the kindness of my heart.

He's a difficult little bugger to like. He grizzles quite a bit when he's ordered to change the wheels or it's his turn to cart the ammo. He has a real talent for rubbin the NCOs up the wrong way. For him to apologise is like gettin blood out of a stone. I've lost count of the number of times he's been confined to barracks for tellin an officer to stick it in less polite language of course. Sad to say but if he was shot dead tomorrow I'd have trouble roundin up enough volunteer pallbearers for his funeral and there'd be very little grievin. Yet I still feel a bit sorry for him.

Bet he hasn't written to you or anyone else for that matter. He never speaks about his family in Sydney and shies away from any mention of his mother. He told me on the trip over here that he was glad he had an auntie from his mother's side of the family rather than his father's. But that was it.

I won't talk too much more about Clarrie except to say a lot of the blokes still rile him somethin terrible about his initials C. S. – as I might've already mentioned they call him Cobra Snake real slow hopin to get a rise. He takes the bait every time and they reel him in hook line and sinker.

I keep thinkin that if he ever got an apprenticeship to learn a trade he'd probably snatch it rather than gettin his ticket after startin a stupid argument with the boss. One of my mates Sandy Campbell from Dalby asks me why I still give Clarrie the time of day and I couldn't answer him for obvious reasons. I thought I'd worked out on the boat comin over what he's stewin' over but can't quite put my finger on it.

All my love
Tasman

29 January, Kota Tinggi

I'd like to say we're givin the Japs curry like we did last Wednesday night back on the Mersing–Endau Road. But from what I heard from a bloke in the Signals Corps in Kluang, they're swarmin all over the Malay Peninsula at the moment but get this he said most of them are on pushbikes. We're always on foot movin sideways or fallin back and can't seem to take a trick.

Sorry to mention Clarrie again when I said I wasn't goin to but he goes around sayin the Japs have got us by the short and curlies. You know the way he likes to talk crude – but I think he's right. I forgot to tell Pop that one in my last letter. He saw Clarrie at your place one Sunday and knows what he's like – he's sure to get a bit of a laugh out of it.

I'm writin this long letter over a couple of nights and won't be sendin it until we reach Johore Bahru or maybe Singapore itself. Hopefully we might be able to raise a decent force down there to give the Nips a real run for their money that's if I don't get me head blown off beforehand. I don't even know if this letter will reach you. There's rumours the army's going through all the mail sent back home and maybe even holding it back altogether.

Pass on my love to Pop, Mum, Morrie, Auntie Beryl, Bert Tully's brother Lionel and cousin Dulcie. If you run into Lionel tell him Bert's still fit as a fiddle now in charge of the ammo storage and dartin around all over the place like a blue-arsed fly.

Best wishes from the 2/10th,

Tasman

CHAPTER
TWENTY-SIX

SINGAPORE ISLAND, MID-FEBRUARY 1942

'WHY YOU LIMPIN LIKE THAT, CLARRIE?'

'It's nothin' Tassie, just skinned me heel … only saw it when I was pullin' me boots off. They got clogged up with that mud, remember? As we were fallin' back through the swamp around Kranji River, about a week ago?'

'Well, I've heard we're all bein' herded towards Selarang Barracks at Changi. It's about 15 mile down the road. If your foot gets any worse, I reckon we should wave down one of the officers' cars, maybe one of those trucks full of Argylls? They'll give you a lift.'

'No way I'll do that. With the wounds some of the blokes have copped, I'd be a big sheila if I complained about a bit of a blister on the back of me foot, wouldn't I. Look at those geezers up ahead – some of 'em look like they're still carryin' pieces of shrapnel.'

'Don't be stupid about that foot of yours! If you leave it too long, it'll get infected. Campbell told me how to recognise a tropical ulcer before sepsis sets in. What you've got is probably the exact type of injury he was taught to look out for when he went on that basic first-aid course last October. He said lame blokes can lose their foot, even their whole leg if they're not careful. He's up ahead. Go and see if he can clean it up for you.'

'Ok, but I've always thought Campbell was up himself, a bit hoity-toity, someone who always looked down on me.'

'That wouldn't be too hard, he's gotta be around six-three, and what are you, five-eight? Even though you might be still growin', you won't get much past five-nine, I reckon. Anyhow, you've got the wrong idea about Sandy. He's got a big heart under that barrel chest and broad shoulders. You should try an' get to know 'im better. Whatever you and Merv think about 'im, it's high time you put things right, isn't it?'

'I'll give it a go, Tassie. Suppose it won't kill me. Nethers lost most of his right arm from a mortar shell on the Jurong Road, not enough to kill *him*, that's for sure. Even with two good arms, you wouldn't find him hoistin' a white flag like Martindale did. Funny thing though, one of the ambulance drivers said Merv didn't really curse the Japs at all from his hospital bed – said he was mostly dirty on the Brits for chuckin' it in too early. I don't know what he was on about … most of those Pommie soldiers showed plenty of guts fightin' the Japs right to the end. I always said Merv was a dead-set commo, and that proves it!'

'It's a wonder I saw you on the road strugglin' to walk. Our regiment seems to have split up, and some of the blokes may've got trapped around Bukit Timah village.'

'Yeah, I know. I got a lift to the Padang from there in an ambulance. Bloody lucky, that was! The Japs bombed everything in sight – the water pipes, the airfields and the oil storage tanks. Look at the sky – it's still burnin'! Word has it that Dalziel got away at the last minute on a sampan. If that's true, what a mongrel!'

'That's the story. I bet hearin' that must've cheered you up no end. But on the positive side, ol' Starchy's still with us – *he's* no deserter. Can't tell you what happened to Captain Peters, but Campbell's definitely up ahead. And, talkin' of bets – you might have to pay me back some of that 30 bob, Clarrie. Sandy's been helpin' out heaps of blokes along the way. I've heard they've even started to call 'im a saviour, greet 'im with a hallelujah. He's got quite a following. You never thought he'd come good, did ya?'

'That was on board ship. If he's as good as you say, he might be able to give the back of my foot the once-over? It shouldn't be too hard to spot him?'

'Well, if you do, as I said, you could try gettin' on with him a bit better for a change. He's a bloke who's hard to dislike. He ended up surrenderin' with what remained of the 2/9th at the last modified field hospital still goin'. They'd all been forced back and had to set up in the grounds of that big church near the Padang. He laughed and said he thought he'd left St Andrew's for good five years ago.'

'Who else have you caught up with?'

'I haven't laid eyes on Leffler, Stiffy or any of his crew, if that's who you're wonderin' about. Wouldn't surprise me if Wally had a little fishin' boat lined up to avoid capture, just like Dalziel? If I know him, he likely sold tickets to get on the boat as well, and you can bet ya life they wouldn't've come cheap. There's no money-making trough around that Leffler hasn't put his greedy snout into. Then again, he's probably not the only bloke who'd see our surrender as a business opportunity.'

Both shuddered at the sound of the word surrender. It was hard to stomach. Everyone preferred to believe they hadn't personally given up but had in fact been ingloriously surrendered to the Japs by their own officers. The 2/10th Artillery had continued firing around Bukit Timah Hill amid a sea of infantry deserters. They didn't stop until the enemy was almost upon them and were ordered to fall back to the Tanglin Golf Course. The following morning the ceasefire was called, and they had to lay down their arms. As the last bit of firing died away during the night, those soldiers still at their posts swore they heard the sound of someone hammering away on a piano near the governor's residence.

Total capitulation to Lieutenant General Tomoyuki Yamashita's forces was the last thing the Australian infantry would have contemplated, even after their last-ditch defences around the RAF Tengah Airfield were breached and ultimately abandoned. What remained imponderable until 15 February 1942 was that somewhere around 1,900 personnel from the 8th Division were either confirmed dead or missing in action since the invasion had started a mere 70 days before.

The road to Changi was filled with thousands of British, Indian and Australian servicemen advancing in strangely silent disjointed columns, the sound of gunfire and the groans of injured mates ringing in their ears. The seriously wounded managed to be transported in ambulances and lorries. All along the way, mostly Chinese onlookers had gathered in some places three deep, and to those soldiers whose eyes were not downcast, the crowd appeared to be quietly jeering at the total collapse of white prestige that the army's capitulation represented.

'Get a load of these gloating bastards, Clarrie. Their eyes seem to be smilin', but they're not bloody Irish ones.'

The grubby faces of small children emerged from between adult legs, making the sense of humiliation and the sound of wordless taunting even more acute. No-one had joined up to become a prisoner of war, to be gawked at from the side of the road by possible enemy collaborators or sympathisers. In the ordinary soldier's mind, the fall of Singapore would always be remembered as a dishonourable betrayal first and an unparalleled military debacle second. The contempt for both was as measureless as the overwhelming sense of shame.

As Clarrie stumbled through the broken lines of dejected soldiers, he spotted Bomber Campbell moving towards him.

Campbell was on the lookout for the lame, the sick and wounded, especially from his old artillery regiment. As he parted the oncoming tide of men, he recognised Cobra Snake immediately and noticed he was favouring one leg. 'Hey, Gunner Roberts, what brings you here?' he joked.

'I didn't think I'd ever be sayin this … but I was hopin' to find *you*. Tassie said you were up ahead and could work wonders with the blisters on me heel.'

'Well, you sure are a lucky fella, as Tassie often says. I think I've got just enough left in my medicine kit to treat you. I've managed to smuggle some of the injured blokes down to Changi Beach to bathe their minor wounds in salt water. So far, the guards haven't noticed us slippin' off along a track you wouldn't know was there. Just follow me,

I'll show you the way. You might be one of the last poor buggers I'll have time to treat down there, before they lock us all away.'

———

The first weeks of captivity were semi-organised mayhem. Several battalions of Australian troops occupied the former British barracks at Changi, which included a dilapidated gaol that was built to incarcerate only a few hundred inmates. European civilians, women and soldiers of other nationalities were interned in separate prison camps nearby. All the foreigners were more fortunate than the thousands of local Chinese civilians who were arrested, mostly men between the ages of eighteen and fifty. They would be indiscriminately massacred in the first few weeks of the Japanese Occupation, randomly accused by hooded quislings of collaborating with real or perceived enemies.

The army prisoners in Changi were assembled into their various units by their respective commanders. Australian officers were placed in charge of the 8th Division's various units and imposed their own harsh disciplinary measures for insubordination. After a few weeks, the units were fragmented into designated work parties around the island. Some unloaded stores in the godowns around Keppel Harbour and the quays along the river, while others were tasked with repairing the only recently shelled roads and buildings.

In those first few months following the surrender, the Japanese guards at Changi were surprisingly scarce, and the area outside the newly erected, barbed-wire perimeter fencing was rarely patrolled. The guards were primarily on the lookout for overambitious and underprepared escapees, rather than the detection of those risking no more than a bit of elicit trading with the local villagers through the wire.

For most of the internees, boredom was soon replaced by the relentless search for food and the fight against the broad spectrum of diseases that stemmed from malnutrition. That meant scavenging anything reasonably edible to supplement the paltry rations of a dixie of boiled rice topped with the occasional slither of vegetables. A deficiency in protein, fibre and vitamins was a constant, inevitably leading to beriberi. The poor quality of the water supply resulted in the wide-spread outbreak of dysentery.

Remnants of the 2/10th Field Artillery Unit were assigned to clean-up parties at Adam Park along Havelock Road, and ironically, were stationed at one of the former amusement parks in early April. From there, hundreds of men were sent out every day to re-establish the roads and utilities devastated by the warfare. Some were involved in erecting a shrine to dead Japanese soldiers on Bukit Timah Hill, sabo-taged, they hoped, by the contamination of the soil with containers of white ants covertly buried beneath the shallow and exposed wooden foundations. The prisoners there were guarded by some ruthless Japanese and turncoat ex-Indian Army soldiers. Following the capitu-lation, the latter were often faced with the 'choice' between being gaoled, hanged or shot by firing squad, unless they colluded with the occupying forces and 'volunteered' to patrol outside Changi prison's barbed-wire barriers.

The deployment of outside work parties came to an end after a few months, but not before much contraband had been successfully smug-gled into the prison camp at Changi, around twenty miles from the harbour. For those who had scant interest in attending any of the self-improvement instructional classes conducted by the well-educated among the prisoners, the tedium of daily life had become almost unbearable. Some, like Gunner Roberts, spent most of their idle hours whining about their misfortune, acting like a teething child throwing its toys out of the crib. Clarrie increasingly turned his thoughts to plan-ning an escape, and suspected Campbell shared a similar view on the matter.

———

'I've gotta get outa here, Sandy.'

'Yeah … and then what? Buy a one-way ticket on that ocean liner we came over on, now bound for Sydney?'

'Look, I'm grateful for you fixin' up me blisters. Tassie said you could work miracles, and I'll go along with that now, but why aren't you so keen on tryin' to escape?'

'Maybe I *am* interested, but haven't let on to *you* about it? And don't claim all you had were a few blisters. If you hadn't got me to treat that ulcer properly, within no time bacterial infection would've spread and gangrene set in.'

'Ok, as I said to Tassie ... that's one I owe you.'

'Speaking of Gunner Walls, what if I told you that your only mate already knows of my plan to escape, and one of our officers is actually organising the details?'

Clarrie suddenly displayed an uncharacteristic degree of attentiveness. 'Come on, if that's true I want to be part of it. Tassie's said nothin' to me about any escape plan. I know a spot behind the Selarang hospital building where the barbed wire hardly touches the ground. Len Kelly and Chocko have both gone under it a couple of times. I've heard all they do is scrounge for pawpaw and palm tree cabbage from around the villages. They just lay low until sunset before sneakin' back in. They've had no problems – the guards would be flat out seein' Chock at nightime, anyhow.'

'Some of that's true, but you're a little out of date. It's good that Tassie hasn't told you anything. I'll briefly let you in on our plans, on the understanding that what I tell you goes no further.'

'Mum's the word. I know when to keep me trap shut.'

'I haven't seen much evidence of *that*! As it turns out, we've been thinking about you as a possibility to join us for a while now. In saying that, the fact that you don't seem to have any problem drawing attention to yourself in the barracks, might be a more serious sort of problem for us on the outside. Tommy Quinn was never within a bull's roar of getting a look in at any time, despite your shitty comment about his ability to evade detection in the dark.'

Clarrie suspected they were still in two minds about taking him on, and he would've been close to the mark.

'We already know the place you mentioned. And because you're such a scrawny little bugger, we reckoned you might be useful helping us crawl under the wire without getting too many cuts. You can duck under it, then hold it up so me and the captain can squeeze through without getting badly scratched.'

'Captain Peters, eh? Whoda thought? If you think all I'm good for is holdin' up barbed wire, you might as well ask Kelly to have another go.'

'Hang on, you don't have to get snakey about it!'

Clarrie was about to say, *you think you're smart saying that, don't you,* but Campbell beat him to the punch. 'You can boast about your escape to Tassie whenever you meet up again after the war. I only found out recently he keeps a big book on you. I don't know how he's managed to keep it out of sight. I've got a notebook too, a fair bit smaller, mainly about what I've experienced on leave. Tassie's the only one I've shown it to. But I'm not interested in making notes on what *you* get up to. Tassie said he'd already jotted things down about your stories, whether they're boring or just plain bullshit. But he says he's made *me* the centre of his attention since my seasickness on the boat coming over. Anyhow, escaping from Changi will count as a real feather in your cap. It's a big chance for you to be part of a team effort, as well as demonstrating real courage – that you're not all front?'

'Bloody hell. Tassie never told me about any book. He'd better not try to flog it off to anyone?'

'Why not? What are you worried about? And anyhow, who'd want to read it, unless you've committed some act of bravery … or cowardice? Are you feeling courageous?'

There was no response.

'Nobby says you can scurry around like a frightened rabbit when it suits you. Apart from disobeying orders, *that's one of the few things that little runt is good at,* he said. At least that's what *I thought* I heard him say? Tassie also said you've got a bit of history getting out of scrapes and leaving in the nick of time. Got experience going AWOL too, I've heard? So, successfully breaking out might be right up your alley. At least escaping will keep you out of the strife you get into in here, I suppose. But you'll still have to follow orders.'

'That's why I've got to get out, bomber, me ol' mate, me ol' china. I'll end up throttlin' one of those Jap guards if I don't. Fancy havin' to kowtow in front of those slit-eyed monkeys, whenever they show up at the gates! You're right, I'm no good at takin' orders from the NCOs either – it's like being forced to have a spoonful of castor oil every mornin' before your bowl of porridge. Me ol' man would do that as a punishment and a warnin' for us kids, even if we did nothin' wrong! But escapin's another matter. I've always been sort of lucky and managed to head off at the right time from places and people holdin' me back. I'm good to go and you can trust me to back you up.'

'Well, all I can tell you at this stage is we intend to slip out in a day or so. A lot depends on the captain's contact on the outside. He's promised to help us get to a camp north of the Causeway. He's a Chinese nationalist – a member of the local anti-communist KMT and supported by the Chinese Chamber of Commerce. I've met him already.'

'How'd *that* happen?'

'It's a long story, but I spotted him talking to some important-looking men when I was on leave in Chinatown last October. I had an idea he was more than the hard-working trishaw owner he made himself out to be. He's known as Mr Lim.'

'Hang on … I've heard there's heaps of chows who'll dob you in to the Japs, quick as a flash. How do ya know if that Chinese commo's not goin' to do just that? And, outside the wire, we'll stand out like sore thumbs, so how do we disguise ourselves once we're out in the open?'

'Don't worry. Captain Peters has guaranteed Lim's loyalty – they've been in contact for several months now. And how many times have I got to tell you, Lim *isn't* a commo? He's getting us food, clothes and a map. I reckon you've still got that coin you took from Tassie on that ship coming over. That'll come in handy too. And by the way, I know how you won that bet! Feeling a bit guilty now, are we?'

'Yeah … well, I was forced to buy some grub and baccy from Wally's sly canteen and had to pay to get into his two-up school, so I've only got about 15 bob left. Why would I give it back?'

'Come on, hand it over. We'll find a use for it on the outside, if you're still interested in joining us. I'll put it in my medical kit for safe keeping. Lim deserves every bit of it, for starters. The captain said Lim was a Chiang Kai-Shek nationalist party spy, based in Singapore. Their main guerrilla forces have retreated to the mountains in western China and are being supplied with arms by the Americans through Siam.'

'When did you learn about that sort of stuff?'

'I picked it up while I was driving the officers from Mersing in the staff car, and from Captain Peters, of course. Until he took me into his confidence recently, I had no idea Peters was deliberately placed in the position of adjutant by the powers that be in Canberra. That explained quite a lot. He was briefed by officials in the Department of External Affairs, who told him that Lim was a reliable anti-Japanese activist, known for his espionage, and credited with sabotaging parts of the Jap supply routes in southern China two years ago. They'd either meet up at the Adelphi hotel, or at a tailor's shop in Endau.'

'Talk about covering your tracks! I guarantee even the colonel still thinks his adjutant's nothing more than an over-promoted bookworm. He's also unaware that part of Captain Peters's job is to take notes on everything he hears, sees and learns, then using his skill at intelligence gathering, to report back to Canberra on Dalziel's level of cooperation with his battalion commanders.'

'Who'd have guessed all that?'

'You're damn right! Peters has had to pretend he was something other than his real self for quite some time, disguising his identity. He had to overcome his Presbyterian guilt at living a life of lies and dissimulation, as he called it. He even managed to convince *me* he's a wowser! That must've been even harder to keep up in the officers' mess. It helped, he said, that his father was a strong supporter of the Temperance movement, so there was never a drop of alcohol in the house he grew up in.'

'Nothing like the place where I lived,' Clarrie murmured.

'Although Lim's apparently planned for almost everything, he can't plan an escape from dengue fever, malaria or dysentery – so we're all on our own there, except for my medical kit. Are you still game to stick your neck out and join us?'

'Is the Pope a Catholic?'

'What? I'm being serious about not sticking your neck out. You must've spotted those swords the Jap guards are wearing? I'm sure if you get caught it's a death sentence, and there'll be nothing above your neck to put a hat on. It's a very short sentence and it always ends in a full stop is the joke doing the rounds at the moment. I wouldn't mind betting they'll fancy your big head, even if *I* don't.'

Clarrie almost smiled.

'What I'm saying Clarrie, is this is a whole lot more dangerous than what Kelly's been up to trading Leffler's cash for food and tins of condensed milk smuggled in from the warehouses along Boat Quay. Peters has tried to downplay the danger, but I've been working with the major three days a week in the infirmary, and I've seen some of the injuries inflicted by the Kempeitai on the first few unsuccessful escapees. As you've apparently found out, Kelly normally doesn't stray too far. He often barters with the locals over the barbed wire for coconuts and yams, rather than going under it. Wally gets him to do it, to restock his little canteen. But what you probably *don't* know, is Kelly was caught outside by the guards yesterday. As it turned out, he only got bashed and had his money and tobacco taken. But even though he'd *nothing* on him, Tommy Quinn not only got bashed, but was dragged away unconscious and bleeding.'

'Why weren't they both dragged away?"

'No idea. But I've always thought any darkie put in gaol is gener-ally there because of the colour of his skin. It's something he can't escape from, and the few living rough around the town of Dalby, where I come from, were locked up as much for that than for commit-ting break-ins and thieving stuff. Kelly said Chock had made things worse for himself by prancing around and throwing a few left jabs at one of the guards, like he was sparring or shadowboxing. After bobbing and weaving a bit, he ended up not landing a single punch before his head met the butt of a rifle and was dragged away – we'll probably never see that poor bastard ever again.'

'They won't catch me doin' that! Prancin' around, ya say? Chock was always mad as a meat axe – an' Kelly? – he'd probably just got out of the rathouse before joinin' up. Blokes say he's got a face as ugly as a hatful of monkeys' bums, so the Japs probably figured out they couldn't worsen his looks by hittin' 'im with a rifle butt.'

'You've sure turned out to be a nasty little bastard, Clarrie.'

'Yeah, well, if you'd had my father, you'd 'ave turned out the same. I shoulda known you were up to something. I've seen you talkin' a couple of times with that four-eyed captain. Looked like you were best mates, gettin' on like a house on fire. I remember sayin' to Stiffy I didn't think you two were just rehearsin' your lines for the concert party next week or workin' out which one of ya puts on a dress to play the tart. Turns out I was dead right. I was surprised to see you two together. Tassie told me you couldn't stand the bloke – that you'd once said if you're ever unlucky enough to be roped into havin' a yarn with the captain, it'd be like spendin' the evening at the Cloudland ballroom full of beautiful-lookin' sheilas an' havin' to dance with your buck-toothed country cousin all night – somethin' like that.'

'That might've been the case before the fall of Singapore. You can forgive people, Clarrie, even if you can't forget what they did. Someone once said to me that we don't always know who a person really is; that we assume things based on appearance, rather than our understanding. I'm trying hard to understand *you*, without much luck. Anyhow, we're both focused on escaping now, and he's got a plan to get us off the island and head north of Kuala Lumpur.'

Clarrie grew quiet after Campbell had spoken about appearances and understanding. He couldn't help recalling a certain murder story reported in the *Gwydir Examiner* – and how he'd been taken in by Miriam, Jack Nevins *and* Flash Billy.

'I'll see what the captain finally decides. He likes to use big words, and in the last couple of days he's even called you *recalcitrant*. I'm pretty sure I know what it means, and it's *not* a compliment. For some reason, Cruikshank and Tassie always seem to give you a good rap, although both mentioned you were a bit reckless and, given your history of upsetting the NCOs, could be a risk to the safety of others. I must've heard the captain say, "I dunno," a dozen times, whenever your name comes up. He said you were a screw loose, and there was a strong element of danger recruiting you for an escape – said he'd only take you on as a last resort. You'll need to tighten that screw and be less bloody-minded, if he gives you the nod. You know that, don't you?'

'Yessir, yessir, three bags full! So, when do we get the go ahead?'

'Don't *you* get ahead of yourself … cool your heels a bit. That's something you might recall I helped you with on Changi beach. All in good time. If the captain finally decides to give you the thumbs up, he'll pull you aside when he comes out here from the officers' barracks later today. You haven't got plans on going anywhere else tomorrow night, have you? And make sure you stump up with that 15 bob.'

———

It was the unofficial, implied duty of every prisoner of war to attempt to escape. Yet, for the first few months, to be selected in one of the numerous work parties around Singapore Island and on the docks not only offered some temporary respite from the tedium of imprisonment, but paradoxically, also discouraged any attempt at escape.

But after the reconstruction and clean-up details had run their course, the Japanese tightened security around the perimeter of the main prison compound. They also reduced the daily food rations and repeated the threat to transfer all captured escapees to Outram Road's nineteenth-century era penitentiary near Chinatown. Once locked up there, you'd likely face starvation, torture and an indefinite period of solitary confinement – the routine punishments, if you managed to avoid death by hanging, firing squad or decapitation.

These details had been gleaned from the accounts of some of the first POWs captured outside the perimeter. Many were so badly beaten that the presiding officer at Outram Road, Major Kenji Saitō, had given approval for the worst of the injured to be transferred for medical treatment to Changi prison's makeshift hospital. He did this, not so much for humanitarian reasons, but to increase the likelihood that the prisoner would recover sufficiently to return and serve out his full sentence in his gaol. It was not considered honourable if a significant number of prisoners died in their cells.

Those in charge of Outram Road were part of an autonomous military police outfit called the Kempeitai. Such was their reputation for brutality that even high-ranking officers in the Imperial Japanese Army deferred to their direct management of serious disciplinary matters. Peters had also confirmed what was happening there in his written recording of the long-term injuries of transferred convalescing prisoners. Even though he was aware of the probable consequences of capture, Peters chose to downplay the extent of the risk to Campbell and Clarrie. Like the improvised operating areas in the prison hospital, information about the rampant illnesses and injuries at Outram Road was partially sanitised.

Lieutenant Colonel Manning, who was not a full colonel at the time of surrender, was placed in charge of the Australian POWs in Changi. All the highest-ranking officers, including General Martindale, Brigadier Vernon and Air Vice-Marshal Stretton, had been shipped off to Formosa, Manchukuo and various ports, mining and industrial sites in mainland Japan. Molyneux was fortunate enough to have been relieved of his duties and recalled to London in early January.

Manning's firm disciplinary attitude and concern for battalion morale, provided an extra hazard for his adjutant in defying orders by secretly planning an escape. Even Wake reluctantly conceded that his old friend's positive attitude had progressively deteriorated and he'd become an irritable curmudgeon. Manning remained deeply dispirited by Dalziel's actions before the surrender. He'd resorted to legalese in calling it *an act of moral turpitude*, saying: 'It was nothing short of desertion in the face of enemy fire. It showed disrespect not only towards the wounded survivors, but also to those brave servicemen and women slain in battle. He should've gone down with the ship.'

The colonel had said this more than once following the capitulation ordered by General Martindale. He also reminded himself of what he'd said to Peters about the Sultan of Johore. It was now clear the *soi-disant anglophile* had ultimately decided to hunt with the invading Japanese hounds. *All those doubts I had about the sultan's loyalty to the British Crown have proven to be justified,* he grimaced. Nor had he ever been taken in by the depiction of Singapore as a fortress – now exposed as a total myth – underlining the colony's unpreparedness for the invasion he'd warned Pym about in October. It had taken the enemy only a couple of weeks to ruthlessly exploit this calamitous situation.

As a result of the seeming futility of escape attempts, and his overarching duty towards the welfare of those under his command, Manning believed non-violent resistance to being broken by internment to be the more prudent course of conduct. He felt personally responsible should there be any further casualties under his command. His lifelong self-assurance was starting to flag, and every day he struggled to find a suitable biblical epigram to bolster his diminishing reserves of optimism and resolve.

While he once might have been admired for his common touch, the present situation demanded a much heavier imprint. He'd ordered that if any soldier learnt of a planned breakout, he was obliged to personally report it to the provosts, who were authorised to immediately foil any such attempts. Manning became a dejected figure, wishing he could approach his new, unwanted duties with the same degree of élan and dedication he'd once brought to clearing a backlog of litigation, or drafting submissions of fact and law in Selborne Chambers in Sydney, before the war.

———

'When we headin' off, captain?' Clarrie said, a little too loudly for Peters's liking.

'I'm not telling you a time, so stop asking ... and keep your voice down! Be ready *any time* tomorrow night. Campbell won't risk waking you up if you're off with the fairies. There's only the three of us breaking out – less chance of the provos getting wind of it.'

'That's fine by me,' replied Clarrie in the closest he'd ever come to a whisper.

'Actually, there's more than us involved. Campbell may've already filled you in. I've a Chinese contact outside the wire, who'll guide us part of the way to a nationalist guerrilla camp near Johore Bahru. After that, he'll leave us and, using his maps, we'll have to continue the trek by ourselves to Ipoh, north of Kuala Lumpur. From there, we're not assured safe passage to the coast either – and if we make it that far, we'll have to pay to get on board a *prau*. Lim said it's a type of small Malay fishing boat that'll take us to Bengal. That's what lies ahead.'

'Yeah, Campbell mentioned most of that. Crikey, that'll test our jungle survival skills. Sounds a bit tougher than those bivouacs behind Caloundra. But hey, that's the first I've heard about a boat trip. How come Campbell's been chosen? He was crook as a dog on a much bigger boat comin' over – Merv used to call him a lovely boy, not a seafarin' one, and I took thirty bob from Tassie, bettin he probably was the muscle-bound pansy Nethers used to call 'im behind his back.'

Peters's contemptuous look and massive eyeroll filled the silence. 'I'll tell you something, Gunner Roberts. He won't own up to it to *you*, but Campbell actually *supported* your joining the escape. I don't know why, but he told me he's even forgiven you for spreading all those slanderous rumours you passed on from Merv Nethercote. "Clarrie doesn't know what he's doin' or sayin' half the time," was the way he put it.'

'So, wake up to yourself!' he continued. 'Obviously that little stint you had in our brigade's lock up a few months ago, had no effect. Get this straight – Campbell's no *pansy*, to use your crude description. He's got plenty of courage as well as very useful first-aid experience. He's somehow managed to ferret away a half-jar of marmite – a last resort to treat some tropical illnesses, he said. I've changed my mind about him quite radically. He told me that working as a medical orderly in the heat of battle had completely altered his attitude towards life. For the first time it had real meaning, he said. He spoke with the quiet assurance of someone who'd undergone the sort of spiritual conversion my father used to talk about. Major Wake recounted his acts of bravery, transporting the wounded in ambulances under enemy fire. He couldn't be certain but thought he saw Campbell reduced to tears while retrieving the bodies of those who'd died. It made him sound as courageous and compassionate as Simpson and his donkey in those Gallipoli trenches. I realised there and then that I'd been way off target with my limited understanding of his character. Yet, despite this positive reassessment, he wasn't my first choice, someone else was.'

'Yeah ... who?

'Never you mind. It's a fact that Campbell and I didn't get on that well when he acted as the colonel's staff driver last October. He wasn't to know I was putting on a big act. I'd already witnessed the way he calmly handled provocation under pressure, coping with aggressive cyclists and bullock-cart drivers outside Kota Tinggi. He also demonstrated initiative and selfless behaviour in offering medical assistance to one of those coolies who collided with the car.'

'How was I to know all that, captain?'

'You weren't. But I can assure you, Sandy's heart's in the right place. But, more importantly, he was recommended by my contact Lim Chi Cheng, and *that* was the deciding factor. As Sandy has probably told you already, Lim's a member of the local Kuomintang, the KMT, and had an opportunity to size him up as an individual while Campbell was on furlough in Chinatown. He'd demonstrated calmness under pressure during an incident, Lim said, which occurred inside a tailor's shophouse. That happened well before war broke out.'

'There's no way I could've known that, either.'

'Even if you did, would it 've made any difference? As I've already said, the major praised his level-headedness as an orderly in the same glowing terms. I have to say, in recent months, after getting to know him better, Campbell's encouraged me to become less judgmental and to get rid of the grand words I can't help using. Who knows, his good qualities might even rub off on *you*, once we have to rely more on one another.'

'Yeah, sure, but you could've still got Tassie to be a part of it as well?'

'Lim would only help *three* prisoners escape – says it's very dangerous getting off the island, there's Jap sympathisers and informers everywhere. He oughta know. He told me he was fortunate to escape being rounded up himself in February. That's when thousands of Chinese men were falsely accused of being anti-Japanese then massacred around the Siglap area, just a few miles from here. He called it *jian zheng shi jian* in his native dialect – victims of a purge, using a sham identification process. He said the whole operation was ruthlessly carried out by the Kempeitai.'

'So what! I still think you should've offered Tassie the chance. You shouldn't've made up your mind on what some chow on the run told you.'

'That's only *your* opinion. Unlike you or your unsavoury fair-weather mates like corporal Nethercote, I can gauge the true measure of the man. Anyhow, I'd be surprised if Nethercote doesn't thank Sandy each day for dressing his shattered arm. He probably now regrets slandering that same man when they were unavoidably thrown together on the *Queen Mary*. But, if it gives you any comfort, Sandy himself was initially lukewarm about breaking out. He said he'd discovered a higher purpose in life caring for the sick and wounded in the mobile hospitals he'd worked in. He even described what he was doing as enabling him to better cope with the folly of war. I gather he managed to save *your* life from the effects of tropical ulcer as well.'

'Yeah, that's probably right. I've already thanked him for that – said I owed him one. But I still can't understand why he'd want to stay a prisoner in this place?'

'It might have something to do with compassion ... perhaps an alien concept for you? Think about it for once. There's twelve hundred sick or injured soldiers being treated in the camp hospital and only 600 beds, so *I* can understand his wish to do more. There could be a couple of battalions, maybe up to 5,000 weakened men, who could come down with any number of serious illnesses in Changi sooner or later. He'll have his work cut out, but who knows how many might benefit from his care? But I only had to mention the name Bosanquet to finally get him really interested in joining the escape attempt.'

'What ya talkin' about? There's no Australian in Changi that I know about with that sort of poncy name. It must be made-up?'

'That's funny coming from someone like you, who's got a habit for calling people all sorts of names. But you know, Clarrie, I don't care one little bit what his name sounds like to *you*. You need to do yourself a favour and concentrate on things that are more important in life. Lim told me Bosanquet, along with Churchill's emissary Jeremy Pym, were both recalled to London in January. Pym's family had already departed, and all their household servants laid off. He said Bosanquet had been attacked in Orchard Road before he left and hoped he'd one day meet up with Sandy again. What's important is that after I dropped the name Bosanquet, and told him most of what Lim had said, he was keen as mustard to escape. He seemed even more determined once I reluctantly broke further news that the Englishman had been repatriated as an invalid, one of his cheekbones and an eye socket smashed in like a crushed table-tennis ball, as Lim described it. Sandy's emotional reaction forced me to question my narrow conception of love and supposed immorality.'

'I don't know what you're on about. Why're you tellin' me all that stuff? What I'm hearin' is, I owe being selected to Campbell *and* Nobby Cruikshank, not you, Tassie or that Pommie Boesiekay … was it? You wouldn't credit it! I'm still surprised Nobby didn't really sink the boot in when *my* name came up.'

'He wasn't overly complimentary, but in the occasional chat they both independently vouched for your stamina, survival instinct and bullheadedness. I think the expression rat-cunning was also thrown around. That convinced me to take you on trust, against my better judgment and despite serious reservations about your lack of self-discipline and what I'd call your *intransigence*.'

'What's that mean? I thought you just said you'd got rid of those big words?'

'Don't concern yourself about it. I'm sure you can guess what it means. Nobby told me your poor attitude is already known to the provos, and I wouldn't be surprised if the colonel has ordered them to keep an even closer eye on you. He's mentioned your insubordination before during our trip to Singapore a few months ago in the staff car.'

'I can't take being bossed around and can't help it if I've got a short fuse.'

'Well, I'll put it this old-fashioned way – sometimes it's a whole lot smarter to toe the line and follow orders than be needlessly defiant. We had to insist your mate Tassie keep the possibility of escape a secret, and the sergeant major thought it better for prison morale if you were gone. I can't understand why he said that, can you? So, make sure you keep *your* trap shut, and try not to play up for at least the next day or two.'

'I've been told to do that by scarier blokes than you, captain. If I can smell real danger, I'm pretty good at layin' flat as a tack and holdin' me tongue – Tassie's heard a few true stories about me doin' just that *an'* pullin' me head in before I signed up for this bloody useless war – so y'can bloody well bank on it.'

CHAPTER
TWENTY-SEVEN

'HOW THE FUCK did we end up here, Sandy? Where've *you* been hidin'? An' isn't that Chock at the front of the line? How'd he manage to keep that rough head of his on his shoulders? Must've come up with a bit of black magic that worked for once, eh?'

'This isn't the time to be crackin' jokes, Clarrie.'

It was mid-morning and already boiling hot. They'd both been separately interrogated by the local head of the Kempeitai, Major Kenji Saitō, and now found themselves thrown together for the first time with other prisoners in the walled and shadeless inner courtyard of Outram Road gaol. They were being nudged along by Commandant Shinjirō Ikeda to a spot where they'd receive a small cup of dirty-looking water and two scoops of nutrition-free polished rice. If today's food was anything to go by, their relatively healthy condition wasn't going to last.

'We must've been spotted hiding in the Lalang grass – what was it, only a few miles from the wire? Looks like you've copped a bashing too, Clarrie? Your face's a little swollen, like mine. I must've passed out when that Jap hit me with his rifle butt. You saw who the other guard was, didn't you?'

'Yeah, it was a big Indian-lookin' bloke ... even if he wasn't carryin' a rifle, I would've 'ad trouble layin' a glove on him with that long reach of his. I wasn't prancin' round either! The last thing I remember is calling him a fuckin' swami on stilts when his back was turned. He must have understood English because he then king hit me from yards away – I didn't see it comin'.'

'Well, those particular words would've upset him more than you could've imagined. His name's Manjit Singh and Captain Peters identified him straightaway, and so did I, even without his usual turban. He's a proud Sikh, *not* a Hindu swami. He used to work at the reception desk at the Adelphi Hotel and his English is better than yours, Clarrie. The Jap officers have since taken over that place as their headquarters. After Manjit knocked you out, the captain tried to reason with him, said he must've had trouble fitting into his new uniform ... kept saying stuff like that to get a reaction. He called him *concierge* many times, but the big bastard refused to own up to being recognised. Peters kept on pleading with him but got nowhere. He then started calling him *durwan*, which didn't seem to improve things greatly. For a moment there I thought the Jap was going to pull out his sabre and put a full stop to the talking once and for all.'

Both found themselves mumbling out the side of their mouths as they were pushed towards the front of the line.

'Where's Captain Peters now? And what about that commo, Lim?'

'For all I know they're probably still being done over in the cells.'

'I've been here a coupla days. I wonder why they didn't bash me for longa, like you?'

'All I can say is, you've got a reputation as a lucky bastard. But then you already know that. I had a hard time just getting them to believe my name, rank and enlistment number, especially after they discovered the cigarette case I was carrying as a keepsake. I had a hell of a time trying to convince them my surname wasn't Esq.'

'Hang on ... you don't smoke?'

'Yeah, but a whole lot of things have changed with me since I left your artillery regiment. I lost sight of Lim in the dark early on, near that abandoned bungalow with the white shutters we stopped at ... remember that? He might be the only one of us who got clean away ... who knows?'

'Someone must've dobbed us in about a possible breakout – they were onto us before we'd even worked up a sweat.'

'More likely it was all that noise you made crawling on ya belly that gave us away. What got into ya head, trying to beat off those swarms of mozzies you must've disturbed in the long grass? You don't seem to accept any responsibility for the guards probably detecting the noise you made. Nobby was right – you can't help drawing attention to yourself, can you? You also kept whingeing about that sore foot of yours too – the one I thought I'd fixed up?'

Their hushed conversation abruptly ended when both received a jarring blow from a bamboo rod to the back of their knees.

'*Shizuka-ni shiro-yo! ... hanashi wa mō yamero! ... damare-yo! ... uruse!*' *Shut your mouth!* was the commandant's decreasingly polite message. By the tone of voice, he didn't need to say it four ways for its meaning to be painfully clear. This was every new prisoner's introductory lesson to commandant Ikeda's elementary textbook on sadism.

———

Several uneventful months passed, during which time both soldiers were confined to their putrid cells on the ground floor of the gaol. It was becoming difficult to distinguish between the stench from an unemptied latrine bucket and the aroma of their unwashed bodies. The number of Australians from different regiments had increased only slightly, mainly those captured in the Dutch East Indies.

Except for the sporadic hosing down for lice, the rare scabies bath in the yard and limited physical exercise in the prison passageway that separated the cells on either side, most of the day and all the nighttime was spent in solitary confinement. Whatever meagre amount of food was provided came on a small metal tray pushed through a narrow slot in the door. The cells were empty of direct sunlight and furniture, except for the latrine bucket, the *benki*, and a few loose wooden boards pushed together to form a bed. Each prisoner was forced to face the door and remain seated in a Buddhist-like cross-legged position while eating. But the greatest deprivations were that of idle conversation, the absence of mateship, and the slow disintegration of any thoughts of a heroic escape.

Normally the daily rations were delivered by grunting Japanese guards or Tamil Indians pressed into employment as food trusties by the Japanese. Each one of the Japs barked orders as if infected with chronic laryngitis. But that day, Campbell heard a far more reassuring sound on the other side of the door. It was Captain Peters's voice.

'Christ, it's good to hear you, captain! I thought you might've been done for.'

'Not yet, but it was touch and go for a while there. Listen up, Sandy … the guard on this floor's been called away, and my assistant trustie down the other end is a lazy Tamil bastard who doesn't speak a word of English, but all the same, I'd better watch out. Saitō tried to get me to confess to being an anti-Japanese agent, not just a captured escapee. Those partisan clothes Lim supplied us with didn't help much. Sorry to say, but Lim was caught too. He must've got as far as Kranji, I reckon? He was executed here, after only a few days locked up.'

'What? Bloody hell! That doesn't look too good for the rest of us. Was he forced to identify anyone else who escaped with him?'

'I don't think he did, or we'd be dead already. Saitō seemed very pleased to let me know Lim's fate, stared at me for a long time, but I was determined not to show any emotion one way or the other. Someone like Manjit Singh, who knew all the names of the nationalist sympathisers in the Chamber of Commerce and the China Relief Fund members, could've dobbed him in? I would never have believed the Manjit I thought I knew could be capable of such a betrayal until he attacked us along with that Jap guard.'

'You're not the only one who's been led up the garden path! The minister's secretary we all met at the Adelphi gave him plenty of work, even called him *adorable* … *first rate*. Can you imagine that? Can't believe he was so easily taken in.'

'Unfortunately, I *can* imagine it. As you now know, I've had to practise a fair bit of deception myself – I would've once called it *subterfuge* – but nothing approaching his level of betrayal. Saitō remained unsure whether I had connections with the nationalist guerrilla groups in central Malaya, which I denied for hours on end. I had to repeatedly disavow any knowledge of Lim.'

'Sounds like he didn't betray us, even if he was tortured?'

'Yes, and he's one brave man if that's the case. I copped a few bashings tied to a chair. Saitō started inflicting the punishment personally, but his fingers and knuckles are so soft and bony that compared to his personal guard Kobayashi, who can give you a decent wallop, he doesn't have the power to leave you with anything more than a bit of a sting around the head ... He has a basement storeroom set up with bright lights. Never turns them off during the night. You're kept awake by that guard, who could rush in at any time. I call it *the lighthouse*, even though this one doesn't protect the unwary from danger. Kobayashi seems to be the only guard on night duty, never goes to sleep and likes a bit of cruelty. He puts a noose round your neck like he's about to hang you, but his purpose is just to frighten you even more. It's impossible to doze off. I was starting to get blurred vision – Major Wake referred to something similar as retrobulbar neuritis. The only cure is marmite, he said. But I can tell you the Jap won't have any of that handy unless he's grabbed it from your medicine kit?'

'You remembered?'

'For sure. I had to open your medical case in the Bentley on that trip from Mersing. And to think at one stage I only ever thought of you in terms of subverting public morality.'

'We might have a talk about what you mean by all that later, captain, but for the moment I'll take what you said as a sort of compliment.'

'Let's just say, you've shown me what it's *really* like to keep a secret, as well as revealing the true meaning of Christian forgiveness.'

'I see you're still carryin' round a dictionary in your head, but now it seems to be full of religious and medical terms!'

'As I said, I heard those medical terms used by the major at the hospital. You must've heard lots of them while working there too? I've got to keep Saitō impressed by teaching him new English words otherwise he'll see no use in having me around. He kept me locked up in that windowless room at the YMCA for what seemed an eternity, hoping to break my spirit, until for some reason he gave up a few days ago. Maybe he was showing me some respect for my resistance. I'd almost reached breaking point when he moved me into a large cell with a handful of Japanese army deserters and petty criminals on the second floor. I don't know what else they did – could've been looters or profiteering with stolen currency on the black market – but their numbers are slowly dwindling. We're kept apart from other prisoners. That's why I didn't know you were here with Clarrie until yesterday. It's worked out reasonably well for me. They give me language lessons, mainly isolated swear words to help pass the time. I can understand more of what they're saying, but I'm still hopeless expressing anything meaningful myself.'

'What made him bring you back here, doing this lowly job? You've got to be the most senior officer in this prison by a long shot.'

'Well, my rank was probably the reason why he kept me out of solitary confinement like you in the first place. I reckon that's how I got this job too. When Saitō finally accepted I was really an officer, that the cigarette case probably belonged to someone else, and I spoke some basic Japanese, he must've thought I'd be more useful as a trustie than rotting away in a cell.'

'*Shh!* … hang on a bit, I thought I heard the guard coming back … no, it's fine. What were you going to say?'

'So, you're now handing out those tiny rations of rice and that brown warm water they call *chah*?'

'That's right. I think some of the guards are more interested in withholding food from the prisoners and slapping them about, than encouraging good order and discipline. Saitō obviously doesn't want too many dying in the cells, and maybe he thought an English-speaking officer could instil discipline and order more effectively, without having to kick the prisoners' heads in. I reckon that's as close as he gets to embracing any notion of compassion.'

'So, he's *nice* to you, is he?'

'Don't get me wrong, that Jap's a bona-fide sadist. He doesn't care whether you live or die, unless your death's a bit sudden because the guards have gone too far trying to extract the type of information that guarantees your death anyway. He basically holds all soldiers who surrender in contempt, and says when a samurai warrior had an empty stomach, it was a disgrace to feel hungry. I guess that's how he justifies the small portions of food everyone gets. Funny thing though, one time he revealed a more *cultivated* side – I wouldn't say *nice* – when he spoke in a sort of broken American English about getting a childhood education in Hawaii. For a while he was unexpectedly civil, even told me his father abandoned his mother and she'd raised him by herself back in Nagoya. Following this conversation, I swallowed my pride and tried to become more friendly.'

'You were pretty game doing that.'

'I had to give it a go. It worked for a little while – even practised giving him a deep bow. He eventually told me he attended a military academy that normally led to a commission in the Imperial Guards – even showed me pictures of the place. When I innocently asked him why he'd only ended up in the military police, he ripped off my glasses, threw 'em on the floor and crushed one of the arms with his boot. I initially thought his reaction may have been caused by my poor Japanese, but I've now come to realise it likely had more to do with his unpredictably malicious streak than my mangled grammar? When I humbly questioned why he treated me like that, he gave me the type of look that would've sent a chill through even Nobby Cruikshank. I can tell you, honestly, I was petrified, and there weren't any more questions from me after that.'

'Is that guard still away?'

'Yeah, I'll hear his boots if he's on the way back.'

'I can vouch for the Jap's cruelty, captain, but not much else. Last night, I think Clarrie was forced to kneel for hours without moving. He must've back-answered the guard, or maybe Saitō himself was there and took it as an insult? I overheard everything going on. We all know Clarrie's tone of voice is not the best at disguising his disrespect for authority. He might still be suffering the effects of a beating. He'll be mincemeat if they discover the tiny wooden shiv he's hidden somewhere in his cell. I haven't seen it, but when we went outside for the scabies bath, he held out his third finger and told me the shiv's not much broader and a little bit shorter than that. He said whenever he gets the chance, he binds and rebinds one end for something to grip – he's managed to unravel the stitching in his shorts to wind round the base and been sharpening a pointy bit with a piece of metal he found in the yard. Talk about bull-headed! Must have taken him ages.'

'It mightn't do him any good. I reckon he's not long for this world anyhow. There's some almost indecipherable *kanji* painted above his cell door – I asked one of Jap prisoners what it meant. I think he said it was an old Chinese *on* reading, an *onyomi* it's called, indicating a prisoner earmarked for death. But then again, it could've been painted there a good while ago for someone who's already been executed.'

'Hang on a tick.'

Peters stopped speaking, then swivelled his neck from side to side, trying to pick up the sound of approaching footsteps. He finally said: 'No-one's comin' … the Tamil's still got his back to me, sittin' at the end of the passageway, hoein' into your breakfast, lunch and dinner.'

'You know, Saitō forced me to attend one of those be-heading executions. In the end, I had to turn away. He seemed to particularly enjoy the final moments of this ritual. The condemned are dragged to a spot outside the wall, forced to their knees facing a hooded swordsman they believe is about to kill them. But you know what happens? The real executioner, commandant Ikeda himself, unexpectedly comes up from behind, and *whoosh*, the head's gone, clean as a whistle. There's no mucking around with blindfolds, prayers with a chaplain or last-minute appeals for clemency in this place!'

'Thanks for cheerin' me up, captain. Bloody hell, now you say that I haven't heard anything comin' from Clarrie's cell since early this morning. It sounded like he was hurlin' another insult before everything went quiet. He'll never learn! Your old *mate* Saitō might have executed him already?'

'He's no mate of mine. I'll forget you said that! No, Clarrie's still alive, but he was black and blue when I looked through the peephole a little while ago. He struggled to answer me. A temporary reprieve is just another one of Saitō's sadistic pleasures. I think he made me witness that execution as a reminder of my own precarious situation.'

'Speaking of pleasures, can you get me some decent food, captain? I'd leap at a crust! What's put in our bowl is worse than the gruel Oliver Twist had to eat.'

'Hahaa! I see you've not lost your sense of humour. You'll never get bread in this place. The only things around here resembling a warm loaf of bread are the flagstones in the yard baking in the sun! All I can promise is to try and retrieve some vegetable peelings from the pit and carry the *meshi* tray around here as often as possible. The Jap guards set aside the best food scraps for their own army prisoners up on the next floor, so it might be tricky. I can't guarantee anything. Hang on … the Tamil's on the move … I'd better go.'

———

During his first few months in charge, Major Kenji Saitō rarely visited Outram Road unless officiating at an execution. But recently, he'd received notification that thousands of POWs were to be transported to Bampong and Kanburi in Siam to build a railway line through dense jungle to Burma. He quickly realised the viability of his gaol could be significantly affected once that decision came into effect. With Manning's successful clamping down on attempted escapes from Changi, and no more civilians being arbitrarily accused of treason or sabotage, fewer prisoners would be invited to attend the Kempeitai Christian Association, as it was facetiously called. Saitō feared he might be transferred, or else receive an order to close the gaol entirely at short notice. It wasn't guaranteed that only the relatively healthy, able-bodied prisoners in Changi would be transported to build the Burma Railway.

Increasingly paranoid about his future, and at the mercy of his inse-curities, in the days and weeks following the notification, he started to fill his spare time furtively observing the detainees from the comman-dant's narrow office window at the gaol. Given the declining need for sustained interrogations, he was able to indulge his peculiar taste for voyeurism on an increasingly regular basis.

Normally, he spent most days in his accommodation at the rear of the former YMCA building. He'd had his rooms gradually fitted out in the traditional Japanese style, *washitsu*, comprising *tatami* flooring, rolled-up *futon*, sliding *shoji* and *fusuma* panel screens, and a centre-piece *tokonoma* and shrine. These furnishings had been systematically removed from former Japanese residents' homes left vacant after the occupants quickly fled Singapore following the outbreak of war in Malaya. His industriousness in this regard had caught the top officers of the IJA unawares – for several weeks they were obliged to sleep in the unfamiliar Western-style rooms of the commandeered Adelphi Hotel.

Upon the Japanese occupation, the traditional recreational pastimes of the former Christian organisation in Orchard Road, of which the Governor, Sir Percival Townshend himself was the patron, had been replaced by activities of an altogether different complexion. Of an evening, Saitō would shed his uniform, his highly polished full-length leather boots and his cane, for an *haori* half-coat and the *hakama*, skirt-like culottes. At the end of each week, he would daub his face with *oshiroi* white make-up like a *geiko*, add streaks of red, and dress in full samurai regalia to affect the stage allure of a *kabuki*-style warlord. Then he would meditate and seek spiritual sustenance for what he'd always aspired to become.

But, several months after the fall of Singapore, as increasing numbers of his Japanese guards began to be transferred back to regular army duty on the Malay–Siam border, he'd decided to take a closer personal interest in the running of the gaol and less time dressing-up or relaxing in his *ofuro* hot bath. His wraithlike appearance could be glimpsed surveying the line-up of prisoners in the courtyard, which was by now dominated by long-term, haggard and compliant internees.

Saitō was in fact conjuring up new ways of implementing his sordid imaginings. It wasn't long before he ordered the gaol comman- dant, Captain Shinjirō Ikeda, to identify any particularly uncooperative detainees for special treatment. His only stipulation was for those chosen to be no more physically impressive, nor significantly taller than himself. Eager to please his superior officer, it took little time for Ikeda to enthusiastically single out Gunner Roberts as satisfying minimum requirements. Clarrie had already earnt the ire of the guards and had been beaten several times for refusing to adopt the seated, cross-legged posture in his cell. He was the preferred choice to be the first recipient for whatever the major had in mind.

At the same time, he'd felt duty-bound to pass on a rumour spread by an Indian guard who'd defected to the IJA. The guard had claimed that one of the Australian soldiers now imprisoned at Outram Road had engaged in unnatural acts at the Adelphi Hotel with a British official months, before the surrender of Singapore. The soldier's exact identity had remained unconfirmed due to a conflicting trishaw reservation listing two different names that day. Ikeda sought no further proof from this former Adelphi employee and, despite more obvious candidates standing out, he took malicious delight in identifying prisoner Roberts as the particular soldier involved. Captain Peters had been forced to supervise the commandant's arbitrary selection process. He made sure he serviced Clarrie's cell first on his rounds, and as he shoved in the food bowl, he said: 'Listen closely, Clarrie. Ikeda's been ordered to release a few prisoners from their cells at various times during this week, starting today. The decision is supposedly in honour of General Yamashita's birthday next Sunday, and you're the first prisoner to benefit. Don't ask me why they chose *you*.'

'Where'm I goin'?'

'You're to go with me and a guard to the major's private quarters, where I've been told you'll get a hot bath, fresh clothes and a decent meal. If that's the case, at least you'll be rid of the stench of urine in your cell, if only for a short time.'

'I was offered that same sort of deal when I was carrying a swag around Moree. Things didn't turn out so well back then. I'll believe it when I see it, captain. He's gotta be up to somethin'? Who the hell's Yamashita anyway? I'd bedda be prepared for anythin'.'

In fact, Clarrie was so scared about the move that he wasted no time retrieving the shiv he'd hidden in the space he'd laboriously hollowed out in one of the three bed planks in his cell. For a short while, he practised holding the shiv tightly in his closed fist before the escort party arrived. However, he knew he'd have to conceal it completely during any supervised wash, so built up enough courage to ease it into a place where the sun didn't shine. He hoped it was a place where the rising one wouldn't shine either, unless he were forced to bend over?

Although one end was bound with old cotton stitching, whenever he tried it, the shiv's insertion hurt like blazes, but was almost painlessly retrievable by gently pulling on a single thin thread left dangling from his anus. He'd unpicked part of the seam around the crotch of his shorts, producing a slit just wide enough to enable his thumb and index finger to locate the thread.

———

Clarrie's understandable scepticism about this sudden display of generosity towards the prisoners was quickly confirmed. After arriving at Kempeitai headquarters, no sooner had he been stripped, bucketed with cold water and fed with the major's leftovers, than he was steered by Peters and Saitō's personal guard, Private Saburō Kobayashi, towards a large, separate room within the building. He'd been kept naked, then bound to a chair at the wrists, seated back to front.

After several minutes Saitō appeared from behind a concealed side door and signalled the other two to leave the room. He was wearing only a *yukata* and *zōri* sandals, and as he slowly circled the prisoner, he loosened the *obi* girdle, exposing his small, uncircumcised and flaccid penis in the process. It wasn't altogether clear what his ultimate intentions were, but Clarrie reacted to the obscene premonition with all the revulsion he could muster.

While Saitō pleasured himself and edged closer, Clarrie managed to wriggle just enough to unbalance the chair, forcing it to topple over onto the floor. Despite the pain from what could possibly have been a badly sprained if not dislocated shoulder, he was not in the least regretful that his body weight had been finally taken off his backside. If it had indeed been Saitō's ultimate intention to sodomise the prisoner, it would've been even money which one of them would've received the greater shock in the performance. The noise caused by the fall was enough to draw the guard back into the room, who immediately struck the prisoner with the butt of his rifle.

As Saitō was leaving the room, he ordered the guard to continue beating the prisoner, who remained bound to his chair on the floor. He re-entered ten minutes later in full Kempeitai uniform, the knuckles of his right hand tightly wrapped in a cloth bandage. After ordering the guard to raise the chair to an upright position, he gave Clarrie one merciless blow to the side of the head with his padded fist. Along with his old clothes tied in a bundle, Clarrie was then dragged away unconscious to the basement. This was where the sessions of prolonged physical and psychological punishment were conducted. Peters knew the room intimately, though there wasn't that much to know. The space was dominated by what resembled two large airfield landing lights positioned on stands in such a way as to cause maximum discomfort to any restrained occupant. He knew Clarrie was destined to be transfixed in their concentrated glare over many nights, without respite.

———

'Do you know what's happened to Clarrie?' Campbell asked in an urgent voice.

'Yes, of course. Saitō delights in telling me all the details of his latest perversions,' Peters replied despondently.

'I hope you like this. I've managed to mix in a tiny bit of what looks like chicken meat into your rice ball today … I can't guarantee it's chicken, it could be fish? It's still only half the size of a rissole, so don't swallow it all at once.'

'Yeah, thanks. But what about Clarrie? What's goin' on?'

'He's been roughed up as I suspected, and kept in that basement room with those lights I told you about. It appears he's being doubly punished for failing to satisfy the Jap's depraved sexual cravings. But I sense Saitō's losing patience simply toying with him and, as far as I can tell, may decide to execute him in the coming days. I can't see Clarrie getting a reprieve for his resistance by being put to work as a trustie, can you? Unless they gag him, it's not difficult to predict how it'd all end up.'

———

Sandy pleaded with the captain to regularly report on Clarrie's plight. After surviving a further two weeks in the lighthouse, Clarrie's physical condition and willpower to survive had become seriously depleted. He was denied any exercise inside or outside the cell, his neck permanently tethered by a rope with a noose-knot, the other end secured to one of the two iron rings that were mortared into opposite walls of the cell. The rope's length allowed him to reach the latrine bucket, but not much else without risking strangulation. The food was slid in on a dish across the floor, as it might be served to a dog. It was of a slightly better quality than the routine Outram Road menu as it occasionally contained unfamiliar, assorted scraps from Saitō's dining table.

Clarrie's eyesight was failing and he'd become delirious due to the constant dazzle of the lights and sleep deprivation. His ankles were badly swollen, one of the early symptoms of beriberi, and recently Peters likened his deteriorating appearance to that of a slightly warmed-up cadaver.

As a medical orderly, Campbell had witnessed many injured soldiers die a slow, agonising death in the mobile hospitals and dressing stations, notably during the collapse of the Gemas–Muar rear-guard action in southern Johore in January. But *none* of those patients were beaten, starved or restrained by a noose while being drained of life. He soon became tormented by the image of his fellow escapee's degradation as much as by his own inability to do anything about it. Acutely aware of Clarrie's probable medical prognosis and the profound humiliation he'd already endured, he decided he *would* do something about it. The next occasion on which he could speak freely to Peters in the passageway, he said: 'I've had plenty of time weighing things up, captain. What if you tell Saitō I'm someone who'll play along with his sexual games in exchange for sparing Clarrie's life? Do you think he can be trusted to honour that type of bargain?'

Peters recoiled at the suggested depravity, so nauseated by the lurid imaginings it aroused that he refused to answer. Meanwhile, the Tamil trustie at the far end was finally alerted to the hushed conversation and looked like he was coming to investigate. Recognising this, Peters continued his rounds.

Over the following days, he struggled to understand why Campbell had volunteered for greater punishment to benefit the most fractious and least deserving prisoner in the gaol, but he eventually overcame his initial revulsion and reluctantly modified his attitude.

During that time, he'd picked up the words *tsugi no kinyōbi* in something Saitō said to an appreciative Commandant Ikeda. The context strongly suggested that Clarrie would be executed the following Friday. He told Campbell what he'd eavesdropped on his next round along the passageway.

'I can't believe it's come to this. If it works, this'll be the second time you will've saved that little bastard's life! And to think – after what he's said about you in the past, wallowing in all those slanders – you can still show compassion and forgive him? Mark my words, Sandy, if he's spurned you once, he'll probably do so again. I'll put your proposal to Saitō, but there's no telling how he'll react. I'll have to make sure it doesn't sound like another insult.'

———

Clarrie banked on a whole lot of things going right whenever he practised removing the shiv from his rectum. No unexpected visit from the guard, for a start. He had to work with his eyes almost closed, which made cutting the rope at the wall an arduous process. It was necessarily a furtive exercise, measured in stolen minutes over non-consecutive days. Even when he finally felt the remnants of the last few strands attaching the rope to the iron ring, he couldn't be sure they'd give way when he needed them to break clean. He was so feeble, he feared he might only achieve this by deliberately falling on his side, like he did before in Saitō's office. He'd be relying on all his now severely depleted strength to be successful.

At first, he thought he was hallucinating when just before daybreak on the Friday morning, Private Kobayashi entered his cell. He was slowly hauling in a bleeding, semi-conscious Sandy Campbell, who already had a rope attached to his neck. His torturer's contempt for the Australian soldier's probable resistance was expressed in one final act of indignity. Campbell's head was crowned with a blood-stained, bullet-ridden slouch hat, which had somehow fallen into his sadistic torturer's hands. Traces of blood had trickled down his forehead and onto his shoulder, and his legs appeared fractured and motionless, like lumps of lead. Through blurred vision, Clarrie saw the guard crouching down, starting to tie the end of Campbell's rope to the metal ring on the opposite wall.

Shit! I hope that monkey doesn't come over here and check my knot too closely. Without waiting for such a fatal discovery, Clarrie lunged at the guard from behind with all the strength and momentum he could summon. As the rope gave way, he fell on top of the guard, retrieved the shiv and thrust it deep into Kobayashi's neck. He repeated the stabbing action several times, despite the victim at no stage threatening to resist his assailant's murderous blows.

Almost immediately, the guard lay still, his neck bathed in a steady flow of blood. There'd been no persistent groans, no writhing body, just a gentle twitch of his wrist, fingers and lips … a brief gurgling sound, then … nothing. Clarrie struggled to regather his senses and eventually managed to wipe the blood from his hands all over the guard's uniform. He'd let go of the bloodied shiv, which had brushed against Campbell's kneecap as it dropped. He then proceeded to untie Campbell's loosely fastened rope from the metal ring in the wall. He'd just enough energy left to remove the bloodied hat and lift Campbell's noose, before slumping onto the floor, utterly exhausted.

'Do you know what you've done, Clarrie?'

'Yeah! I've saved you from gettin' bashed in the head anymore by that fuckin monkey, that's what I've done!' he said, inhaling large breaths. 'You must be badly cut 'cause he tried to cover up your bleeding with one of our slouch hats.'

'What? … No! Forget about the hat! … I'll tell you what you've done. We're now *both* going to cop it for *you* killing the Jap. It was that turncoat Manjit who beat me – didn't like it when I said I saw through him way back at the Adelphi. I think the guard's head hit the wall after you fell on him, and it must've knocked him out stone cold. It was potluck with your eyes barely open, but your little blade over there probably struck his carotid artery first go? You must've sensed he was a goner, but you went into a frenzy and stabbed him at least *four times.* Why did you do that? It was like you were killing something that refused to die?'

'I dunno … it was just instinct, I suppose … I got panicky because I was blinded, dizzy, felt like my head was on fire from those burning lights. All I know is, I've gotta somehow get outa this place quick smart before Saitō comes round.'

'What about me? You're not leavin' me here, are you? Didn't you say back in Changi you owed me one? You might've thought about my busted shins before killin' the guard. Everyone says you're a screw loose and it's true, because now we're both in deep shit. If you wanted to get outa here by yourself, why didn't you get rid of the rope around your *own* fuckin' neck first?'

'C'mon, Sandy, help me turn him over. I need to grab his key. I can feel it on the side of his belt.'

'Why do you want the key? The cell's unlocked.'

Clarrie had managed to dislodge the key, but after a moment's reflection, threw it in Campbell's direction in a bitter reaction to his own stupidity and started to almost feel his way towards the door.

'Hang on, Clarrie. Me legs have gone all numb ... an' what about your blindness? How come you're better? You still won't get too far without me ... c'mon, lend me a hand.'

Within moments, Saitō appeared waving a small calibre pistol. He ordered the morning duty guard to reattach Clarrie's serrated rope to the ring before removing Kobayashi's lifeless body from the cell. He then picked up the bloodied shiv and the large key, close to where Campbell's foot was resting. He immediately noticed that Clarrie's noose was still attached at the neck, while Campbell's was removed, and the end of his rope untethered. It was sufficiently clear to him which one of the prisoners had somehow overpowered the guard, then removed his own noose before cutting the last strands of Clarrie's rope.

CHAPTER
TWENTY-EIGHT

SINGAPORE, AUGUST–SEPTEMBER 1945

THE WAR officially ended in Singapore on 12 September 1945 with the Japanese surrender before Lord Louis Mountbatten in Singapore's Municipal Building. But, for the soldiers of the 8th Division, it could be more accurately described as the end of the grotesque deprivations experienced during imprisonment. For many who were soon to be discharged, the effects of wartime internment would never end.

When Emperor Hirohito ascended the Chrysanthemum Throne in 1926, it ushered in a period of Japanese history referred to as *Shōwa*, Illustrious Peace. Given the emperor's collusion in the militaristic expansion of the nation from 1931 until the complete devastation of the Japanese empire by the end of 1945, one could hardly imagine a more inapt description.

The surrender of the Japanese in Singapore had resulted in surprisingly few reprisals for the many years of brutal treatment suffered by those imprisoned during the occupation. Some Japanese soldiers who otherwise would have been condemned to death for their war crimes, chose to deny their captors any opportunity for redress. Upon hearing the emperor's radio message of surrender on 15 August, Major Kenji

Saitō was one of those who found honour and surrender to be totally irreconcilable concepts.

The following day, he cleansed his body thoroughly before dressing in a ceremonial white kimono. He then knelt on the floor facing the *tokonoma* in the shrine, his body resting on his heels ready to perform ritual disembowelment, maintaining a position that ensured he would fall forward to his death. The commandant of the prison, Captain Shinjirō Ikeda, being his second in command was acting as the *kaishaku*, and stood motionless at his side. He remained ready to perform the beheading that would bring a dignified end to the excruciating pain that followed the initial cut across the belly. Ikeda had already been given plenty of practice wielding the sword from behind. Death would come swiftly.

Deep within his soul, Saitō had accepted that he'd dishonoured the strict moral code of the feudal warrior caste to which he felt he belonged. *Seppuku* was the only way to be absolved from the permanent shame, and the iniquity the allied victors would surely attach to his conduct. *Cowards die many times before their deaths, the valiant never taste of death but once* – in some respects, Caesar's prescient observation would not have been far removed from Saitō's understanding of the uncorrupted ethical precepts of *bushidō*, and the extreme nature of penance it invoked. It served to harden his resolve before he made the long incision starting from the left-hand side of his abdomen, with the nine inches and a half *wakizashi* blade.

———

By the time his regiment had disembarked from the *Highland Chieftain* in Brisbane on 9 October 1945, Gunner Clarrie Roberts had not only avoided death but would soon be financially compensated for the unpaid 1,711 days he'd been on active service overseas. However, it was only one of those days – Friday 20 November 1942 at 3.00 pm in the 17th year of the *Shōwa* era – that would come to define Clarrie's life in the armed forces. It was the day Alexander Campbell was beheaded for the presumed killing of the Kempeitai guard. The circumstances that led to his execution still preoccupied the thoughts of at least two of his close comrades on the slow voyage home.

'I keep askin' meself, David, how come Sandy copped it, but Clarrie somehow survived? He must've convinced Saitō that he couldn't've killed the guard because he looked weaker than Sandy and had likely gone blind? Or maybe he was right all along when he called himself a lucky bastard? How he also managed to get transferred back to our prison hospital months before the Japs surrendered beats me.'

'Yes, those thoughts crossed my mind as well. But didn't you often say, you'd never come across anyone who's squandered so many second chances to do something right as Gunner Roberts? I've got a feeling this time luck had little to do with it, and good fortune didn't necessarily favour the brave. Perhaps it's *me* who's really the lucky one? I now know I should be grateful you went for Clarrie instead of me to be part of your escape. If it'd been different, I might've ended up either being the one left to explain things, or the one who ended up dead. Clarrie's never fully explained what went on in the lighthouse that morning.'

'On the other hand, you could've made it all the way to Ipoh. It's a bit late to go over all that stuff again, Tassie. I think Cruikshank argued it'd be better for prisoner morale if you'd stayed rather than Roberts – I can't remember exactly.'

'Well, all Saitō told me was that there'd been a stabbing. I didn't dare question him further about what happened, but I could tell the whole incident had badly affected him. That's possibly the reason why Sandy, along with those two Jap prisoners who apparently assaulted Ikeda in the yard and tried to break out, were the last ones executed at Outram Road. After Clarrie's description of Sandy's blood-stained appearance when dragged into the cell that morning, I can't help thinking he resisted being forced into committing some act of depravity, and Saitō resented it like mad? It's a long shot, but maybe in sparing Clarrie from the sword, Saitō was honouring the terms of that disgusting pact with the devil Sandy asked me to negotiate to my eternal discredit.'

'How can it be to your discredit, David, when what you agreed to do, might've saved Clarrie's life? Should I put all that in the diary? I've still got blank pages all over the place.'

'Why not? Who's gunna believe it? I retrieved Campbell's notebook from his locker at the infirmary, so you may as well add some of its contents to your diary whenever you can. I've kept it secure ... no-one's going to dig any deeper about what he really got up to during the war – especially his time at the Adelphi – without that information. I know he wanted to remain discreet about certain things in his past, not wanting to disappoint his father. Perhaps he stands for a different kind of heroic death, one not suffered on the field of battle but through an isolated, selfless act that went unrecorded, the surrounding circumstances so morally unpalatable as to render the act uncelebrated?'

'Those twenty-pound words are creeping back, David ... but yeah, all that's a possibility. But it'll haunt me forever whenever I think about that tiny wooden shank Clarrie apparently sharpened for ages in his cell. Surely the Nips couldn't've thought it was Campbell's? How could he have managed to keep hold of it and summon enough energy to kill the guard after being knocked around so much beforehand?'

'Yes, I admit things don't quite add up. It all points to Clarrie as somehow managing to do the job. He's always been a cheerless fella, but I haven't seen any other soldier looking so gloomy and withdrawn after being released from prison. Even those who've lost limbs were overjoyed at their first taste of freedom in nearly four years. The fact he clams up about what happened in the cell that morning suggests he's still plagued by bad memories he can't damn well erase. I guess if anyone else gets to read the entire diary one day, they might be able to figure it all out, if they've a mind to?'

CHAPTER
TWENTY-NINE

SYDNEY AND MELBOURNE, LATE NOVEMBER 2015

WHEN I GOT the news of Clarrie's death, it felt more like a long-awaited salvation than a bereavement. He'd lasted longer than I expected, refused to die even after being helped along by the supposedly lethal properties of pentobarbital. Perhaps I'd been given a raw deal, deceived by undetectable impurities in Sicario's illicit concoction. *It's gunna be hard complaining to the consumer watchdog about this dodgy transaction,* I thought.

Marginally worse than that earlier trip to his hospital bed, I knew once I decided to show up at his funeral service I'd have to contend with a host of pussies' bum faces of barely recognisable relatives. As far as I could remember, the majority of my father's five siblings had been proselytised by door-knocking Pentecostals in the late fifties. They must have been ripe for trading in their old Baptist dogma for a shiny new Billy Graham-style crusading zeal. Despite religious convictions unmolested by self-doubt, their missionary outreach never got quite far enough to embrace brother Clarrie, however.

My father's bigotry in matters of religion was well-known, and his virulent form of atheism inevitably led to our estrangement from practically everyone on his side of the family. From time to time around the dinner table, he'd feel the urge to rattle off by heart all sixty-six books of the Protestant Bible in perfect order from Genesis to Revelation. In later years, I wondered whether he'd worked out some catchy mnemonic in order to win a bet on the *Queen Mary*. He obviously thought this parroting exercise gave him a bit of cachet with the wife and kids as his performances were generally accompanied by a smug, self-congratulatory grin. He also had a repertoire of asinine, heathen jokes, such as a description of the priest's preparation of holy water for the Mass: "You fill up the kettle with water from the tap … put it over the gas flame … and then boil the Christ out of it!" he'd say.

He found that so hilarious his eyes watered every time it was boringly reprised. It didn't take me long to realise he knew fuck-all about religious faith and the sacraments. His own father had been nominally Baptist, but the only teachings he'd received were of the narrow, sectarian persuasion. Not laden with unadulterated dogma, mind you – there was no inclination to adhere to their recommended teetotal regime.

Despite the celebration of his nuptials in what's called the One True Holy and Apostolic Church, a Roberts family tradition demanded you despise those who professed the Roman Catholic faith – the tykes or micks as Clarrie took delight in labelling them. Of all the denominations, they were uniquely stigmatised as the most incorrigibly gullible followers of that whole religious mumbo-jumbo he fancied he'd become expert in deriding.

My mother's silence in putting up with this ignoramus broke my heart. Having been brought up a Catholic, why did she never speak up when Clarrie paraded his deep attachment to irreligious beliefs? It must've had a lot to do with his assertion of power over her. Unsurprisingly, he liked to think of himself as a blaspheming hard man who liked a drink and a smoke, the family dreading his return from the RSL after work for his tea, full as a boot. Everyone quickly learnt to tell how many schooners of Resch's he'd already sunk that afternoon, as the level of menace rose in direct proportion to the number consumed. Had he learnt nothing from his own father's corresponding behaviour as a child growing up in Bexley?

When he arrived home for dinner, my mother acted as dependable cook and hovering servant, his hot meal delivered on a large plate, which she tightly clasped around the ends of her upturned apron. Its preparation and arrival were timed to coincide with his enthronement at the head of the narrow rectangular dining table. It was only after those unforgiving years that I came to fully understand and silently grieve for the demeaning role my mother had stoically endured and was never motivated enough to openly challenge. One by one it seemed her friends had dropped away. Who could blame them if they always found an excuse not to visit a home where they might be met with a husband's cold indifference to their attempts at friendship. They'd only ever visit once.

I kept asking myself, why should I go to Sydney again, this time for his funeral? I've made some bad calls in life, and attending this predictable sad-fest was bound to be another shocker. Knowing the character of my younger brother Norman, once he'd assumed his self-appointed role of chief mourner, he'd probably organise a no-frills funeral, the centrepiece of which would surely be an effortlessly inept attempt at a eulogy.

Who was this brother I hadn't seen for decades? Indulging my mischievous bent, I said to myself, *I can't wait to inspect Normie's current hair arrangement.* Over forty years before, he'd planned to defy heredity by having plugs inserted around his receding hairline. The transplanted tufts of hair were only slightly more attractive than an adhesive-free toupee made from AstroTurf, or the windswept comb-over parted just above the ear.

As for the quality of the funeral ceremony itself, I could guarantee it would be devoid of any reference to the immanence of God. But above all, I just knew it'd end up being an unashamedly skewed appraisal of Clarrie's undistinguished life. In fact, the whole show turned out to be much worse than I'd anticipated. I felt so hollowed-out and disoriented afterwards, that like Camus's Meursault, I too could have murdered that Arab on the beach in Oran, experiencing a rush of blood, dazzled by the sun.

378   E. J. JOHNSON

To get the show on the road, a pasty-looking regimental padre from the nearby Holsworthy Army Barracks had been recruited for the solemn occasion. It didn't take long to conclude he was no master of ceremonies. He'd answered the call and delivered his regulation homily in the non-denominational chapel within the grounds of the Woronora Cemetery in the Sutherland Shire of Sydney. There were few of the usual obsequies, or *mala fide* attempts to put a positive spin on the very modest achievements of the deceased. The padre's words conveyed no more spiritual meaning than he thought necessary, and he applied the standard of necessity strictly. The only way you could plausibly explain why he had taken up the cloth would be to subscribe to the theory that God's mystery is revealed in all things.

This rent-a-padre was followed in quick succession by the gruff vice-president of Clarrie's branch of the local RSL. This earnest individual simply parleyed some unremarkable military footnotes to the proceedings. In common with the padre, the brevity of his resume eloquently demonstrated that he also didn't know Gunner C. S. Roberts from a bar of soap.

What passed for a liturgy booklet came with a photocopied snapshot of Clarrie on the cover above his span of years. He'd been allocated considerably more than the biblical three score and ten. At least there was no photoshop deception practised here, rather the greyish tufts of hair around the bald pate and his quizzical grin almost succeeded in rendering him as someone kind and grandfatherly. Little else was included in the order of service beyond the names of truncated readings, a couple of hymns, and the clichéd words of a soulless prayer printed on the inside. Reproduced on flimsy paper with a wobbly staple in the middle, it looked as if it had been thrown together as an afterthought the night before, up late following a hastily arranged audience with Monseigneur Google. Classy effort, Normie.

Brother Norman would've thought he'd pulled off an organisational coup getting those two military-accredited jokers to front up. For me, the ceremony had all the refinement of a Las Vegas-style drive-through wedding in a stretch limo, serenaded by a heavily perspiring Fat Elvis impersonator. I hazarded a guess that those two celebrants must have only agreed to go through the motions for the payment of a modest honorarium. But the fact that they didn't hang around for the exchange of awkward pleasantries outside suggested they might've had more lucrative funerals to attend. The pall of mediocrity that enveloped the service had Normie's fingerprints all over it. What was remarkable was that this whole experience was so, *unremarkable*. I was half-expecting a scratchy recording of 'Wind Beneath My Wings' to draw the ordeal to a close. Mercifully, that manufactured treacle from West Coast America didn't seep that far today.

My lips started to curl when everyone was invited afterwards to the nearby Forget-Me-Not Cottage for light refreshments, as if I could ever imagine it possible to forget. It was attended by the implied threat of further insincere condolences, schmoozing and glasses of lemonade all round. A proper send-off is surely enhanced by several shots of whisky to assuage the poignancy of death, not just the dredged-up recollections from a group of wowsers over cold ribbon sandwiches and a lukewarm cup of tea. To top it all, my own son suddenly appeared on the raised dais, and I was transfixed, reduced to staring daggers. He said nothing. He hadn't known my father at all. Who or what had pushed him so much that he'd decided to go behind my back, to disrespect my enmity towards my own father in this way? Like father … like son, I suppose?

Clarrie was around ninety at his death, the ever-diminishing number of former comrades would probably be complete invalids by now, insolvent or wound up like their defunct newsletter, *Barbed Wire and Bamboo*, which had sought to keep internment alive. It was just the extended family now in whom all memory reposed, apart from the anger-free, verbatim records of Tasman Walls. Why did Clarrie's supposed best mate not come to the funeral? Was everything that could be said, finally revealed in that diary I hadn't yet opened? Nonetheless, I felt Walls's ghostly presence everywhere, imagining him pulling at his collar, contorting his neck, unused to wearing his Sunday best, or fearful of the chop. In the end, my fleeting glimpse of history walking away in that hospital corridor was all that remained.

———

It goes without saying that I'd been completely excluded from any input into the funeral planning, and consequently, serious reflection upon the first twenty years of Clarrie's married life was conspicuously absent. I realised then and there that I was destined to walk alone with the so far unknown details of his overseas service. Norman spoke to me only once. He said his dad's last words were, 'Sorry, Mum.' What the hell was I to make of *that*? Ol' Cobra Snake was a stranger to the apology, and it was a bit late to be expressing some form of regret, wasn't it?

Normie had said nothing of what his father may have divulged about life before marriage and would've been awarded the John Cleese Medal for not mentioning the war. *What else could you expect from Normie boy,* I thought. After all, he still embraced a wilful denial of my psychological distress during early adolescence. It soon became obvious that his weeping children were the designated star descendants that day, chosen because they were clearly ignorant of any unsavoury aspect of their grandfather's character. Fancy imagining in the first place that these goofy children could impart anything of real substance to the assembled mourners, as they sniffled on the mock pulpit. Yet I really couldn't blame them, I suppose? The only image that emerged from their tear-laden, incoherent blathering was that of a docile old man who'd built them a makeshift billycart and had happily allowed my mother to pull them around for hours on end in his treeless backyard. While amused by all of this, the experience was no sweeter than picking at a piece of cracked icing from the top of a very stale sponge.

Normie did not appear deeply mournful; he'd long ago drowned in his emotional shallowness. It precluded any real understanding of what I'd experienced in childhood, despite our cohabiting under the same roof during all those years. For him, my brutalised treatment was a nullity. As a child, he'd never copped a hiding for *anything*. True to form, he just left me to stew over the past, all on my lonesome. Five years younger and sheltered from physical abuse, he'd convinced himself that the reason for my aloofness was derived from an innately arrogant nature. He believed I sought to exaggerate the frequency and extent of family violence, from which he'd been fortuitously spared or had wilfully ignored. Was he expecting *me* to seek forgiveness, offer up a bogus mea culpa? *Well, fuck him and his silent complicity in what I alone had to endure.*

But my greatest disappointment, as I've already said, was witnessing my own son join the array of simpering children on the raised pulpit. I continued to wonder why he was determined to turn up today behind my back. Does treachery run in the family? Surely he knew I despised his grandfather? This indelible insult meant he'd be permanently pushed out of my life. If I'd said this to him at the time, maybe things might have panned out differently. Was it a misplaced sense of pride, or an unstated desire to be the willing plaything of fate that had promoted these family estrangements? Why was even death unable to erase the rancour and the miserable obsessions that had brought successive father–son relationships to such a pitiful conclusion?

I was kidding myself if I didn't already know the answer. I'd invested so much emotional capital in misplaced contrariness, that there was nothing to show for it but prolonged misery. Ostracism had revealed itself to be the ultimate form of self-punishment, the forever enemy of forgiveness.

CHAPTER
THIRTY

WITH THAT IMAGINED conversation with my traitorous son still floating in my consciousness, following my return to Melbourne I finally decided to read Mr Walls's hefty diary. It took several days to finish. I reread the long note he'd placed inside, ashamed I'd missed the opportunity to bring up Sandy Campbell's story while ol' Cobra Snake was still alive and wriggling.

Dear Simon

It's Sunday night, and I'm leaving with you this personal record of your father's time in my artillery regiment while we were stationed in Malaya.

Most of the later details, either myself or Sandy Campbell personally witnessed. Where the time and events pre-date our enlistment in May 1940, things were added from what Clarrie let slip over time. Luckily, I'd left many pages at the start of the diary simply blank. This enabled me to go back and fill in bits and pieces of Clarrie's story from the time he hit the road and set out from Sydney to Brisbane in late '39. I can't guarantee the complete accuracy of what's been included. He was known to brag and never told you the whole story about anything. But you can read between the lines all the same.

After the war, I kept the diary's contents to myself, apart from only one army officer from our battalion. I promised never to release it to any remaining members of the POW Association, to family or any other interested party. It's full of many unsavoury episodes, but not all involve your father. I owed a pledge of secrecy to our colonel's adjutant, Captain David Peters, who kept his own regimental records, and added my recollections as well. He and Campbell were the source of my notes on the senior officers, and the Poms in Singapore. I've also included some old letters I wrote to my Aunt Florence during the war. She'd kept every one of them, and I was lucky to get hold of them before she passed away.

David was in his nineties when he died at the Eventide Aged Care Home in Sandgate, Brisbane. That finally released me from the burden of secrecy. Out of respect for Sandy's memory, we'd both agreed it was best if the official account of his death, like his eventual grave site in Kranji cemetery, remained undisturbed. So, we made a solemn commitment to indefinitely withhold some little-known facts and details, which might suggest another story. I tracked down your contact number and disclosed my identity in that voicemail message last week. It was quite strange when I heard your recorded voice, it was as if ol' Cobra Snake himself were speaking.

Hanging on to the battered old diary for so long was driving me nuts. During the war, I had to conceal it in some very unlikely places, especially when Clarrie was around. Most of the time in Changi it acted as a very hard pillow. If I'd been sent to work on the Burma Railway it would've suffered the same fate as a lot of my mates and not survived. It probably turned out to be heavier than some of those blokes ended up weighing. Luckily, I was in hospital with malaria, and Clarrie was still in Outram Road gaol when our D Force was sent to Hin Tok camp in Siam in March '43. After he was brought back to Changi, Clarrie let slip a bit more about his past after I convinced him the guards had discovered the diary I'd been adding to on the sly. I told him they thought it was full of secret messages and seized it for their experts to decipher before being destroyed.

Back in Brisbane, I was starting to feel the diary was holding me captive; that it was like some bloody great sword hanging above my head, ready to lop it off at any moment. I couldn't cope and started using it as a doorstop. That's why now, quite a bit after Captain Peters's death, I've decided I can no longer bear being its sole custodian.

Towards the end, there's stuff only David knew or thought about. Everyone in our regiment could testify to the captain's honesty, integrity and his freakish recall of past events. While he abstained from many things, the gospel truth was not one of them. It's interesting how his relationship with Sandy flourished during their time in captivity. They'd obviously forgiven one another for their earlier jumping to conclusions about each other's true character. David often said no-one's without sin, and who are we to pass judgment?

He never married, and was, like me, a bit on the prudish side. He was brought up under a strict moral code by his parents – his father was a Presbyterian minister – but despite that, the captain was no God-botherer. David thought that if it were ever to be released, the diary should go to Clarrie's eldest son, if he existed? I was determined to find that out. He called it a right of primogeniture – he remained addicted to his twenty-pound words! Anyhow, it's now for you alone, Simon, to deal with the entire contents as you see fit.

When I first visited your father in hospital yesterday, he was dirty on me for bringing the diary along. He called it a relic, then said it was probably all bullshit and to throw it away – or better still, burn it, rather than leave it in the hands of his son, Simon. I had no idea you weren't on speaking terms. When I mentioned Sandy Campbell, he refused to say anything about him. I thought that more than a bit odd, but I think once you read the diary, you'll probably figure out why. He still carried some of that haunted look he had on the trip home in '45, as I recall.

I left in a bit of a huff, and you know, I almost did toss it away after his reaction. The second time I came in – today, Sunday – I think he pretended to be asleep. It looked like he was turning his back on me, after all we'd been through. I will never forgive him if that's the case. The nurse in charge on weekends will arrange for the diary to be left for safekeeping where she's stationed. I'm travelling back to Brisbane on Monday, after one last visit to see if he comes good or not. That's why I decided to write this long note beforehand, in case I missed you.

Silly old bastard I was. I stupidly thought age and sickness may have mellowed him. He can't have that long to live? Anyhow, my family quack said I may not live long enough to make it to my own funeral, let alone Clarrie's. So please, Simon, don't waste your time trying to message me, unless it's to say you got hold of the diary and want to clear up some things. Sorry it's come to this.

Yours sincerely,
Tasman Walls

———

Over the phone, I'd already foreshadowed to the psychiatrist what the diary had disclosed about my recently deceased father. I told him that what'd been left unsaid among the fragmentary jottings simply leapt off its fragile, yellowing pages. We arranged a time to discuss things face-to-face before Christmas. I planned to convince him I now had insight into the cause of my tendency to be overly judgmental, although I still had trouble asking his God for forgiveness. As for Sandy Campbell, who could've predicted the sort of man he'd become by the time of his death. It seemed almost everyone he met had left his presence a changed person. Wished I'd met him. Can't get over his deceiving so many people that he wasn't queer. Lucky he was, because if you believe what happened in that diary was true, I mightn't have been born at all.

As a result, I'd decided to seek out a publisher for the diary's story, in which Campbell had clearly emerged as the heroic protagonist. I didn't agree with my work colleague Christopher, a fellow atheistic creative who insisted there was *no* hero, just a series of flawed and outdated one-dimensional characters. In his opinion, it was no more than a rather bloated and fictionalised memoir, depicting a diverse bunch of big-headed racists, crooks and losers, no more inspiring than those simpletons who still believe in the nativity story of the baby Jesus, Joseph, Mary and the wee donkey.

He claimed it didn't have the broad appeal of gritty stories of survival set in a drug-infested, violent dystopia, or the latest gripping crime thriller. 'Intergenerational abusive relationships are a dime a dozen,' he said – 'as original as those spurious accounts of visitations by the Blessed Virgin Mary, and phoney prophesies of the second coming of Jesus Christ. Besides, what romantic fantasy-addicted female, let alone a Gen-Z post-feminist, is going to fall in love with a naive bisexual farmer of admittedly uncommon virtue, who loses his head while in prison? Campbell might've initially come across as more handsome and macho, but at least Mr Darcy kept his head on!' In commercial terms, Christopher said the story lacked marketability, like trying to flog the Book of Common Prayer to a congregation of pimps in a whorehouse. 'It's no page-turner, and I couldn't pinpoint one single cliffhanger,' he laughed. 'If you wanted a bestseller, you should've developed Lady Celia's outrageous eroticism into a steamy bodice-ripping bonkbuster. If you'd produced that, I imagine there'd be lots of things more likely to be uncovered in the long grass of the Yorkshire moors than a clutch of brooding game birds,' he facetiously suggested. At least he appeared to have read one part of the story.

'Screw you, Chrissie,' I said, not realising until then that his level of cynicism surpassed my own. I wasn't surprised when he told me the last thing he'd read was purchased online from among the plentiful self-help book-of-the-month releases. It'd obviously had little effect.

This left me more determined than ever to honour my promise to the psychiatrist to unburden myself of all the distressful memories my father had evoked, and present them as dispassionately as possible during our long-postponed second consultation. I'd even gone back to Doctor Kuczmierowski, asking him for an updated prescription for a course of ibuprofen!

I had it all down pat but never tired of rehearsal. I'd tell Mendelson none of my emotions had remained unexamined. I'd weaned myself off the soothing drug of self-deception and removed the noxious clumps of bigotry root and branch. Contrition was well on the way to becoming my middle name. To get to this stage, I'd managed to go cold turkey, no longer blaming my psychological condition on heredity, unafraid of now telling everyone that some of my best friends were shrinks.

As I entered the waiting room, several comfortable-looking Scandi chairs weren't the only part of the decor that'd been given a new lease of life. No more picture rails but prominently displayed on one of the freshly painted walls was a curious reproduction. Rather than the predictable chiaroscuro bowl of fruit, this one depicted a balding, bespectacled man in a suit descending a red spiral staircase suspended in the clouds leading to … heaven only knows.

Any further observations on the surroundings were interrupted when a rather dishy young receptionist with a beehive arrangement of frizzy black curls winding down past her shoulders, bounced out to greet me. She was wearing an oversized, loose-fitting white shirt pulled in around the waist by a wide belt, which then dropped over a tight skirt that hugged her thighs several inches above the knee. Her black eyeliner and mascara were far more wicked than those false eyelashes that accompanied every Amy Winehouse performance. What I could only describe as an angelic smile washed over her glossy lips as she cheerfully announced, 'Jake will see you now.'

That was music to my ears. Anyhow, I'd resolved not say a word that could possibly be construed as offensive. The malicious fun I'd once enjoyed in blaspheming had become, well ... *sooo yesterday.* Through a delayed process of self-evaluation, I'd finally come to know myself, convinced that a little less impertinence could only benefit my establishing positive, respectful relationships. Putting this realisation into practice would become my one and only new year's resolution.

But, as it turned out, complete renunciation of past immature behaviour and profanity proved easier said than done. Unfortunately, as soon as the receptionist had spoken, I experienced an irresistible urge to sing out, 'I believe in miracles ... since you came along ... you sexy thing.'

The phone alarm went off, and as I rolled over in bed, I realised I'd only been dreaming. Well, I'll be damned! For all its brevity, the little that I did recall of this waking dream didn't remotely defy interpretation. It meant that Mendelson would not be ready to see me before Christmas.

All the same, I was comforted by the thought that New Year's Eve was still a good month away.

AUTHOR NOTE

Accounts of the Japanese occupation of Malaya and the Fall of Singapore are plentiful. I wish to acknowledge the many non-fiction writers, war historians, biographers, memoirists, journalists and military figures who, over several decades, have contributed to our knowledge and understanding of this conflict.

A bibliography of scholarly journal articles on this topic alone would likely extend to hundreds of pages. There is also no shortage of writers of fiction who have provided their insights into the reasons for the decline of British colonial rule, using various settings in what was known as the Far East.

Although the novel *Blight* is also a work of fiction, I am especially indebted to the following sources for their helpful content embedded in fact.

- The Australian War Memorial Research Centre, Canberra, for access to the official history of the 8th Division's 2/10th Field Regiment.
- The National Archives of Australia for access to the war records of Australian service men and women.
- *BiblioAsia*, the quarterly review produced by the National Library Board of Singapore.

- *The Kamilaroi/Gamilaraay Dictionary* by Peter Austin and David Nathan (dnathan.com/language/gamila-raay/dictionary/GAMDICTF.HTM).

Each of the following three non-fiction works provides harrowing accounts of the brutal treatment and resultant psychological illnesses of Australian prisoners of war, either during or after World War II.

- *The Story of Billy Young*, Anthony Hill (2012).
- *Stubborn Buggers*, Tim Bowden (2014).
- *The Battle Within*, Christina Twomey (2018).

In addition, *Remembering the Myall Creek Massacre*, edited by Jane Lydon and Lyndall Ryan (2018), provided me with the historical perspective from which to approach the question of frontier violence, the forcible removal of children and the dispossession of traditional land experienced by First Nations communities in Northern New South Wales. Aspects of these discriminatory practices are briefly depicted in the novel.

I would also like to acknowledge the unstinting support of my wife April, who graciously weathered my increasing self-absorption in the rather solitary process of writing.

www.ingramcontent.com/pod-product-compliance
Lightning Source LLC
Chambersburg PA
CBHW031742180726
48283CB00005B/1636